Saved by the Rancher

Saved by the Rancher

Book One: The Hunted Series

JENNIFER RYAN

AVONIMPULSE
An Imprint of HarperCollinsPublishers

Excerpt from *Lucky Like Us* copyright © 2013 by Jennifer Ryan.

Excerpt from *Seduced by the Gladiator* copyright © 2013 by Lauren Hawkeye.

EPub Edition MARCH 2013 ISBN: 9780062268020

Print ISBN: 9780062268037

HB 05.25.2023

Dedicated to my three children, who never really mind when Mom's a bookworm.
To my husband, Steve, who after twenty years of marriage still makes me laugh and believe in love and happy ever after. I'm keeping you.
A special thank you to Mom and your red pen. Your steadfast belief in me that "I can do it" has always given me the strength and confidence to try anything.
For George. You're the dad I never had and always wanted. The grandfather my kids deserve and I always hoped they'd have.
I'm so lucky to have all of you in my life.

Prologue

DAVID SAT BEHIND his massive desk, his hand wrapped around a tumbler of whiskey instead of his high-priced, highly educated, but still incompetent lawyer's neck.

"She outmaneuvered us, Mr. Merrick. If we'd known about—"

"You should have known!" he bellowed, barely able to contain his temper. "I lost half of everything to that bitch!"

"At least it didn't go public."

"Get out." Voice low, it resonated with his inner rage.

Alone, David stared out the windows of his thirty-sixth-floor office at Merrick International. His company, and now she'd taken part of it. The fire of fury from that single thought shot through his veins, enraging him more. He tipped the drink to his mouth and swallowed a deep gulp, welcoming the familiar sting down his throat.

Three men entered. He tracked their progress toward his desk with their reflection in the window. He'd used his elite security team to investigate many corporate deals, but now he needed them for something much more personal.

His back to them, he ordered, "Whatever it takes. Find her."

They marched out eager to do his bidding.

David turned his focus from the city lights inside to the anger eating away at him. How could she do this? He'd make her regret winning today in court. She'd pay for besting him. No one got away with taking anything from him. No woman left him, especially not his wife.

He held his drink aloft and toasted the San Francisco skyline. "The game is on."

Chapter One

Two years later . . .

Is HE STILL here? Lurking, waiting.

Jenna opened her heavy eyelids a mere slit. She lay sprawled on the cold wood floor, shivering, snow falling everywhere. Inside? She squeezed her eyes closed and opened them again, trying to focus on the things around her. Her sight adjusted, the double images coalescing into a morbid scene she didn't want to see. Feathers from the pillows on the bed floated on the air and rained down, creating a white blanket over the devastation in the room.

The ringing in her ears quieted, allowing her to better focus on the bedroom of her rented cottage. Shards of glass from the smashed antique dressing mirror lay scattered around her. Some of the pulled-out dresser drawers landed on the floor, others hung open crookedly. Her clothes, though few, lay slashed and strewn everywhere.

The overwhelming sweet scent of jasmine perfume mixed with the metallic scent of her blood made her stomach clench and pitch until bile rose and stung the back of her throat, leaving a sour taste on her tongue.

She took a few shallow breaths to stave off the inevitable, at least until she got to the bathroom.

His worst rage yet. Mind-sharpening memories of the last hour flipped through her brain like a morbid slide show.

Him, grabbing her from behind on the front porch when she returned from running. He clamped his gloved hand over her mouth, grabbed her around the waist, and hauled her through the door. Him, spinning her around and with a backhanded slap sending her reeling backward and crashing into the dining room table. Pain radiated from her hip and down her leg. He grabbed her wrist, pulled her forward, and squeezed her so tight to his chest she couldn't breathe. Pain along her jaw, she opened her mouth to scream in terror, but he clamped his hand over her mouth, cutting off her air, and the scream rising out of her disappeared in the back of her throat. Him, shoving her away. She hit her head against the wall and stars exploded on the inside of her eyelids. Pain in the back of her head, a large throbbing bump swelled under her skin.

Nothing but him and pain. And, oh God, more to come.

Forcing her into the bedroom, he held her in his tight grip, grinding his hips and hard arousal against her bottom, inciting even more fear.

He liked her scared.

She stood helplessly frozen. Tried to get her mind to work, think, tell her body to flee, but her limbs didn't heed the wild thoughts in her head.

Him, snatching her belt off the dresser, pushing her onto the bed. She landed on her stomach and his fingers dug into her skin, bruising. She curled up, tried to make herself as small a target as possible. The belt lashed across her back and buttocks, her screams disregarded, her thin tank top and nylon shorts no protection against the bite of the leather whip and metal buckle.

The dressing mirror smashed to the floor with a loud crack. He wielded a shard of broken glass, his lips pulled back in a feral smile, he slashed her thigh, tearing the flesh in a jagged line of searing pain. She screamed in agony. Him, sitting on her bloodied, welted back, pulling her hair and hacking at it. She tried desperately to scratch and claw at his hands over her head. Him, shoving her off the bed and onto the floor with a resounding thud. Him in a mindless rage, demanding over and over again, yelling at the top of his lungs, *"Say you'll come back. I'll stop. Say it. Say you'll come back."*

Him, whispering in her ear, his knee grinding into her spine, *"You're mine. Wherever you go, I'll find you. You promised before God you'd be my obedient wife. Till death do us part. Death, Jenna. Say it."* The last he said with such menace, his voice became calm as a flat sea.

Her whisper, softer than his gasping breath, broke into his raging mind when all her screams went unheard.

"Never."

Fear gripped her mind and heart like a vice, making it near impossible to speak the word.

"If you're not with me, you might as well be dead."

Him, hitting her in the head. Blessed blackness enveloped her.

How long have I been on this floor?

Alone, the silence and stillness in the small cottage reassured her. She couldn't believe he found her again. God, had she really complained about the flowers left on her doorstep just to let her know he'd found her again, or the threatening notes left in her locked car or house? The late-night phone calls and hang-ups. His showing up at unexpected times and places. Those things were scary. This was . . . madness.

The first time he slapped her, she made the biggest mistake of her life and stayed with him. Because of his pleas and pretty words, she became his prisoner until his ugly words and petty jealousies forced her to flee. Now he had turned the game into a hunt. He would find her and release her, only to hunt her again at his whim.

She didn't know how he found her, but he did . . . again. This time she remained hidden for over five months, longer than their marriage lasted. All she remembered of the last two years, always on guard, running for her life, never truly alive or safe, and once again it came down to this. He wanted her to know no matter where she went, she belonged to him, and he could find her anywhere.

Sometimes he begged her to come back. Be a family with him. They'd have children. Other times, he yelled and threw things. He blamed her for everything, including his hitting her. This time went beyond verbally abusing her and shoving her around. He raged. She would never be safe. One day he'd make good on his promise and kill her.

He certainly came close this time.

She took a moment to inventory all the aches and pains combining into the pounding throb throughout her body. A gash on her head just above her temple from the candlestick he used to knock her out. Blood dripped over the silver base to the floor where it lay beside her. The welts on her back hurt like hell. How many times did he lash her with the belt? Enough that the blood pooled along her spine. Her severely bruised ribs would heal in a couple weeks. He didn't kick her that hard, probably because she was already out cold. Not as satisfying to kick her if she didn't grunt and squeal in pain.

The most serious injury, a long cut on her upper thigh. Probably needed stitches. Not the first time she needed them. Wouldn't be the last, the gruesome thought came to mind. Once the numbness wore off, she'd feel like a lump of soggy mud.

Sticky blood coated her right hand where it lay next to her leg. Like moving hundred-pound weights, she pressed herself up onto her hands, dragged her knees up under her, and sat back on her heels.

Well, I'm almost off the floor.

She waited a moment for the room to stop spinning and her stomach to settle. She grabbed the bedpost, hauled herself up to standing, her back and thigh screaming in agony. Deep breaths, the pain subsided in small increments. She'd learned to ignore it.

Get out. Get away. Hide.

Adrenaline pumping through her veins, the need to run, escape, overtook her and gave her the strength to do what needed to be done to flee to safety. The fear lay beneath all the pain, but she had to ignore it, too, and keep her head.

Jenna made it to the bathroom in time to puke her guts out. She rinsed her sour mouth and throat and refused to look at herself in the mirror above the sink. Pulling her hacked hair back, twisting it on top of her head, she knocked over the toothbrush holder with her shaking hands, and found a clip to hold her hair away from her bruised face. Hopefully, no one would notice her chopped locks. Hastily, she scrubbed the blood from her hands and face before moving back to the bedroom to dress.

She pulled clean clothes out of the closet he'd thankfully missed during his rampage. She stripped off her bloody running shorts and tank top. Bending over to pull off her shoes and socks proved to be a challenge with her back in such terrible condition. Her muscles tightened. She wiped away the majority of blood with a slashed T-shirt she grabbed from the floor. The thick cotton staunched the flow of blood from the cut on her leg. She tied another piece of T-shirt around her thigh to keep it from bleeding, until she tended it better. She finally pulled on a loose floral skirt and burgundy tunic and slid her feet into a pair of sandals.

Dressed, breathless, scared and shaking, she searched the wreckage for the phone and found it amid a broken crystal vase.

"Stop right there." Gun drawn, the officer blocked the open bedroom doorway.

Jenna froze, eyes wide, a new surge of adrenaline pumped through her veins. Telephone in hand, she'd barely had time to dial nine. "This is my place," she rasped out, her voice raw from screaming.

Gun still pointed at her, the officer asked, "What's your name?"

"Jenna Caldwell." She left off the Merrick. If she gave that name, the press would be here in ten minutes, the story splashed all over the papers.

Thank God she'd had time to clean herself up and toss the bloody clothes in the corner of the closet before the cops saw the real damage.

"Do you have ID?"

"In my purse on the table by the front door." She scanned her surroundings. "At least that's where I left it."

He exchanged a look with his partner, who withdrew to the other room to find her purse. "Who were you calling?"

"You. The police. Why are you here?"

"We received a report about a break-in." His gaze went from the smeared blood on the floor to her bruised and swollen face. "You okay?"

She ignored his question and focused on the problem. How to get out of here without being dragged to the police station, or God help her, the hospital. "A break-in. So that's why he trashed the place." Her gaze fell on the bloody candlestick. Bastard probably thought he killed her and needed to cover it up.

"What happened here?"

For the next twenty minutes she answered their grueling round of questions. She kept to the point without embellishing or adding any unnecessary details. The police found her uncooperative and attributed it to what happened with many women caught in this cycle. They called for help, then changed their mind and refused to press charges. She wanted to press charges, but knew she didn't have the evidence needed to bring him down. Right now, she had one goal, escape. As quick and as soon as possible.

"So, nothing's been taken and you never saw his face?"

"Like I said, he wore a mask."

"How can you be sure it was your ex-husband?"

"I know."

"Do you want to press charges for the assault?"

"Against who? The masked man? Even I know the charges would never stick. He'll have ten people lined up to provide an alibi and a dozen lawyers to drive a truck through my testimony. Sorry, been there, done that." If she sounded bitter, she'd earned it after years on this merry-go-round.

"At least let us call an ambulance to take you to the hospital to get checked out."

"Just some cuts and bruises," she lied. Not convincingly, judging by the officer's frown. "Nothing major. I don't need an ambulance. Just fill out your report and dump it in the this-will-go-nowhere file." She pressed her fingers to her temples in a futile attempt to stop the pounding.

"Do you have someone who can stay with you tonight?"

"I'm not staying here." To prove it, she turned her back on them and called a cab, using one of the many emergency numbers she'd memorized. On average, a cab arrived within seven minutes at the cottage. She'd timed them. She would head to the fitness club, grab her emergency supplies, and get lost.

Second, she called her lawyer, Ben Knight. When his secretary, Annie, answered, she said one thing, "Rabbit's on the run," hung up and got ready to bolt.

"What was that all about?" the officer asked, finally moving toward the door.

"Recurring nightmare."

"You know, if you help us, we can help you."

"No offense, but you can't help me. The man who did this knows how to stay in the shady gray of the law."

"Like wearing a mask and making this look like a botched robbery."

"You're catching on."

"You should press charges," he coaxed again.

"My word against his. I've filed for restraining orders multiple times and been denied. The anonymous notes could be from anyone, the phone calls all come from disposable phones, and there's never a witness to any kind of abuse. No judge will side with me against him."

"He goes to a lot of trouble to keep this thing just between the two of you."

"It's personal, and he's got a lot to lose."

"Say he did this, a judge will listen."

"He's a rich businessman who runs an international company. His face is splashed all over the society pages, the image of a corporate mover and shaker. I divorced him and took a big chunk of his assets with me, and he ruined me in the press, playing me off as the gold-digging whore. Who do you think a judge or jury would believe?"

"With your face looking like that? You."

"Botched robbery, remember."

"This is some twisted shit. Excuse the language," he said, frustrated. She felt for him. He saw this day in and day out. She lived it.

"You have no idea."

"We'll follow-up, give him a call, see if we can rattle him into an admission."

Jenna forced an indulgent smile. "It's your time to waste." She grabbed her purse and headed for the door. Tired to the bone, her feet scuffed along the hardwood.

The cab pulled up outside and she rushed into the back seat. "Bayfair Fitness, please. Quickly."

The police pulled out of the drive and her adrenaline kicked in again. No protection. She turned and checked out each window, making sure he wasn't coming after her. She couldn't let her guard down. He might be out there, following her. She had to get away. Fast. Her mind screamed at her, *"Hurry! Run! Hurry!"*

"Are you all right, lady? You don't look so good."

"I'm fine. Please, just hurry. I need to get out of here." Her voice shook and rasped out after all the screaming.

"Looks like someone beat you good."

Jenna held his gaze in the rearview mirror, unable to think of a single thing to say. She caught sight of her own face and winced. She looked like a wounded animal backed into a corner, shaking, her eyes wide and watchful.

"I hope the other guy looks worse than you do, missy." She must have indicated she didn't have the pleasure of beating the other guy bloody because he went on, "The cops'll get him. You make that bastard pay." He gave her a stern look.

Jenna wished she could make him pay. One day she would. Right now, she wanted to lie down and go to sleep. Impossible, at least for several more hours. Probably not a good idea anyway with the splitting headache, telling her she had a mild concussion.

Now, the long process of running and finding someplace safe to hide began. Ben, the only person she allowed herself to count on, would help her. That's what she paid him to do. After all, this was the sixth, no seventh, time she had to run. With all her practice, they had come up with a system. And it worked this last time. Or so they thought.

She never accessed her bank accounts directly. She didn't use any credit. She had several aliases set up. None of it mattered. Rich and spoiled, he would use all his influence and power to hunt her down for his own sport. No one ever said no to him. Until she stood up to him and dared to say no. The more times she refused him, the worse things got for her.

Those first few times he found her, he sent her pretty gifts and notes, showed up unexpectedly while she was out shopping or eating in a restaurant. The police couldn't do anything to stop him. Stalking laws were specific— and often inadequate to protect victims. Each time he showed up, she left and found a new place to hide, never giving him an opportunity to truly stalk her. He never left enough damning evidence for the police to collect and arrest him. *If* they'd arrest him.

She simply couldn't endure his unwanted attention. Then he got tired of playing contrite and demanded her return. With her resounding *no* came a shove, a push, a slap, a punch. Again, the police did nothing. He shielded himself behind his wealth, family name, and a battalion of lawyers, leaving him untouchable.

She'd waged a futile battle trying to get justice in a system not set up to protect against a powerful man's obsession. Other stalked women suffered similar circumstances, oftentimes listening to the police say the same thing she'd heard too many times—until and unless he hurts you, we can't do anything. Even then, they didn't help her. Her ex had the ability to make people say what he wanted them to say and evidence disappeared at his convenience. Money can buy silence.

"Hey lady, we're here." Frowning and looking unsure, he said, "Maybe I should take you to the hospital and have them take a look at that cut on your head."

She appreciated the thought, but couldn't take the time to tend to herself. She had to get away. "I'll be okay. What do I owe you?"

"Twenty-seven fifty-eight."

She handed him a fifty. "Keep the change and forget you ever saw me."

"No problem. I hope you'll be okay."

He smiled, but sadness filled his eyes. The sympathetic expression told her he wished he'd never seen her battered and bloody face. "I'll be fine. I just need to find a new hole to hide in," she added under her breath and exited the cab.

Slamming the door, she headed for the side entrance of the twenty-four-hour fitness club. The few people at this end of the club stared, but she kept her head down and walked directly to the locker room and her hidden emergency supplies. Relief swept through her when she palmed the orange plastic-handled key she found in her purse. The small suitcase and satchel, containing her camera bag, money, IDs, and a secure cell phone were still inside. Ben had friends in high places and guaranteed the cell phone was untraceable. Securing the bag on top of the suitcase, she rolled it behind her back out to the curb, hailed another taxi, and headed for the airport.

Next stop, the airport rental car counter. She used one of the credit cards and IDs under an assumed name to rent a car. She exited the terminal and found the waiting vehicle. Finally, safe behind the wheel, she drove out of the city and away from the terror. Constantly looking in the rearview mirror, she tried to rein in her emotions. Her head pounded, pain and exhaustion slowed her mind and body. On her way to parts unknown, after all these years, it didn't matter where she ended up. So long as she escaped him, she would drive.

Two hours later she dug out the cell phone and called Ben. Annie answered.

"It's Rabbit. I need Ben." Annie put her through without a word.

"How bad is it, Rabbit?" Ben's anguished voice came on the line.

"I'm okay. Is my identity still safe from your staff?"

"Yes. No one knows who you are, just what to do if they hear the password. Now, how bad?"

"Pretty bad." Tears filled her eyes. She refused to cry. Not now. Not when running meant safety, meant her life. Later, when she was safe and able to take the time to fall apart. She blinked back tears. "I'll send the pictures when I can. Promise you won't open them. Just stick them in the book."

"Rabbit, you know I can't make that promise. Now, tell me how bad."

His genuine concern prompted her confession. "I have a bad gash on my head, bruises from him slapping and punching me, a bad cut on my thigh, and welts on my back."

Silent tears streamed down her face. Her voice so soft, detailing all the injuries. She sounded like a small child reciting her lessons. The weakness in her voice irritated her. She'd held it together with the cops, but with Ben she let down her guard.

Barely able to pull the car over to the side of some quiet suburban street, she parked.

"What do you mean welts on your back? Did he punch you in the back?"

"A belt," she whispered, knowing he probably didn't hear her.

"What did you say?"

She spit out the ugly truth. "I said, a belt."

"Oh, God. Oh, God, Rabbit. Do you need to go to the hospital?"

"No. No hospital. He'll only get angrier if I do." Her anxiety kicked in again and the adrenaline pumped through her veins and amped up her system. When it finally wore off she'd crash. Hard.

"I can't explain away these kinds of injuries. They'll have police and reporters there asking more questions. They'll find out who I am. He doesn't want the publicity. He'll take me from the hospital and do worse to me." He'd kill her if she went to the hospital. She knew it like she knew her name.

"I don't know what happened this time. He worked himself into a rage before he even got me in the door. I can feel the gash on my leg oozing blood, and I can barely sit down in the seat to drive this car for the strapping marks across my backside." Her whole body shook and she sucked back a wracking sob.

"Rabbit, I'm so sorry. Tell me where you are. I'll come get you. Protect you. I promise." His voice pleaded and the sadness overwhelmed her.

"Please no. So far, we've been lucky he hasn't discovered you're helping me. You know what he did to my bodyguard. I couldn't stand it if he came after you, or hurt you too. All I can do is give you the evidence and wait for the right time to end this."

"Please, Rabbit, he's going to kill you."

She swiped the tears away with the back of her hand and took a deep calming breath. "I need to do this my way. It's the only way. Have you started making arrangements?"

Resigned to the fact she refused to let him come and get her, he resumed with their business arrangement.

"I contacted the Berringers. They told me about the cottage and the police. They'll total the damages and send me the bill. They've agreed to throw out your belongings. Most were destroyed anyway. They're worried about you."

"I hope you told them how truly sorry I am for what happened. The rest, well, it was only clothes. Oh, if he didn't destroy my computer, try to get that back." Her mind shut out the pain and terror and shifted to more practical matters. Easier to think about the mundane than her crazy, evil ex. Time to put the attack on the back burner and get on with hiding again.

"I spoke to the police. They're not happy you left. If you refuse to identify him as your attacker, they can't move forward. Let's file charges, fight him in court, and let people see what a monster he is."

"He wore a mask and gloves. No prints. No other witnesses. My word against his. Play that scenario out in court and I lose."

"We can build a case based on past behavior and the evidence we've collected."

"It's not enough." She sighed, the weight of the last few years too much to bear right now. "Ben, I'm tired. Get me to a safe place."

"Actually, I thought ahead this time and already have a place ready." His voice was filled with how much he hated anticipating another attack and the need for a new place to run to. All he could do for her, all she'd let him do.

"Just so happens, a friend recently moved back to his family ranch in Hidden Springs, Colorado. A huge spread, about three hundred and forty acres. I've secured a cabin for you on the property. Jack says it's away from the other buildings, across one of the pastures. He's a friend, but he doesn't know anything about you."

"If he's your friend, I don't want to put him in jeopardy."

"He's an old college buddy. I haven't seen him in years. When we ran into each other, I asked about his place and thought it would make a great hiding spot for you if you needed to run. I paid the rent for the next year. I'll call Jack and tell him you're coming. Don't worry. You'll be safe there. Jack is ex-military. He'll protect you, Rabbit."

"No one can protect against his kind of madness." A chill ran up her spine. What she wouldn't give to have someone in her life to protect and love her, instead of hurting her all the time.

"Either way, it sounds nice. Thanks for working so fast. I'll spend the next few days driving around a few of the southern states. You know, the usual misdirection and roaming should get him, or anyone watching me, off my trail, so I can safely get to Colorado."

"I'll send your usual stuff to the ranch. You'll have plenty of money and your accumulated mail. There's a card from your mother. You should call her."

"No. If she doesn't know where I am, he can't hurt her and get information from her. You've been checking on her? She's okay?"

"All is well. I make sure she has enough money. She's

getting along fine. She has her friends and her Thursday night poker parties."

Jenna thought fondly of her mother. She hadn't seen her since all of this began. The thought of her sitting around playing poker with a bunch of rowdy men and women from work made her smile. Her mother, always the life of the party, loved with her whole heart and treated everyone as a dear friend. She missed their long talks and confiding in her. After her father died, they'd grown very close. Now, she didn't let anyone close to her, not even her mother. He destroyed everything in her life, and she wouldn't let him destroy her mother's, too. "I miss her."

"I know. I'll let her know you're okay."

"Tell her . . . I'm sorry. I should have listened when she said he was no good for me."

"He's one of the wealthiest men in the country, who knew he's such a bastard?"

"Money can't buy you happiness, or sanity. Look at me. I got one of the largest divorce settlements ever awarded, and I'm on the run, hunted by my ex-husband. What I wouldn't pay for peace and safety. But money can't buy my way out of this. Nothing can." She rested her forehead on the steering wheel. "Sorry, the past is haunting me. Thanks, Ben, for everything."

"You know, Rabbit, Jack might be able to help you. Trust him."

"I don't trust anyone. Except you. I'll call if I need anything, or if the hunt begins again."

"I hate it when you say that. You don't deserve this."

"To him, I'm only the prey. Unless or until he kills me, I don't think this will ever end."

"Then let me do more than just find you a new place to hide." His words came out tight with frustration.

"How is my project coming along?" she asked, reminding him he was doing more.

"Slowly."

"Then all I can do is run. For now," she said, hoping to placate him.

"Stay safe, Rabbit."

"I'll try, Ben."

She disconnected the call and turned off the phone. Staring out the windshield for a moment, she tried to gather her strength for the long drive ahead.

Birds chirped in the trees outside. The neighborhood was quiet with charming houses that probably had loving families living in them. Just like the one she grew up in. Sad, she'd probably never have a home and a family of her own. He would never allow it.

Unless she stopped him.

Chapter Two

"THE POLICE DON'T have a thing on you. They will not pursue the matter further," David's lawyer guaranteed.

David hit the END button on his cell phone. Attacked by a masked man, Jenna had survived, but couldn't positively identify him . . . without lying, or making herself look the fool. The airtight alibi his lawyer supplied the cops ensured he wasn't a suspect.

"They can't touch me. I win again, Jenna."

He smiled at his reflection in the shabby motel's cracked mirror over the rust-stained sink, not far from Jenna's most recent hiding place. He wrinkled his nose against the smell of stale beer, sweat, and moldy carpet. She'd brought him to this dilapidated place and it pissed him off. Already shaking from the adrenaline wearing off, he fisted his hands, blood dripping into the sink from the cut on his palm.

He moved his hand through the air, imagined cutting

Jenna's thigh again, and felt the rush of power and satisfaction that line of blood down her pale skin had invoked.

David inhaled deeply to settle the charge of energy memories of making Jenna pay unleashed in him. He smelled the blood, tasted its coppery scent on his tongue, and smiled at himself in the mirror.

No doubt Jenna was on the run again. Good. He so enjoyed finding her.

Chapter Three

JENNA SAT IN her car outside a diner in Hidden Springs, Colorado. The last four days a haze of highways and back roads. She exhausted herself zigzagging all over the south before heading west toward Colorado. She changed rental cars three times, finally buying a new SUV in Kentucky. Ben arranged for the vehicle using one of her many trusts.

The trusts hid her name behind company after company. At this point, she didn't know which were real companies, or just on paper. Ben hid her name and whereabouts, using the millions from her divorce settlement. Funny how the money she used to hide came from the very man who hunted her. The irony wasn't lost on her.

In the last four days, she'd slept about ten hours. When she had to, she slept an hour or two in the car at truck stops, having stopped at only one fleabag no-tell-motel the first night to tend her wounds as best she could with her limited first aid kit. She would buy fresh bandages in town before heading to the cabin. She longed to be at the ranch, relatively safe, able to relax and rest.

The welts on her back and legs throbbed after sitting in car after car. The cut on her thigh pulsed with heat and pain, probably infected; no amount of ibuprofen took the edge off. She'd been eating it like candy. To top it off, she had a fever.

Jenna eased out of the car, careful not to move too quickly and send her back muscles into spasm again. Stiff, she limped on her right leg because of the cut. She slid on her sunglasses to hide the dark circles and bruises. She didn't have anything to cover the cut above her temple, or hide the dark bruise along her jaw where he slugged her. She made her way across the street to the local grocery store. For the first time, she noticed the quiet street and picturesque town. She inhaled deeply the crisp clean air, hoping to revive her tired body and mind.

Surrounded by beautiful mountains, the town had an old west quality. The buildings weren't large, but small storefronts lining the main street. In addition to the diner, the quaint storefronts offered a jewelry store, bank, ice cream parlor, hair salon, clothing stores, and antique shops. Just what you'd expect to find on Main Street in a small town. Benches and pots of red and white flowers sat in front of some of the stores and several people window-shopped.

The grocery store was the largest, most modern building with a big parking lot on the side. She shopped for bandages, medicine, and a few essential food items for the cabin. In a few days, she would come back and stock up. For now, the most important thing on her mind was mending her leg and getting some sleep.

The teenage checkout girl stared at her face, unable to hide her curiosity. She knew the picture she made; everyone she passed gawked. After all the times she had been bloodied and bruised, she expected the stares. In a small town like this, people would talk about the battered woman who came into the store, but they wouldn't get involved.

She just didn't care anymore. Not today. Her nerves were shot, and she wanted to get to the cabin before she really lost it. She paid the girl with shaking hands, grabbed her bags of groceries, and headed back to her car aware that people watched her every step.

JACK WALKED DOWN Main Street with Sally to the diner and noticed the new SUV parked out front. Not many new cars in a small town like Hidden Springs. The woman sitting in the driver's seat had her head back, eyes closed. At first, he thought maybe she fell asleep, until she shifted awkwardly and opened the car door. Moving more like an eighty-year-old woman, she eased out and limped toward the grocery store. About five-six, skinny as a beanpole and pale as a ghost. Though he missed getting a good look at her face, especially after she put on her shades, he did notice her nicely rounded curves. Her hair, knotted on top of her head, deep brown, until the sun shone on it, flashed red, like bark catching fire.

He'd like to see it by firelight and watch it come to life. He shook his head to dislodge the thoughts taking root and shoved them away. He didn't need complications in his life. Women were usually a complication—at least the ones he'd dated.

Still, he watched her walk, unable to help himself. Something about her drew him. Pale, but probably beautiful on a good day. Maybe she had the flu. It had been going around town for the last few weeks.

Jack entered the diner and took his usual back corner booth. Sally, his golden retriever, took up residence on his boots under the table and settled in for a late afternoon nap.

"Hey, Mary. How's business today?"

"Not bad. A little slow right now, but the dinner crowd should be coming in soon. Do you want the usual?"

"Yeah. Thanks."

Mary brought him his cup of coffee, saying his burger and fries would be out shortly. Jack read the paper, drank the strong brew, and waited for his lunch.

The bell over the front door rang and the young woman from the SUV came into the diner. Careful of her movements, she lowered herself onto a stool at the counter. Very pretty at a distance, up close, she made some ember spark to life inside him.

"I'd like a cup of coffee and a turkey sandwich, please." Her hoarse voice reinforced his earlier assumption she suffered some ailment.

"Are you okay?" Mary asked.

"I'm fine." She lowered her head and took off her

glasses, laid them on the counter with her purse. Mary poured her coffee and put in her order with her customary efficiency.

Jenna put her shaking hands around the hot mug and drank deeply, hoping the coffee would breathe a little life and warmth back into her. Not many customers in the diner at this hour. The fewer people around her, the safer she felt. The other customers, including the nice-looking man in the corner, didn't seem to notice her. Sandy blond hair, a day's growth of beard, and the bluest eyes she had ever seen fixed on the paper he was reading. Relaxed in the room and with himself, he conveyed strength and confidence. Nothing bothered him. It was in the way he took up the space in the booth. She envied people like him. She used to be like him. Once.

Jack couldn't stop staring at her over his paper. She turned her head his way and he stopped breathing. Dark circles under her eyes marred her sickly pale skin. A dark bruise bloomed along her jaw, and a bad cut ran up her temple to her forehead. He took a closer inspection. Bruises speckled her arms, several more on the part of her legs revealed beneath the hem of her skirt. Her green eyes and face remained blank. *What the hell happened to her?*

Mary asked after her. She replied with an automatic *fine*, but Jack saw a lot during his life in the military and knew she was far from okay. She tried to hide it, but not very well. He wondered if he shouldn't take her to the hospital. He checked the impulse to go to her and at least try to make her smile. She looked lonelier than he'd felt the last several months.

Mary placed his order in front of him and he asked under his breath, "Is everything okay up there?"

"I don't know, Jack. She says she's fine, but did you see her?" Mary whispered back.

"Yeah, I see her." He couldn't not see her. He tried, but everything inside him had focused on her.

After leaving his order, Mary, pity and sadness set in her lips and eyes, grabbed the woman's late lunch and set it on the counter in front of her. The woman worked up half a smile, but it took effort. She nodded her thanks and ate her sandwich in silence with her head down. Judging by the way she put away her lunch, Jack figured she hadn't eaten a decent meal in a while.

"Excuse me, do you know how to get to Stargazer Ranch?"

Mary turned from making fresh coffee. "What do you want with Jack Turner's place?"

"I rented a cabin on his property."

"Mr. Turner is sitting in that booth over there. He'll give you directions."

She laid a twenty on the counter, stood, kept her hand on the back of the stools for balance, and walked over to him. She stopped about four feet away and cleared her throat to get his attention from the paper he pretended to read.

Not wanting to make it obvious he'd been watching her the whole time, he asked, "Can I help you, ma'am?"

"Mr. Turner?"

"Yes. What can I do for you?"

"I'm Jenna," she said, leaving off her last name. "Ben said he rented a cabin for me at your place."

Sally got up from under the table and sat guard at Jenna's feet. Sally rubbed against Jenna's leg, and unless he hadn't been looking at her face, he would have missed the small wince of pain that crossed her eyes. She hid it quickly and bent to pet the dog on the head. Soft, loving strokes. Jack liked her for that alone.

"Ben and I go way back. I saw him a few months ago. He rented the place, paid for a full year, but never said when to expect you. He called a few days ago, said you might show up soon. I guess you're here." She wasn't exactly what he expected.

"I am. Would you please tell me how to get to your place? Perhaps you have the keys, or someone at the ranch can give them to me."

"You look like you're about to fall over, why don't you sit down."

"I really just want to get to the cabin. I need some sleep."

"Looks like you need a hospital," he coaxed in a soft voice.

Her eyes pleaded with him. "Mr. Turner, please. Directions to the cabin, that's all I want." The fragility in her voice tore at his heart.

"Follow Sally and me back to the ranch. We'll get you settled. And it's Jack. Call me Jack."

"I don't want to cut your supper short, Jack."

"No trouble. I'll take the rest of my food to go, and we'll get you to the ranch." He asked Mary to box up his meal. She made quick work of the job and handed over his lunch.

Jack exited the booth and stood up tall in front of her. Just to see her reaction, he took a step toward her. She took two quick steps back. Sally stayed in front of her. Just what he thought, she was afraid of him—men. His anger flashed, and he narrowed his eyes. Some man did this to her. For reasons he didn't want to identify, tenderness welled in his heart. She reminded him of a wounded bird. Skinny as one, too. Great legs from what he glimpsed below the flowered skirt. As wrinkled as she appeared, he guessed she'd been on the road a long time.

He took another step toward her. She took one back, Sally keeping pace with her.

"Don't worry. I won't touch you." He dropped his voice to a near whisper. Her eyes grew large and the deep green softened to jade. He took a good long look into those pools of green. For a second, he thought he recognized something essential in them.

"Um"—she held her hands tight together in front of her—"I don't like people being too close."

"It's all right." Voice soft, he coaxed, "You go out first, and I'll be right behind you."

Unable to stop looking at her, something pulled them toward each other. He thought she noticed it, too. They started for the door together, but she peeked over her shoulder twice to make sure he didn't get too close.

"Shouldn't you pay your bill?"

Jack gazed into her sad eyes. "I own the place."

"Oh."

"Don't you want your change, miss?" Mary called after Jenna before she exited the door. She turned so abruptly she almost ran straight into his chest. She took a quick step backward and so did he. He gave her enough space so he didn't crowd her or make her feel threatened. Sally stayed at her side.

"Keep the change." Jenna half smiled, unable to meet Mary's eyes. The tip wasn't for the service, but for caring about her well-being. He liked her for that, too.

They exited the diner and Jenna headed for her SUV with Sally on her heels. Jack's truck sat parked a few spaces past hers.

"Hop in my truck. I'll drive you and send one of my guys to pick up your car later. You look like you're about to fall over. It's dangerous to drive when you're exhausted."

"I'm okay. I made it this far, I'll make it the rest of the way."

"I'd hate to see you fall asleep at the wheel and crash. I'd never get a chance to get to know you," he added, without really thinking.

The last made her take a step back, like even the thought of getting to know him made her want to distance herself. Still, something in the way she looked at him, just for a split second, made him think she might be interested in getting to know him too.

"I'll be okay. Shall we go?"

Standoff. No way to convince her to get into his truck with him, a man she didn't know and feared based on some other asshole's unholy acts. Shit. Afraid to let her drive herself, but he relented. What could he do? If he tried to force her, she'd probably take off. "Come on, Sally, in the truck."

Sally didn't budge. She stood at the door of the SUV next to Jenna, who stared down at the dog.

"Go on, girl. Go to the truck."

Sally refused. Ornery, she sat on Jenna's feet.

"Sally, come on. Get in the truck." Jack let his impatience tinge his voice. He wanted to get Jenna to the cabin and off her feet. She wouldn't be standing much longer in her condition.

"Jack, if you don't mind, she can ride with me. It's no trouble." Jenna opened the door and Sally jumped in.

Jenna carefully raised herself into the high driver's seat. He wondered what her clothes were hiding. The cut and bruises on her face were probably not her only wounds. The way she moved indicated her back bothered her and the limp pointed to an injury to her leg. The skirt went down to just below her knees. Her thigh or hip must be injured.

His anger simmered and a knot fisted in his stomach. He wanted to kill whoever did this to her. He wanted to take her in his arms, kiss every inch of her, and take all the hurt away.

Nice, Jack. Real nice. She's hurt, and you've got her undressed to tend a hell of a lot more than whatever wounds she's hiding.

Alone for a long time, too long maybe, he preferred it that way these days. Didn't he? His last relationship ended in disaster when he finally closed his wallet and asked to share something more than his credit card. He wanted what his sister had, love, a family. Instead, he got a woman who took and gave nothing back. Jenna didn't seem that way. Shoot, she'd left Mary a fourteen-dollar tip on a six-dollar meal just because Mary was nice to her. Now, that's saying something. Reminded him of his mother, her warmth and kindness innate. He found it rarely in the women he dated, but seeing it in Jenna . . . well, it made him want to break his dinner-for-one streak and ask her for a date. His mother once told him after a particularly bad breakup that true beauty shines through from a warm heart.

Jenna leaned over the console, wrapped her arms around Sally, and hugged the dog close. Her eyes closed when Sally nuzzled against her neck, offering the comfort Jenna so obviously needed and wanted. Funny, he wanted to give it to her.

Well, she is staying at his ranch for the next several months. Plenty of time to get to know Jenna with the sad green eyes.

Chapter Four

JENNA HARDLY NOTICED the dense woods, the pungent smell of pines, the green grass, or brilliantly blue sky. She concentrated on the two-lane highway and the silver truck in front of her. Whenever her eyes drooped, Sally barked.

"What a smart dog you are, keeping me awake." She gave Sally a nice pat on the head and rubbed behind her ears. Sally wagged her tail and kept an eye on her as she drove.

They turned off the main highway onto a deserted road that wound up through the hills and down into the next valley. A huge ranch with green pastures filled with horses spread out before her. The main house sat off to the right of the property with several cabins tucked behind the huge white barn. The barn looked new, and from what she could see, well maintained. Jack, obviously, ran a tight operation.

Across a large pasture and off to the left, tucked into the trees, another cabin stood, its pointed peak reaching to the high limbs. Beautiful, all wood with large windows, rustic, but not run down. Near the cabin, a creek ran along the back side and through the far end of the pasture where it met the trees again. She imagined hearing the rushing water while she slept. She couldn't wait to explore.

Jack headed toward the cabin, Jenna followed. The cabin's gravel driveway split off from the main road just after the gates to the main ranch.

Jack exited his truck and headed over to Jenna's SUV. He opened the door for her and stepped back a good two feet, allowing her to exit on her own. Barely able to move, when she stood up, she wavered. He made a grab for her arm, but she braced herself with a hand on the door and the other held palm up to stop him before he touched her.

"I'm fine. Just tired." Sally jumped out and ran up the steps to the cabin door, waiting patiently for them to let her in.

"I'll get your bags," Jack offered, giving her the space she needed, but keeping an eye on her just the same.

"You don't have to do that. I can manage."

"I'll be surprised if you can get up those five steps to the door," he offered with a smile to soften the frustration in his voice. He grew more disturbed with every tired movement and sigh she made.

Too tired to argue with him, he was only trying to help, and she was being stubborn.

He isn't a threat. She repeated that to herself again. And again.

Jenna walked toward the cabin at a snail's pace, her body rebelling against her brain's commands. Her leg was getting worse, her back and shoulders stiff. Every move made her muscles ache. Feverish sweat broke out on her forehead and between her breasts.

Jack passed her, went up the steps and into the cabin before she made it to the first step. By the time she made it up to the third, he passed her on the way back to the car and brought up the rest of her bags and groceries. He never said a word about her slow progress, but his warm eyes remained watchful. She had no doubt if he thought she was really in trouble, he'd come to her rescue. Not such a bad feeling, she thought.

She finally made it in the door. Jack stood in the kitchen, putting her groceries in the cupboards.

"You only bought fruit and dry goods? Nothing for the refrigerator?"

"I'll go back to town in a few days for more. I didn't know how long it would take to get here, so I only bought essentials."

"What's with all the bandages? Are you hurt?" Ridiculous question. The bruises, her exhaustion, her inability to move normally proved she hurt. He needed to know how bad. All the bandages and medicine made him nervous. He didn't think she'd give him a straight answer, but she surprised him again.

"I have a cut on my thigh. I'll put a fresh bandage on it. It'll be fine. No problem."

Yeah, right, no problem. He should put her up over his shoulder and drag her to a hospital. Let a doctor get those clothes off her and see what they were hiding, find out what was hiding under that pale skin. He hoped she didn't have any internal injuries.

Jenna ignored his penetrating scrutiny and focused on the beautiful and spacious cabin. The kitchen was off to the back of the living space. Everywhere her gaze fell on wood: wood walls, cabinets, floors, and furniture. She loved it. A large loft with a queen-sized bed framed by massive windows sat at the top of a steep set of stairs. A brown leather sofa faced the fireplace with a cream and navy blue rug under the pine coffee table. A gorgeous river-rock fireplace invited her to set a blaze and curl up in front of it for the next week. That's just what she needed, someplace soft and warm to lie down and sleep.

Her gaze fell to the wood floor. Flashes of memories poured over her: her lying helpless, bleeding in the cottage, all the pain and destruction. She inhaled sharply. Jack stared at her with blue-gray eyes that saw far more than she wanted him to see.

She tried to cover her behavior. "The cabin is wonderful. I love it. Thanks for renting it to me."

He frowned, not buying her false exuberance. "I'm glad you like it. It gets cold at night this time of year. I'll build you a fire and let you get some rest. There's plenty of wood here and more on the back porch. If you run low, just let me know."

"I'd love a fire. Thanks."

He took another long look at her and at the stairs leading to the bed. She wanted to sleep. He wanted her off her feet. He didn't even want to acknowledge the little daydream he had going of undressing her and laying her out on the cool sheets upstairs and them making a fire of their own.

"Can you make it up those stairs?"

She frowned, the longing for the bed clear in her eyes. "I'll crash on the couch for a while. Once I've had some sleep, I'll be better."

"Right. Better is probably relative in your world," he said under his breath. Her eyes narrowed when she didn't hear him, and he said, "I'll help you up to the bed."

"No," she protested and took two steps back and put up both hands this time, despite the fact he stood five feet away and never made a move toward her. "I'm sorry, I'll be fine."

"That's what you keep saying, but you don't look fine, sweetheart." He shoved down his instincts to take care of her, carry her up to bed, tend her wounds, and tuck her in for a good long sleep. He mentally kicked the shit out of his insane thoughts of wrapping her in his arms and holding her. Instead, he gave his hands something better to do and kneeled in front of the cold fireplace and stacked heavy logs and kindling, sparking a match, and setting them to blaze.

That's one way to keep her warm and give her some comfort. His imagination mocked him with several more.

Jack put a heavy log into the fireplace, and Jenna watched the play of muscles in his arms with fascination. His shirt stretched across the wide expanse of his back and shoulders, making her catch her breath at the sight of his handsome features. It had been a long time since a man piqued her interest and made her think about how his skin would feel against her palms, or how all that strength turned to gentleness. She averted her eyes and pet Sally to distract herself from this man.

He stared into the fire, poking and shifting the logs to catch and flare. He turned back toward her, studying her like some kind of experiment under a microscope.

"Thank you for everything. If you don't mind, I'd like to be alone." He stared, a touch of pity replacing the male interest she caught earlier. Everyone always pitied her. She just didn't have anything left inside her to care, to offer up explanations, or false excuses for what that bastard did to her. "Please, Jack, just go. Let me rest."

Nothing else to do, she wasn't any of his business. Shocking himself, he thought, I want to make you my business. Time to do some serious thinking about how he'd gone to town for a burger and ended up mixed up with a woman like Jenna.

"Okay, but if you need anything, my number's by the phone in the kitchen along with the keys to the cabin." He hated to leave her alone. "Do you want me to call someone to come and look after you? I've got a sister. She can come by later and check on you."

"I'll be fine. You can go."

Tears clogged her throat, making her words stilted. She valiantly held on to her bravery, doing her best to get him out of there, so he wouldn't see her break down. He'd give her that courtesy and reluctantly head for the door. The last thing he wanted was to see her cry.

"Um, Jack. Do you know where I can get a haircut?"

A haircut? About to keel over, and she wanted to know where to get a haircut. He shook his head, bewildered by her request.

"Just so happens my sister works at the local beauty salon. I'll send her by later tonight, around eight. You can have the nap you desperately need, she can check on you and cut your hair here. That way you don't have to go back to town until you're feeling better." With a resigned sigh, he added, "I'll feel better knowing someone made sure you're still alive."

Jenna ignored his last comment, frowned and looked away to let him know she didn't appreciate his harping on her about her condition. Too bad. If he could help himself, he would.

"I don't want to inconvenience her by asking her to come all the way out here."

"She lives in a house just over a hill behind the main house. She won't mind."

"I really don't want to be any trouble. If you're sure she won't mind, then thanks."

"No thanks necessary. It's my pleasure. Come on, Sally, let's leave Jenna alone."

Sally didn't move. She stayed in between him and Jenna. Guarding. Jack opened the cabin door and waited. "Come on, girl. Let's go."

Again, Sally didn't move. "Let her stay. I'll send her home later."

Jack shook his head again, looked at his dog guarding his new tenant, deserting him, and walked out the door before he did something stupid. Jenna left the car door open. He went to shut it and noticed the blood on the driver's seat. The cut she mentioned must be bleeding. He hoped she cleaned and bandaged it before she fell asleep. He thought about going back in and getting a look at the cut himself. He took a couple steps toward the cabin, then thought better of it. Not his responsibility. She said she's fine and wanted to rest. He'd let her and hope when Summer came to give her the haircut, she'd be feeling better.

She's not my business, he scolded himself again. And again. And again. So, why did the band around his chest get tighter and tighter the more he tried not to think about her?

Chapter Five

JENNA WANTED TO get cleaned up before she slept for the next two days. She dug out her silk robe and toiletries from her emergency suitcase by the stairs. She grabbed her camera bag and headed for the bathroom, making sure both the back and front doors were locked. She curbed her obsessive need to check the locks again. Sally settled in front of the fire, watching Jenna move around the cabin.

Happy the bathroom was on the first floor, she stepped inside the lovely room. It boasted a spacious tub and separate shower. The thick towels were navy blue. A turquoise rug brightened the slate gray floor. Her favorite part, a large window made of frosted glass blocks and the skylight above the tub. At night, she could watch the stars while she soaked in the bath. Jack sure had great taste. Simple. Nice.

She stripped off the clothes she'd been wearing for four

days. She should burn them. Frantic, she hadn't stopped unless absolutely necessary. She took off the white gauze pad and tape she'd hastily used to cover the gash down her thigh. She should've taken better care of it by now. At least cleaned and closed it with some butterfly bandages and put some antibiotic ointment on it. Instead she'd left it open and caked in dried blood. But when things like this happened and the panic set in, she forgot everything, except escape—run far and fast.

Of course, he'd never hurt her this badly.

The cut flared an angry red, infected. It stung and throbbed when she touched it. She needed to put medicine on it and try to close the wound. For now, she piled everything on the tile floor and stepped into the shower. She adjusted the spray to lukewarm, so as not to burn the raw abrasions and welts on her back. She avoided looking down as the water, red with blood from her back and thigh, ran down the drain and disappeared. She took the clip out of her hair and let it fall down to the middle of her back. Even that hurt. She washed her hair, her arms and legs heavy as lead weights.

Out of the shower, she gingerly dried herself. The shower boosted her spirits. She felt better being clean, but her whole body shook with fatigue and weariness as the fever intensified. She needed to lie down before she fell down.

First, she took care of business. She pulled the camera out of the bag, and using the full-length mirror on the wall by the tub and the flip around screen, she snapped a photo of the front of herself. The photo would show the bruise on her jaw, the cut on her head, and all the bruises on her ribcage. Then she turned around. She moved her wet hair over her right shoulder, placed the camera on her left shoulder, and snapped a picture of her back. Unenthused, she checked both pictures and ensured the date stamp and time were correct. She would email the photos to Ben, once she got a new computer. One of these days, the authorities would make good on her complaints and restraining order requests and they would arrest him. She held on to hope, even though it was like trying to catch fog.

She wrapped a towel over her hair and put on her robe. She grabbed the camera and shuffled out toward the fire, carelessly tossing it on the coffee table.

She grabbed the slate blue blanket draped over the back of the couch and a couple of the large pillows, moving mindlessly, like the walking dead. She laid the pillows on the floor in front of the fire and lay down on her stomach bringing the blanket over her legs. Asleep as soon as her head hit the pillows. She hardly registered the feel of Sally curling up next to her, guarding her while she slept. Oblivion was sometimes necessary for survival.

SUMMER TURNER KNOCKED, no *pounded*, on the door for at least five minutes. The woman slept on her stomach by the fire, never moving or acknowledging the loud thuds.

"Well, damn. Jack said to come and check on her and give her a haircut. The least she could do is answer the door." She pounded on the wood again. Nothing.

"That's it. I'm calling Jack."

She dug out her cell phone and dialed her brother. "Jack, I'm at the cabin. I see the woman, but she won't wake up and answer the door."

"What do you mean she won't wake up?"

"Like I said, she's asleep by the fire. She's got a towel on her hair, and she's wearing a really pretty white robe with red roses on the back. I've been knocking for five minutes. She won't wake up and the place is locked up tight. Sally is curled up next to her watching me out here like I'm crazy."

"I'm on my way over. I have the spare key. Keep an eye on her."

"Like she's going anywhere. She's not even moving."

Jack hung up and hauled ass out of the barn to his truck. He sped down the driveway, hoping Jenna was all right and knowing in his gut something was terribly wrong. He shouldn't have left her. He should have taken her to the damn hospital, even if he had to drag her by that hair she was so concerned about getting cut.

The trip took only a couple minutes, but Jack worked himself into a panic. He flashed back to days in the field, soldiers bloody and dying as he tried to help. Stomping down the military memories and trying to stay focused in the here and now, he launched himself up the stairs toward his waiting sister. Smart, she stood back as he barreled for the entrance. He unlocked the door and crossed to Jenna in a few long strides. They weren't red roses on the robe like his sister described, but blood. Fresh blood. His sister came in and kneeled by Jenna's head and unwrapped the towel from her hair. It spilled over the pillow, flashing red in the firelight. Summer ran her fingers through the wet strands and pushed them away from Jenna's bruised face.

"Jack, what the hell is this? She's bleeding and it looks like someone took hedge clippers to her hair. No wonder she wanted a haircut. Who did this to her?"

"I don't know. She showed up today. Ben rented the place for her a few months back. Never said when she was coming, just paid for a year and asked me to keep the place ready for her."

"She needs an ambulance. She's so pale. Her skin is hot and slick. It's not because of the fire, either. She's sick."

Something inside him warned not to do the obvious thing, but protect Jenna. "I'm calling Ben." He stood to dial his phone and spotted the digital camera on the table. He picked it up, hit the power button, and swore vividly. He'd known her clothes hid something, but never expected anything as bad as what the photos revealed.

"Ben, what the hell is going on? It's Jack. Jenna showed up today out of the blue. She's unconscious on the floor, bleeding."

"What? She told me she'd be okay. She said . . ." Ben's voice trailed off.

"She took pictures of herself. She's got slash marks across her entire backside and a cut about a foot long on her thigh. Nearly every inch of her is covered in bruises. Now, tell me who she is and what happened to her."

Jack vibrated with anger and concern for this poor woman. Summer pulled the blanket off Jenna's legs. She accidentally bumped the cut and Jenna moaned with pain. Jack's stomach turned. Summer stroked Jenna's hair and whispered, "You're okay. We won't hurt you. We'll take care of you." Jack's throat closed up with emotion.

"She took the photos for me. I'll put them in the book with the others."

Jack interrupted and spoke very slowly and deliberately. "What do you mean the others? How many times has this happened?"

Ben's heavy sigh whooshed into the phone. Jack felt his frustration. Jenna moaned again, and he died a little inside.

"Once is too many," Ben expressed, a weary sigh to his voice.

Jack agreed with the sentiment.

"Never this bad, according to what you and Jenna have told me about what happened. But still ... I don't know how she survives.

"I don't even know what she really looks like. I've never seen her in person. I've seen pictures of her, but my mind always goes to the images of her bruised and bloody. The photos she sends to me, I try not to look too close. It's so damn hard to see her ... to know ... Will she be all right?"

Summer managed to get the robe off Jenna without disturbing any more of the wounds. She used the bandages Jenna bought to clean some of the injuries and stop the bleeding. He saw all the damage now and it made him ill. He kneeled down next to Jenna and placed a hand on her calf next to one of the many old scars marring her body. Her skin burned with fever beneath his palm. Still, that something extra that flared between them shot up his arm and danced across all his nerves.

"Ben, she needs to go to the hospital. She refused my offer before, but now it's not an option. She has a fever and her leg needs stitches. It's infected."

"No. You can't do that. If he finds out she went to the hospital . . . He'll kill her next time. I know he'll kill her."

"Who? Who is doing this to her, and how would he find out if she went to the hospital?"

"Her ex-husband. I can't explain it all now, but he'd find out. Either that or the police will discover who she is, and the media will report she's there in Hidden Springs. Then he'd surely know where to find her. Please, Jack. You're trained in combat emergency medical care. You can stitch her up, get her well again."

"I can, yes, but she needs a hospital."

"She needs you. That's why I sent her to you. Please, Jack, as a favor to me, help her. Protect her. She won't let me. Hell, she won't let anyone near her. You're my last hope that she'll survive."

Jack wanted to dump her at the hospital, let them care for her, and not think about her ever again. Stick to his safe, normal life on the ranch. After he left the military, he swore he'd never hold another person's life in his hands. He'd never lose another friend.

He didn't want to let her into his life. Shit. Too late. She was already living on his property. He'd been the one to bring her here, even after he saw the bruises at the diner and knew what they meant. Steeling himself against that, hc answered resignedly, "Fine. I'll take care of her. I'll call you later, and you'll tell me the whole story."

He shoved the phone back into his pocket and gave himself over to the new feelings resonating within him. He couldn't give her over to anyone else and pretend he'd never seen her. He'd never forget her. Hell, the truth was he couldn't not help her. She needed him. And, damnit all to hell, he felt something for her. He hadn't felt anything in a long time. And he resented her for making him feel. Why her? Now? She moaned in pain. Giving himself over to fate, he'd do everything possible to help her and make her well. He'd make sure no one ever did this to her again.

Chapter Six

"I'VE NEVER SEEN anything like this, Jack."

Jenna lay moaning in pain, never actually waking up, her body wracked with fever. Summer kept whispering to her and smoothed her hair like she did with her daughter. "This poor woman, someone beat her."

Jack placed a hand on Summer's shoulder to reassure her. He needed the touch as much as she did. "I'll take care of her."

"No, we'll take care of her. No one should end up like this." Summer shook her open hands at Jenna. "How can we live in a world where someone gets away with beating someone, cutting them?"

Summer, the baby of the family, grew up loved and protected. She couldn't fathom being in Jenna's condition and ending up in a new place alone. She couldn't conceive of lying down hurt, knowing no one was coming to take care of her, because she had

Jack, their brother and parents, and a husband who loved her.

"Doesn't she have someone to care for her?" Summer ran a shaking hand through the side of her hair and the shine of tears filling her eyes spilled over her lashes. She swiped them away and sighed.

Jack ran his hand over his sister's hair. "Ben says she's been on the run for a couple of years. This isn't the first time she's been hurt. And no, I don't think she has anyone. More likely, she won't allow anyone close to her for fear they may be hurt, too."

Jack's voice calmed and went soft. He didn't even notice he kept stroking Jenna's calf, holding on to his sister's shoulder.

"What are we going to do?" Summer asked, unsure where to begin.

"Go out to the truck and open the passenger door. I'll carry her out and we'll take her to the house. I can take care of her there. Call Beth and tell her to get the guest room ready."

"Do you think we should move her? How will you pick her up without hurting her back?" Summer bit her lip, unable to really look at the welts and cuts.

"I don't have a choice. Hopefully, she's so out of it, she won't know or feel any pain. God help me if she wakes up." He narrowed his eyes and frowned down at Jenna. "Go. Hurry. Call Beth. Get the truck open. We need to get that cut on her leg cleaned and her fever down."

Summer ran out the front door with his phone to her ear. Jack went up to the loft and grabbed a fleece blanket from the bed to protect Jenna from the cold outside. She didn't have any clothes on, nor could she with her body in that condition. Desperate to get her to the house and his medical supplies, he hadn't felt fear like this since before he returned from the military. He didn't think he could feel anything anymore. Not until he laid eyes on Jenna.

Sally never left Jenna's side. Jack softly put the blanket over her and Sally nudged Jack's arm with her nose.

"Don't worry, girl, I won't hurt her."

Jack gently tugged Jenna's arms to try to turn her over. Jenna stirred and murmured something over and over. Jack put his head down close to her lips.

"No. No more. Stop. I won't go with you. I'll run. I'll run. Please stop." She tried to protect herself from her imagined attacker, raising her arms to cover her face.

Jack pressed his forehead to hers, lightly restraining her arms so she wouldn't hurt herself any more. He whispered to her. "Don't worry, Jenna. No one will ever hurt you again. I'm taking you home now."

"No home. No safe place."

He knew how she felt. She'd been running for so long, she had no home, no place or person to make her feel protected and safe. Jack knew just how that felt, being in some foreign country, fighting for freedom and always being on guard, and wishing for home.

"Come on, honey. When I lift you up, it's going to hurt, but I promise you'll be safe."

Jenna cried out when Jack lifted her from the floor. Then her eyes rolled back in her head and she passed out. Jack let out a heavy sigh of relief. Limp in his arms, her head resting on his shoulder, he rushed her out the door and eased into the truck. Summer closed the cabin door after Sally ran after him. Sally and Summer jumped in the driver's side and they sped off toward the house.

Jack rested his cheek on Jenna's head and spoke reassuringly to her the whole time. Summer tried to avoid every bump and hole in the gravel driveways, but the drive was anything but smooth. Jack held tight to Jenna, still talking to her softly and letting her know she was safe.

Beth ran down from the porch to open the door for Jack as soon as they arrived. Jack got out with Jenna, still unconscious in his arms. Sally followed him up the steps. At the top, he turned to Summer, who ran up behind him.

"You and Beth go down to the barn. In my office is a large green military medic bag behind my desk. Bring it. If it's too heavy, have one of the guys help you carry it, but hurry."

Summer and Beth were already running for the barn.

Jack made his way into the big house. He took Jenna up the stairs to the guest bedroom. Beth had turned back the covers on the bed. A lamp cast a soft glow from the bedside table. Jack carefully set Jenna on the bed, gently rolling her onto her stomach and out of the blanket he wrapped her in. He went into the bathroom and came back with a towel, a couple ibuprofen, and some water. He placed the towel over her bottom, and had just managed to get her to swallow the pills when Summer, Beth, and one of his ranch hands, Pete, came in with the Army medic bag.

"What the hell?" Pete gaped at Jenna.

Jenna opened her eyes wide and screamed, "No more!" She tried to get up from the bed, but couldn't even manage to get her arms under her.

"Get out," Jack shouted at Pete. He put a calming hand on Jenna's head, encouraging her to lie down, and leaned close to her ear. "You're all right. No one will hurt you. Stay still. You're hurting yourself, baby. Please, stay still."

Summer and Beth stood like toy soldiers at the foot of the bed. As he spoke, Jenna's body relaxed and Jack's knotted muscles unwound.

Pete left the room as ordered and Beth went after him. Jack overheard them on the stairs. "What the hell was that all about? I ain't never seen Jack look that way, or yell at me like that."

"I know, Pete. I don't know who that woman is, but Jack won't let anyone near her. I've never seen anything like it. Did you see her back? What did that to her?"

"Not what. Who." Jack heard Pete's furious words, "A man. And if Jack gets his hands on the scum, he'll kill him."

Amen, Jack thought.

Chapter Seven

DAVID TOOK THE call in his office, sitting behind his desk. He turned his hand palm up and stared at the healing cut, remembering his time alone with Jenna fondly. The police tried to question him again, but his lawyer held them off. Untouchable. The thought made him smile.

"Where is she?"

"I lost her in Tennessee," a deep voice came over the phone, clipped and to the point.

"You lost her." He reined in his fury and responded, "I see."

Rattled by the dead calm tone, his man offered up an excuse. "I thought I picked up her trail heading out of state, but I lost her at a gas station where three major highways converge."

"You mean she lost you." He both loved and hated how smart and clever she could be. It made it difficult to find her, but it made the chase that much more interesting and challenging.

"Yes, sir."

"Find her." Less calmly, he shouted, "And don't take five months to do it this time!" Rage simmered in his gut, feeding his need to find her. The longer it took, the more impatient he grew, which had disintegrated his control this last time. Next time he'd keep his wits, take his time, play out his plans, and enjoy every minute she was at his mercy. A shiver of anticipation ran through him and made him hard. With that thought in mind, he ended the call by saying, "You know what to do. She'll make a mistake. She always does."

And then I'll find you.

Chapter Eight

SUMMER CAME OUT of the bathroom with a bowl of cool
water and a washcloth. Jack sorted out antiseptic, bandages, syringes, medicines, and other things to fix up
Jenna, determined to make her well.

Summer knelt next to the bed by Jenna's head and
placed a cool washcloth on her forehead. "What are you
going to do with all this stuff?"

"First, I need to clean all the bleeding wounds with antiseptic. It'll hurt, but I've got to clean the wounds. I'll stitch
up her leg. I have some medicine here that will numb it for
the most part, but she'll probably know what I'm doing.
Then I'll bandage her up the best I can and hope she sleeps
and her fever breaks. Tell Beth to go down to the barn and
ask one of the guys to give her a bottle of antibiotics."

"The medicine you use on the horses?"

"Trust me, it'll work. She needs them now before this
nasty infection spreads."

"Shouldn't we call Doc Stanton and ask him to come and treat her?"

"No. Ben said no hospitals. She doesn't need anything I can't do for her. If she gets worse, we'll have Doc take a look. Now, please, send Beth. The sooner we get the antibiotics into her, the faster we can stave off this infection in her leg."

Summer took off out of the room. Sally jumped up on the bed and lay across Jenna's left side and on her arm. Jack tried to get her to move, but Sally wouldn't budge. It didn't appear to bother Jenna, so Jack washed out cuts and wounds starting with Jenna's shoulders and moving down her back. Jenna stirred and moaned a few times, but Sally and he held her arms down. He began a chant of "You're okay. You're okay, sweetheart."

That's how Summer found him when she returned, Jack crooning softly to her as he tended her wounds. "I don't know how much more I can take. The anguish in your voice, I hate seeing you so upset."

"I passed upset when I saw her at the diner. Now I'm just furious with myself for leaving her alone at the cabin when I knew she needed medical attention."

Summer rinsed out the washcloth and replaced it on Jenna's head. "You couldn't have known—"

Jack cut her off with a glare. No excuse in his book for not doing something when he knew it needed to be done.

He'd already tended the worst of the wounds on Jenna's back and bottom. The abrasions and welts would heal with the ointment he put on them. Summer cut up bandages and Jack taped them in place. Jenna lay silent, her breathing ragged. She gasped in pain sometimes, but for the most part she lay still, too weak to fight them.

"Okay, it's time to do the cut on her thigh. She will not like this, Summer. Take hold of her feet and make sure she doesn't kick. I don't want her opening up the cut even more."

"Jack, I don't know if holding her down is a good idea. She freaks out every time someone touches her, or comes near her."

"We need to finish and clean and close the cut or it'll get worse."

Summer grabbed Jenna's feet and Sally growled.

"It's okay, girl," Summer crooned. "I won't hurt her." Sally licked Jack's arm. "What is up with the dog? She won't let Jenna out of her sight."

"Sally knows Jenna is hurt and needs help. She's gone into guard-dog mode. It's kind of sweet. I've never seen her act like this. It's as if Jenna's her puppy."

That brought a smile to his face. It made for a sweet picture in Jack's mind. Summer smiled too. She pet the dog's head for reassurance and went back to holding Jenna's feet.

"Okay, here goes. Jenna, if you can hear me, don't move your leg. I'm going to clean the cut out. Do you hear me, Jenna? Don't move."

Jenna mouthed, "Okay."

Jack poured some antiseptic on a cloth and began cleaning out the cut. Open about a quarter of an inch and deep. He grabbed the tweezers to remove a few shards of glass. He swore under his breath for each sliver he took out.

"Okay, Jenna. All clean. I need to give you several shots near the cut to numb it, so I can stitch it up."

Jenna didn't respond, but tears seeped out from under her closed lashes. Jack brushed them away with a gentle swipe with the pad of his thumb.

"You're doing great, baby. You're so strong. Keep it up. Almost done. Then I'll leave you in peace."

Jack stuck the needle in her skin in several places along the foot-long cut. He gave the medicine a few minutes to work.

"Why didn't you use that stuff when you were cleaning the cut? You idiot."

"Because it only lasts about ten minutes and I want to make sure it stays numb while I stitch the cut closed. Do you know how many stitches it'll take to close up that cut?"

Bile rose in Jack's stomach just thinking about it. Training set in, and he got to work. Jenna struggled for a few of the stitches, finally going quiet after number five. He stopped counting after fifteen, disgusted with the whole situation. He died a little bit with each stitch. Looking past all the wounds and old scars, she was the most beautiful woman he had ever seen. Her green eyes would haunt him for the rest of his days.

Summer's amazed voice broke the silence. "I can't believe you've done this and so much more to save lives, yet I never really understood what it takes for you to do it. You really care. I've never been more proud of you."

Again, Jack didn't comment on her words. He couldn't. His feelings were too raw at the moment. Jenna needed his focus and his strength to endure and get the job done.

"Finished." He leaned down to Jenna's ear. "Jenna, can you hear me? I'm done. No more stitches. There's a bandage on your leg. Don't move around, or you could tear the stitches. Can you hear me, baby?"

Jenna didn't move, her breathing slow, but constant. Jack knew she had probably gone inside herself to escape. He didn't blame her. He needed a drink.

"You've seen a lot in the Army. How bad is this?" Summer asked.

"She'll be all right. What you need to understand is that in combat, or special ops, you know what you're facing going in. Your enemy assumes the same risk you do. Jenna didn't ask for this. She didn't sign up and say, 'Let's go fight.' Someone beat her and tortured her because she's weaker and smaller and couldn't fight back. I can't make sense out of that, the way I can rationalize combat. What this person did makes me sick."

He shared a look with his sister. They had always been close, but he'd been distant for a long time, keeping everyone at arm's length. He had never felt closer to her than he did at this moment. He had Jenna to thank for that.

The front door crashed open to the shouts of Lily calling for her mom and him.

"Stop her before she comes up here. She'll be scarred for life if she sees Jenna looking like this."

Summer rushed out the door and down the stairs to intercept her daughter and husband.

Caleb took one look at his pale and exhausted wife. "That bad, huh. Pete called," he answered her unspoken question about how he found out.

"Worse. Go up and see Jack. Don't say anything, though. When she heard Pete's voice before, she panicked. Just see if Jack needs any help cleaning up. Tell him I'll come by in the morning. I'm taking Lily home."

They shared a long kiss, Summer holding him as tight as she could, Lily squirming between them. Caleb returned the embrace, knowing she needed the support.

Chapter Nine

CALEB MADE HIS way up the stairs without a sound.
He'd served with Jack in the Army and saw a lot of things
himself. They'd both been in the Rangers and had special training in emergency medicine. Nothing prepared
him to see his long-time friend holding a woman's hand,
the same haunted look he'd seen in his eyes when he sat
beside their friend's burned and bloodied body. Dead
from a roadside bomb, Jack unable to save him. Caleb
hoped to never see that look on his friend's face again.
But here Jack sat, the past haunting him.

Caleb took in the woman's injuries and how Jack had
tended all of them. A bandage covered her entire thigh.
Caleb knew whatever happened, it was bad. As steady as
they came, confidence under fire, the one person Caleb
could count on to get him out of any type of dangerous situation. Here Jack sat, staring at a woman, a single
tear sliding down his cheek. Struck speechless, Caleb

wouldn't have been able to say anything, regardless of his wife telling him to remain silent.

Sally gave Caleb's presence away when she let out a low growl. Stunned, Caleb had never heard the dog growl at anyone. Jack scrubbed both hands down his face. He held his finger up to his lips to make sure Caleb stayed silent. Caleb nodded and went into the bathroom and brought out the trashcan. Jack gathered the bloodied bandages and used medical supplies, dumping them inside. They repacked Jack's medic bag and headed for the door and downstairs. Before Jack made it to the door, he turned back to the bed and leaned down to the woman.

"I'll be back. Sleep now. You're safe."

"Rabbit's on the run," came her soft whimpering voice.

Jack didn't understand her meaning. He didn't understand any of this. He kissed her hair softly and joined Caleb at the door.

"What did she mean, Rabbit's on the run?"

"I don't know. She hasn't been really clear the last hour or so."

They went downstairs in silence. Jack led the way to the bar in the Great Room. While pouring a double shot of whiskey, he rubbed at the back of his neck, then lifted the glass and drained the entire thing. He thumped the glass back onto the bar and with both hands, raked his fingers through his hair. He poured another double for himself and handed a second to Caleb.

"You okay?"

"Do I look okay?" Jack snapped.

"No. Who is that woman upstairs? Pete called the house, said Summer might need me here, and you have some beat-up woman lying in your guest room. What the hell is going on?"

"Jenna Caldwell. That's all I know. Her name. Well, that and the fact she mentioned driving from God knows where for the last four days. Can you imagine sitting in a car with her back in that condition for four days? She's the tenant who rented the cabin for the next year."

"I thought your college friend Ben rented the cabin for a friend of his."

"She's the friend. 'Client' might be a better term. Apparently, that's what she pays him to do, find her safe places to hide out. For the last two years, that's what he's been doing. I'm about ready to lose it, I want to punch something."

Tonight the dam had broken and Jack's emotions were ready to explode, despite his ruthless struggle to contain them. If they slipped the leash, Jack could do some serious damage. Thankfully, he wasn't Jack's target.

"Someone's been beating her up for the last two years?" Caleb asked to keep Jack talking.

"No. She apparently divorced some jackass and hid from him afterwards. Over the last two years, he's found her multiple times. This, apparently, was the worst one, according to Ben. For God's sake! She takes pictures of herself and sends them to Ben, so he can keep a record. Why hasn't anyone stopped this guy?"

Caleb didn't know the answer. He didn't understand what drove someone to torture another person, especially a woman. He'd seen a lot in the military, traveling to other countries where women were treated as second- or even third-class citizens with few rights. He just didn't understand what drove a man to hurt a woman simply because he could.

Jack threw himself into a chair and let out a ragged breath. Defeated, he said, "I fixed all her wounds, but I can't get to the person who hurt her." Unclenching his fists, he took his cell phone out of his shirt pocket and dialed Ben's number.

"Hello."

"Ben. Who did this to her?"

"Jack, I've been waiting for your call back. How is she? Is she better? Did you bandage her up?"

"Who did this to her?" Holding the phone so tight his fingers ached, he mentally counted to ten and reminded himself Ben wasn't the enemy.

"I told you, her ex."

"I want his name."

"I can't give you his name. She won't let me. If you want to know, ask her, or figure it out on your own."

"Tell me his name."

"I'm Jenna's attorney. I can't give you that information. As much as I want to help, Jenna is my client, and she wants her privacy—and especially her name—protected. Ask her. If you've gained her trust at all, she just might tell you. I'll tell you this though, he's very rich and powerful. That's how he's gotten away with this for so long."

Ben sighed and chose his words carefully. "I sent her to you, and you deserve to know what you're up against.

I'll break this confidence. You obviously already know she's being abused, so I don't think it matters if I give you some of the details.

"The first four times Jenna tried to have him arrested, he paid off people and the evidence disappeared. He had some people visit the hospital staff and convince them, in not-so-nice ways, Jenna had never been there. Any pictures, records, or medical evidence disappeared, destroyed. That's why she sends the photos to me. She doesn't involve anyone in this because she doesn't want anyone else to get hurt.

"She had a bodyguard, once. He turned up dead one morning in the pool at one of her hiding spots. Accidental drowning. Yeah, right, he'd been on his high school's swim team for four years. Two days after the drowning, her ex grabbed her and did some serious damage to her that time, furious she'd put someone between them.

"He switches between trying to romance her back into his life with notes and flowers and gifts and threatening her, smacking her around when she doesn't do what he wants. It's a game. His game. And he makes her play. She managed to hide for five months this time. That's the longest he's ever left her alone."

"I think I'm going to be sick." The story and the whisky made his stomach roll.

"I can't do this anymore, Jack. I can't stand by and do nothing to help her. She won't even come see me for fear he'll do something to me. We've managed to keep a lot of secrets, but he finds out more than we can hide. I didn't want to involve you, Jack, but you're my last hope. If you can't help her, I don't think anyone can. She'll have to keep running for the rest of her life. I'm convinced he'll kill her. It's only a matter of time."

"By the looks of her, he almost killed her this time."

"Is she going to be okay?" The fear in Ben's voice disturbed him, made the situation all the more real and terrifying. He might have patched her up, but she wasn't out of the woods.

"If I can get her fever down and the infection in her leg cleared up, yeah."

"If you need anything, call me. Oh, you'll get an overnight package tomorrow for her. Just the usual stuff I send her when she runs."

Something sparked in Jack. "What does 'Rabbit's on the run' mean?"

"That's her code when she needs help. She calls my office and the entire staff knows to get me anytime, anywhere. She's being hunted like a scared rabbit. Her words, not mine. That's how she refers to this whole mess."

"Hunted. That's a vivid description."

Caleb winced and downed the last of his whiskey.

Jack ended the call. "I'll expect the package and take care of Jenna."

"Have her call me," Ben said, his words desperate. "I need to hear her voice."

"I'll tell her. It'll probably be a few days before she's feeling better."

Jack hung up and dropped the phone on the table beside him. He downed the last of his whiskey and sat in silence.

"You going to be all right?"

Jack ignored the question, knowing he'd never be the same. In some ways, he guessed, that was a good thing.

"How does someone go through life feeling like they're being hunted? Even when we were in combat situations and running special ops, I don't think I ever felt hunted. More like a strategy, you against them. For her, it's run and be captured and tortured and run again, find a new hole to hide in before he finds her again. I can't stand it." He shot up and paced.

"Jack, come on, man. I've never seen you like this. She's okay, safe in the room upstairs."

"Safe, for how long? I don't even know who the hell is after her, or if they know she's here. How can I protect her when I don't even know who I'm protecting her from?"

"You hardly know this woman, and yet you're acting like she's your wife or something. Take a step back. Get some perspective. She'll be fine in a few days, and then you can decide how deep you want to jump in this thing with her."

"I'm drowning, is how deep I am in this thing. I can't turn my back on her. I just can't." He'd always been this way. If someone or something got hurt or fell sick he had to take care of them, and it always took a piece of himself. Maybe that's why his military career took such a toll. Each horror took a piece, until each of those pieces added up to a huge gaping hole of hurt.

"I was afraid you'd say that. Okay. You know I have your six on this. I always do. Let me know if you need my help with anything."

"Thanks, man. You always have my back. I know I can count on you. Now go home. Kiss Summer and Lily. Make Summer laugh, she had a hard time tonight."

"I will. Summer said she'd be by tomorrow."

"Night, Caleb."

Caleb slapped Jack on the shoulder and gave him a look, telling him without words he was there for him. Jack appreciated the sentiment and the support.

BETH WALKED IN the front door as Caleb left, holding a glass bottle in her hand. Jack stood in the Great Room and turned to stare out the window toward the mountains. His hands buried in his front pockets, his shoulders sagged, weighed down by the gravity of Jenna's situation. He gazed up to the stars, his mind a million miles away with them.

"Jack? Here's the medicine. Sorry it took so long. I thought you'd still be up with her, and the guys asked a lot of questions." When he glared, she added, "Don't worry, I told them to mind their business. Besides, I don't know anything."

Yeah, well, he didn't know shit either. "Thanks, Beth. I appreciate your help."

"No problem. Anything for you, boss. How is she? Any better?"

"No. But maybe once I get these antibiotics into her, she will be." Jack accepted the bottle and took the stairs up two at a time.

Beth called after him. "Do you need me to stay tonight?"

"No, go on home. She'll probably sleep through the night."

Jack climbed the rest of the stairs, knowing he faced a long night watching over Jenna.

Chapter Ten

SALLY RAISED HER head and followed his progress around the bed to Jenna's side. She moved off Jenna's arm, but still lay down at her left side. Jack spoke softly to his beloved dog.

"How is she, Sally girl?"

Sally slapped her tail on the bed softly.

"That good, huh. She hasn't woken up?"

Again, Sally slapped her tail.

"Good. Let's give her another shot and hope it doesn't wake her."

Jack prepared the needle with the proper dose for a human, not a horse. He grabbed an alcohol wipe out of his medic bag and swabbed a small spot on Jenna's bottom between two nasty welts. He stuck her with the needle, sending the antibiotics into her system. Hopefully, they would help break the fever soon. He trashed the needle and alcohol pad and rinsed out the washcloth on Jenna's forehead. He washed down her face, rinsed the cloth again, and placed it on her head. He pulled the sheet over her, careful of her back and leg, and turned off the bedside lamp. Moonlight spread across her like a glowing sheet.

Jack slumped on the chaise lounge by the window. His elbow rested on the arm, he put his hand on his brow and massaged the ache building behind his eyes. Tall, his right booted foot hung off the end of the long chair. He bent his other knee and planted his foot on the floor and watched her sleep for a long time. Hours later, too tired to fight it any longer, he drifted off to sleep, his mind tired from trying to sort out everything he found out about her and all the feelings racing around inside his heart.

The barking didn't really register at first, but he didn't mistake the scream shattering the quiet night. Jack shot out of the chair. Jenna thrashed in the bed, moaning and screaming, fighting off her dream. Jack laid a hand on her shoulder to try to still her. He leaned over and in a low honey of a voice soothed her.

"Jenna, it's Jack. You're safe. Stop moving. You'll hurt yourself, baby. That's it, sweetheart. Calm down. You're okay. Be still."

"He's coming. He'll get me. He's going to kill me. Run!"

"No, Jenna. You're safe with me. It was just a dream. Calm down." He kept his voice low, calm. In a panic, if he could get her to listen, maybe she'd quiet.

"Jenna, I'm the only one here. You're okay, baby. I won't let him get you. Calm down. Stop struggling. Remember your stitches."

Jenna's eyes flew open and locked on Jack.

"Stitches? What stitches? How did I get stitches? Please, you didn't take me to a hospital. Tell me you didn't take me to a hospital." She tried to get up, but Jack gently pressed on her shoulder. Completely out of strength, she could barely keep her eyes open or struggle with him.

"Jenna, calm down. No one took you to the hospital. I stitched you up. I even gave you a shot of antibiotics. You'll be feeling better in a few days."

Her eyes drooped, ready to close again.

"Where am I? I never seem to know where I am," she said weakly. Yet she remembered Jack without reservation.

"You're safe. You're in my house where I can take care of you."

"Never safe. Always running. Always alone. Have to run. Rabbit's on the run." Her eyes fluttered shut and she drifted back into sleep.

"No, Jenna. Rabbit's safe. You're not alone. Not anymore. I'm here with you. Rest, baby. I'll keep you safe."

"Safe," she said mockingly. "I don't want to be hunted anymore."

He almost couldn't hear her soft plea. "I'll keep you safe."

The single tear slipping through her closed lashes told him she didn't believe him. He'd prove it to her.

Jenna's breathing slowed and she fell into a deep sleep. Sally settled back at her side. Jack took up his guard in the chaise by the window with an overwhelming urge to crawl into bed next to her and hold her. Then she'd know the feel of safety again. He couldn't. Not only because of her injuries, but because he feared frightening her. She'd stayed a good distance away from him in the restaurant and backed up with every step he took toward her. No, he couldn't rush her into trusting him, but she would. He'd work at it until she did. He couldn't let her go, when for the first time in years he actually felt something warm burning in the cold pit that used to be his heart.

Chapter Eleven

JACK WOKE THE next morning sprawled on the chaise with a sore neck and a pounding headache. Water splashed in the sink in the bathroom. Summer came out with a bowl of water and a fresh washcloth. Jenna lay asleep in the bed, her hair and the sheet soaked with sweat. Her fever kicked into high gear. She lay perfectly still, except for the slow rise and fall of her back as she breathed. Sally hadn't left her side.

Jack rose and followed Summer over to Jenna's side. She pushed the quilt on the end of the bed to the floor. Sally refused to leave willingly, so Summer grabbed her collar and yanked her off the bed. Sally took off out the door and down the stairs.

Summer pulled the sheet off Jenna and tossed it on the floor by the doorway. She used the warm water and washcloth to gently wash Jenna's face, arms, and legs, wiping away the salty sweat.

Jack grabbed a needle and the antibiotics and stuck Jenna again. Each time he had to jab a needle into her, it made him cringe.

Jack stood by watching as his sister silently took care of Jenna. She brushed Jenna's hair away from her face and into her own hand. Then she separated it into three pieces and braided it down the length. She tied if off with a rubber band she pulled from her wrist. Then she twisted the braid into a circle on the back of Jenna's head and used a pin to secure it. Good idea. That would keep the tail of the braid from rubbing on Jenna's sore back.

She glanced at Jack and smiled. Jack couldn't smile, but he nodded with approval. They very carefully changed the sheet Jenna lay on. They rolled her as little as possible to get the sheet out from under her and replaced it with a fresh one. Jack grabbed the clean sheet to go over her and gently placed it over her legs and up to her waist. Her arms, bent at the elbow, lay by her head. He kissed Jenna's shoulder and left the room quietly with his sister, disturbed by how quiet and still Jenna remained.

Beth waited for them in the kitchen at the large island chopping celery, carrots, and onions, probably to make a pot of soup for Jenna. She had the coffee on and breakfast ready for him and Summer. The smell of bacon made his stomach rumble to life.

"Want some coffee, you guys?"

"Thanks, Beth, I'll pour." Jack reached for a couple of mugs and filled them, inhaling the rich scent. He handed over Summer's and she sat on a stool at the island by Beth. Sally scratched at the back door to come in. Beth must have let her out. Jack let her in and filled her bowl with food. She ate greedily. Neither he nor Sally ate dinner last night.

"How is she this morning?" Beth asked and continued chopping. She watched Jack with her dark brown eyes, inherited from her Mexican mother.

"Her fever hasn't broken. She's passed out cold. She'll probably sleep the day away."

"I'll check on her throughout the day. If you want, I'll sit in the room and watch her while you go to work."

"No. Just check on her. Like I said, she'll probably sleep through the day. I'll eat and go down to the barn, catch up on paperwork, and check on the horses and the crew. I'm sticking close to the house today. I'll send Caleb to check the pastures and herds."

He scooped scrambled eggs and bacon onto two plates and handed one over to his sister. After she set her plate down, she grabbed him around the waist and hugged him hard, squeezing the air out of his lungs. He almost dropped his plate. He put his own plate next to hers and wrapped his arms around her head, resting on his chest.

"Honey, it's all right. She'll be okay. What you did for her this morning, it was sweet."

"It's the least I can do. I feel bad for her."

"I do, too." He let his sister go and sat on the stool beside her.

"How did she do last night?"

"She had a few bad moments. She woke up and panicked at one point when she thought I'd taken her to the hospital to get those stitches. I calmed her down, and she slept well after that. She talked a little in her sleep. Stuff about how she'd never go back, she wouldn't give up. She's strong. She'll get through this." He took a bite of eggs, not tasting them, but knowing his body needed the food.

Sally finished eating and burst out of the kitchen heading for the stairs. Jack knew exactly where he'd find her later. He checked the impulse to follow.

Summer and he finished their breakfast in silence, watching Beth put together her soup in a huge pot on the stove. She got the fixings out to make bread. By the afternoon, the scent of fresh baked bread would fill the house. Jack's mouth watered thinking about a slice with hot melted butter.

Jack gulped down another cup of coffee before he stood to go upstairs and shower and walk down to the barn.

Before he left the kitchen, he asked his sister, "Where's Lily?"

"I sent her down to the barn with her daddy to see her pony. I'll pick her up and take her to preschool on my way to work."

"Okay. Don't let her upstairs. I don't want her to see Jenna."

"She's curious about the 'lady upstairs' and wants to meet her."

"Not now. When Jenna's better."

"I agree. I'll come by after work and check on you guys before I head home. I'll see you later."

"Tell Caleb I'll be down shortly."

"I will."

"Beth, come get me if Jenna stirs."

"Count on it. Get cleaned up. Go to work. I won't let you down."

"You never do." Beth's eyes glassed over at his praise and confidence in her. Jenna had made a big impact on his life. He'd been a hard, cold man for too long. Jenna was bringing him back to his true nature and it showed this morning. It took her arrival and knowing she'd spent the last couple of years isolating herself from everything and everyone around her to make him see he'd done much the same in his own life.

Sure enough Sally lay on the bed next to Jenna, watching the door. Jenna hadn't moved. He passed her door and went down the hall to his own room. He pulled his shirt over his head and made his way to the bathroom. He sat on the toilet and worked off his boots and socks. He got up and turned on the water in the big marble shower. Steam filled the large bathroom. Jack stripped off his jeans and boxers and stepped into the shower washing away his hard night. He wished it could wash away the images of Jenna's beaten body from his mind.

Chapter Twelve

JACK ARRIVED TO the barn later than he normally would any other day. His crew took care of the stalls and fed all the horses. Many of the horses were being groomed. Others were out in the pastures and up in the hills, ridden by his crew checking on the cattle. Caleb stood by Jack's horse's stall.

Blue was a huge gray stallion Jack couldn't pass up at auction last year. Ornery as hell, mean to everyone but Jack. He'd bitten several of Jack's men. Anyone close enough to him better watch he didn't get kicked. Jack couldn't explain it. He loved Blue's defiance and spirit. They suited each other. Jack's crew thought he should shoot the beast. It just made Jack laugh.

"This horse is going to hurt someone one of these days. He snapped at the groom and it took two people to move him out of the stall so they could clean it."

"He's not so bad. Just a little cranky is all."

Caleb laughed. "That's how I'd have described you over the last year. How is she? Better yet, how are you? You look like crap."

"I'm fine. And thanks, you look like horseshit yourself, but that's normal." Jack put all teasing aside and turned serious again. "She's sleeping. The fever hasn't gone down. Beth will keep an eye on her. I'll stay close to the house, check on her when I can."

"Summer thinks you have a thing for her."

"Summer's a smart woman." He did have feelings for her. He just wasn't sure what they were exactly, besides a tangled mess with his anger toward the person who had hurt her. The one thing he knew for sure, when he saw her, touched her, something inside him eased and reached out at the same time. Like the way he felt about Blue, he admired her spirit and grit.

"Well, I'll be damned."

"I already am."

"Is it serious?"

"I don't know. Something inside me broke loose yesterday when I met her. Every time I look into those green eyes ... I don't know ... It's something I haven't felt before." He tossed his hands up in the air and let them fall. "I can't explain it."

Caleb smiled. "You think she'll stay?"

"I'm not sure, but I'll try to convince her." He needed to know what this thing between them was. She felt it too, just for a moment in the café. They'd both felt it. "All I know for sure is that I need to find out who did this, and do everything I can to make sure he never gets to her again. I can't stand by and do nothing. I think that's why Ben sent her to me. Besides the fact the ranch is isolated, he knew I'd protect and keep her safe against any threat, no matter who it is."

"You know Summer and I will do everything we can to help."

"Thanks. I think she's starting to trust me a little. She doesn't seem to mind when I'm in the room, or when I touch her. Course, she's half out of it. We'll see how she reacts when she's fully awake. She's got guts. I'll give her that."

"I'm heading out. Call me on the CB if you need anything. I'll be in the south pasture, then I'll check the fencing to the east. The crews have all been sent out. Everything's running like clockwork."

Caleb left the barn through the large open doors at the end of the stalls. Jack opened Blue's stall door and stepped in to groom him. The physical work would do him good, and Jack knew horses were sensitive to emotions. Maybe spending some time with Blue would help him sort out his feelings.

Blue put his huge head over Jack's shoulder. Jack rubbed his hands down both sides of Blue's neck. Blue rubbed his head against Jack's head.

"Yeah, big guy. I know. You missed me. A pretty lady needed me. Just like you." Maybe that's what finally broke the dam in Jack's heart. Jenna needed him and he wanted to be needed for something deeper than his wallet.

Jack continued to stroke Blue, working a brush over his whole body. All the strokes and exertion were helping

Jack finally relax. Blue shook his big head up and down happy, letting Jack know he appreciated the effort.

Jack finished grooming him and made sure he had feed and water. As he closed the stall door behind him, he gave Blue an apple.

"You're a fine friend." Jack felt better.

One of the grooms worked inside a nearby stall, and Jack ordered, "Take Blue into the pasture later, so he can get some exercise." Jack wasn't riding anywhere today and the big stallion liked a good run.

He headed into his office at the end of the barn and found Pete waiting for him.

"Everyone's been talking about the lady you got up at the house. She okay?"

"She will be. What's everyone saying?" Jack asked.

"All kinds of things. Mostly they think someone beat her up and you saved her. I saw her last night. Never seen anything like that. You get the guy who did it?"

People were talking because Pete let it be known he'd seen Jenna. Jack's behavior last night had been unexpected and Pete and the others wanted to know if the boss had himself a new woman.

"I don't know who did it. And I didn't save her, she saved herself. I just patched her up. Hey, if you see anyone around the property who doesn't belong, you let me know."

"No problem. Me and the guys, we'll keep our eyes open. She staying here a while?"

"If I have anything to say about it. Tell everyone to stop talking about her. I don't want her to feel self-conscious or embarrassed. She's scared right now, but she's tough. She'll get through this."

"If you need anything, we're all here to help."

"I know, Pete. Pass the word that I appreciate it."

"Sure, Boss. I'd better get back to it."

Jack sat and leaned back in his chair, put his head back, and contemplated the ceiling for a while. Tired after the long morning, he gathered up the papers on his desk and worked his way through them. He spent hours working on the computer, entering figures and printing out reports. The ranch was doing well and turning a profit. Jack intended to keep it that way. He started on the paperwork for the diner when the office phone rang.

"Jack, it's Beth. You're two hours late for lunch. Get up here."

Time slipped away from him. He hated doing the paperwork. He'd rather be out in the fields with the horses and cattle. He needed to check on Jenna and felt guilty he'd lost track of time.

"She still asleep?"

"Yeah, now come have lunch."

"I'm on my way."

Jack usually went around the house and entered through the kitchen. Today he went in the front and up the stairs to check on her first. She hadn't moved, was still sound asleep. Beth had put another cool cloth on Jenna's fevered head. He prepared the antibiotics and gave her another shot and tucked the sheet around her so she wouldn't get the chills.

She stirred and called his name. He brushed his hand

over her head and held it over her soft cheek. "I'm here," he whispered. She relaxed again and settled into sleep. He rubbed his fist over the ache in his chest.

Sally licked his hand. "You're a good girl. Keep an eye on her."

Jack kissed Jenna's shoulder and lingered over the task. Her skin, so soft. He brushed his lips over her. He hated to leave her, but he needed food and headed downstairs for lunch, knowing she pulled at him even as he left her sleeping.

"She's fine, Jack," Beth said when he entered the kitchen. "Your face is hanging so low, you look like a hound dog. Don't worry. She hasn't stirred all morning, or afternoon."

"I know, but that fever hasn't gone down."

"I have to leave in an hour. So you'll need to stay with her, or have one of the guys come up to the house."

"She wouldn't like having a strange man around if she wakes up. I'll stay."

"Dinner's in the fridge. Just pop it in the oven for half hour and you'll be good to go. If she wakes, there's soup in the fridge for her and fresh bread in the box on the counter."

"Yeah, I've thought about that. I need to get some fluids into her before she wastes away."

"Why don't you call Doc Stanton and have him come check on her?"

"If she isn't better by tomorrow morning, that's exactly what I intend to do, whether she likes it or not."

Chapter Thirteen

JACK SETTLED ON the couch to watch a ball game on the big screen TV. Beth left a few hours ago, and evening set in. He tried to get his mind on the game and off the woman upstairs. No good. He couldn't muster up any enthusiasm despite his team leading three to one in the third inning. Sally ran in and jumped on his lap, whining and pawing at his chest.

"What's up, girl? I didn't think you'd ever leave that room. You need to go out? Hungry?"

Sally kept pawing at him and whining. He stood, practically dumping her off his lap, and walked to the front door to let her out, but she ran and stood by the stairs and looked back at him. Her warning registered and he ran upstairs to Jenna's room and found it empty. Jenna wasn't in the rumpled bed or the bathroom. Sally scratched at the door to the walk-in closet, whining, determined to get in.

Jenna's anguished sobbing came through the door.

He knocked and called out, "Jenna, it's me, Jack. I'm opening the door and coming in. You're okay. I won't hurt you."

His stomach in his throat, Jack opened the door into the dark closet. Sally ran in and lay down by the wall and Jenna. He hit the switch for the light and found Jenna huddled in the corner, wrapped in the sheet, her knees pulled up to her chest, her head on them as she rocked back and forth sobbing. Her hands covered her head. She'd done a good job of pulling most of her hair out of the braid.

Jack slowly walked toward her. Plenty of room in the empty closet for both of them. Jenna sobbed harder the closer he got to her in the back corner. Jack bent down on his knees a couple feet in front of her. She put a hand up to stop him from coming any closer. She never stopped rocking and sobbing.

The past few days had crashed down on her. Inevitably she'd break down and have to let it all out. Every sound of misery tore at his heart and twisted his gut.

"Jenna, I won't hurt you. You're okay. Let me help you back to bed."

She continued to rock, her body shook, and sweat broke out on her arms and what little he could see of the side of her face. She buried the rest in her knees and the arm she wasn't holding up to him covered her head. He didn't know what to do.

"Jenna, baby, come to me. I'll put you in bed. You're okay."

"I won't go back. I won't go back. I won't go back," she sobbed and chanted.

"No, honey. You can stay. Stay with me." He added the last on a whisper.

Jack moved closer and ran a hand over one of her hands and down to her shoulder. She pulled back and tried to curl up more. No place for her to go, she stuffed herself into the corner.

"Come here, sweetheart. I'll keep you safe. I promise."

He kept stroking her arm. She rocked and sobbed, shaking from the exertion.

"I won't go back. I won't go back."

"Come on, sweetheart. Come to me. Please," he begged.

Jenna tilted toward him and Jack took the initiative. He grabbed her from around her back, putting his arm around her knees. He picked her up enough to move her between his legs, his back to the wall. He scooted himself into the corner with Jenna between his up-drawn knees. He crossed his ankles, making a circle around her with his long legs, and wrapped his arms around her and held on to her while she cried.

She put both hands under his right arm and held on to his bicep, burying her face in his chest. Jack wrapped himself around her like a cocoon, letting her soak up all his warmth and protection. She cried it all out. Nothing else for her to do, he'd found her with all her defenses down. Too far gone, she didn't have the strength to put up her walls and push him away.

Summer stood in the doorway. Jack lifted his face

from Jenna's hair and met Summer's sad eyes. He nodded they were okay and for her to go. Summer silently agreed and left.

Jenna settled down after a while and her exhaustion took her into a deep sleep. He needed to get her back into the bed. Sitting on the floor probably hurt her, and he hoped her stitches were still intact. He rubbed his fingers back and forth over her soft skin on her shoulder. He didn't want to let her go. Not yet.

He listened for a long time. Her breathing evened out. The wracking breaths from crying subsided. Safe to take her back to the bed. His legs were half asleep, so he stretched them out and accidentally kicked Sally. Jenna didn't stir. She did have a good hold on his arm and nothing had ever felt better than the feel of Jenna against him. He hated to let her go, but he couldn't sleep with her on the floor of the closet all night.

He scooped her up close to his chest and, bracing his back to the wall, rose as best he could from the floor without disturbing her. He carried her to the bed and lay her down on her stomach. Even with the sheet wrapped around her, he managed to pull it up her thigh and check the bandage and stitches. Still swollen and red, none of them were torn, making him grateful for that small mercy. Sally jumped up next to her and took up guard. He shut off the lights and crashed in the chair by the window. Tonight took an emotional toll on him. He never wanted to hear anyone cry like that again. He fell asleep watching over her.

Chapter Fourteen

THE SUN SHINED through Jenna's eyelids and she opened her eyes to a strange room. She recognized the tall, lean, handsome man asleep in the lounge chair by the window. Jack. Little memory of the last two days, but she remembered him doctoring her back and leg, murmuring in her ear, and holding her while she cried. He'd said comforting things that made her feel warm inside. She would never forget that low, soothing voice, or how she felt safe in his arms. Safe, a feeling she hadn't had in a long time. She'd be grateful to him the rest of her life for giving her the small respite from reality.

She tried to move, but a paw pressed down on her shoulder. Sally gave out a soft bark. Jenna turned her head and came nose to nose with the golden retriever.

"Good morning, Sally. No barking, you'll wake up Jack."

"Jack is awake."

"Now see what you did." Jenna turned her head again and stared at Jack.

"How are you?" he asked. He took a measuring look at her. "Your face has a little more color. Your eyes are bright and clear. Fever must be down."

"I'm a little groggy, and I hurt everywhere. How did I get here? The last thing I remember is lying down by the fire in the cabin. After that, bits and pieces. A stinging pain on my back, something poking my thigh over and over again . . . you talking to me. I don't really remember what you said, but I heard your voice." She paused to gather her emotions. "Thank you for taking care of me."

"Let's start at the cabin." He leaned forward and laid his forearms on his knees, his big feet planted firmly on the floor. "My sister pounded on the door, but you wouldn't wake up. She came to cut your hair, which at first seemed kind of strange considering your condition. But then, when she took the towel off your head and revealed the mess someone made of your hair, well, it became clear." Eyes boring into hers, fear flashed and turned to fury in an instant. Not sure she'd seen the first, she didn't miss the second. "You scared her half to death, so she called me."

Anger laced his voice and every word. Tightly controlled, but underneath his icy gaze and matter-of-fact tone, he was livid. Familiar alarms went off in her head and the recognizable tingling feeling crept up her spine.

"I used my key to get in. That's when we saw the blood down your back and leg, not to mention the fact you were unresponsive and unconscious."

"I hadn't slept much over the past four days."

"Yeah, I got that. How you sat in a car and drove for four days in your condition is another matter entirely. Anyway, the short version is, I called Ben. He said not to take you to a hospital, that it would just make matters worse. So I brought you here and fixed you up." His tight control slipped.

"You're angry. I'll go. I promise. As soon as I can, I'll go."

He couldn't stand to hear her pleading with him. Her voice changed to that of a child begging. He got up and stood over her. He spoke before he could control the tone of his voice and it sounded harsh even to him. "You're not going anywhere. Do you hear me?"

It happened so fast; he couldn't believe she could move that fast in her condition. She rolled onto her left side and pulled her knees up to her chest into the fetal position. She threw both arms over and around her head to protect herself the only way she could. A bright red bloom of blood spread across the sheet where she tore the stitches in her thigh.

Everything inside him shattered, crushed under the weight of his guilt. He never meant to sound so harsh. He just wanted her to know she didn't have to go. Now he'd scared her half to death and made her tear the stitches. He caused this. He didn't know if he could live with himself at that moment.

Sally came around to Jack's side and blocked him from Jenna, growling low and menacing.

He spoke softly, hoping to reassure Jenna and gain

back what little trust he managed to forge over the last two days. "Jenna, please listen to me. You're bleeding again."

"I'll go. I promise. You won't ever see me again. I'll go."

Slowly, he managed to move Sally from between them and kneeled next to the bed. "Listen to me, Jenna. I don't want you to go. I'm sorry I yelled. I'm not angry with you. I'm not. I'm angry this happened to you. I'm angry with the scum who did this to you. Not with you, never with you. Stay here with me, I'll keep you safe."

Jenna peeked out from between her arms. "Do you mean that? It's okay for me to stay?" She hadn't known how much she wanted him to ask her to stay until he asked. Overwhelming hope bloomed inside her. The kind of hope she hadn't felt in a long time. The kind of hope that was dangerous, because it left her open to more disappointment and hurt. She didn't know if she could take any more.

"I want you to stay."

She stared into those eyes, staring back at her and filled with so much warmth. She remembered the way he enveloped her and held her while she cried. Something unspoken passed between them. A bond, a promise, a connection shared.

Tired of being alone, here was a handsome, rugged man offering her a lifeline. Scared to reach out for it, even more afraid not to and give up a chance to have something good and decent in her life.

She laid her hand on Jack's soft, lightly waved blond hair. When was the last time she touched someone? She stroked her hand down his head to his scratchy cheek and rested her hand against his warm skin.

"I'll stay."

Tears sprang to her eyes and Jack lovingly held her hand and kissed her palm, her fingertips, and her knuckles. She ran her hand back through his hair. He had great hair. She could bury her fingers in it. He closed his eyes and put his brow to hers.

"Jack?"

"Yeah," he said without moving away from her. Her breath feathered across his face, so close he could kiss her.

"Something's wrong with my leg. It's killing me."

He pulled back and spread his hand over her hip above the cut on her thigh. "I'm sorry I made you do that."

"It's not your fault. Most women don't react like I do when someone snaps at them. It's just that my sensitivity is heightened after *it* happens. Takes me a few weeks to find some inner calm and readjust to being around people. Please understand, it's not you. It's not anyone here. It's just me."

A soft knock at the door made Jenna jump. Jack put his hand over hers.

"It's okay. It's probably my sister coming to check on you."

Jack stood from the side of the bed and walked to the door. Summer carried a tray with bacon and eggs, fresh juice, and coffee and stepped past him into the room.

"You are the best sister ever. I'm starving," Jack said with as much of a smile as he could muster.

"Kiss the chef."

Jack gave his sister a peck on the cheek and took the tray from her. They both came into the room as Jenna tried to get into a sitting position.

Jack yelled, "Stop!"

Jenna froze, her eyes wide.

He hated to put that look on her face again. "You'll open up the cuts on your backside," he said more gently. "Lie on your stomach, or your left side. Damn, your leg needs to be stitched again."

"It can wait until after you have your breakfast," Jenna said.

"That's your breakfast. Hi, I'm Summer. How are you feeling today?"

"Sore," Jenna said wearily.

"I'll take care of the leg first." Jack hated to stick a needle in her again. He'd take her place in a second. "Then you get another shot of antibiotics."

Summer set the tray on the end of the bed. "You look better today."

"I guess you've been helping Jack take care of me. Thank you for being so nice." She had a hard time meeting Summer's eyes.

"Don't worry about it. We all need help sometimes."

"The coffee and food smell wonderful." Her stomach rumbled. Starving, he'd barely gotten more than water and soup down her over the last two days.

Difficulty moving, Jack noted the wince of pain that crossed her face when she shifted and pulled the sheet up to keep her breasts covered.

"Where are my clothes?"

Jack smiled with a wicked grin. He wondered how long it would take her to realize she was naked and he'd seen her. Several times. "You weren't wearing any."

"I was wearing my robe. Where is it?"

"In the trash. It was covered in blood."

Jack moved closer to the bed carrying the needle for the antibiotics and the supplies to stitch up her leg.

"What are you doing with that?"

"Giving you a shot, then I'll fix those stitches."

"Are you a doctor or something?"

He wondered why she looked so upset. "No. But I have medical training, and I stitched up your leg the first time."

"I don't like shots," she said emphatically.

She had a comical look on her face, absolutely serious about not wanting a shot. "Too bad. You've had lots of them over the last two days, and I'm not stopping now. The antibiotics have kicked in, and your fever is down, but it's not gone."

"I don't like shots, Jack."

"Sit still, or I'll have Summer hold you down. Either way, you're getting this shot."

Outnumbered, Jenna sat still with her eyes squeezed shut and let Jack give her the shot. He peeled off the bandage and touched her cut. She screamed out a protest.

"Stop. Don't touch it." She did her best to push his hands away, but he wouldn't be deterred.

He ignored her protests. He had to. He needed to fix her leg. "You're lucky. You tore only four of the stitches. I'll fix them, then you can eat."

"Stop touching it, you're hurting me."

Jack took her hand when she tried to swat him away again. He leaned in close and kept her hand between both of his. Their eyes locked. Both of them aware of the heat shimmering between them. "It's okay." He didn't know if he meant her leg, or this strange connection between them. "I'll fix it fast. I'd never hurt you on purpose."

With no choice left to her, she gave in with a hesitant nod. Instead of obsessing about the needle, she concentrated on how warm Jack's hands had felt around hers and the deep, penetrating way he looked at her.

"All done," Jack announced, his hand on her thigh. She glanced down and got the shock of her life when she saw how many other stitches he put in all together.

"Oh, God. Look at that. Look what he did," Jenna cried. Summer held her hand and stroked her hair. Jack brushed his hand down her leg in a long soft stroke.

"I got the glass out of it, cleaned it really well, and closed it up. The antibiotics are helping with the infection. It looks much better today."

"He wouldn't stop," she sobbed. "He found the belt on the floor, and he wouldn't stop. He wouldn't get off of me. He took a shard of mirror and sliced it down my leg. He hacked at my hair and pulled it so hard I saw stars. He threw me down and hit me in the head with a silver candlestick holder. I woke up on the floor and I ran."

Summer and Jack stared as the horrible words spilled from her mouth. Summer stroked her hair, and Jack laid his hand on her calf. Funny, she was getting used to that simple gesture.

Jenna pulled the sheet closer around her and wiped at her eyes. She took a deep breath and felt better for getting it out. Finally, telling someone what happened.

"Sorry, I'm fine now."

Jack didn't speak. Touched, Jenna understood they knew someone had done this to her, but hearing her tell them how it happened turned Jack quiet and introspective.

Jenna continued to stare at Jack's face, trying to figure out why he cared so much. In her experience, people were usually reluctant to get involved in other people's business. Not Jack. He'd come to her rescue, brought her into his home, fixed her injuries, and appeared to genuinely care about her well-being and safety. Leary, she'd thought good things about her ex. Boy, had she read him wrong. But Jack . . . He seemed different. Genuine.

"You should get it out. You'll feel better for it," Summer reassured her. "Have some food. You must be starved. Jack, Beth is keeping yours warm in the kitchen. Go down. I'll help Jenna get cleaned up after she eats."

Sorry she'd put that sad look on Jack's face, she tried to smile when he stood to leave. He hesitated, opened his mouth to say something before he thought better of it. When he did speak, his words were matter-of-fact, but his voice held a trace of something she wished she could place. It made her heart reach out as if it had arms that wanted to hold on to him and never let go.

"I'll bandage up your thigh after you eat something. Eat slowly. You've had a shock and you don't want to make yourself sick." Without looking back, he headed out the door, Sally at his heels. Even though Summer remained, Jenna felt the familiar loneliness she'd lived with for years. When Jack was with her, she didn't feel it at all.

Chapter Fifteen

"Is Beth Jack's girlfriend or wife?" Jenna asked, embarrassed for being so completely obvious. He didn't wear a ring, but what did that really mean these days. Now she felt silly for asking and maybe dreaming of something so foolish.

"No. Beth takes care of the house and cooks for Jack. He hasn't had anyone in his life for a while," Summer offered with a knowing smile. "I've never seen him so"—she paused and tilted her head, thinking before saying—"connected to someone. He's definitely attracted to you, but it's something deeper," she added.

Jenna let out her breath on a soft sigh. Sure something was happening between herself and Jack. Relieved he didn't have another woman in his life. Odd to be relieved, since at some point she'd have to run again.

The thought of running and never seeing Jack again made her sick. She hadn't felt a spark of wanting someone since she started dating her ex-husband. Young, she wanted to have a husband and family someday. Dreams she thought she'd given up. Maybe it was time to dust off that dream, or at least explore the possibility of letting Jack into her life. God, how she wanted to feel his arms around her again. Feel safe. Something else she hadn't dreamed for herself in a long time.

Summer helped Jenna move the tray so she could eat. Careful not to bother any of her wounds, Jenna managed to drink the coffee and eat most of the food. They chatted about everyday things. Jenna tired quickly, but she liked the sense of normalcy, sitting and eating breakfast with someone else.

"Do you think you can sit up? I'll help you out of bed and to the bathroom. Two days in bed, you must need to pee."

Jenna smiled. "Thanks. I do, and I wasn't quite sure how I'd get there."

"Well, come on, lean on me and I'll help. We'll clean you up a bit, and I'll fix your hair. No shower today, though. Maybe tomorrow when you have more strength."

"I must look awful."

"Not so bad. A couple more good meals and some rest and your color will come back. So will your strength."

"You're really kind. Jack, too. You guys didn't have to do this for me."

"I don't think anyone could stop Jack now. Not after the way he looked at you when you were at the cabin. As for me, I'm really lucky to have a husband like Caleb. He's sweet and gentle and loves me more than anything.

You'll meet him and Lily later. I can't believe someone who supposedly loved you did this to you."

"It wasn't love. It's obsession. And it's eating away his sanity the longer I take to willingly go back to him. I won't do it though. No matter what he does to me, going back would be worse."

The stitches down the back of her leg made it difficult to sit. Summer didn't seem to mind helping, so Jenna gave in and let her, too weak to do it on her own anyway. She stood in front of the sink mirror and Summer redid her hair.

"It's a mess."

"I can fix it. You have great hair. Long, soft, full, a great color too, deep brown with a flash of red. I'll come again tomorrow. I'll give you a really pretty, simple style. No one will know it ever looked like this."

"Thank you."

"Don't thank me. I hardly ever get to work on someone with such great hair."

Summer helped Jenna wash her face and body with a washcloth at the sink. Wobbly, Jenna held on and Summer helped her back to the bed. Once settled, Sally ran into the room and jumped on the bed, Jack right behind her.

"All set?" Jack asked.

Cleaned up, his hair was still wet from his shower. His jeans were snug in all the right places and his white t-shirt stretched nicely over his broad chest. He noticed her noticing him and his eyes lit up, sky blue. A slow smile changed his unreadable face, made him more relaxed and approachable. Her insides melted from the heat of his returned stare.

"You look better. A little food and getting cleaned up looks good on you," he said with that same wicked grin she'd seen earlier.

"I've got to go, you two." Summer didn't try to hide her amused grin. "I'll be back tomorrow, Jenna. It's my day off, and I'll help get you more settled. Bye, Jack."

Alone together again, Jack stood next to the bed where she lay on her stomach, Sally next to her. "I'll wrap a bandage around that leg."

Responding to Jack's easy demeanor, she asked, "Do you have to replace the front door every day?"

Smiling at him, not a big smile, but a smile nonetheless. It warmed Jack from the inside out.

"What are you talking about? I told you, you're safe here."

"Are *you* safe here?"

"What?" He didn't understand what she meant, but he liked her sweet smile.

"Women. They must beat down that door every day to get to you."

He cracked up with laughter. "You think so, huh."

"Oh, yeah."

"I think you're pretty damn beautiful yourself."

"Yeah, right. I hear bandages and bruises are in this year."

"You're beautiful."

They stared at each other, that invisible but undeniable something passing between them. He wanted to touch her, but knew now wasn't the time. As forward as she'd been joking with him about women beating down his door, she shied away from acknowledging this thing between them. He broke off the look first and dug out his supplies. He wrapped a bandage around her thigh, trying not to think about the softness of her skin or the fact she was naked under the sheet.

Her eyes fluttered shut. He bent down and kissed her on the forehead. She placed her hand on his cheek. Such a simple gesture. He leaned into her palm, felt her fingers brush against his skin. How long has it been since a simple touch affected him so deeply? Reluctant to leave her, nonetheless he drew back and her eyes remained closed. He took her hand from his cheek and placed it on the pillow next to her head.

He nuzzled at her ear and whispered, "Beautiful. Believe it."

Chapter Sixteen

JACK LEFT JENNA sleeping in his house and went down to the barn to work, lighter after seeing her soft smile this morning. She'd actually teased him. A good sign after she broke down during the night, and it did his heart good.

He returned for lunch to check on her. She slept through the afternoon, and after he showered and changed into clean clothes he went in to wake her. Wrapped in the sheet, she sat in the chair he'd slept in for two nights, looking out the window, her mind a million miles away. He crossed the room and sat at the end of the chaise, his forearms braced on his thighs, his hands clasped together between his knees, so he wouldn't reach out and touch her the way he desperately wanted to.

"Where did you go?" he asked. He ignored her instinctive flinch away when he sat, and held on to the way she settled at the sound of his voice.

"This is a beautiful room. I like the soft green walls

and the cream carpet and the colorful oil paintings of roses. The antiques are so pretty."

"I'm glad you like it. You can stay as long as you want." In my bed would be better. He'd settle for her in the same house, for now.

"I liked the cabin, too. Did you decorate everything yourself?"

"I took an extended leave from the military about eight years ago for the summer and spent it building the cabin. I needed the time to sort some things out. I like working with my hands. It's a good way to relieve stress."

"Why did you go back to the military?"

"Because that's where I needed to be at the time. Caleb and I were part of the Rangers. We thought we were doing some good in the world."

"Why did you finally leave?"

Not one to open up, her genuine interest and openness in her eyes made the words fly out of his mouth. "That kind of life takes a toll on a person. A little over four years ago, I decided I had enough. Caleb and I were buddies. My parents wanted to go out and see the world, so he and I came back and took over the family ranch.

"He took one look at Summer, sparks flew, and all of a sudden my best friend is marrying my baby sister. Kind of strange at first, but you could see how much they loved each other. I couldn't help but be happy for them. Of course, I had to punch him when he said he was marrying my sister."

"You didn't punch him. Your best friend."

"I did. Then we shared a couple of beers." She laughed

and smiled with him. His belly tightened. "She's my sister. No one's good enough for her. Caleb comes close though. They got married four months after they met and had Lily nine months later. Besides my parents, I've never seen two people so right for each other."

"So what about you? How come there's no lady of the house?" Jenna asked, curious. An open expression on her face and in her eyes made it easy for him to open up and answer. He wanted to see her smile again. He liked being the reason she smiled.

"I dated a few women when I came back. Turns out my wallet appeals to them more than I do."

"I find that hard to believe," she said shyly.

"Startling, isn't it?" With a grin, he went on. "They find out about the land, the cattle, the horses, the diner, all of a sudden they think I'm an ATM. Their eyes light up with dollar signs."

"So you're rich, huh?"

"I do okay." Yeah, he did better than okay, but he downplayed it, afraid to see those dollar signs light up her eyes. He didn't want to feel that pang of disappointment, like all the other times. "Why, you need a loan?" he asked, half kidding.

She laughed, making his belly do that strange jump. "No," she scoffed. "So, I guess you're looking for something more meaningful than bank statements and charge cards."

Read his mind. "Let's just say I envy my baby sister, and that's a first for me." He liked her laugh. He liked it even more that when she said she didn't need a loan, it actually sounded like she meant it. She didn't want his money.

"Why the diner? Seems like the ranch would be a lot of work on its own."

"Don't laugh, but the only thing Caleb and I can cook up is trouble. There aren't a lot of fast food places around, if you didn't notice. This far out of town, delivery is nonexistent. Anyway, the old, rundown diner in town barely scraped by on a few loyal customers. The owners were about to give up and board it up for good. I bought it, renovated the old dive, and Caleb and I could eat something better than chewy spaghetti and scrambled eggs. As good as we are at the BBQ, even that got old after a while. The town appreciated the new place. It does a good business. I don't have to do much. Mary, the waitress, runs things well enough."

"But now you have Beth?"

"Well, Caleb married my sister and I got tired of barging in on them and watching them kiss over the dining room table. Driving into town all the time got old, fast. So, I hired Beth. Now the house is always clean, and she's a kick ass cook."

He gave her a huge grin. "See why I'm such a catch. I've got money and a housekeeper who cooks. What wife wouldn't like that?" Half kidding, he wanted her to know that for the first time in a long time, he was open to a relationship. Her smile encouraged him even more.

"You're funny, Jack. Those things aren't important to me."

"What is important to you?" Serious now, he really wanted to know how to make her happy.

"Kindness. You've shown me a lot of kindness, Jack. You'll never know what that means to me. I've been on my own a long time. This is probably the longest conversation I've had with someone over the last two years other than Ben. That's a long time to be without kindness."

She broke his heart when she talked like this. The simplest things were missing from her life.

"I'd never hurt you. Never."

"I know that. Please don't mistake my skittishness with thinking I'm afraid of you."

For the first time since he entered her room, he reached out to touch her, resting his hand over hers on the back of the chaise. She jumped when his warm skin touched hers, but immediately relaxed.

"I don't think you're afraid of anything, or anyone."

"I am scared of him and what he wants to do to me."

"You face him with courage despite that fear, like a soldier facing a battle."

Sensing her need to change the subject, he asked, "Tell me something about you?"

Giddy, nervous, expectant . . . this felt like a first date and he wanted to know about her. She wanted to know everything about him, greedy and anxious to learn everything. "Well, I'm twenty-six. How old are you, by the way?"

"Thirty-four."

"You don't look it," she said.

"Yeah."

"Yeah. All the sun-streaked blond hair, those blue eyes, the tan skin from being outside all the time. Nice."

The cocky grin spread over his face, brightened his eyes, made him look mischievous.

"God, you're cute. You're flirting with me. You must be feeling better."

Ignoring his wide smile and teasing, she changed the subject completely and hoped the butterflies in her stomach settled. Though if he kept brushing his fingers over the back of her hand like that, she'd melt into a puddle.

"I run my own business. I'm a computer graphics artist, and I do a lot of programming. I have a website, and I take jobs through the Internet and email. Obviously, it would be difficult to have an office with the way I move around. I like it, and I work when I want."

"You must do well for yourself."

All for the truth, sometimes she found it best to skirt full disclosure. "I do it because I like it. I don't have to interact with a lot of people. So long as I have a laptop, I can run the business. Ben takes care of all my legal and money matters."

"How did you meet Ben?"

"I never have in the normal sense. I've never seen him in person."

"What do you mean? I thought you guys are really good friends."

"After the divorce, well, there began the first of many incidents. That was the first time I went into hiding. It isn't an easy thing. You leave a trail of records wherever you go. I needed help, so I went on the Internet and did my research. I found Ben. He had all the qualifications I needed."

"What qualifications were those? How to hide someone 101?"

"No." She smiled, but it died when thoughts of her past intruded. "As a lawyer, he had to keep my situation confidential. He runs his own private firm. While he has other lawyers working for him who specialize in a great many things, he also has people who are investment specialists and CPAs. All of which I needed, and Ben oversees everything. The clincher, though, I found a bunch of human-interest stories about, 'Small town boy makes good and gives back,' about him. Did you know he provides free legal services to women staying at battered women's shelters in San Francisco?"

"I didn't know. But he told me once that his father abused his mother."

"That's right, you guys went to college together."

"Yeah. We were dorm mates freshman year. I dropped out and went into the military. Ben went on to law school and look at him now."

"You haven't done so bad for yourself. After all, women are chasing after you and your bank account."

He couldn't help laughing. "Now you're making fun of me." He shrugged his massive shoulders and added, "Looking back, I guess it is kind of funny. I wasn't interested in marrying any of them," he admitted. Their eyes locked, time spun out, stalled in the quiet room. "So, what else?"

"Well, Ben never worked for my ex-husband, nor have they ever met."

"Tell me who he is?"

"Not tonight," she said wearily. "I don't want to speak his name. Once you find out, well, let's just say you'll be astounded."

"Will you tell me soon? I can help you."

"I'm tired, and it's too much to get into tonight."

"For now, I'll accept that. But we will have this conversation soon. I can't protect you and my family if I don't know who I'm up against."

"I didn't lie when I said this is one of the longest conversations I've had with someone. I haven't let anyone into my life. I haven't even spoken to my mother in two years. Not directly, anyway. I need some time."

"Take all the time you need. I'm not going anywhere, and I'm not letting you go anywhere either. You know what I need—food. Let's have dinner."

Jack glanced at his watch, his fingers brushing against her skin as he turned his hand. "I can't believe we've been talking for so long. It's almost eight. I'll go down and get dinner and bring it up. We'll eat, we'll talk, and after you can rest."

"I'm starving," she admitted.

"Back in a minute."

Sally and Jack went down to the kitchen. Jenna managed to get herself to the bathroom and freshen up. About to sit in the chair again, Jack carried in a huge tray of food.

"Are you ever going to bring me my clothes from the cabin? I can't wear a sheet the rest of my life, you know."

"Now, what would possess me to bring you clothes?" His eyes roamed over her body with lazy satisfaction, and a flush rose from her breasts to her cheeks. "I like you in only a sheet. Besides, honey, I've seen you naked. Every beautiful inch of you. Two days of pure torture touching you, but not touching you." He paused, his blue eyes smoldering, he swept his gaze from her face, down her body to her bare feet. Her breasts tingled, she squeezed her thighs to stop the jolt of heat. It didn't work, and his eyes moved up her legs, stopped on her squirming hips, slid up to her peaked breasts. His eyes met hers, she felt singed by the heat in his. "I really want to touch you." He gave her his now-familiar wicked grin, enjoying her discomfort and diffusing the intense moment.

She clamped on to the lightness in his smile, unable to push past her fear that, despite his kindness, she'd read something wrong in him. Ridiculous, a voice scolded. He's harmless.

"Payback's a bitch, Jack. I'll get you for this. I want my clothes."

"Later. Maybe." He cocked up one side of his mouth in an adorable grin. "Eat."

She tucked the sheet closer around her aching breasts and looked at the plates of food Jack had brought up. A huge bowl of soup for her with fresh bread and melted butter. Jack's plate disappeared under a huge steak, mashed potatoes, and green beans.

"You're a real meat and potatoes man, huh?"

"Beth cooks, I eat. She makes all kinds of things. Besides, I'm a rancher. Tonight happens to be steak. She made the soup especially for you. How's your stomach, any queasiness?"

"Not really. The soup is excellent. Now, give me a bite of that steak."

"Bossy. You must be feeling better." He handed over a forkful of succulent steak.

She closed her eyes and savored. "That's good."

His eyes on her mouth, he stared, shook himself out of his lusty thoughts about her mouth on him and ordered, "Eat your soup. It's good for you and easy on your stomach."

"Now who's bossy?"

They ate and talked about their lives. They'd been talking for three hours, and Jack couldn't remember any other time when he'd sat talking to a woman. Well read, she could talk about anything. She even liked sports. They shared a lot of the same interests. Best of all, she was a good listener. She asked him question after question, interested in everything about him. He couldn't learn enough about her either and time got away from them. The heavy darkness outside the windows and the quiet of the house surrounded them.

They sat inches apart, yet Jack never touched her. Relaxed with him, he didn't want to push. He enjoyed just being that near to her and knew with every passing minute of shared conversation—and a few intense, heat-filled moments—he gained her trust little by little. He wanted more than anything to touch her, but she asked for time. He'd give her what she needed and gain what he wanted most. Her complete trust and understanding that he'd never hurt her, no matter what.

Her eyes drooped and she yawned several times,

completely worn out. He helped her walk to the bed and settled her in.

"You're getting your strength back. Maybe tomorrow I'll take you for a walk outside, get some fresh air. It'll be good to work your muscles again."

"I can't wait to see the ranch. I didn't really see anything when we drove in. Too sleepy. Like now."

Jack prepared another needle with the antibiotics.

"You're not sticking me with that."

"Come on. It'll only hurt for a second, and I'll get to look under that sheet again."

"Jack, I'm not kidding. I don't like shots. Enough already."

"You need the medicine. Now gimme your cheek."

"Ha. Ha. Very funny."

She let him give her the shot and stuck her tongue out when he finished. He loved how easily she made him laugh.

"Smart ass."

"Sore ass is more like it."

He chuckled again. Even in her condition, she showed her playful side. Quite something, she trusted him enough to joke, play, and show him glimpses beneath the guard she kept up and reinforced when it slipped and she forgot and caught herself.

Sally lay curled next to Jenna sound asleep. "Looks like you aren't the only sleepy one. Lucky dog. Good night, honey."

"I like it when you do that."

"Do what?"

"Call me sweet names."

"I was talking to the dog." He gazed down at her, trying his damndest not to smile or laugh.

She cracked up. "Ha. Ha."

He leaned down and planted a smacking kiss on her forehead. "Sleep tight, baby."

"Night, Jack."

He trailed his fingers all the way down her uninjured leg as he walked the length of the bed toward the door. He'd slept in his bed alone for too long now. Having Jenna this close and not tucked beside him sent him through his dark, lonely room and straight into a cold shower.

Chapter Seventeen

DAVID HID HIS disappointment and annoyance with the woman beside him as the party continued around them. A nice substitute, but the woman he really wanted remained out of reach. He inhaled and imagined the musky scent beside him was softer, tinged with sweet floral notes and Jenna's elusive scent. He missed the way Jenna smelled, the way her hair flamed red in the sunlight and deepened to rich chocolate in the dark spread over a pristine white pillow, her skin soft and supple beneath his hands. He ached to spread his hand over her creamy stomach, slide it up to cup her rosy pink tipped breast, higher to her elegant throat . . . and squeeze, until she begged him for mercy.

"I see the mayor. Let's say hello. My family helped get him elected," she bragged.

"Go ahead, darling. My grandfather is headed this way, something's on his mind."

"Patricia, you look lovely this evening, my dear," his grandfather said, kissing her cheek.

"Thank you, Charles. It's nice to see you again. Excuse me." With a pretty smile for his grandfather, she excused herself.

"She's perfect, David. Beautiful, educated, wealthy, *connected*. You could do worse."

"You mean Jenna."

"You changed when you married her . . . And not for the better. Forget the past. Focus on your future." His grandfather raised his glass, indicating Patricia across the room. His future, according to his family.

Not according to him. He would get what he wanted. He always did.

Chapter Eighteen

THE NEXT MORNING Jack sat at the breakfast bar drinking coffee, desperate for the caffeine to jolt his system after another long, restless night, dreaming about Jenna and talking himself out of walking down the hall to her room and crawling into her bed. That argument lasted deep into the night and early morning.

Caleb and Lily came in through the kitchen door. "Uncle Jack. I got to see my pony. She's brown and white, and she ate a carrot out of my hands."

"I know your pony is brown and white. I bought her for you, goofy."

"Where's the lady?"

"She's upstairs sleeping with Sally. Stay down here. She's not feeling well, and she needs to sleep. Morning, Caleb."

"Morning, Jack. All the crews are working. No problems this morning, except for Blue. He wants to go out for a ride. You've had him cooped up for too long. Stubborn horse."

While they sat in the kitchen discussing the ranch, Lily snuck upstairs. Jack and Caleb realized, too late, Lily escaped. They bolted from the kitchen and reached to top of the stairs in time to see Jenna's back to the door and Lily next to her. They paused outside the door on the landing, enthralled by the innocent scene in the bedroom.

REST, FOOD, AND the medicine worked wonders in making Jenna feel better. She lay in bed listening to Sally snore and stared across the room to the windows and the trees outside. The beautiful morning bloomed with bright sunlight. Lying on her left side, a little blond head popped up next to the side of the bed.

"I snuck in here. Daddy and Uncle don't know."

"I see."

"Who are you?"

"I'm Jenna. Who are you?" Had to be Lily, but she loved the lyrical sound of this tiny nymph's voice. She couldn't help smiling at this bright angel of a child.

"I'm Lily Bowden, like the flower. I'm three."

"Stargazer lilies are my favorite."

"Like Uncle's ranch. Stargazer Ranch."

"So it is. I hadn't thought of that."

"Can I come up there with you?"

"May I come up there. And yes, you may."

Lily climbed up and lay down facing Jenna. She put her hands together and tucked them under her cheek. Angel baby, smelling of spring and strawberry shampoo.

"Daddy calls me sunshine sometimes. Mommy's name is Summer. He says I'm Summer's sunshine. That's funny," she giggled. "Daddy brings mommy flowers he picks in the fields. He puts them in a vase on the table. Then he kisses her."

"Very romantic. People should always do nice things for others, especially the ones they love."

"No one brings me flowers. What does the Stargazer look like? Maybe I can find one in the field."

"I don't think you'll find one. Stargazers are a really big lily. They start out closed like this." Jenna held up her hand, palm up, with her fingertips touching. "Then, they open like a star and inside they are dark pink and they smell really, really good." She spread her fingers to show Lily how the flower opens.

"Is there a flower shop in town?" Jenna remembered several stores on the main street by the diner, but couldn't remember what kind. Her arrival in town had become nothing but a blur, except meeting Jack. Him sitting in the booth at the diner showed crystal clear in her mind.

"Yes. Next to mommy's work. It always smells really good."

"When I feel better, I'll go into town and see if they have any Stargazers. If they do, I'll buy you some, so you can see. Maybe mommy will let you keep them in your room."

"Really? I can have flowers?"

"Yes. You have your Uncle's and Mommy's blue eyes." Lily's were very close to Jack's, but his had deep blue flecks.

"Daddy has muddy brown eyes. I like blue ones better. Yours are pretty. They're the same color as grass."

"Yeah."

"That's Sally behind you. I named her when I was one. Uncle said it wasn't fair Mommy got a baby and he didn't, so he got a puppy. She used to lick my face and I would call her silly, but Uncle Jack thought I called her Sally, so that's what he called her, Silly Sally. Isn't that funny? Silly Sally."

Lily burst into laughter over her own joke. Jenna couldn't help but smile and giggle with her.

Lily turned very serious. "Do you have a big owie?"

The sheet covered her, but one bandage high on her right shoulder wasn't hidden. Just a white bandage, no blood, she didn't think it would frighten Lily.

"I got a bad sore and your Uncle Jack put the bandage on to help it get better."

"That's a big owie."

"Yes, it is."

"Did you go to the doctor? I don't like the doctor. They give you pokey shots. I get a lollipop, so it's not so bad. Mommy kisses it better."

"I didn't go to the doctor, but your Uncle Jack gave me lots of pokey shots right in the butt. I didn't get even one lollipop from him. Can you believe that?"

"You should at least get a lollipop."

"Yeah. Well, he's coming back in here later and try to give me another shot. I'm not letting him if I don't get a lollipop this time."

"Yeah. That's not nice that you didn't get one."

"It's okay. I bet your Uncle doesn't have lollipops anyway," Jenna giggled.

"He might. He hides candy in a special jar for me in the pantry."

"You know what I like to have for breakfast sometimes? Chocolate covered peanut butter cups. They're really good with a cup of coffee."

"You get to eat candy for breakfast. Mommy won't let me. She says I have to have cereal or fruit or something."

"That's the good thing about growing up. You can have anything you want. Sometimes I eat rocky road ice cream for breakfast."

"I can't wait to grow up," Lily said with an exasperated sigh.

"Well, that's the problem. In order to grow up you need to eat good things for breakfast. But once you do grow up, all the ice cream and candy you want."

"I like you."

"I like you, too, sweetie." Her voice shook. The loss of the last two years grew heavy in her heart, though Lily's sweet presence went a long way toward making things better. It felt wonderful to be around a family after years of running and living on her own.

CALEB GLARED AT Jack. "You hide candy in the kitchen for her."

Jack shrugged. "What good is having a niece if I can't spoil her?"

Time to get Lily. Caleb and Jack entered the room.

Jack gazed down at the two beauties in bed, lying face to face. They sure made a pretty picture, the two of them talking about pokey shots, lollipops, and ice cream for breakfast. For just an instant, his mind and heart showed him a picture of a bright future he once thought would be cold and lonely. His Jenna. Their daughter. He shook off the thought, but acknowledged this sense of wanting a family had really settled inside him. He waited for the nerves, the sound of shackles clamping down. Nothing. Just the same sense of ease he always felt around her.

Lily launched herself off the bed into her dad's arms. Caleb scooped her up and gave her a big kiss on the cheek.

"You must be Daddy with the muddy brown eyes." The sad look in her eyes vanished with the smile she gave Caleb.

Caleb chuckled. "Yes. Caleb. And you're Jenna?"

"Yes. Your daughter is wonderful. Thank you for sharing her with me. She's the best medicine."

If Jack hadn't already been amazed by the sweetness of this woman after listening to her talk with Lily, her thanking Caleb for sharing Lily with her clinched it. He couldn't take his eyes from the deep pools of green, awestruck.

Warm hearts shine through, his mother's voice whispered in his mind.

Summer walked in and tickled Lily's ribs. "You can stop staring at her now. You're married, for God's sake." She elbowed Caleb in the ribs, grabbed her daughter, and planted a kiss on her chubby cheek.

Jenna laughed and it did Jack's heart good to hear the lighthearted sound from her.

"Seems I'm still underdressed for this party. Jack, will you please bring me my clothes?"

"I already told you, I'm not crazy, or stupid." He couldn't help egging her on. Too much fun to play with her.

"I did, however, bring you these." He held up a prescription bottle. "No more pokey shots. Doc Stanton dropped by the other day when you were passed out. He checked on you and left these antibiotic pills."

"Uncle Jack, you didn't even give her a lollipop when you gave her pokey shots. That's not nice," Lily scolded.

"Yes, Uncle Jack." Jenna said. "That's not nice, and neither is eavesdropping."

Caleb and Jack exchanged guilty looks. "Busted." Jack handed Jenna the pills and a glass of water from the bedside table. Jenna took out a pill and downed it without protest.

"Much better than a pokey shot. Thank you, but . . ."

"Don't worry. He won't say anything about seeing you. He's a friend," Jack assured her.

"Enough, you guys, out." Summer took charge. "I'm getting Jenna up and giving her a haircut. Jack, go over to the cabin and get this girl her clothes and other things. It doesn't look like she'll be going back any time soon. Hey, what are those two boxes by the front door?"

"Oh, yeah, those are for you, Jenna. They arrived yesterday. I think they're from Ben."

"Would you bring them up? Oh, and make sure you grab my purse at the cabin. I need my phone."

"Anything else, ladies? I'm at your beck and call," he responded sarcastically.

"Please, Jack," Summer and Jenna said in unison.

"I'm outnumbered. Come on Caleb, you get to help."

"I want to stay with Mommy," Lily said.

Summer and Jenna exchanged concerned looks. Nobody wanted Lily to see Jenna's back. "Sunshine, you go with Daddy and Uncle. Make sure they bring all of Jenna's things." Lily beamed, excited to be in charge of the task.

"Are you really going to get me flowers?"

"As soon as I'm able to go to town, I will, okay?"

"Okay."

Lily's smile made Jenna smile in return. Jenna gave her a conspiratorial squint of the eye and told Lily, "Make sure Uncle Jack brings my clothes."

"You're spoiling all my fun," Jack teased and left with Lily slung over his shoulder, giggling.

She had to think about Jack and what he could mean to her life. She felt like she had two ghosts whispering to her. One said, take a chance on love. The other said, don't be selfish. You're putting him at risk. Afraid of the first, she wanted to ignore the second all together. Too bad they were both right. Falling for Jack could be a chance for love, but it also put his life at risk. All their lives at risk.

Chapter Nineteen

"WHAT'S THIS ABOUT flowers?" Summer asked, curious about her daughter's question.

"Oh, nothing. We were talking about her name and the fact that Stargazer lilies are my favorite. She wants some, and I told her if I could find them, I'd get her some. I hope it's all right?"

"You don't have to do that."

"I want to. You have a great daughter, and it's such a small thing to make her happy. I don't have anyone to spoil," she said, her sadness drawing her lips into a frown. Her thoughts wanted to drag her to the past and all she'd lost, but she focused on Summer, the here and now in Jack's house.

"Only if you want to."

"I do."

"Let's get you into the bathroom. After Jack and Caleb bring your stuff, you can get dressed and come downstairs for breakfast, maybe lunch," she said and eyed her watch. "The morning seems to have gotten away from us."

"Are you sure you don't mind doing this? I can wait and come down to the salon to get my hair cut."

"It's fine. Can you get up on your own?"

"Yeah, I'm feeling much better today. I walked around the room a little last night. Jack and I stayed up late talking. It's been a long time since I got to know someone. I had a nice talk with your daughter this morning. I love her sweet personality."

"Yeah. Wait till she finds out she's getting a sibling."

"Really?"

"Yes. Caleb is so happy." By the sheer joy on Summer's face, he wasn't the only happy one. "He can't wait to tell her. Jack knows, but we want to wait a while longer to tell Lily."

"Congratulations. When is the baby due?"

"In about five months. February first."

Jenna had trouble getting out of bed and into the bathroom. Summer took off all the bandages.

"Actually, most of these look better. A lot of the welts have gone down and aren't red anymore. We won't need to put so many bandages back on. Your back is in full bloom, purple, green, and yellow. The stitches look good, too. I think it will be okay to take a shower. Just be careful. Do you need help washing your hair?"

Summer undid the braid. Pieces stuck out everywhere, because of the many lengths. Summer would have to cut a lot off to even it out. Jenna loved her hair. She didn't mind a shorter style. Her vanity could take the hit, but she hated her ex taking one more thing from her, even something as small as her hair.

"I'll manage. If I need you, I'll call."

"Okay. While you shower, I'll change the sheets on the bed. I don't know about you, but I love fresh sheets when I'm not feeling well."

True, sometimes it was the littlest things that brightened your day. She'd lived on little things to help her cope for a long time.

The shower relaxed her. Her arms and legs were fatigued but blessedly clean, and she felt almost whole again. She took a quick survey in the mirror. Lots of bruises everywhere, but her back looked a lot better. The stitches were sore and itchy, but even the cut didn't look so angry today. Jack did a nice job. Despite his good work, she'd have one hell of a scar to add to her collection.

Wrapped in a big, soft towel when Summer knocked, she entered the spacious bathroom, carrying a stool. "Take a seat and let's fix your hair." Summer placed a nylon wrap around Jenna's neck to keep the hair trimmings off her.

Jenna's hair (well, the longest part, anyway) went down to just past the middle of her back. Summer pulled out several strands on each side, testing the lengths, assessing the damage.

"Okay. Any requests? Is there a style you want?"

"I like to keep it long. No bangs. Basically, just make it look nice. I trust you."

"Thanks. I'll do my best. You'll love it."

Summer worked quietly for half an hour. She ended up cutting it to just below her shoulders. Which, actually, better suited Jenna's thick, heavy hair. She parted it off center, toward Jenna's right, and added some long layers. She blew it dry and with the soft waves and fiery color, it suited Jenna perfectly. Summer sprayed it to hold the hair in place and off Jenna's face. She stepped back and took an assessing look at the finished product.

"You're beautiful. I hate you now."

Silent tears slid down Jenna's face. Summer panicked. "I'm sorry, you don't like it. Oh, God. Now, you hate me."

"I love it. You're right. It's beautiful. Perfect. Thank you."

"It's not too short. I cut off a lot, but I really think it suits you."

"I love it. I don't mind that it's shorter. Makes it easier to dry."

Summer sighed with relief. "Well, okay then. You like it. I'm so glad. You had me worried there for a second."

Jenna dried her eyes. "Now the question is, do I have any clothes?"

"Let me see if Jack brought them up."

Jack came in with Jenna's suitcase, secretly wishing the thing had disappeared. He couldn't keep her in a sheet forever, but a few more days would be fun. Fun: when was the last time he thought about pulling pranks and joking around . . . with a woman, or anyone?

The suitcase dropped out of his hands when Jenna came out of the bathroom wrapped in a towel. Her breasts swelled over the top. Her hair framed her pretty face and fell to her shoulders. Jack's mouth went dry, he couldn't breathe. He stared, thunderstruck.

"Summer, leave us alone." Jack never took his eyes off Jenna.

Summer's gaze went from him to Jenna and back again before she pivoted on her toes and headed for the door without a word. Jenna stopped near the bathroom door and he drank in the sight of her, unable to move or speak.

"You don't like the haircut?"

"God, you're beautiful." Jack closed the distance between them, some invisible force pulling him across the room. She didn't back away, but stood looking up at him, nerves and wariness in those big green eyes.

"Jack?"

He didn't bother answering. Instead he cupped her face, turned it up to his, lowered his head, and touched his lips to hers. She didn't respond at first, except for a slight jolt. He brushed his lips to hers, rubbed his thumbs along her jaw, and settled into her. She stiffened and flinched with surprise. He expected her timid response. He brushed his lips over her cheek, her temple, her forehead, letting her know she was safe and cherished, not overpowered. Soft little touches. When his mouth found hers again, she kissed him back. He deepened the kiss, using his tongue to trace her lips. She opened on a surprised sigh, inviting him in, closer, and he smoothed his tongue over hers. Sinking fast, and in more ways than one. The feel of her, the taste, her smell, everything drew him in, filled him up, made him feel . . . good, right.

How long had he been living feeling indifferent and

apathetic? Stuck in a rut for far too long. Time to try something new with someone who stirred up all kinds of interesting things inside him.

She responded by grabbing his shirt and pulling him closer. She held on to his biceps and matched his kiss with her own. His hands slid down her neck, and he trailed his fingertips along the swell of her breasts. She moaned into his mouth, and he stroked across her breasts again, just above the towel. Lost in her, she tasted so sweet and smelled so fresh. Flowers, sweet and heady.

His hands made a journey up her throat and into her hair. He held her head and tilted it, deepened the kiss. Her nails dug into his arms.

She moved them up his shoulders and linked them behind his neck, pulling him closer. Closer to where he wanted to be. His hard shaft pressed to her belly. She pushed closer and a soft rumble came from his throat. He put his arms around her, about to lift her off her feet and carry her to the bed. She yelped out in pain.

He immediately released her and took two steps back. She almost fell toward him, he'd released her so quickly. With his hands outstretched, he steadied her by the arms.

"I'm sorry. I lost my head. Did I hurt you? Are you okay? Stupid, I shouldn't have touched your back." He raked his fingers through his hair and took a deep breath to try to calm his overheated, unruly body.

"Jack, calm down. I'm all right." Shy and hesitant, she stepped close, put her hands on his cheeks, and pulled him down for a soft lingering kiss. He pushed his fingers through her soft, thick hair and held her head, too.

"I'm sorry," he said against her lips.

She settled back onto her heels and bit her bottom lip. Her tongue swept across her kiss-swollen lip. Tasting him, her eyes met his. Though he appreciated the passion, it was the trace of wariness that held him back from diving in again.

"I'm all right. Are those my clothes?" Jenna needed a minute to settle her insides. The man could kiss. He made everything inside her mind turn off and her body turn on. The only thing she could think and feel was Jack. Intense and scary and wonderful all at the same time, she took another deep breath and smelled him, soap, leather, hay, and horse. A nice combination.

"You're always trying to get your clothes on. Right now, I just want to get my clothes off."

A deep laugh bubbled up her gut and burst out. "Down, boy."

"He doesn't want to go down. He wants to come out and play." Absolutely serious, but aware she needed the levity and time. She appreciated his attempt, despite the tightness in his face and body, telling her he was as aroused as her.

"Funny. How about I let you wrap my thigh before I get dressed?"

"Do I get to kiss it and make it better?"

She smiled. "Be good," she ordered.

"Oh, honey, I am," he teased back.

She turned the opening of the towel to her back and stood in front of him. His ragged sigh made her laugh again.

"You're killing me, you know."

"Somehow, I think you'll survive."

Resigned, Jack grabbed the bandages and knelt on the floor to tend her wound. He checked the stitches and made sure the cut wasn't still damp from her shower. He covered the gash with ointment and taped a bandage in place.

He trailed kisses along the side of the cut from the bottom up to the top of her thigh. Every touch of his open mouth shot sparks of heat through her system. His big hands rubbed up the front of her legs from her ankles to her hips. Everywhere his hands roamed, her body heated and pulsed. She sighed, felt her heart jump when his fingers closed on her hips, his fingertips inches from the heat pooling low in her belly.

He wound gauze around the bandage and her thigh. Her entire back displayed to him, he bandaged two of the bad welts and cuts. The rest he put ointment on.

The whole time his hands made soft caresses up and down her back as he worked, sending shivers of heat racing over her skin. He kissed all the bruises. When he stood to kiss the bruises on her shoulders, she shook with anticipation as his breath caressed her skin a moment before his mouth tasted.

She closed her eyes and enjoyed the lazy travel of Jack's mouth and hands over her body. He moved her hair to the side and kissed along her neck and shoulders, nearly sending her to her knees.

"Better than a lollipop?"

She smiled. "Oh, yeah."

"Good. I'd much rather kiss you than give you a shot."

His hands traveled over her shoulders and arms. She nearly dropped the towel. Long forgotten need awakened with his every touch. Any second, she'd collapse against him. A warning sounded in her head to be careful, cautious. Instead of leaning back into him, she stood her ground, but couldn't bring herself to step away.

"Not that I want you to, but get dressed and come downstairs and eat."

Grateful he understood her signal, she turned, reached up, and caressed her hand over his strong jaw and cheek. He leaned into her palm and turned and kissed her wrist. Her heart slammed into her ribs at the sweet gesture. "I'll be down in a minute."

Strange, she'd never been affectionate with her ex-husband, not even when they first started dating. Not like she wanted to be with Jack. With him, she felt free to be herself. She'd tried to live up to her ex-husband's high standards of class and decorum, since the first moment she'd met him. Well-educated and extremely smart, but he never made her feel like Jack made her feel. Jack wore his masculinity so easily, and because of that, she felt more like a woman when she was with him than she ever had in her life. It was a powerful feeling to know he wanted her. She wanted him just as much. She feared she needed him. Dangerous, because needing him made it that much harder to run to save herself. To save him, she'd do anything. Even leave the best thing that had ever happened to her, leave the one man she might actually love the rest of her life.

Chapter Twenty

JENNA SORTED THROUGH her emergency suitcase for something to wear that wouldn't rub on her back or thigh. Not much to choose from, she only kept three outfits and a pair of shoes in the case. At least she'd get to buy some new clothes, one of the small pleasures she had in her life. She decided on the black jogging suit with white stripes down the side. A bra would hurt, so she put on the tank top and zipped the sweatshirt to just below her breasts.

Fully dressed, feeling much better, and her hair looking great, Jenna made her way downstairs. Careful as she descended, it took her a little longer, since she favored her injured leg. Sally stayed at her side the entire time. Comforting, she liked having the dog with her.

She never got a chance to see any of Jack's house, except for the guest room. Lovely, much like the cabin. Wood everywhere. At the end of the stairs facing the front door, a Great Room lay off to the right. A huge fireplace dominated one wall, cozy furniture in soft muted tans and browns mixed with touches of blue. Jack must like blue. Of course, a big-screen TV completed the room.

The windows in the Great Room looked out to majestic green mountains and the valley. Through the front windows, she saw a large porch. No one in the Great Room, she headed left. She went through another sitting area, past several closed doors, and passed through the dining room and found everyone in the huge kitchen. They all turned from the big island to stare at her.

She stopped in the doorway and placed her hands on her fluttering stomach. "Is something wrong?"

Summer came off her stool toward Jenna, grabbing her arm, she led her to the island.

"Nothing at all. We're just surprised to see you wearing clothes and standing up. You've been in that bed for so long, it's a surprise to see you looking human again. I'm so jealous. You could be a model with that exceptional figure."

"Oh. Well, thanks. But I have nothing on you. Your blond hair, blue eyes, and stop-a-man's-heart figure are nothing to sneeze at. I hope I look as good as you after having kids." She also remembered Summer was four months pregnant. True, pregnant women glowed. Summer sure did.

Caleb winked at his wife before saying, "That's my wife, she stops my heart every time I see her."

Summer smiled and blew her husband a kiss. "Charmer. Jack made you lunch. Come eat."

Jenna walked over to the plate on the counter next to

Jack, who held Lily on his lap. She laughed when she saw what Jack made her. Next to her turkey sandwich sat a huge pile of chocolate covered peanut butter cups and a cup of coffee.

She smiled at Jack and Lily. "Now that's my kind of lunch. I'll say it again, eavesdropping is not nice, but it can be productive."

Jack smiled. "One candy for every shot. I didn't find any lollipops in Lily's stash, but you said you liked those, too."

"You are a kind man, Jack."

"You make it easy to be kind."

"Not everyone is." Silence settled over the group for a moment, thick as gravy. Everyone thought of the reason she'd been in bed for days. Kindness shared nothing in common with the rage that put her there.

She stood next to Jack and ate her sandwich, sharing her candy with Lily, who was excited to be with everyone in the kitchen. Everyone talked and enjoyed their meals. Jenna didn't like intruding on this close-knit family, but she cherished the fact they made her feel welcome and part of things.

"Why don't you sit down?" Lily asked.

Jenna didn't want to tell the little girl why she couldn't sit on the wood stool. Instead, she kissed the little girl in Jack's lap on the forehead. "I've been in bed for a long time. I need to stand for a while. I also have an owie on my leg and the stool will make it hurt."

Jack moved his thigh, resting it against her hip. Waves of warmth spread through Jenna at the contact of his body to hers. She wished she could feel that warmth every second the rest of her life, and so she didn't move away, but settled into him.

Caleb and Summer gave each other a look and a knowing smile. Some kind of silent conversation and agreement between them. Jenna understood the undertone. Sparks flew and the air crackled any time she and Jack were close. She'd never felt this kind of attraction before, but she didn't want to lose it. After everything she'd endured, most of all the loneliness, she desperately wanted to hold on to the feelings Jack stirred in her.

"Today's Friday, right?"

Everyone agreed.

"Summer, do you work tomorrow?"

"No. Why?"

"Would you like to go shopping with me? I don't have anything, and I need to buy some new clothes. It'll be a whirlwind shopping spree, lots of fun. Wanna go?"

"Are you kidding? I'd love to."

"Great, I'll make all the arrangements."

"Arrangements?" Summer asked, confused.

"Trust me. It'll be great."

"Okay. I have to take Lily home for her nap. Come on, Sunshine."

"Jack and I need to head down to the barn and check on some of the horses. I'll be home later, honey." Caleb kissed his wife and daughter goodbye. A touch of jealousy zinged through Jenna's heart. They were a real married couple, something she'd experienced too briefly . . . if at all.

"I need to make some phone calls. I guess I'll see you all later." She put her empty plate in the dishwasher along with her coffee cup. She turned and almost ran straight into Jack. Instinctively, she took a step back and threw up her hands between them to ward him off. Completely unnecessary, and the slight frown he gave her told her how much her backing away hurt him.

"Who are you calling?"

She dropped her hands and answered without acknowledging what she'd done without thinking. "Ben. I need to take care of a few things with him."

"What things?" Jack was afraid she'd call Ben and hightail it right out of his life now that she was feeling better. He didn't want to see that happen when he was just starting to realize how much she could mean to him. Already did mean to him, judging by the zip of alarm that shot through him.

"Jack, I don't let people into my life. For very good reasons. Let me do what I have to do."

"As long as it doesn't include running away from me."

"I have no reason to run away from you. But I'll do everything I can to protect you and your family from the person who did this to me."

"Protect us from whom?"

"We'll talk about that later. I'm not ready yet. Time, Jack. Give me a little time to settle, to let the thoughts and pictures in my head clear."

What she meant was time to trust him with her secrets. He'd already set his mind to earning that trust. So he'd wait, but he didn't have to like it.

"You're making this hard. I can't protect you, or my family, if I don't know who's after you. This is my ranch, my family." He bent and kissed her lightly on the mouth. This time, her hesitation lasted a split second and vanished. Progress. "Stay with me. Let me help you."

Stay with me. Those words hadn't come easy for him. Trusting him didn't come easy for her either.

"I'm trying. I've been alone a long time. Asking you to help me opens you and your family up to the nightmare I live. Let me call Ben. I'll settle some things and figure out what's best. Then we'll talk. That's the best I can do right now. This is hard for me. I don't want to involve you and your family, but I can't bring myself to walk away from you either."

She took a deep steadying breath. "I care about you, and it's tearing me up to think I might have put you in danger by coming here." She thought acknowledging her feelings and telling him would make her nervous and anxious. It didn't. Instead, it settled her and centered her in a way she didn't expect. "It's only been a matter of days, most of which I've been passed out. Every instinct tells me something special is happening here, but another part of me is scared to trust those instincts."

Because she'd trusted another man and he'd turned on her. "I'd never hurt you."

"I know that," she said too fast and with a hesitant note to her words.

"No, you don't. Not really. One day you will, and until then I'll spend every moment proving it to you."

"I'm sorry. I'm sure it seems I'm pulling you close and pushing you away all at the same time. I'm not playing games."

"I never thought you were."

"If there's one thing I've learned, it's not to waste time. Unfortunately, I haven't had the luxury of taking time to build new relationships with people. In order to at least try to make this happen and explore this thing between us, I need to take care of and set up a few things to protect myself and you."

He slipped his hand around the back of her neck and held her close. "I won't let anything happen to you. Promise, promise me you won't run away."

"I can't make that promise. If he comes for me, I won't let him touch you, or Caleb, or Summer. I won't let that evil get to Lily."

"I don't think I can live without you, now that I've found you," Jack admitted on a ragged whisper.

"You woke me up from a nightmare. I want a life, a real life. I don't want to be afraid. I want to know I'm home." She ran her hands over his chest, just the small contact to steady her world and let her know this is real. He's real. "Let's talk about this later. Caleb is waiting for you down at the barn. Go. I'll make my calls, and then I think I'll take a walk and get some exercise."

He bent his brow to hers. They stood nose to nose. "Are you staying?"

She placed her hands on his cheeks and held him to her. "Yes, Jack. I want to stay here with you."

"That's a good place to start."

"Are you going to bolt?" she teased, because guys tended toward retreat when commitment was on the line.

"Not a chance. Any other time, any other woman, and the thought of them moving in would make me run for the hills. It's different with you." He gently brushed his fingertips along her bruised jaw. "You're different. I'm not sure what this thing between us is, but I know I don't want to lose it before I know for sure." He kissed her forehead and pressed his cheek to her head and held her for a moment before he reluctantly released her. "Be here when I get back."

Chapter Twenty-One

"It's Rabbit. I need Ben."

Efficient as ever, his staff put her through to Ben immediately. Even when he was in court, they managed to get him for her with relative ease.

"Ben, you're going to earn those big bucks I pay you today."

"I guess you're feeling better." Relief tinged his words. "It's so good to hear your voice, and more so to hear you sounding like your old self. I've been worried about you. Jack's kept me apprised of how you're doing. Everything okay?"

"So far. Do you know where he is?"

"Paris. Some business or other."

"How long will he be gone?"

"At least another week. He's negotiating buying some company. The soonest he'll be back, maybe three days."

"Right. I saw that in my email from the company

detailing the purchase. Do you know what his schedule is after Paris?"

"No, something's going on at his office. My source hasn't been able to dig anything up. That's why I don't know for certain his return date."

"Okay. Three days gives me time to get my wits back and decide what to do."

"What do you mean, what to do?"

"Not just me, you're going to help. It's time to end the hunt. I need to figure out the best way to do that without getting myself killed, or anyone here hurt."

"You know I'm with you, Rabbit. You're my best client, not to mention my friend."

She smiled and sighed wearily. "Thanks. That means a lot. You've been a good friend to me over the years and the only constant in my life. I wish I could repay you for what you've done."

"Something's different. You sound hopeful. I mean, you usually have a great attitude, but I don't know. I can't put my finger on it."

"It's Jack. He's the best gift you could've given me. You were right about him. He saved me in more ways than I knew I needed saving. His quiet strength and unflappable confidence rubbed off on me, I guess you could say. Being here with him and his family has shown me what a real life could be like having people around who care about you, really care deeply and unconditionally."

"You deserve so much more than what you've gotten over the years. I hope you've found some happiness."

"I'm starting to feel like everything that's happened has led up to this. It's time to stop running and do something. That's where you come in."

"What do you want me to do?"

She started back up the stairs. Slow going, her leg hurt each time she used it to lift herself up a step, but she needed to exercise the muscles. "First, did you send me a new computer?"

"Didn't you get your packages?"

"Yeah, I just haven't opened them yet. I will. Is the computer in there?"

"Yes, your usual laptop, twenty thousand in cash, your mail, copies of statements and business papers. Look those over, there've been a lot of changes."

"How's my project with Mike going? Has he kept things quiet and hidden?"

"So far, we've seen no outward signs anyone has taken notice. He's got things split up between several of your trusts, which have your name buried deep. Someone would have to dig to find out they all belong to you. Of course, they'll know interest in the stock has increased."

"How long until I have what I want?"

"I don't know for sure. Mike's kept things fairly spread out over the last two years. He doesn't want to send up any flags. You don't need that much more. Once you have it, we can change all the trusts back to your name whenever you want. What will you do once you've got this?"

"Show him that he can't get away with hurting me."

"You're playing with fire."

"No. So far, I've let others tie my hands, tell me to be patient and let the system work for me. While I wait, he comes after me again. Enough. This is the only way to hurt him."

"What do you want me to do? All your long-term plans are moving along."

"I want you to draw up a new will and a couple of new trusts. I'll email you all the specifics. Can you send the papers to me tomorrow morning to sign? Double copies. You'll see why when you get the email. I'll need a set and the others can go back to you. I want them before I leave to go shopping with the girls."

"Shopping with the girls?"

"Yes. I intend to be a normal person tomorrow. I'm taking Jack's sister, Summer, and niece, Lily, out for the time of their lives."

"Do you need me to do anything for that?"

"I'll put it all in the email."

"Sounds like you're enjoying this."

"I am. It's time I had fun. I'm going to do something good. Wait till you see the email. After all the time you've known me, I think this email will be a shock. Look for it in a few minutes. Get to work. I want those papers tomorrow. And thanks, Ben."

"I'll look for the email in ten. I hope I get to hear you like this more often."

"I hope so, too. Call me when all the arrangements for tomorrow are done."

"I will."

She held the phone in her hand and gazed out the window to the trees beyond. For the first time in a long time, things were going her way. In control of her life, her direction, she savored the powerful feeling. She had Jack to thank for her newfound determination.

Chapter Twenty-Two

JENNA OPENED THE boxes from Ben and found the new laptop. She used her cell phone to connect to the Internet and her email account and sent Ben instructions to carry out her plans. On course to complete her goal, she'd give her ex the shock of his life if she pulled this off. She had to pull it off. Time to take a stand. Bodyguards, walls, gates, time, distance, nothing had protected her. She'd always known the only way to end this was to give her ex a very powerful reason not to come looking for her again. Thanks to Ben and his team, she had that reason.

She found it difficult to think of what her life could be like without her ex-husband hunting her like a wild animal. This life is all she knew now. She thought of Jack and decided life could be wonderful. Images of them happy together for years to come were so easy to conjure, it scared her.

After replying to several emails, tired of her own company, she took her cell phone, left her pretty room, and went outside with Sally. The fresh air smelled of grass and honeysuckle from the bush by the front steps. The sun warmed her face, and she gazed up at the bright sky and took a deep breath and relaxed.

"Where should we go?"

Sally barked and took off to the barn.

"Okay. Let's go see Jack," she said, talking to air. Sally disappeared through the wide doors. Jenna made her way down the gravel driveway to the huge building at her own slow pace.

The face of the barn was made of river rock, up from the ground three feet. The rest was wood painted white with dark blue trim. Jack really had a thing for blue. Outdoor paddocks led inside to stalls down both sides of the building. Some of them held gorgeous brown quarter horses. The top level of the barn had lots of windows and a hay-filled loft. The scent of hay and horses enveloped her as she stepped into the corridor and let her eyes adjust to the dimmer light.

Unsure where to find Jack and Caleb, she walked down the spacious center aisle that led back to some rooms at the far end. Jack must have an office down the way.

The horses moved and shifted in their stalls. Some peeked their heads over the doors. A few men worked in the barn, taking care of the horses. She smiled but kept her distance, Sally keeping pace beside her.

She came upon an open stall door with only a thick rope across it to keep the huge stallion inside. He moved to the opening and blocked her path with his big head. The most gorgeous horse she had ever laid eyes on.

He bobbed his gray head up and down, stomped a hoof, and blew through his nostrils into her hair. She immediately reached up and rubbed her hands over his long nose and along the side of his face. She stood in front of him stroking his neck and talking softly. He put his head over her shoulder and let her stroke behind his ears. She nuzzled her head against his. The scrape of boots fast approaching startled her.

A man carrying a strap in his hand drew closer. Panic stole her rational thoughts and she moved toward the horse, away from the threat.

"Miss, get away from him. He bites and might stomp on you. I don't want you to get hurt."

Jenna put up a hand. "Don't come any closer." Her voice weak, panic rose and took over her senses.

Sally barked several times and Jenna ducked under the rope into the stall. The big stallion went along with her. She backed up to the far wall. Every cell inside her screamed run. Trapped, fear overtook her, freezing her in place inside the stall behind the huge horse.

"Miss, that horse is mean as can be." He stood at the open stall door, blocking her exit, and called to her. "You gotta come out."

Jenna's focus zeroed in on the strap hanging from his hand. Unable to move, her knees went weak. She crouched down with her back to the wall, the horse moving, so he stood completely over her. She kept her eyes glued to the man with the strap and folded her arms around her knees.

Jack stood in the middle of the paddock, lunge line in

hand, as the yearling ran circles around him. Whenever the youngster tried to buck or prance, Jack coaxed him back to his training. Focused on the task at hand, it took a second for Jack to hear the change in the other horses. They neighed and stomped in their stalls, restless. Blue fussed, and Sally barked and growled. Jack's eyes met Caleb's and he recognized the same alarm he felt. Jack untied the yearling and he and Caleb ran inside. They spotted Pete at Blue's stall. Sally barked and refused to let him get closer.

"What's going on, Pete? What's wrong with Sally and Blue?"

"It's the woman from the house. Blue's going to kill her. She's in there with that demon horse, and she won't come out."

Jack ran to where Pete stood and stared unbelieving into the stall, Caleb right behind him.

"Oh my God, Jenna." Literally, she crouched under Blue, who stomped his front hoof warning everyone to stay away. Sally wouldn't let Jack in the door. Jenna stared at Pete with huge eyes filled with fear. Terror radiated off her and pounded at his heart.

"Jenna, honey, please come out. Blue might hurt you."

"I won't go back. I won't go back. I won't go back."

Not a good sign. She'd been doing so well this morning, and now she chanted that phrase over and over again, rocking back and forth. Just like the other night in the closet when she'd broken down.

She didn't move, just stared at the men in the doorway. Actually, her eyes were locked on Pete's every move. "Pete, tell me what happened," Jack demanded.

"She stood here rubbing Blue's head. I thought maybe he'd hurt her, so I told her to get away from him. I guess I startled her. She turned, said something I didn't hear, then when I came closer, she backed herself into the stall with your beast."

Jack didn't know what to make of it. She must have gotten scared from seeing a strange man. "Jenna, come out. No one will hurt you. Caleb and I are here. We'll take you to the house."

Caleb moved next to Jack. "Come on, I'll call Summer and Lily. They'll look after you. Would you like that?"

Jenna rocked back and forth, still chanting, "I won't go back." Her eyes unfocused, lost in some imagined terror, Jack didn't know how to pull her back to reality.

Frustrated, Pete said, "I don't want to lose my job, or make you mad." The slap of leather against Pete's thigh pulled Jack's attention from Jenna to Pete. "I didn't do anything to her," Pete said, pleading.

Jenna's eyes got even bigger, her face paler as Pete continued to smack his thigh. Jack finally understood what held her attention. Not the man, but the leather in his hand that looked very much like a belt.

"Pete, slowly hand that strap to Caleb, and then I want you to walk away. Go into the kitchen and have yourself a cup of coffee."

Pete handed the strap over, not realizing what he'd done wrong. He walked away from the stall and down to the kitchen. Jack would explain later. Right now, his priority sat precariously under a tempestuous thousand pounds of ornery, devilish horse.

Caleb's face mirrored Jack's inner turmoil. Knowing Jenna needed reassurance, Caleb spoke softly. "This is just a strap to fix a horse bridal. That's all. Pete would never hurt you. I'll put it away." Caleb walked away slowly, making sure Jenna saw him taking away her worst nightmare. Jack's stomach turned as her eyes followed Caleb's back as he left.

"Please, honey, come out of there. If Blue kicks or steps on you, he could kill you."

Her ex's image superimposed over the first man, and now Caleb. She kept seeing her ex coming at her with the belt, heard the sound it made when it whistled through the air and the snap of it when it slapped across her back. The stinging pain of it biting into her skin. Flinching, she tried to shake off the memory. Her focus returned, and Jack stood in the doorway before her. Locking on to him, she barely managed to say, "Hi."

"Hi, honey. You okay now."

Jenna regained her senses, and little by little her body relaxed. Her eyes weren't so huge and she didn't hold her knees as tight. Blue stood guard over her, still, for now. He turned his big head down, looked underneath himself and neighed at Jenna.

"I was looking for you."

Jack could almost breathe easy again. "Did you miss me?"

"Yeah. Nice barn."

"Thanks. You know it's making me really nervous watching you sit under one of the meanest horses who ever came into this stable."

"He's not mean. He blew in my hair, and I was giving him some love when ..." She stopped and locked eyes with him. "I got scared."

"Well, you're scaring me now. Honey, come on, get out from under Blue."

She combed her shaking hands through her hair. "His name is Blue?"

"Yes." Jack couldn't take much more. While talking, color bloomed back into her cheeks, but she still wasn't safe. If Blue decided to kick ... He didn't want to think what would happen if he kicked her.

"You named him Blue?"

He didn't know why his horse's name concerned her so much, but if it took her focus off being scared and got her out of the stall, he was all for talking about it. "Yes, honey, come out."

She broke out into a full belly laugh.

"What the hell is so funny?"

"You really do like blue. The cabin, the house, the barn trim, and now the horse, all blue." She continued to laugh, trying to catch her breath. He didn't mind, even if she sounded a little hysterical. She released some of the pent up tension in both of them.

"Would you get out here, please?" Jack bent under the stall rope. Sally calmed and sprawled in the hay. He walked to Blue, careful not to spook the animal, and stroked him down his neck the way he liked.

Jenna stopped laughing and took a deep calming breath. Jack put his hand down to her and she grabbed hold and came out from under the horse. She wrapped her arms around his neck and gave him a huge hug, holding on as hard as she could. They stood there for several minutes, his hands resting on her hips.

"I'm sorry. I don't know what happened. I saw him coming toward me with the strap in his hand, everything closed in around me, and I panicked. I was back in that house, and he was hitting me, and . . ."

Jack grabbed her and held her tight. Her whole body trembled against his.

"Ouch!" Jenna squealed then squirmed.

Blue smacked him in the back with his head. Jack let go of Jenna, and they almost toppled over from the force of Blue hitting him.

"I'm sorry. I forgot your back. Damnit, Blue, knock it off."

"I like Blue. He's beautiful. Aren't you, sweetheart." Jenna walked around Jack and grabbed Blue's head. She gave him a squeeze and stroked him. Blue nuzzled her neck and shoulder. Then he placed the front of his head down the front of Jenna, from her breasts to her belly.

Caleb stood watching from the stall door. "I've never seen the stubborn beast cozy up to anyone. He tolerates Jack, but it looks like love with you, Jenna."

The stress and strain left Jenna's body as she stroked the huge animal. Horses had that effect on people when they connected with you.

"Well, I'll be damned. That horse doesn't like anyone, and here he is all snuggled tight to you," Jack said, surprised.

"You're just jealous." Jenna gave him a sweet smile.

"Um, yeah. Come on, let's get out of here."

"I'm really sorry I made such a scene. I don't know why I did that. You must think I'm crazy."

"Maybe you should talk to a doctor, someone who helps women in your situation," Caleb suggested.

Jack agreed, he and Caleb had both had their fair share of post-traumatic stress. He thought Jenna could use some help dealing with everything she'd been through.

"I'll think about it. I got a lot done on the phone with Ben, and I thought I'd go for a walk, get some fresh air, see you guys. Then the past and the present got mixed up, and my brain shut off and the panic took over."

"It's okay, honey." Jack caressed her neck with his fingertips. "You've had a bad couple of days. You're entitled to be out of sorts. I'm here now. You have nothing to worry about. Come on, I'll introduce you to Pete. You'll like him. Then if you see him around, you won't be scared."

"I'd really like to apologize to him. I must seem like a crazy woman."

"Someone hurt you. It's natural to be afraid, especially in a new place with new people." Jack held her hand and walked down the aisle toward the kitchen with her.

"I don't know how you put up with me."

"You keep smiling at me like that, and hugging me like you did in the stall, and I'll drag you to the house and show you how I put up with you."

"Jack! Caleb is standing right there."

"Caleb didn't hear anything."

"Yes. Caleb didn't hear anything," Caleb mimicked back, snickering at Jenna.

"Besides, he's sleeping with my sister. And he's gone and knocked her up—again."

"I do my best." Caleb and Jack smiled at her, lightening her mood and making her feel much better.

They entered the small kitchen. Pete sat at a round table, contemplating the steaming cup of coffee between his hands, looking dejected.

"Miss, really, I wasn't gonna do anything to you. I didn't mean to scare you."

"I know. I've had a rough time lately, and I panicked. It had nothing to do with you. I'm really sorry."

"Shoot. No need to apologize. That horse could have killed you."

Jack didn't want to go there. Seeing Blue standing over Jenna scared him half to death. He held her hand tighter, reassuring himself she was fine.

"Pete, I'd like you to meet, Jenna. Jenna, this is Pete. He oversees all the horses."

"It's nice to meet you, ma'am." Pete stood and offered his hand.

Jenna took it without reservation. "It's nice to meet you, too. Again, I'm really sorry."

"Oh, enough. Any time you want to ride, I'll get you a real nice horse to take out. Jack has some real beauties."

"I'd like that, but not until my leg is better."

Jack hadn't thought about her leg. "Did you tear those stitches again? I don't want to keep sewing you up."

"I think they're fine."

"Come into my office, and I'll check them to be sure."

Caleb and Pete excused themselves, while Jack and Jenna went into the office. Jack's domain had an oak desk and file cabinets, a state of the art computer system, and posters of muscle cars—Camaros, to be exact—covered the walls. Stunned, Jenna turned a circle to look at all of them.

"You being a horse man, I'd have figured you for Mustangs rather than Camaros."

"My dad had a '69 Camaro when I was a kid. I hated when he sold it. I always wanted that car. There's this place a few towns over. They restore classic cars. Caleb and I go down there sometimes and drool. Caleb's a Mustang man. He likes the '67 Fastback. They had a red one at the shop about six months back. I didn't think I'd get Caleb out of there."

"Why didn't you ever buy a Camaro?"

"Didn't have the money. Didn't have the time. I don't really know. I guess I could now. Maybe I will." He shrugged.

The name of the shop was printed on the calendar behind Jack's desk. September had a picture of a '69 Camaro, black with silver racing stripes up the hood and over the roof. Of course, the requisite blond bombshell in a bikini stood beside the car with a sultry smile.

"That's a nice car. I love fast cars. I used to have a Porsche. I loved to speed down the back roads."

"A Porsche, huh. That's an expensive car," he stated, a touch of curiosity in his voice.

"The SUV I have now is okay, but there's nothing like speed."

"God, I like you. You're not like any other woman I've ever known. You like cars, horses, even sports. You don't even mind my dog following you everywhere and sleeping in your bed."

Jack leaned back on his desk and drew Jenna in between his legs. She settled against him, locking her arms behind his neck. Jack gently grabbed her hips and pulled her closer. Again, the slight hesitation lasted a second and disappeared.

"I just want to touch you, but it seems whenever I do I end up hurting you."

"It's okay. Hold on to me."

He did. They stayed snuggled together for a long while. Jenna stroked the back of Jack's hair and absorbed his warmth. She needed to be close, to be held. To let the last of her fear dissipate and Jack's strength seep in and fortify her resolve.

She'd had so little physical contact over the years. Being in Jack's arms reminded her how comforting cuddling with someone could be. Before her ex-husband, she dated, had other boyfriends. She remembered feeling close, but this was so much more.

He kissed her neck and worked his way along her jaw. She tilted her head back to give him better access. Her hands traveled through his hair, down his neck, and over his strong shoulders. The ringing of her phone finally broke through the spell they weaved.

"Don't answer that," Jack grumbled. "I finally have

you to myself." He made a grab for her phone, but she quickly held it away, laughing at his little-boy antics.

"I have to, it's Ben calling me back with some business."

Jack let out a frustrated grunt, and she answered the call.

Chapter Twenty-Three

"HELLO."

"All your instructions have been handled. Looks like you'll have a great time with the girls tomorrow. I set up an account at the stores, in addition to the other items you included in your email. All the paperwork is completed and on its way. Special messenger will deliver them to you tomorrow morning bright and early. He'll get the originals back to me. Are you sure about the will? As your attorney, I have to advise you the changes you made are sudden. Maybe you should take some time to think it over."

"I'm sure. What about the other papers? Are they done?"

"All set up. The name on the one set can be changed as soon as you know what it is. The accounts are in place, too."

"Perfect. Listen, I have something else I want you to do. I'll send you an email, and if you can take care of this for tomorrow, you have no idea how much I'll appreciate it. Expect good things at Christmas."

"Well, that'll be something, considering you're the most generous person I've ever known."

"You've earned it. And if you pull this off, you'll make me, and a few others, very happy."

"Okay, send the email. It's getting late in the day and whatever you want done might take some time."

"Give me five minutes."

She hung up with Ben. Still in Jack's arms, he'd watched and listened to her every word.

"What's all that about? What kind of business do you have with Ben?"

"Just some personal things I asked him to take care of for me."

"What things?"

"A few surprises for tomorrow, that's all. How about we ask Summer, Lily, and Caleb over for dinner tomorrow night after the girls and I get back from shopping? Would that be all right? I know it's your house and all, but I'd like to spend the evening with everyone. It's time we had that talk. Since they're involved with me, with you, I want to make sure they know about my past. I need to warn them. Well, all of you."

"Dinner's fine. I'll have Beth whip something up. Caleb and I can barbeque. I've been waiting for this talk. Are you going to tell me who your ex is?"

"Tomorrow. I'll tell you everything. I need to send Ben an email. Will I see you soon?"

"I have some work. I'll be up for dinner, then maybe we'll crash on the couch and catch a movie."

"That sounds like heaven."

"Jenna, the house may be mine, but I want you to feel at home. And I don't mean with you in the guest room." He pulled her hips snuggly between his legs and let her feel exactly what he meant.

"I got the hint." She put her hand to his face. "We'll get there. With everything that's happened—"

Jack laid his finger over her lips to silence her. "Let's stick with, 'We'll get there.'" She nodded and kissed his finger, making his eyes narrow and smolder. "I'll see you at dinner." He set her away gently and softly slid his hands over her shoulders and down her arms. He clasped her hands in his and just held them for a moment while he studied her upturned face. He didn't want to let her go, but knew he had to in order to get anything done.

"Go. You're distracting me."

Jenna withdrew reluctantly and went back to the house and sent the email off to Ben and took care of her last customer. She finished her design work before the incident had put her on the run, but she hadn't sent off the finished product to her client. She emailed everything to them, including her hefty bill. She spent some time pouring over her other emails and checking inquiries for new business. Might be a good time to take a break. After all, being your own boss had its advantages, and she didn't need the money.

Chapter Twenty-Four

JENNA AND JACK had a cozy dinner in the Great Room next to the fire. They watched a couple of movies curled up together on the couch. Jack sat in the corner, his feet propped on the coffee table, with Jenna resting her head on his leg to keep off her thigh and back. He stroked his fingers through her hair and even held her hand. They watched movies like they had done it every night of their lives, content just being in each other's company.

He saw her to her door and kissed her goodnight like the end of a date. Sally curled up on the bed waiting for her. Jack glared at Sally and grumbled, "Lucky dog," before leaving her with a mumbled goodnight. As she got ready for bed, she listened to Jack moving around his rooms, taking a shower before he settled into his bed. The quiet enveloped the house and night, but didn't bring her any comfort.

Restless and plagued by nightmares, she woke from

the last dream, sweating, a thunderstorm disrupting the quiet night. Wind and rain battered the roof and windows. The noise and swirling shadows frightened her. Her mind conjured her ex lurking in the murky corners and every creak was his footsteps, him sneaking up on her. Usually she'd have gotten up, told the little girl inside her to suck it up, lost herself in work at her laptop or in a book, and waited desperately for the sun to rise. Tonight, she thought of Jack—gentle, kind, safe, and good—only a room away.

She went back and forth in her mind, trying to decide how much she should allow herself to rely on him. In the end, she talked herself into the indulgence. Feeling stupid for letting her imagination get the better of her, she mustered her courage and climbed out of bed. Sally right behind her, she made her way to Jack's room. The door stood open a crack, and Jack's soft breathing pulled her forward. She snuck in. Sally jumped on the bed and lay at Jack's feet. Jack didn't stir, giving Jenna courage to climb up on the empty side of the bed and curl up next to him on top of the blankets. A clap of thunder made her jump, but the soft sound of Jack's breathing relaxed her. She watched him sleep, comforted just having him near. Drowsy, the rain subsiding outside the windows, she slept.

Jack woke up, barely, when the alarm radio went off at six. He didn't open his eyes, but lay still, slowly coming awake to the Eagles' *Hotel California*. His awareness stretched. Sally must have come in during the night and curled up in her usual spot at his feet. Recognition bloomed again, and he turned to the now familiar pull of the woman curled up next to him, burrowed in at his rib cage. Not even covered with a blanket, wearing nothing but the t-shirt he'd given her last night, goose bumps broke out on her bare arms and legs. He stroked her hair away from her cheek with his fingertip. Touching her silky skin was quickly becoming an addiction.

Hands pressed under her chin, she lay curled in a tight ball, trying to stay warm. Without jarring or hurting her injuries, he drew the blankets out from under her and settled her under the covers with him.

He nuzzled his nose into her neck and hair at her ear and whispered, "Jenna, honey. Wake up."

"Uh, uh."

"Wake up, honey, you're freezing."

"I had a bad dream, the storm woke me, and I snuck in here in the middle of the night." Her voice groggy with sleep, she wiggled and snuggled closer to him. He held her close and let his body heat seep into her.

"Why didn't you get under the covers?"

"Because I didn't know if you'd mind."

"Mind having a beautiful woman sneak into my bed. I thought we discussed this, I'm not crazy or stupid," he said on a laugh. The tension in her built, but he hoped his light tone settled her nerves. Relieved, she stirred awake and settled her head on his chest, draped an arm across him, and threw her bandaged leg over his thigh and between his legs. Every part of her cool skin pressed to his warm body. She snuggled closer, eliminating any space left between them, and he held her close. Content, he settled into the moment and her and the undeniable connection between them.

"You're naked."

"You're overdressed," he teased.

"We have to get up."

"I already am." He tried to keep things light and make her laugh despite his rising ardor.

"The messenger is coming with my papers. Caleb, Summer, and Lily will arrive soon, so we can go shopping. You have a surprise today."

"I'd say the nicest surprise is waking up with you in my bed. Though it would have been better if you woke me in the night." He kissed her on the head and held her close, loving the feel of her body pressed down the length of his. He inhaled her flowery scent and thought this is where she belonged.

"We'll have plenty of time for that later. Behave yourself. Now, don't you want to kiss me good morning?"

"You just said to behave." He kissed her anyway. Long and slow. Their lips met again and again. Warm, sweet, soft, she responded to every caress of his lips to hers. Drugged beyond reason, Jack's endurance snapped and he took her mouth in a demanding sweep of his tongue, branding her as his.

Opening her mouth to accept his invasion, Jenna relished every taste and kiss. He rolled toward her and pressed her into the mattress. His erection pressed against her belly, her nerves tingled with awareness and apprehension. She hadn't had sex in a long time and Jack was a big man, in every way.

The heat between them built. Jack cupped her breast and kissed his way down her neck. He pulled up her shirt and his thumb made slow circles over her aching breast, finding his way to her taught nipple. His rough palm against her sensitive skin made her breasts grow heavy. Jack groaned with pleasure and she arched into his touch, responding to the heat and need rolling off him and sweeping her away. Her heart beat so fast, her head spun. His weight settled into her, pressing her into the mattress, trapping her. Unwarranted fear raced through her mind, stealing away the pleasure of the moment. She pressed her palms to Jack's chest and gave a half-hearted push. A voice inside yelled pull him back. Fear won out, and she hated her ex for doing this to her, taking one more thing from her.

"Jack, stop. Stop."

Jack pulled back, pressed up onto his hands, and shook off his blinding desire. "Are you okay?"

"It's just that, um, I haven't done this in an extremely long time, and we have to get up, and you're making me really nervous, and I don't think I'm ready for this," she rambled on.

He tried to lighten things without moving from where he needed to be. The thick head of his cock pressed to her entrance. He shifted and pressed harder. Her thin panties adding to the friction of the caress. Her eyes went soft and drooped closed as she sighed.

"You're not ready yet, but give me a few minutes and you will be," he said, his voice husky with pent-up desire. He buried his face in her neck and kissed a trail to the soft spot behind her ear. God, she tasted better than she smelled.

She gave out a giggle. "Jack, I'm serious. Get up. People are coming over."

"You're killing me, you know that." He rose above her on his hands, the lower half of his body keeping her trapped. He narrowed his eyes, deadly serious, he said, "We will finish this later."

"We will," she assured him, cupping his beard-roughened jaw in her hand to soothe him. As always, he leaned into her touch. "Seriously, I haven't been with anyone since, well, a long time. I'd like us to take our time. Learn how to enjoy each other. You're, uh, a really big guy, and you're scaring me a little bit," she admitted.

The last thing he wanted to do was make her pull away. Then he thought about what she was telling him. She hadn't been with anyone since her ex. Jack couldn't believe a beautiful, wonderful woman like Jenna hadn't been with another man in so long. It amazed him she'd chosen him. His size and strength had frightened her more than once already. As much as he wanted her, he wanted to take his time. He didn't want her nervous, or anxious, the first time they made love. As much as it hurt, and he was hurting, he'd wait and know she wanted him as much as he wanted her. Next time, he'd make sure she didn't feel anything but pure pleasure, no nerves, no fear.

"We'll wait until the timing's better. About the other, I'd never hurt you, Jenna. Never."

"Thank you for understanding. It means the world to

me you're willing to give me the time and courtesy I need right now."

He could seduce her. She wanted to be seduced. That much he knew for sure. Making love was a natural expression of what they were feeling for each other. Each passing hour the need they shared grew between them until it was palpable. With the amount of heat between them, it was only a matter of time before they came together in a blaze. Right now, he had to put her needs above his own.

He let loose the pent-up groan in the back of his throat and settled beside her, missing the feel of her skin against his. He allowed her time to get up first and head back to her room to shower. He didn't want to make her any more nervous by getting out of bed naked and aroused. His t-shirt looked great on her, the hem skimming the middle of her thighs, teasing his senses, heating his blood even more. He'd like to spend the rest of his life waking up with her in his arms and her wearing his clothes. Actually, nothing at all. He'd be thinking about her firm round breasts, her supple body, and long legs wrapped around him for the rest of the day.

He showered, shaved, and dressed before Jenna came walking down the hall wearing nothing but a towel.

"See, I knew you couldn't hold out. Come here, darlin'." He held out his hand to her.

She swatted it away. "Very funny. I need you to put medicine on the cuts on my back."

"Now see, you're just no fun."

"Come on, baby, play doctor with me," she said with

a throaty, whiskey smooth voice that could have seduced any man. It worked. She seductively brushed the hair back from her face and lowered her lashes demurely. He lost his breath.

"Definitely killing me." He barely got the words out after she spoke to him with that voice.

"Yeah, well, I'll make it up to you later."

"Promise?"

"Oh, yeah."

Easy enough for her to tease and play with words. The way she held herself ready to bolt at any sudden move he made toward her and the tinge of embarrassment pinking her cheeks as she stood before him in nothing but a towel told him just how uneasy and nervous he made her. The last thing he wanted her to feel when they made love the first time was hesitant. More, he needed her to feel safe enough to let her guard down and be herself, knowing he wasn't a threat in any way.

With that in mind, he tamped down the sexual energy radiating off him and put the medicine on her back. The cuts were almost healed thanks to the ointment, and most of the redness had disappeared or turned to bruises. The stitches looked good, they'd need another five days before he could take them out. In all, he couldn't believe how fast she was healing.

As he finished his task, the house exploded with activity. Caleb, Summer, and Lily arrived through the kitchen and someone rang the doorbell.

"I'll answer the front door while you get dressed." He kissed her on the forehead and headed downstairs.

"Jenna," he called back up. "It's the messenger." He escorted the man to the dining room table and headed for the kitchen to see his family.

EVERYONE WALKED OUT of the kitchen as Jenna finished signing the last of the papers. She handed them to the messenger, who assured her they would be delivered to Ben the next morning. He handed her several marked envelopes containing all her copies and left.

Jenna's phone rang.

"Hello." They stood around the dining room table watching her.

"It's Ben. I got everything taken care of from your last email. Who is this surprise for? Jack?"

"One is for Jack, the other's for Caleb. Will they be delivered today?"

Jack, Caleb, Summer, and Lily listened with open curiosity. Caleb shared a questioning look with Jack to see if he knew why Jenna was talking about them. Jack just shook his head and raised his shoulders. They had no idea what she was up to, and it felt good to surprise them, knowing she'd make them happy today.

"Yep. Jack and Caleb will flip when they see them. The guy at the shop emailed me photos. I am so jealous," Ben said.

"Yeah, well, you never know what Santa will put under the tree for you. Thanks for doing all of this. I signed the papers this morning. You should get them tomorrow."

"Okay. Have a good day. Rabbit, you are the most amazing woman. I hope Jack and his family know that."

"I think he does, and they do. I'll talk to you later. Thanks, you're a real friend."

"It's nice to know you're having some fun. Bye, Rabbit."

Everyone's curiosity pricked. She played it cool. She wanted to watch their faces as she revealed her plans.

Calmly, she scanned all their faces. "Good morning, everyone."

"What's with all the legal documents?" Summer asked, concerned. "Are you in some other kind of trouble?"

"You will all find out later today. Summer, Lily, are you ready to go? This will be a shopping trip you'll never forget."

"Is Santa coming today?" Lily wanted to know.

"Have you been a good girl?" Jenna teased.

"I've been a really, really good girl," she said excitedly.

"Well, then it's your lucky day, because I'm playing Santa today. Let's go, little one. We have a lot of shopping to do, because I don't have anything to wear. Jack and Caleb, expect the delivery of your lives today. Sign for them, and we'll see you when we get back. Don't forget to sign the papers. Ready, Summer, Lily?"

"What delivery? What papers?" Jack and Caleb asked in unison.

"You'll see. Have a good day, boys."

"Where do you want to go shopping?" Summer asked as they stepped out the front door. "I can think of several stores in town, but I'm not sure what you're looking for specifically."

"We're going to the Cherry Creek Mall. I hear they have some nice stores."

They were getting into Jenna's SUV. Lily buckled into her car seat looking around the shiny new vehicle.

"Jenna, Cherry Creek Mall is in Denver. That's at least six hours away. We'll never get there and back by dinner."

Jack overheard Summer; concerned, he addressed Jenna through the driver's side window. "Honey, you can't drive to Denver today. Your leg and back will be killing you if you sit in this car all day."

"Who said we're driving to Denver? We'll see you guys back here at six. Enjoy your surprises today." At that, she gave Jack a quick kiss and took off down the driveway and handed the directions over to Summer.

"Where are we going?"

"To the airfield in Gates. I've chartered us a flight."

"What?"

"Like I said, this will be a shopping trip to remember."

Chapter Twenty-Five

ONE HELL OF a day. Jack and Caleb sat on the porch in rocking chairs, drinking ice cold beer. Jack's thoughts strayed to Jenna. They did all day. His gut knotted when he thought about her out there somewhere, shopping, having a day out with the girls, but still in danger from her ex-husband.

She's okay, he reminded himself for the hundredth time. She'll be home soon. Home. Already he thought of it as their home. So simple to picture her here with him always, long into the days, months, years to come. Absurd something like this could happen in a matter of days, but his life had lacked the absurd, so he embraced it. Hell, why not. It felt damn good to think about her, even better to think about touching her like he had this morning in his bed. Exactly where he wanted her tonight. If she'd only get her pretty bottom home.

"What did she mean they weren't driving to Denver?"

Jack wondered about that all day, and the mysterious delivery. So far, nothing arrived.

"I don't know. Did you see how mischievous she appeared this morning? Reminded me of Lily when she's done something she doesn't want you to know about."

Jack hadn't known her long enough to understand all the little things about her that would tell him what that smile on her face really meant. "Yeah, well, I don't know what she's up to, but she said she'd explain everything tonight. She's even going to reveal the bastard's name. And where the hell is this delivery?"

No sooner had Jack gotten the words out when two flatbed tow trucks lumbered down the driveway. Each with a covered vehicle on the back. They pulled up in front of the house and positioned themselves to unload the vehicles.

The man in the first truck got out and said, "This Stargazer Ranch?"

Jack replied, "Yeah."

"You the owner, Jack Turner?"

"Yeah."

"Delivery's for you, man."

Jack and Caleb came off the porch, staring at the trucks and the man. "Whose cars are these?"

"Yours. Sign here, please."

Jack signed and the man got out two pink slips. "Who gets the Camaro?"

Caleb and Jack looked at each other blankly. "She didn't," Caleb blurted.

"If the *she* you're referring to goes by Jenna Caldwell, then yes, she did," the delivery man said.

"Uh, the Camaro is mine, I guess." Jack couldn't believe it. She bought him a car.

"Okay, sign here." Jack did and took the pink slip.

"Is the Mustang for you?" the delivery man asked Caleb.

Caleb opened his mouth, closed it, then said still unsure, "Uh, yeah, I guess it is."

"Sign here and we'll get them unloaded."

"Jack, she bought me a car. Why did she buy me a car?" Stunned, they could only stare. "This can't be real. People don't buy other people cars. Not like this."

"I don't know. She bought me one, too," Jack said, dumbfounded.

The drivers hauled themselves up to the back of the flatbeds. They uncovered the Camaro first, rose the front end of the flatbed, and backed the car down onto the driveway. They repeated the process with the other flatbed, uncovering the Mustang next and unloading it.

Jack and Caleb stood in awe, unable to believe what they were seeing.

The driver handed the keys to him and Caleb and took off. First thing, they both popped the hoods and stared at the amazing machines. They shoved at each other and grinned, slapping each other on the back.

"Look at these beauties. Can you believe it? They're our dream cars, a blue '69 Camaro and a red '67 Fastback Mustang. But why did she do this? How did she do this?"

"I don't know, man, but she did. We'll ask her when

she gets here." Jack leaned over the engine wondering how she'd done this, how she could afford to do this, and what else she had planned for them. He wasn't used to women buying things for him. This was something beyond even that. She'd made one of his dreams come true and brought back cherished memories of him with his dad flying down the highway, nothing but speed and fun.

He needed to see her. He wanted an explanation. Nothing about Jenna added up. He was a man who liked to know exactly how things fell in line, how the pieces added up to make a whole.

JENNA SMILED TO herself as they passed the tow trucks on the main road. The guys must have gotten her surprise.

Summer drove, the back of the vehicle loaded down from their shopping trip. Lily napped in her car seat, crashing from too much sugar and fun.

"Summer, how do you like driving this big car? I know you're used to your little four-door, and I really appreciate you driving home."

"What's not to like about driving this thing? Leather interior, all kinds of buttons and gadgets."

"So you like it, huh." She smiled secretly to herself.

"Yeah. It drives like a dream, even though it's big."

They reached the front of the house and witnessed the perfect display of boys with their toys. The two cars were parked next to each other. Hoods up, the two men were looking at the engines with their backs to Jenna and Summer. They had a perfect view of Jack and Caleb's butts hugged snugly in their jeans as they bent over the cars.

"Now that's what I like to see. A couple of nice asses bent over a really hot car."

"Jenna! You didn't. You bought them cars."

"Yep. Cool, huh."

Summer gently woke Lily and got her out. She rushed over to her dad.

"Daddy, guess what? We got to go on a plane. A jet. I got to see the pilot and sit in the cockpit. It was so cool. Then, we got to ride in a huge limo. You could fit a whole bunch of people. It even had a TV. Then, we went shopping and the people helped us. Their job is to shop with you. Isn't that neat?

"Jenna bought us all kinds of stuff. Diamonds, too. See my earrings. And I got a jeep. It's in the car. You have to put it together. Then, we had a really fancy lunch, and we came home on the jet again. See my new dress and my shiny shoes. Aren't they pretty? Jenna bought them for me. Not only this, she bought me play clothes too and toys. I like the Jeep the best though. Will you put it together now?"

"Slow down, baby. It sounds like you had a great day. You went on a plane?"

"A super fast jet the pilot said. He was really nice."

"I see. And you got new clothes, diamond earrings, and a Jeep." Caleb picked up Lily. "Those earrings are very pretty, you'll have to be extra careful not to lose them."

"I got more toys, too. Jenna said I could have anything I wanted. She got it all for me. Mama got stuff, too."

Beautiful in her new floral dress, Summer also wore her new sparkling diamond earrings. Caleb stared, appreciating his stunning wife. Jenna stood back admiring the family, feeling a pinch of jealousy along with a sense of utter happiness.

"Did you have a good time, honey?" Caleb asked his wife.

Summer smiled and laughed. "Are you kidding? Who wouldn't like being a Rockefeller for a day? She's crazy, you know. A jet. We had personal shoppers picking things out for us and bagging them up. She's insane, wouldn't take 'no' for an answer. It was, I don't know, the most amazing experience of my life."

They stared at her and she smiled back at all of them, feeling ten feet tall. She wore her new blue silk dress. Blue for Jack, it had a thin collar around the neck and the fabric draped down and skimmed her body to her knees, leaving her shoulders and arms bare. She wore her new diamond earrings, too. Diamond earrings for all of them, something to remember the day by. She figured it was time to do some explaining, but Caleb spoke first.

"The cars, Jenna. How? Why? Not that I'm complaining, but this is too much. How can you do this for all of us?"

"Yes, Jenna. How can you afford to do this for everyone? Jets, limos, cars, diamonds, shopping sprees?" Jack couldn't take his eyes off her. She looked like a million bucks in that dress and his mouth watered just looking at her. This was the real Jenna. Dressed like she was, smiling, enjoying herself. He didn't know what to make of it.

"Jack, you asked me several times who I'm running from. You neglected to ask who I am."

She wore a huge smile on her face, like the joke was on him for missing that fact. He guessed it was.

"You may be rich, but I'm filthy stinking rich." She let them absorb that little bombshell. Still smiling like the cat who ate the canary, she took in their shocked faces.

"What I did today was just money. I could do this every day until I die if I wanted to."

Stunned into complete silence, she smiled even more.

"Okay, here it is. You guys took me in and cared for me. A stranger. You didn't know anything about me, except someone hurt me. You nursed me back to health and gave me something back that I've been missing for far too long."

She turned to Caleb. "Friendship."

To Summer. "Caring."

And Lily. "Hope."

She faced Jack again. "Kindness. That's all I ever wanted. You know that. You all gave it to me, expecting nothing in return, without knowing who I am, or what my circumstances.

"I'm returning that kindness. You all have my love and friendship, but I wanted to give you something to show you how much I appreciate having you in my life." She raised her hand and gestured to the cars. "So, every boy should have a really cool toy. Hence, the really cool cars. I hope you like them.

"Every girl should get to go on a marvelous shopping spree. The jet and limo were just, well, lots of fun."

They all spoke at once, saying it was too much, and they couldn't accept.

She held up both her hands to stop all the protests. "These are just things, and I give them to you with all the love in my heart. Accept them. Enjoy them. Seeing you happy makes me happy. That's another thing I haven't felt in a long time.

"Now, the appropriate response is, 'Thank you, Jenna.'"

Heads turned this way and that as they all came to a silent agreement and in unison said, "Thank you, Jenna."

She laughed.

Caleb couldn't stop admiring his new car and Summer tapped him in the ribs. "Nice Mustang. Both my babies got new cars," Summer joked with her husband.

"That's not true. The keys in your hand are yours, and so is this." Jenna took an envelope out of her purse, the pink slip to the SUV she'd signed over to Summer and handed it to her.

"Jenna, no. I was kidding. The shopping trip was enough. Really, I was only teasing."

"I'm not. The car is yours." She looked down at Lily and then at Summer's slightly swollen pregnant belly. "You need it. I'll buy another one."

Summer came over and hugged her, tears spilling from her eyes. "You're too much. This is too much. Thank you. I don't know what to say."

"There's nothing more to say. You've given me more than you know."

Summer released Jenna and her husband stepped in and gave her a hug. "Thank you. My dream car. I can't believe it. How did you know?"

"Easy, Jack's office is covered in Camaros. He mentioned you liked Mustangs and a shop nearby where you guys like to go and drool. A calendar behind his desk had the name of the shop and their website. I'm a whiz with computers, so I logged into the site, found they had the completely restored vehicles in their showroom. I emailed Ben and had him buy them and have them delivered to you today. See. Easy."

Lily danced impatiently at Caleb's feet, begging for her Jeep. Caleb went to the back of his wife's new SUV and got the huge box out. Jenna stood at the front, pinned by Jack's impenetrable stare and his quiet intensity.

"Jenna, which of these packages is yours? I'll take them into the house for you."

"The ones by Lily's car seat are mine."

Caleb hauled out the packages, lots of them. Saks Fifth Avenue, Neiman Marcus, and Victoria's Secret. "I hope Summer's stuff includes a Victoria's Secret bag."

Summer gave her husband a playful slap on the arm. "Knock it off. Take Jenna's stuff inside and let's get dinner started."

Alone in the driveway, Jack leaned against his new car with his arms crossed over his broad chest. His silence made Jenna nervous that he might be upset about the gifts.

She walked over and stood in front of him. "Are you mad at me? Don't you like the car?"

Jack's face gave nothing away. His eyes turned cool blue, staring at her. "I love the car, but you didn't need to buy it for me."

"I wanted to say thank you, show you how much I appreciate what you did. You took care of me," she explained without really conveying how deeply she felt about what he'd done for her.

"No one has ever done anything like this for me, for my family."

"You said you always wanted one. It just so happens they had the '69. A blue one," she said with a smile and winked at him.

"Yeah, I like blue. I guess you figured that out. Nice dress, too, by the way."

"It wasn't that hard to figure out. But if you don't like it, they had a really great black one. We could take it back and get that one if you want."

"I like this one. Come here." He reached out for her, his gaze locked with hers.

Jenna stepped into his arms, their faces inches apart. Looking deep into her eyes, he said, "I'm seriously falling hard for you. I can't seem to stop myself."

"Is this because of the car?" She only half teased.

Still serious, he answered, "It's just you."

She'd seen it in his eyes, felt it in the way he touched her, but now it radiated from him intensely. "I'm falling pretty hard for you, too, Jack. I only wanted to make you happy."

"You make me happy. Just you, Jenna. You shouldn't have done all this." He was smiling now, a really big smile. "But since you did, it's a really awesome car. Thanks."

"You're welcome. Want to take me for a ride?"

"Absolutely, but later. We have dinner still, and you have some more explaining to do."

"I know, and I will after dinner. I have a few more surprises still."

That same mischievous smile she had this morning appeared on her face, and it made him nervous. "Are you kidding me? What surprises?"

"You'll see. Kiss me, Jack."

He didn't need to be told twice. Not when it came to Jenna. He kissed her, long and passionately, burying his fingers in her hair. She held on to his shoulders. They lost themselves in each other. Jack trailed kisses over her forehead, down her nose, her cheek and jaw, and down her neck. She gripped her hands in his hair, holding him to her. Her body pressed against his.

Jack mumbled against her throat, "Ever since I saw you get out of that car wearing this dress, I've wanted to get my hands on you. You're so beautiful."

"Summer and Caleb are waiting for us."

Silencing her attempts to stop him, he crushed his mouth to hers. Sliding his tongue over hers, savoring the taste of her.

Jack slowed the kisses and they ended on a long slow steady joining of lips. A breath away from his face, her eyes slowly opened. He pressed his forehead to hers and gazed into those green eyes that haunted him. "I missed you today," he admitted.

The longer he knew her, the more intense the feelings inside him grew. The easier it was to tell her how he felt.

Open and honest, she made it easy to be with her. No games. No pretenses. Maybe because he'd taken care of her when she was most vulnerable, they both felt they could let down their guard and just be themselves with each other. Something inside him acknowledged what a rare gift that was. She was a rare gift.

They started back to the house, Jack holding her hand. "Do I get to see anything on you from the Victoria's Secret bags?"

"Everything. Later." She gave him a wicked grin and winked.

"God, you're killing me." Jack put his arm around her shoulders and drew her close to his side and kissed the side of her head. "I'm glad you're home."

"Me, too."

Chapter Twenty-Six

DAVID SAT AT the center of the table, his grandfather and parents to his right, his fiancé on his left with her immediate family. Colleagues and close friends filled the rest of the long table. The restaurant was crowded, everyone's eyes on the newly engaged couple.

The diamond solitaire sparkled on Patricia's hand, mocking him. He brought her fingers to his lips, kissing her knuckles above the offending ring.

"You look beautiful tonight, darling, though I prefer the blue dress to this green." He traced his finger along her cheek. "The blue matches your eyes."

Patricia's pout at his first comment turned into a shy smile with the last. She'd learn how to please him in time. He'd make sure of it.

Seeing Patricia in green reminded him of Jenna's eyes, the pale shade so soft and unique. His family may have believed he was moving on, but he had no intention of giving up his true wife.

"Are you enjoying the dinner?" Her eyes pleaded with him to say he was pleased with the small party she'd put together to surprise him. He hated surprises.

"I'm looking forward to enjoying you later." Her eyes darkened with anticipation and a touch of apprehension. She wanted to be romanced and made love to in the bedroom. Maybe he'd take her on the living room floor from behind. Tonight, he'd continue to teach her to bend to his will and demands when he wanted her. Wherever and however he wanted her.

The guests tapped their utensils against their wine glasses, signaling the couple to kiss. David leaned in, pressed his lips to Patricia's, and thought of nothing but kissing Jenna.

Chapter Twenty-Seven

DINNER WAS A ruckus family affair with lots of laughing and joking. Jack tucked away the memories they made tonight. He loved having his family around, but adding Jenna into the mix made the night that much more special. She fit. With him. With his family. In his life. He'd have to give some serious thought about how comfortable and easy it was to have her living with him and what that meant for his future. Their future.

Everyone moved into the Great Room after dinner, some entertainment news program playing on the TV. The coffee table and carpet were littered with boxes, plastic, tie wraps, and toys. Caleb and he had already put Lily's Jeep together. Lily couldn't wait to try it out, so she'd been driving it around the Great Room before and after dinner.

Expectations ran high as they waited for Jenna to join them and explain who she was, and reveal her ex-husband's name.

"Look, that's David Merrick. He's one good-looking man. Rich. Runs some huge company." Summer watched the TV from the sofa along with Caleb, Jack next to them on the love seat.

"What's the matter with Jenna?" Lily asked.

Jenna stood still behind the sofas, unable to take her eyes off the image of that monster on the TV. Jack jumped up and moved to her side. He cupped her face in his warm hands. The instant he touched her, everything inside her focused on him. Afraid of the image of her ex on the TV, she reached out for Jack and the safety, security, and comfort innately a part of him.

"What's wrong, honey?"

"That's him." Barely able to speak, she saw Jack, but her mind switched to images of David hurting her and she flinched away. Jack refused to release her. "That-that's him," she stuttered. An eerie shiver ran through her whole body. She clamped her hands to Jack's wrists near her face and held tight.

Summer pointed to the TV. "He's been the most eligible bachelor for years now. He's getting married to some socialite, they said. That's the man who did this to you?"

"I'm going to be sick." Jenna's stomach pitched and rolled at the thought of some poor woman marrying that monster.

"No, you aren't." Jack tipped her chin up for her to see him. "Take a breath." She tried, but couldn't suck in enough air. Jack's warm lips brushed a kiss to her forehead. The heat from his body, so close to hers, warmed the chill from her bones. She leaned her forehead against his chest, inhaled the familiar scents of horses, leather, hay, and just Jack. He kissed her head. "Come sit down," he coaxed, and led her to the love seat and sat her down before she collapsed. His strong arms wrapped around her, protecting her from imagined ghosts.

Shocked, but trying to keep it together, she glanced at Lily playing on the floor.

"Summer, why don't you take Lily for ice cream with Beth in the kitchen? She shouldn't be here for this. I'll wait until you get back to explain."

Summer took Lily away. Jenna settled into the sofa, but Jack stood and paced the Great Room, pent-up anger vibrating around him.

Unable to keep silent, his temper flared. "I can't believe that's the guy who's been hurting you. I swear to God, I'll find him and kill him."

Summer returned. "Jack, sit down. Let Jenna tell her story. Then you can rage."

Jack glared at his sister, furious, then fell onto the sofa beside Jenna. After taking a very deep breath, he took her hand and squeezed it, offering her support. Softening, he brought her hand to his mouth and kissed her palm. "Tell us everything, sweetheart."

"Now you know who, David Merrick." Just saying his name left a bad taste in her mouth.

She took a deep breath and began her story. "He and his family run one of the largest corporations in the U.S. and globally. I'm sure you've all heard of Merrick International. I met him when I was twenty-four, attending the University of San Francisco, my last year studying computer science and graphic art. He's eight years older than me. He was visiting the college and gave some speech on business. His family also donated a large sum of money to the business program, which I found out later. Anyway, he was walking with a group of students, talking, and one of them ran into me and I dropped my books. Upset the person wasn't paying attention, he apologized for the guy and helped me pick them up. We spoke briefly and he asked me to dinner. I accepted. Ordinary, simple, an attractive and charming man asked me for a date."

She took another deep breath and continued. "After several dates, he told me about his business and family. He was like a prince, rich and powerful, and he liked me. He took me to all kinds of places, dinners, the opera, and charity benefits. Very overwhelming, but wonderful. After three months and a whirlwind courtship, we eloped. His family was furious. They couldn't believe he'd married me so fast. When they confronted him, he said, 'I'm obsessed with her. I can't live without her.' At the time, it seemed sweet. He loved me so much, couldn't live without me, and he stood up for me to his family.

"After two months of wedded bliss, things changed. He changed. At first, it was subtle. He'd make a disparaging comment about my hair, or my dress. He'd dismiss my opinion, or do something big without consulting me. The changes went from subtle to aggressive very quickly. Any time I talked to another man, he got jealous. He wanted to know where I was and what I was doing when I went to school. Soon, he made me leave school. He said I needed to be more involved in his life and business.

I wanted to be a good wife, so I gave up school to make him happy. As a result, I lost touch with my friends. That was the beginning of his campaign to isolate me and keep me all to himself.

"His temper became volatile, so I thought it would be easier to give in. Soon, the jealousy turned to rage. We got home from a party late one night, his anger had been simmering for hours underneath the public persona he projects. He accused me of flirting with every man there, said I must be having an affair, and he slapped me. He said no wife of his would sleep around. I had stayed by his side the whole night, making his accusations completely irrational." Lost in her memories, it took her a moment to break free of her past. "Anyway, that was the first time he hit me.

"Several more incidents happened. I ended up in the emergency room a few times. They never did anything. He'd make some lame excuse about his clumsy wife tripping in the garden and banging her head. No one would help me, or more accurately, go against him. He made several large donations to the hospital, and they looked the other way.

"He rarely left me alone. When I wasn't with him, his people were watching. I had lost all my friends and feared telling my family. I feared what he would do to them if they spoke out against him. I feared being punished if I did, so I was alone in my misery.

"The last incident was the final straw. I knew I had to get out, or he'd kill me." With a deep breath, she spit out the words, "He accused me again of cheating and threw me down a flight of stairs. I broke my arm in the fall, and he was forced to call an ambulance. He couldn't stay with me during the X-rays. After they put the cast on, I snuck out of the hospital and took my chart with me. I ran and hid behind bushes and dumpsters, always looking over my shoulder, until I could find a way out of town.

"I hopped on a bus and found a cheap hotel several towns over. I stayed there for a few days until I recovered enough to visit the library and use their computer to find a lawyer. I found Ben. He helped me file for divorce."

She looked at Jack. "Do you remember me telling you about the good work Ben does for battered women? He helped me, kept me hidden, set me up with a top-notch divorce attorney to keep his involvement a secret, and we went to court. The Merricks were furious because David never had me sign a prenuptial agreement. That left them wide open for me to take a large chunk of their empire."

Summer leaned forward in her seat. "I remember now. They brought in a bunch of men who said you were having affairs with them. They also said you were a gold digger, who only married him for his money. The stories were sordid and terrible. They ripped you apart in the press."

"Yes, they did. But in the end, I won. Remember I said I took my chart from the hospital. Ben and my other lawyer waited until the last minute to use the information. The hospital chart detailed my cracked ribs and the broken arm. David's lawyer said I fell down the stairs on purpose, trying to get David's attention. Things like that. It didn't work though."

She took a deep breath before she continued. "David didn't know, but when he threw me down the stairs, I was pregnant. I lost the baby. He killed his own child. He couldn't defend himself against that. Had I brought the charts into open court for the record, David would have been crucified in the press, which would have reflected on Merrick International. He and his family couldn't afford to have that happen. So David was forced to settle with me. And I made him pay. I was awarded an astronomical settlement, including a sizable chunk of Merrick International."

Summer was crying. Caleb rubbed his hand over his wife's pregnant belly.

Jack sat stunned beside her. His eyes were sad as they connected with hers, but his hands were clenched into fists on his thighs, his whole body stiff as he tried to contain his fury. Nothing could have convinced her more of his deep feelings for her than him sitting there about to explode at the injustices she'd suffered.

Summer was the first to speak. "You lost the baby?"

"Yes, and I'll never forgive him for that."

It took her a long time to get past it. She'd learned to accept it was for the best. If she'd had the baby, David would have been a part of her life forever. He'd have had a hand in raising the child, and that was unthinkable.

"That's why I took the money. The press accused me of being a gold digger, but getting a large settlement was the only way I could hurt David. I made him pay me off and hand over part of his precious company. His family was furious. The trial cast a shadow over him in the public eye. More importantly, I've done a lot of good with the money from my settlement.

"Ben's firm partners with a shelter in San Francisco. I donate money and Ben handles the divorce proceedings and restraining orders pro bono. The child custody battles can get very expensive. Without representation, most women end up having to turn their children over to abusive fathers without so much as supervised visits. I pay for those cases. For every dollar Ben bills, I make another donation back to the shelter. Last year, the shelter raised enough money from me and other donors to buy an apartment building they use to house women in need. They also provide the women with vocational training and get them working, so they can support themselves. I give to other charities as well. Along the way, I've helped a few people privately. I turned my situation into something positive for others.

"Since the court case, I've been on the run. Over the last two years, David has managed to find me seven times. Ben employs some exceptional computer and financial guys to hide my assets and me, but somehow David always finds me. We haven't figured out how he does it. I'm very careful about where I go and who I see. That's why you needed to know. I never get close to anyone. I learned that lesson the hard way when he had my bodyguard killed." Summer gasped at the news. "I don't want anything to happen to you guys. I couldn't live with myself."

"I saw some men looking around outside the ranch the other day." Caleb looked pointedly at Jack.

"One of the emails I sent to Ben directed him to hire

men to watch the ranch. If David shows up, my hope is that they'll take care of the matter before anything bad happens. I specifically have a couple of guards watching your house and Summer and Lily."

Stunned, Summer's mouth dropped open. "People are watching us."

"From a distance, and only to make sure you're safe. I don't want anything to happen to you or Lily. So far, he doesn't know I'm here. He's out of the country. I don't know when, or if, that will change. The one thing I can't afford to do is think for a moment that he isn't coming, because I know he will. It's only a matter of when."

She sucked in a deep breath and prayed they wanted her to stay. She loved being a part of this family, in even a small way. Most of all, she didn't know if she could take it if Jack asked her to leave.

"What I need to know, is now that you know who I am and what could potentially happen if he finds me, do you want me to leave? I've put you in a terrible position by allowing you all to get close to me. If you want, I'll leave. He'll never know I was here, and you won't be in any danger. You'll never see or hear from me again."

"No!" They all said together.

"You understand? I know what he'll do to me if he comes. I don't know how far he'll go. He might just come for me. But he could go after you to get to me. I couldn't live with myself if anything happened to any of you." It would kill her to leave them, especially Jack, but if it meant their safety, she'd leave immediately.

Jack couldn't take any more, his voice gruff and laced

with frustration, he said, "You aren't going anywhere. I've told you that a hundred times." He calmed, cupped her cheek, and looked her in the eye. "Hear me when I talk to you. I want you here with me."

She leaned into his hand. Calm one minute, the next the situation got the better of him. "I can't believe you have guards on my ranch."

"Not that many, and only Caleb noticed. I'll call them off if you want, but I want them protecting Summer, the bundle she's carrying, and Lily."

"Jenna, I can't believe all this. How could he do this to you?" Summer asked.

She and Caleb had a wonderful marriage, full of love. Caleb would never hurt her. He'd never raise a hand to her. That hadn't been Jenna's experience, until she'd met Jack. She knew to her soul he'd never hurt her.

"Less than six months of marriage to someone who started out a prince and ended up the devil turned out to be more than I could bear. He's obsessed with me. The first year after the divorce, he would find me and terrorize me. He'd threaten and try to convince me to give up my shares. He can't afford to buy me out with cash, leaving only two ways he can get them. Marry me again, or have me sign them over to him. So, he threatens and beats me, hoping I'll give in to his demands."

"Why don't you just give them back and put an end to this," Jack demanded. "If this is all about something as stupid as stocks, give them back in exchange for your safety," he pleaded.

Jenna wanted to laugh, understanding Jack's need to

think this could be solved so simply. Nothing in life is ever simple. "It wouldn't make a difference, or change anything. Deep down, you know that. The shares are all I have to hold over him. I have a plan for those shares. I won't give them back.

"After the first year, he became less obsessed with the shares, and more obsessed with me. He's gotten everything he's ever wanted, whenever he wanted it. He grew up spoiled and rich. He's had everything and everyone at his beck and call, until I refused him. It's made him crazy. He's turned his obsession into a hunt. It's a game, a challenge for him. He hunts me in between business meetings and playing golf. He thinks he can break me. So far, he hasn't been able to, though I've had a few bad moments."

She thought about her breakdown in the closet and freaking out in the barn when Pete walked up with the strap. In those dark moments, she'd often thought going back would be easier. One way or the other, this nightmare would end. But her fight and resolve would rally, allowing her to keep fighting.

Her gaze fell on Jack. Because of him, she had a lot to fight for now. "Not even this last time has made me want to give in, or give up. Soon, I'll have the means to end the game. Until then, I hide."

She took in all their shocked faces as they absorbed her words and situation. "So, I'll say it again. Now that you know everything, do you want me to leave?"

All of them agreed. Shaking their heads, Jack answered, "No."

"You don't know how much this means to me, but I also want you safe. Do the guards stay, Jack?"

"I hate the fact they're necessary. There just isn't any other choice. I want my family and you safe. So, yeah, the guards stay. We need to figure out a way to end this though. We can't all live here with guards and just wait for something to happen."

"We won't have to wait much longer. Like I said, I set a plan in motion, but it's taking some time. I've almost got everything in place. Once I do, I'll show David he can't get away with what he's done. If I have to, I'll bargain for my freedom."

"Bargain for your freedom. What kind of way is that to talk, to live?" Jack asked, having a difficult time accepting this as the only way to handle things. Ex-military, Jack needed a plan of action. Too bad, at this point in her plan, the only thing to do is wait until all the pieces fell into place.

"It's the only thing I can do. What would you do if you had lots of money, but no power to use it? I figured out a way to get that power, and soon I'll use it. He's made me pay for leaving him, and I'll make him pay for not letting me go."

"What are you going to do?"

"That's a whole other story. Let's save that one for when my plan is complete. Trust me. You will be a part of it, if you really want to help me."

"I'll do anything for you," he said and brushed his hand over her hair. "I'm not letting you go anywhere."

"I would if it meant you'd be safe."

"We don't want you to go." Caleb spoke and Summer nodded her agreement.

"Okay. Now that it's all out in the open, let's move on to something better. I'll get Lily. You guys wait here. I have more surprises for you."

She kissed Jack, stood, and ran a hand through his hair, satisfied when he gave her half a smile.

"What is she talking about more surprises?" Summer asked curious.

"I don't know." Jack stared toward the kitchen where Jenna had gone, wondering how such a kind, generous, wonderful person could endure so much and still manage to smile and light up his world. "Seems like this has been the day for them. Can you believe everything she said?"

"It's unbelievable. I can't believe about the baby. She must have been crushed." Summer ran a hand protectively over her belly, unable to bear the thought of losing the baby growing inside her. Jack felt the same way. One more reason to stop this bastard for good.

"Think of everything Jenna will never have by losing that baby. She never got to see her baby, never got to touch him, or hold him and stroke his hair," Summer went on.

Jack could only imagine. He already knew he wanted to spend the rest of his life making Jenna happy. Now, all the more, he wanted to give her something that had been taken away. The thought of having children with Jenna bloomed into a vivid daydream. One he latched on to and promised himself he and Jenna would make a reality.

Jack put a hand over his sister's swollen belly. Warming to the idea of having children with Jenna, a real family.

"Jenna's got the strength to move mountains. Hell, she's had to in order to survive that man. She deserves a better life, and I'll make sure she has it. I don't know what she's planned, but one way or another, I'll stop him."

Chapter Twenty-Eight

JENNA SENT LILY back to her parents and retrieved the envelopes from her purse and the flowers hidden in the pantry that Beth had picked up for her. She returned to the Great Room with the envelopes in one hand and the flowers hidden behind her back.

"Lily, I have a gift for you." She drew the huge bouquet of flowers out and held them up to Lily.

"Look, Mommy, flowers."

"These are Stargazer lilies, and they are for you." She brushed her hand over the little angel's golden hair, her delight evident in the glow of her blue eyes. The heady scent of lilies quickly filled the room.

"They're so pretty and big."

"Yes they are. This is also for you." She handed over an envelope. "Give it to Mommy and Daddy, so they can read it."

Jenna sat next to Jack and held his hand while

Summer and Caleb opened the envelope. Lily had her arms wrapped around her flowers and her face buried in the fragrant blooms.

Caleb's head snapped up. "Jenna, no. You can't do this," he said, indicating the papers.

"I've already done it. I hope you'll accept. There's enough money in that trust for her to go to college anywhere she wants and live a good life."

Caleb was still getting over the shock when she handed him a second envelope that read: For Baby Bowden. The same trust fund had been set up for the new baby. "Oh, Jenna, you didn't," he said, shaking his head.

"I did. You'll never have to worry about their financial future. Now you can spend all your time being the loving parents you already are."

Jack kissed her hand. "You are an amazing woman."

Summer cried softly against Caleb's shoulder, her eyes on the papers he held. "It's unbelievable. You're unbelievable. You've changed our lives. This can't be real."

"I'm not done yet. I have something for you, Jack. I wasn't sure if you would accept, so I have the papers here for you to sign. I hope you'll accept this as my gift to you." She gave him a half smile and squeezed his hand. "Please don't be mad I snooped."

"Snooped into what?" Jack took the papers and read them. "You want to set up a trust for the ranch? I don't understand."

"You love this ranch. It's been your family's home for three generations. I want you to always have it, and for every future generation of the Turner family to have it.

I haven't had a home in a long time. Everyone should have a home, so I want to make sure you always have yours. You make a profit on the ranch, but there are outstanding loans. As you can see, there's a substantial amount in the trust. The trust pays off those loans and allows the land to stay in your family for every generation to come. If there isn't a family member to take over the land, the trust will go into effect and the land will be held in conservation. The ranch and land will always be here."

"So, according to this trust, I own everything free and clear and my children will get the property and their children and so on."

"That's exactly it. It's yours, as it is now, but this way it will always be here for your family. It will be your legacy."

Humbled, he understood exactly what she'd done for him. She was right, the ranch made a nice profit, but he didn't know what would happen if he were gone. Future generations. He wanted there to be future generations stretching into time, starting with them.

He couldn't believe she'd made it this easy for him to ask her for . . . everything.

"Will you help me fulfill this trust?" Her gaze moved from the papers in his hands up to meet his eyes.

She knew what he was asking. Children. Provide the next generation. After losing her baby, Jenna had a hard time thinking there would ever be another. Looking at Jack, she wanted it all, to win the brass ring. With Jack, it seemed so easy to grasp. "Yes."

"Good, let's go upstairs and start." He kissed her

palm, then draped her arm over his shoulder and leaned in to take her mouth.

"Jack, Summer and Caleb are here. Knock it off. Sign the damn papers."

He kissed her again, silencing her protest. The kiss was long and slow with his hand on her neck, holding her to him. She melted, and only then did he pull back. He did sign the papers. "With my signature, you just agreed to give me everything I've ever wanted and never thought I'd have."

Choked up, she could only lean in and kiss him softly to seal the bargain. It felt very much like the promise made at a wedding.

Jack hadn't considered one thing. She decided to give him a hint and see if he ran with it. After all, one good deed deserves another. She hoped Jack would get the hint.

"Jack, you understand that the trust pays off all the land and buildings, right?" She crooked her head in the direction of Summer and Caleb.

He got what she was saying right away, his eyes went bright with excitement. "Yes, I see what you mean. You did do some snooping, didn't you?"

"Yes, I did, but only in the hope my good deed would allow you to do a good deed. It's within your power. You own the land and all the buildings on it."

"What are you guys talking about?" Summer asked confused by their convoluted discussion.

Not only did Jenna make it possible for him, and generations to come, to have his land, she'd made it possible for him to give his sister and brother-in-law a gift in return, a piece of that land.

"What Jenna is saying is right, I own all the land and buildings on it. That includes your home. You guys borrowed the money from me to build the house, and part of Caleb's salary goes toward paying for the house. Jenna paid off the loan."

"So part of my salary will continue to pay you for the house and you'll get to keep the money," Caleb said. "You'll be making a profit instead of paying off the loan you took at the bank for us. We agreed we'd buy the house from you. We hope to live there the rest of our lives and raise our family."

"That's true, I could do that," Jack agreed. "What Jenna pointed out is that I now have the ability to do the same thing she did. She gave me the land that's mine, now I'm giving you the house and land that is yours."

Summer tried to follow. "What do you mean you're giving us the land that is ours? The ranch belongs to you, Jack. You bought it from Mom and Dad when they decided to go off and see the world. You run the ranch, with Caleb's help, of course, but the ranch is yours."

"The ranch is mine, free and clear now, it appears. So I can do with it as I please. I'm giving you the house and the land it's on. You and your children for generations will have your home. Caleb will bring home every cent of his salary. No more payments. Jenna gave me a gift, now I'm giving you a gift."

"Oh my God, Jack." Summer's tears streamed down her cheeks.

"That's more than generous. We'd be happy to continue paying for the house. You don't have to do this," Caleb said, stunned.

"You're my best friend, and she's my sister. Thanks to Jenna, I can give you something I would have liked to give you in the first place. She's right, you know. What would you do if you had that much money? I'd make sure the ones I love had the things they needed and wanted. That's the gift she's given us."

He reached out and touched Jenna's cheek, brushing his fingers over her smooth skin. "You are the most amazing person I'll ever know. I can see it isn't the money for you. You did this because you love us. Without the money, you'd have shown us in another way."

Uncomfortable talking about love when their relationship was so new, she went around the subject. "The money is just a bonus. It only provided the means for me to make sure *you* had the things you needed and wanted. You made that love grow even more when you transferred that kindness to your sister and Caleb. You didn't have to give them their home, but you did. Kindness, Jack. You have it in spades."

"I'm overwhelmed. You did all of this in a couple days. Amazing," Summer said, wiping tears from her cheeks.

"Ben is an outstanding lawyer. I've also made him a rich man over the years. Time for him to really earn it. He worked like a dog getting this ready for me. Summer, I know you're overwhelmed right now. I want you to take care of yourself. You said earlier that this was life changing, and it is, for all of you. There's one other thing

Jack just gave you, which you haven't considered. Caleb's salary will more than double now that you don't have a mortgage payment. You can work only if you want to. You can stay home with Lily and ..." She nodded to Summer's belly. Lily still didn't know about the baby. She didn't want to spoil the surprise.

Summer glanced at Jack, who nodded at her, then she turned to her husband. He smiled, then kissed her softly. "It's all we've ever dreamed."

"How can we ever thank you, Jenna, Jack? You've truly changed our lives for the better. Summer and I won't have to pinch pennies, she can stay home if she wants, and the kids will have all the money they need to go to college. It's hard to believe all our worries are gone. Thanks just doesn't seem enough."

"Your friendship is thanks enough for me." Jenna stood and hugged the two of them. Lily continued to play on the floor with her dolls, oblivious her life had changed, her bundle of flowers next to her.

"Jenna's right, you're my family. The six of us are a family, and hopefully," he locked eyes with Jenna, "we'll add to our family very soon."

Jenna firmed her resolve to finish her business with her ex-husband. She'd never risk the lives of any of her and Jack's children. Despite the fact things with Jack were so new, she thought of nothing but having Jack's baby. Nothing would make her happier. She wanted to start that future, so ready to have a real life, a normal life. One free of David for good.

Chapter Twenty-Nine

THEY FINISHED THE evening off with cherry pie and vanilla bean ice cream. Jack opened a bottle of champagne to celebrate the good fortune Jenna had bestowed on them. Such a magical day, Jenna was feeling much better now that everything was out in the open.

Summer took Lily home to bed, but not before she cried and hugged Jenna, thanking her profusely for changing their lives. A little after eight, Jenna was already tired after such a long day. Her thigh hurt from all the walking and the high heels she had bought to go with the new dress.

Jack and Caleb stood in the driveway, the cars' engines revving, and talked about their new toys. The lights from the porch spilled down to them. Jenna stood, leaning against the post, watching, enjoying seeing their bond and appreciation of the cars.

"Boys with toys." She smiled from the top step. "You guys look happy."

"What's not to be happy about? These are the coolest cars ever," Caleb said with the exuberance of a teen with his very own custom hot rod.

"You owe me a ride, Jack."

"Honey, I aim to give you the ride of your life as soon as this one goes home to his wife." Jack gave her a wicked grin and closed the hood of his car.

Jenna laughed and smiled. "You have a one-track mind." When was the last time she felt this light?

"Honey, my mind hasn't been off you since I saw you in the diner."

"I got the hint. I'm going." Caleb closed the hood of his car, still purring like a really big kitten. He walked over to Jenna as she came down the porch steps to the gravel drive. He wrapped his arms around her, careful of her healing back, and she wrapped hers around him. So easy to do now that she'd opened herself to him, the whole family.

He bent and whispered into her ear, "Thank you. Thank you for what you gave to my wife, my children, and me. I'll never be able to repay you. If you ever need me, I'll be there for you, no matter what. You can count on me. You're an angel, an absolute angel."

"Get your hands off my woman. You have one of your own at home."

Jack watched his brother-in-law with Jenna. They'd created a close bond, the same as with his sister. She didn't shy away from him when he embraced her; instead she held him and drew on his strength. Caleb would be like a big brother to her. He would protect her.

Caleb drew Jenna away just enough to look into her eyes. He put his hand to her cheek, his other arm still wrapped around her. "Thank you."

"You're welcome, Caleb. You're a good man."

"You make me want to be a better one."

"I just want you and your family to have a happy life."

"We will, thanks in part to you and Jack. You're part of that family now, too. Don't ever forget that."

"Thank you."

"Don't thank me. You're a wonderful person. The best I've ever met." He kissed her cheek and released her, turning back toward Jack.

"I already punched you for kissing my sister. I guess I have to punch you for kissing her now, too," Jack teased. Caleb didn't rise to the bait.

"You hurt her, and I'll be the one throwing the punches." He smiled back at Jack, then walked over and gave him a big bear hug. "Thanks for what you did for me, Summer, and the kids. It means everything to us. I'll see you tomorrow." He smacked Jack on the back before getting into his car. Caleb revved the engine, beamed them an excited smile, and took off like a rocket toward home.

"You going to hurt me, Jack?"

"Not if I can help it. I'll spend the rest of my life and yours trying to make you happy. How's that sound?"

"Like heaven. Take me for a ride."

He raised his eyebrow and grinned, but decided to give her a break. He'd hold off on trying to get her into his bed. She knew that's where he wanted her. Besides, she looked tired and rough around the edges.

"Hop in. I'll show you one of my favorite spots."

Jack took her five miles down the main road, taking a right down a dirt road through the lush trees. They came to a meadow, and beyond, a lake. Jack pulled the Camaro through the meadow and backed up to the shore. He helped Jenna out of the car and they sat on the back of the trunk with their backs to the window. Jack had his arm under Jenna's head, her body pressed against his side. They stared up at the stars and the full moon. A beautiful clear night, crickets chirped in the distance and an owl hooted from the nearby trees.

"It's so peaceful here. This is beautiful. Where are we? Your own personal make-out spot?"

He smiled down at her and kissed her softly. "Not exactly. We're still on the ranch. I love it here, especially at night. This is where I come when I want to think and be alone."

"I can see why. It's as if you're the only one alive out here."

Worried she felt too isolated, he asked, "Do you think you could live on the ranch for the rest of your life?"

"I love the ranch. It's so beautiful. I'd like to ride the horses. I love horses."

"You can ride whenever you want. I'll even get you your own. What I mean is, the ranch is somewhat secluded, the town is small, there isn't much to do. Can you deal with that? Can you live in a small town and on the ranch with me and my family without resenting being stuck here?"

"Jack, if you really want me to stay, I wouldn't be stuck

here. We could travel. I can work anywhere. All I need is my computer. I've traveled all over, and I've been alone for a long time." She didn't feel isolated. More like right where she belonged. "Being on the ranch, with you, with your family, is the best place I could be."

"You mean it. You wouldn't feel trapped?"

"Not trapped, Jack. I'd be part of a family."

"We've only known each other a short time. It's too soon to ask, but someday soon will you be my wife and have babies with me?"

"I want that more than anything. But it's only been a few days. Are you sure you want to make that kind of commitment? With my past, you may decide I'm more trouble than I'm worth."

"I'll take all the trouble you can throw at me as long as I have you. I want to know we have a future together." He couldn't lose her and go back to living the kind of life he'd been living the years before he'd met her. He didn't want to go back to not feeling anything. With her, his feelings were all good and happy and hopeful for their future.

"I hope you know how I feel about you. I told you before, I don't play games. I don't want to waste time beating around the bush. I've lost more than two years of my life. I don't want to spend another day without you."

"I hoped you felt the same way I do." The tightness in his belly eased. He hadn't realized how much he was counting on her to stay with him and give them a chance to really explore the overwhelming feelings they had for each other.

"I know you need time. Time to recover and figure out what comes next. Time to settle in with me at the ranch. We'll take that time to be together without all the craziness of the last few days. Soon, I'll give you a ring and ask you to marry me properly."

"Jack, I don't need all that. I only need you."

"I want to give you a ring, my ring, and I want us to have a wedding with flowers and cake. Most of all, I want you to have the happy ending you deserve. I'll spend the rest of my days making you happy."

Overwhelmed by the words, knowing he meant every one of them, filled her with so much love.

They sat in silence watching the stars for a long time. When they spotted a shooting star, they both made the same wish, for a happy ending.

Jack slid off the trunk and pulled her off the back of the car.

"Let's go home. I've wanted you all day."

He kissed her softly and pushed his body against hers. His thick erection pressed to her belly. Tonight they would finally be together. Anticipation raced through her veins. She held on to his hips, pulling him closer. He groaned low in his throat as she rose to her toes to better align her body with his. He pressed his hard shaft snugly into the apex of her thighs. Heat pooled then washed through her. He kissed her neck and cupped her breasts in his hands. His thumbs rubbed over the soft silk and her hard nipples. The thin fabric added another layer of sensual caresses over her heated skin. She sighed and arched into his touch.

"I don't think I can wait to get you home," Jack rasped against her ear.

"Take me to bed. We have all night."

He released her reluctantly and took a deep calming breath. His hands slid down her arms to take her hands. He drew her to the car door and settled her in the front seat. She gave him one last kiss before he went around to his side and slid in beside her. Thanks to the Camaro's speed, he drove them home fast as lightning.

Chapter Thirty

JACK MANAGED TO hold out until he got her out of the car, up the steps, and through the front door. Then he scooped her into his arms, locked his lips over hers, and headed upstairs and into his bedroom. He set her down, their lips still locked and their hands moving over each other in a frantic need to touch and discover. She kissed his neck, her hands buried in his hair, and her body pressed to him.

"Will I find Victoria's Secret under here?" He worked the zipper all the way down her back. His fingertips followed its progress over her heated skin.

"You'll find me under there, and that's all."

He groaned. "God, you're killing me."

He slipped the dress down the front of her, let it pool on the floor at her feet. She wasn't wearing anything now, except her heels. The bandage wrapped around her thigh didn't distract from her gorgeous body. Neither did the black and blue bruises blooming across her ribs. Generous breasts tipped with rosy pink nipples, puckered and begged for his mouth. Her eyes were so green, he thought of grass in spring. Lit up by the moonlight coming from the window, he'd never seen a more beautiful woman.

Jenna stepped out of the dress. Impatient, Jack sat on the bed and pried off his boots and socks. He rose and stood before her again. Hesitant but brave, she pulled his shirt from his jeans. Her hands shook. Nervous, she overcame it and pressed on, sliding her palms under Jack's shirt. His warm skin against her palms ignited a fresh wave of need. She pulled the barrier off over his head. She wanted to touch him and feel the play of muscles in his chest against her hands. She undid his pants and pushed them to the floor along with his boxers. He stepped out and turned her back toward the bed and stood before her, all confidence.

She couldn't get over his size. At least six inches taller than her, his chest was broad and smooth, and his arms were so strong. His stomach was flat and his waist narrowed down to his powerful thighs. His cock stood proud, throbbing for her. She looked up at him, a bundle of apprehension and nerves. It had been a long time since she was naked with a man.

Unable to hide her nervousness, Jack tried to soothe her by tracing her jaw with the pads of his thumbs. "Don't worry, little one. I promise I'll never hurt you. When we're together like this, you'll only ever feel pleasure. Let me show you."

He lowered her back onto the bed. She scooted up, and

he followed, taking in every plane and curve of her body. He lay on his side next to her, stroking his hand up her leg and over her belly where he found and cupped her round breast. She gasped at the intimate touches. He closed his mouth over her nipple and sucked, bringing it to a hard peak. She arched to him and moaned with pleasure as her eyes closed and a ragged sigh escaped her parted kiss swollen lips. He took the other nipple into his mouth and used his hand to stroke the tight bud he'd just left. His hands remained gentle, while his mouth demanded and coaxed everything from her.

Responsive to his every touch, she arched and buried her hands in his hair, holding him to her. He skimmed his hand down her belly, caressing as he went, his warm fingers tracing small circles on her skin. He slid his palm over her mound and cupped her in his hand. She gasped at his intimate touch. He continued to lick and suck her nipples, moving from one breast to the other as he gently used his fingers to explore her soft, wet core. He stroked the soft petals and entered her, one finger, then two. She rocked her hips against his hand, making those little love noises he coaxed from her with pleasure.

Her hands moved over his shoulders and back, fingers digging into his muscles and pulling him closer. He kissed his way up her neck until he finally found her lips, and using his tongue he explored her sweet mouth with the rhythm his fingers set inside her. He swallowed every moan and gasp as she rose and fell with him. He took her higher, until she couldn't bear it anymore and she moaned out his name and tumbled over the edge.

With a swift shift of his body, she cradled his hips between her thighs. Pressed against her, chest-to-chest, hips-to-hips, their legs tangled together. He crushed her into the bed. She felt so good pressed along the length of him. He couldn't stop kissing her mouth, and moved over her face and down her neck, positioning the swollen head of his cock against her, sliding against her slick heat. She tensed, but he thought it only anticipation. He wanted to bury himself in her hard and fast, but tried to hold back and go slow, giving her as much pleasure as she incited in him.

Without warning, she pushed both her hands to his shoulders and shoved him away.

"Stop," she gasped.

Surprised, he stared down at her beneath him. The fear on her face registered immediately. Her whole body trembled against his.

"Jack, please stop. Wait a minute."

Unsure what happened, her desperate plea froze his insides. He rolled off her and onto his back and inhaled a deep breath to get his aroused body to listen to his brain. He scrubbed his hands over his face, took a deep breath, and tried to gain control of himself before the beast within grabbed her and he really scared her.

"I'm sorry, did I hurt you? I forgot about your back. I lost my head. I didn't realize I was hurting you. Is it your thigh? I'm sorry. Are you hurt?"

She lay looking up at the ceiling feeling emptier than she ever remembered. The loss of his warm and strong body against hers went all the way to her soul. She wanted him back in her arms in the worst way. In order to do that, she needed to get over her fears.

"No, Jack. It isn't that. You didn't hurt me."

He turned his head to her, his eyes still clouded with passion. He asked gently, "What is it?"

"You're so big, and I couldn't move, and I don't know, I felt trapped under you. It's me. It's my fault. I'm sorry. You didn't do anything wrong. I'm so stupid."

She rolled on her side and looked at the wonderful, kind man next to her. Gloriously naked and wonderful to look at, she let her eyes roam over him. She took in every shape and contour of his sculpted body. God, how she needed him.

She watched him with hungry eyes, making it that much harder to keep his hands to himself. "You're not stupid. It's okay, sweetheart. You need more time. I understand. We don't have to do this right now."

"I want to make love to you. I want to be with you. I was fine. Then, I don't know. I felt trapped."

"You want me?"

"Yes, Jack. I hurt for wanting you." She bent over him and kissed him, moving her body against his, firing his passion.

"Try this." He backed himself against the pillows, grabbed her arm and drew her over him. "Put your leg over and straddle me. Sit on my thighs, until you feel comfortable."

Timid and vulnerable displayed over him the way she was, she settled on his lap. His skin warm against hers, he moved his hands up her arms, encouraging her.

Emboldened, she rubbed her hands over his chest, exploring the solid wall of contours. Everywhere she touched, muscles rippled. She felt powerful having him beneath her. The more patience he showed her, the bolder she became.

"That's it. Relax. We'll just start again," Jack said, visibly doing his best to keep his head, go slow, and allow her to drive him crazy.

He took her mouth and devoured. He rubbed his hands from her shoulders down the side of her breasts to her hips. She sighed and let the tension run out of her with each stroke of his warm hands over her body.

Relaxed, in the moment, her passion building, she felt empowered. She set her belly on his erection and he moaned with pleasure. She pressed and moved against him. His whole body tensed, but he continued to kiss and distract her with his every touch. Then he took her hands from his chest and placed them on the top of the headboard, her hips coming up off him, on her knees, bent over him. His hot mouth clamped on to her breast and a wave of heat shot through her system and straight to her aching core. His tongue laved and licked over her tight nipple. She squeezed her hands around the wood, sighed, and arched her back offering up her breasts for him to feast. Jack's hands traveled up and down her sides and over her hips, soothing away the last of her nerves as she bent over his marauding mouth.

One hand lazily smoothed over her stomach with his knuckles, until he found her center. Open for him, straddled over his lap, she hovered over him anticipating his most intimate touch. He thrust his finger deep and found her sweet spot with his thumb, rubbing and sending ripples of pleasure dancing across every nerve. She moaned and moved against him, craving more. One of her hands combed through his hair and held his head to her breasts. Lost in the moment and the pleasure, she rocked her hips with his fingers as they softly played over her heated skin.

She rose to the crest again. This time, he replaced his fingers with the thick head of his cock, pushing against her opening, sinking in barely an inch. Not enough.

"Whenever you're ready, darlin', I'm all yours."

Hers. Inflamed with passion and a deep sense of possessiveness, she lowered herself onto him, torturing them both with the smooth, slow movement of her rolling hips to accommodate him. She stretched around him, filled herself, until she took all of him. The feel of him deep inside herself so amazing, she sat for a moment savoring being one with this wonderful man.

"God, you feel so damn good." Hungry for her, he rose up and that wonderful mouth of his lapped and sucked at her breast, greedy to taste and savor every inch of her.

She rocked against him, rose up, and sank down with a soft moan. He grabbed her hips to urge her on. The more he responded, the more she felt free to enjoy the ride and take him along with her. He groaned her name at her breast and she moved over him, taking him deep, then rising up before he pulled her back.

Giving him pleasure and taking it for herself, it had never been like this. She'd never felt like she was able to give and take so much. With Jack, she let go of everything, except the feel of him and the sensations building inside of her.

The slow and easy rhythm soon gained in speed. He thrust as hard as she pressed down on him. She couldn't take him deep enough. He smothered her gasps with his mouth and his tongue tangled with hers. He waited for her to rocket over the edge first. Her inner muscles locking around his hard shaft, she trembled, and he thrust deep, his whole body tensing and pulsing. He emptied himself with a gruff groan.

The warmth spread inside her as he shuddered underneath her. His arms wrapped tight around her and drew her down to his chest. Breathing hard and ragged, his heart pounding with hers. Locked deep inside her, she held him close, their hearts pressed together, joined in rhythm, just like their bodies had been but moments ago.

"I don't ever want to let you go. I want to stay like this forever, forget the past and just be yours."

"Jenna, God, when you say things like that it just makes me want you again. Come here."

He rolled her to her back. This time she didn't ask him to stop. Still joined, Jack moved, pulling out and thrusting hard and deep. She drew her legs up, wrapped them tight around his hips, drawing him into her even more. She grabbed his face and brought his lips to hers and kissed him with all the passion and love she had. She traced his bottom lip with her tongue and gently sucked it into her mouth.

Her fingers dug into his back. He crushed her into the bed and still she pushed her hips up to meet him, taking him deep and loving the feel of him over her. He buried his face in her hair and neck and thrust into her hard and fast until she moaned his name. She tightened around him, that blissful heat exploding through her body. He increased the pace, harder, deeper, until he spilled himself inside her again.

Jack wanted to collapse on top of her, but supported his weight on his forearms and knees. Her legs went to jelly and slid from around his waist back to the bed. Her arms wrapped around his back, hugging him. He slid both arms around her and rolled onto his back, taking her with him, careful not to hurt her injured thigh. Worried about her other injuries, she didn't complain, and he was too busy trying to catch his breath to ask after her.

"I didn't know I could do that. I don't think I can ever do that again, twice in a matter of minutes. You inspire me, sweetheart."

"I feel really good myself. I liked being on top. I felt really powerful."

"Honey, you can be on top anytime you want. I'm at your beck and call."

"Oh, yeah. How about now?"

"Uh. Please tell me you're kidding? I'm spent." He'd never given himself to a woman like that before. And certainly, he'd never made love to a woman without protecting himself and her from the possibility of a baby. He hoped they'd made a baby tonight. He thought about the gift she'd given to his family just hours before, and he hoped she'd give him another gift—their child.

"I am kidding. You're a big man, Jack. I'll probably be sore for a little while."

"Oh, honey, I'm sorry. Did I hurt you?"

"No, I'm fine. We're a perfect fit."

"Is your back okay?"

"Sore, but well worth it."

His whole body went still. The thought of hurting her upset him. Reading his thoughts, she kissed his chin and gave him a nip with her teeth. "I'm fine. Really." She kissed him on the mouth and moved just enough to disconnect herself from him. Wrapped in each other's arms, their legs tangled together. Jack reached behind her, grabbed the comforter, and pulled it over them, cocooning them in the aftermath of their shared pleasure and blocking out the cold and her past. Tonight, she slept safe in Jack's arms.

Chapter Thirty-One

Ten weeks later . . .

DAVID TAPPED HIS fingers on the cherry wood armrest and leaned back into the soft leather seat. His private jet sat on the San Francisco airport tarmac, waiting for clearance to take off. His cell phone vibrated in his coat pocket, reminding him to turn it off for the flight. He checked the caller ID first. A zing of excitement shot through him. This was the overdue call he'd been waiting for.

"Tell me you found her?" No other response was acceptable. He'd made his wishes clear and the people he hired either did their job, or didn't have one.

"She set up several trusts under a business name we've confirmed belongs to her. I've emailed you the details. She's in Colorado. A town called Hidden Springs, living on a horse ranch. It's isolated, but accessible. There's one problem."

"She's still there, isn't she?"

"Yes, but she has guards spread over the property, watching her house and another."

David heard the hesitation in the man's voice. "Tell me everything."

"She's living with a man, the owner of the ranch."

David's fingers clamped around his phone and a flush of red-hot rage rushed through his veins. Dismissing the need to be in New York for an important business meeting, he ordered the pilots, "Change of plans, take me to Hidden Springs, Colorado."

Chapter Thirty-Two

Two weeks later . . .

JENNA AWOKE IN Jack's arms, just like she had every morning for the last three months. They still couldn't get enough of each other. Though Jack had pointedly said he wanted to marry her and have children, he'd never said he loved her. The words weren't necessary, because he made a point to show her how much he loved her in everything he did and said. David had given her the words over and over, but showed the lie in his every cruel deed.

They'd settled into a comfortable routine. Jack worked in the barn, or around the ranch, and Jenna took on a new client. She worked in Jack's home office on her computer, until he returned home each evening. They'd have dinner together, then sit on the couch and watch TV or read together. Sometimes they had Summer, Caleb, and Lily over. Jenna loved having a house full of people.

She remembered being alone, night after night, lonely for company. Now she could have a house full of guests, or just be in Jack's arms, exactly where she wanted to be most.

Jack's monthly trip to auction was today. Afterwards, he and Caleb were driving to the courthouse to sign and record the deed for Caleb and Summer's piece of the property. On the way home, he and Caleb would deliver a colt to a friend's ranch.

Summer was dropping off Lily before she went to work. She had cut back her schedule to three six-hour days until the new baby arrived. Then she'd take everyone's advice and stay home with her kids, at least for a while.

Jenna looked forward to having Lily for a few hours. She loved the little girl like her own, and if her suspicions where right, she and Jack would welcome a new little one in about seven months.

Jack would be so excited. She needed to confirm her suspicions soon.

Jack had hinted a few times that he thought she might be pregnant. She had discouraged him so far, wanting to surprise him when she was certain. Who was she kidding? In her heart, she already knew Jack's baby was snug as a bug in her belly and she couldn't be happier. Since she had Lily today, she'd wait until tomorrow and go into town and get a home pregnancy test.

Jack stirred next to her. His morning erection pressed to her hip. She thought about letting him sleep longer, but why waste a perfectly good erection. She kissed his chest and moved up his collarbone to his neck and pushed him onto his back. Straddling him now, she pressed a kiss to his earlobe and whispered in his ear, "Good morning, my love." She lowered herself onto him and rocked against his hips. She kissed his neck and shoulder, rocking herself back and forth with long slow movements. Her breasts brushed against his strong chest muscles. Her hard tipped breasts ached for his touch, the sweep of his tongue.

Without opening his eyes, he grabbed her hips and moved with her. When she was ready to peak, he wrapped his arms around her, now healed, back and pressed her close to his chest. He thrust deep, filled her as she fell over the edge with him.

Unable to move, his arms wrapped around her, her face buried in his neck where she nibbled and nuzzled.

"Good morning to you, darlin'," he rumbled out the words, practically purring.

"Mmm. I couldn't resist you. You're all warm with these strong muscles everywhere. I had to get my hands on you."

"Baby, I'll oversleep every day if that's how you wake me up."

"You didn't oversleep, I just couldn't help myself. Every time I'm with you, I can't help but touch you, Jack. You're addictive."

"I hope you never find the cure. I can't get enough of you either." To prove it, he cupped her bottom with both hands and pressed himself deep inside her, setting off a new wave of aftershocks. She moaned as the pleasure crested and washed over her again. He loved it when they were like this together. He'd never felt this close to a woman in his life. With Jenna, he could let everything go and just be with her.

"Ready to go again, big guy?"

"Not exactly." He wrapped her in a bear hug. "While you are inspiring, I've got to get up and get ready to leave with Caleb. You haven't mentioned your surprise."

"While your morning erection and my taking advantage of it are stupendous, I wouldn't consider it a surprise. More a biologic and obsessive kind of thing."

He laughed. "Funny. I meant the surprise I left on your hand while you were sleeping."

Jenna sat up on top of him and gaped. A beautiful four-carat diamond ring sparkled on her left hand. She clamped both hands over her mouth, smothering her squeal of joy. Tears welled in her eyes. She held her hand in front her again and stared, just to be sure it was real. "It's gorgeous."

"You're gorgeous."

Not exactly how he planned to ask her. He intended to wake her, ask her, and then make love to her. He didn't mind her way. Her gloriously naked body sitting atop him, the huge smile on her face, her eyes shining with unshed happy tears. Yeah, her way worked.

He skimmed his fingers down the valley between her breasts to her stomach. "I love you." Those unshed tears spilled over and ran down her cheeks. He'd never told her, but made a point to show her. Proving his love had seemed infinitely more important than telling her. Now he wanted to tell her again and again—for the rest of his life.

"Marry me," he whispered reverently. He swiped the pads of his thumbs across her wet cheeks, pulled her down, and kissed her softly, nibbling at her lower lip.

"Please, Jenna, be my wife," he begged against her lips.

"Yes. Yes, I'll marry you," she said against his mouth. Tears spilled from her eyes to his cheeks.

"I love you so much. You've made me the happiest man these past months."

"Being here with you has been more than I could have ever wished for myself even six months ago. Everything in my life has changed. I'm happy for the first time in years, because of you."

They kissed and held each other for a long time. Savoring each other and the special moment they had shared.

"Come with me today. I don't want to leave you here alone." Jack was concerned every time he left the ranch without her. Ben had said several times her ex didn't leave her alone for long. He hoped nothing would happen while he was away. He never wanted to see her hurt again.

He rubbed his hand over her thigh and the long scar that ran down the back of it. He never wanted to forget what that man was capable of doing. He'd been patient with her, waiting for her to finish things with her ex. So far, she wasn't forthcoming with her plan to take him down, but her long phone calls with Ben told him she was working hard to do it.

"I'll be fine, Jack. You'll be back tonight. Beth and Lily will be with me most of today. I'm going to work on one of my projects later and send it to my client. I have plenty to do. Don't worry. I'll be here when you get back."

"I don't like the hang-up calls."

"Two hang-ups in a couple of weeks is not unusual," she responded, trying to downplay his concerns.

"The guards have mentioned seeing cars stop on the road and hearing strange noises in the woods."

"Animals live in the woods." When he rolled his eyes, she added, "They've never found any sign someone is on the property."

"Come with me." He'd suggested the same more than once. She tried so hard to live each day without letting the fear paralyze her from enjoying her life, but sometimes he caught her looking over her shoulder, or jumping at a strange noise. He tried his hardest to give her a sense of ease and safety when she was with him, but they both knew, so long as David was out there, she'd never be safe.

"We've been over this. I promised to watch Lily today. I'm having some plants delivered. Lily and I will plant them in the gardens. I know you're worried something will happen. That's what the guards are for. Besides, David got married yesterday in San Francisco. I doubt he's thinking about me." She hoped he'd forget all about her, and she'd never see him or fear him again.

"If I ever get my hands on that bastard, I'll kill him."

"Jack, calm down. He's too busy with his new wife. They're probably on their honeymoon. I'm here, safe on the ranch, with you. He doesn't even know where I am."

"He's found you before. Lots of times before. Too many times before. You don't even know how he finds you. How do you know he doesn't know where you are this time?"

"Jack, this is the same argument we've had a dozen times. All I can do is hope he doesn't find me this time. Maybe it's over now that he has someone new in his life. Maybe he's over his obsession with me. It's not like I can call him and find out. All I can do is be careful not to alert him to where I am. That, and my other plans are in the works. When the time is right, I'll use those plans to end this. If I can control the company, I can control him. It's complicated."

"Complicated. This plan is taking too long. He haunts every second of your day, and mine." Resigned that he couldn't keep her locked away, or by his side every second, he relented. "I want your word you'll stay on the ranch while I'm gone. With the guards, you'll be as safe as you can be, I guess." He hoped. God, if something happened to her, he'd never forgive himself. He couldn't live without her.

"I promise, I won't leave the ranch. I know you're worried. I am too. Believe me, the last thing I want is him coming after me again. You know what he did the last time. Next time, I think he'll kill me."

The same chill he felt run through her, danced up his spine and he held her closer. "Don't say that. There won't be a next time if I can help it."

"I don't want to talk about him, or the situation, anymore. He wins every time we make him more important than you and me and our life together." She traced his jaw with her fingertips, her eyes bright with happiness. "You asked me to marry you."

"You said yes."

"You knew I would." She playfully smacked his shoulder and laughed with excitement. "I can't wait to be Mrs. Turner."

"Soon. Very, very soon. I promised you a ring and happily ever after. I'm one down, one to go."

"You're my happily ever after." She wrapped her arms tightly around his neck and kissed him until he wasn't thinking about anything but her in his arms, safe and sound.

Chapter Thirty-Three

CALEB ARRIVED WITH Lily at eight. Jenna and Jack managed to keep their hands off each other long enough to get ready and meet Caleb in the kitchen.

"Where's Lily?" Jenna asked.

"Outside with Beth. The truck with the plants arrived and they're unloading. Lily is supervising. Nice ring by the way. You could blind someone, you know."

"Isn't it beautiful? Jack asked me to marry him."

"About time. Congratulations, both of you. When's the big day?" Caleb hugged her while Jack glared at him. Caleb just smiled and released her, but not before giving her a peck on the cheek to antagonize Jack.

"We haven't decided, but soon. Very soon." Definitely soon if she wanted to fit into a dress before the baby started showing.

"Summer will be so excited," Caleb said. "She's been waiting for this announcement since the day you arrived."

Jenna laughed. "I'll tell her when I see her today. I guess I better go out and help Lily supervise. What time is Summer coming to pick her up?"

"One o'clock. She's been tired lately, she isn't working that long today."

"That's perfect. We'll have lunch before Summer arrives. Beth mentioned taking the afternoon off and tomorrow is her day off. I'll have the house all to myself, while I work."

"Lily has a checkup, so Summer will probably be in a hurry when she comes to pick her up," Caleb added.

"No problem. We'll play in the dirt and have lots of fun. I'll have her cleaned up and ready."

"Let's head out. We have a long drive and the horses are already loaded. You," Jack grabbed Jenna and kissed her, "be good. It'll be late when we get back, but I'll wake you." He winked and gave her his wicked grin and made her laugh. Something to look forward to.

He kissed her again and again, holding on to her. A chill ran up his spine. A warning he hated to ignore, like he'd never see her again. "Promise me you'll stay on the ranch." He leaned his forehead against hers, needing desperately to hear the promise and know it as the truth.

"I will. I promise. Stop trying to spook me."

Jack's concern rubbed off on Caleb. "Has something happened? Does he know you're here?"

"No. Stop worrying. Both of you. Go. I'll see you tonight."

Jack kissed her again, unwilling to let her out of his

arms until he absolutely had to. "Call me if anything happens. Maybe you should have one of the guards stay in the house with you."

"Jack, I don't want, or need, the guards staying in the house with me. If someone is on the property who shouldn't be, they'll know about it. Three men are watching us right now from the tree lines to the left and right."

"The ranch is a lot of ground to cover. They can't watch everything."

"They don't have to watch everything. Just me, which they know to do from a discreet distance."

"It's not enough," he complained.

"What do you want me to do, hire an army to watch the place?" she asked, planting her fists on her hips.

"Smart ass. Fine. Be good. Stay on the property. I want to know if anything happens."

"Yes, sir." She saluted him.

He grabbed her and held her tight, his arms banded around her waist. "You are such a smart ass. Kiss me goodbye."

Their lips met in a soft brush, then settled against each other and went deeper. She poured every ounce of love and assurance into the kiss. Jack responded, his anxiety faded with the heat and love pouring out from her. They broke the kiss and their eyes met. Unspoken, she promised to stay and he promised to relax his protective instincts. Not an easy feat for him when every fiber of his being demanded he protect what he loved, what was his. Her.

She walked him and Caleb out the front door. Lily

skipped around the pots and flats of plants grouped on the driveway.

"Looks like we need a search party to find Lily in all these flowers," Jack said, pretending to look for his niece.

"Uncle Jack. Aren't they pretty? These are blue."

"You're prettier. Give Uncle a kiss goodbye. Daddy and I are leaving now."

He scooped up his niece into his arms and got a smacking kiss from her. He turned to Jenna with a wide grin. "I want one of these."

"When you get back, we'll work on it some more."

"My favorite part," he said with a wide grin. "Count on it."

Caleb kissed and hugged his daughter. "You be a good girl for Jenna. Mommy will be here after lunch."

"Can't I come, too? I want to take the horses to their new house."

"No, Sunshine. I need you to take care of Mommy. Okay?"

"Okay."

Caleb kissed his daughter on the nose and handed her over to Jenna. He kissed and hugged Jenna too. Jack punched him in the shoulder as they walked to the waiting truck and horse trailer. They both waved at the girls as they drove from the barn down the long driveway.

Jack watched Jenna from the truck mirror as long as he could. As he and Caleb passed through the gates onto the main road, his gut tightened. He wanted to go back, stay with Jenna, protect her. He scolded himself for not trusting her and the guards on the property. He couldn't stay with her every moment. Still, something ate at him, and he wished he could relax and know everything would be all right. She'd be fine. Nothing happened the dozen other times he left for one errand or another. This time was no different. Right?

Chapter Thirty-Four

JACK HADN'T TAKEN care of the flowerbeds around the house, so the only things alive were a few hardy bushes. The flowers Jenna had ordered would brighten the porch and patio out back. He'd told her over and over again to think of this as not just his home, but hers too. Difficult to believe after moving from place to place for so long, nothing ever felt like hers. So she had finally settled in and decided to add a few touches. She loved to garden and wanted to spruce up the outside. She'd start there before choosing a room upstairs to turn into a nursery for the baby.

Jenna and Lily finished planting the roses, snapdragons, columbine, dahlias, and daisies in the front yard. Lily liked watering the best. She'd sprayed Jenna a few times for fun. The beds in front of the long porch were beautiful and would be even better next spring. The winter cold would kill some of the flowers, but she would replant whatever didn't survive. For now, they would enjoy it while it lasted.

Lily chased a butterfly. Sally chased Lily. Jenna loaded the wheelbarrow with flats of lovely white, pink, and red impatiens to brighten the back patio and the shaded areas close to the house. What a lovely picture it would make from the back windows off the Great Room.

Jenna came back around the house to fetch the blue and pink hydrangeas that would go behind the impatiens and in front of the trees. The large bushes would be a lovely showpiece in full bloom. Jack would love the blue of the hydrangea flowers. She loaded the six plants and headed for the back of the house.

"Lily and Sally, come in back with me. We'll finish the big plants before lunch."

"Okay. I want to plant the blue ones first." Lily skipped behind Jenna.

"Six bushes, we'll do one blue then one pink. That way we'll spread out both colors."

"They're so pretty. I like the front."

Late in the morning, Jenna knew Lily was getting hungry. She watered the hydrangeas they had already planted while Jenna put the last one in. The row of bushes improved the backyard considerably.

"Once the impatiens are in, the view from the patio will be gorgeous." That earned a smile from Lily.

She and Jack would have to sit and enjoy the backyard more often. Maybe she'd buy a few Adirondack chairs to put out on the lawn so they could sit and enjoy the garden. It'd be nice to sit out at night and look up at the stars. She thought about the night she and Jack had sat on the back of his Camaro by the lake. The first night they had made love.

A noise came from the trees, drawing her out of her memories. She didn't really pay much attention, figuring one of the guards had come to make sure she and Lily were okay and where they were supposed to be. She had instructed them to stay in the background. She wanted Lily to stay blissfully ignorant to the darker side of life, like the necessity of guards to protect her.

Sally lay happily dozing on the lawn in a small patch of dappled sunlight. She didn't move or indicate she sensed anything out of the ordinary. Used to having the guards on the property, Jenna had made sure the guards were introduced to Sally, so Sally wouldn't bark at them every time they were around. Still, Jack's worry from this morning had rubbed off on her. She tried to shake it off, reminding herself that living in fear was no way to live.

Lily watered the last hydrangea and Jenna sat back and surveyed their work. A productive day. Her arms and back were sore from all the digging, but the yard looked so nice she didn't care.

A movement off to the left inside the trees caught her eye. Nothing there now. She scanned the area, spotted another movement, heard the rustle of dried leaves. She couldn't make out anything specific. The stillness and scent of dirt and sweet flowers surrounded her for a moment. Just when she thought it her imagination, David stepped out from behind a thick tree, holding a long hunting knife. The wicked sharp blade caught the light and gleamed, punctuating the ominous moment. Her heart pounded, fear rooted her to the ground. He pointed a finger at her, and then crooked his finger for her to come to him. With a feral grin, he pointed at Lily and held up the knife. A clear threat against the small child. She couldn't let anything happen to Lily and would do anything to save her, including go with the man she feared the most.

A wave of fear shook her whole body. Without taking her eyes from David, she addressed Lily. "Time for lunch. Turn off the water, sweetheart, and go into the kitchen with Beth. Tell her I'm finishing out here and you're ready to eat." She'd tried to keep the panic out of her voice, but even she heard it shake.

Sally stirred, cocked her head to the trees and listened. She put her nose in the air and let out a low growl.

"Aren't you going to have lunch?" Lily shut off the water before heading to the back door.

"I am, but I'll finish the flowers and be in, in a little while. Your mommy will be here to pick you up in about half an hour. Stay in the kitchen with Beth until she comes. Okay. Promise you'll stay with Beth.

"Sally, be quiet."

"I will. Maybe I can have ice cream if I eat all my lunch. Should I take Sally with me, something's bugging her?"

"Yes, honey, you can have ice cream. Stay with Beth. Sally will be fine with me."

"I'll stay and wait for Mommy to come." Lily went in through the door, leaving Jenna by the flowerbed.

Relief washed over her when she knew Lily was safe in the house and out of David's reach. For now.

A branch behind her snapped, making her jump. Jenna turned slowly. David stood just inside the tree line. Sally stood guard at her side, letting out a menacing growl. David crooked his finger at her again. She tried to think through the fear, figure a way out of this. She wanted to run, but she couldn't risk Lily or anyone else at the ranch. Resigned, she fisted her hands and stretched her fingers wide.

Her mind screamed, not again.

Her heart whispered, I'm sorry, Jack.

Her feet carried her slowly into hell.

Where were the guards? Why didn't they stop him? What was he wearing? Short at five-eight with dark brown hair, his lean build deceptively hid the power behind his skinny frame. He could overpower her easily. She had never been a match for him physically, and now she had to worry he might hurt Lily. What about the baby she knew she was carrying? Her hand hovered close to her belly, but she stopped herself from placing a protective hand over her baby. David wouldn't miss the gesture. She couldn't risk his reaction to her carrying another man's baby. Jack's baby.

He wore camouflage pants and shirt, black gloves and hiking boots. The knife in one hand, and in his other he carried a circle of wound rope and a red bandana. She stopped about five feet from him and stared into his cold eyes, knowing this could very well be the beginning of the end. Too much to live for, she wouldn't go down without a fight.

Perspiring from the adrenaline, David had snuck

through the woods, slipped past the guards, and finally had Jenna in his sights. She'd made a mistake when she set up the trust for the land. That was a public record and his investigators had found it buried under three bogus company names she'd used years ago. Well, that and the bits of information a secretary in her lawyer's office was able to funnel to him. The prick lawyer was so closed-mouthed about his precious client. Every document locked in a special vault only he accessed.

Luck, fate, the gods, everything lined up for him today. The ranch buzzed with activity, but he'd been patient and watched for his chance. David's timing was impeccable as always. Even the rancher left this morning. It was a sign.

Nothing and no one would keep him from Jenna. He'd teach her that lesson once and for all. There was no place she could hide that he couldn't find her.

He had her. Never far from his mind, he'd been trying to get her to see reason. This time, she wouldn't refuse him. If she did, it would be the last thing she ever did.

"Come here, Jenna."

"Where are the guards? Did you kill them?"

"You should hire better people if you think those guys could stop me. The guard watching you and that little brat went to check on the other side of the house. We're getting out of here before he comes back."

"Why are you doing this to me?" She tried to stall, hoping the guard would return and save her. "Didn't you get married yesterday?"

"Ah, so you heard. No congratulations? Unlike you,

she does what she's told, when she's told, whatever I tell her to do."

"Go back to her and leave me alone."

"Did you really think I could forget you? My family wanted me to marry her, to take the tarnish off after what you did. She's got money and a good family name, but she's not you. She doesn't have your fire. It's you I love. Come back to me and all this will be over. No more games."

If she came back he'd have everything he'd always wanted. The shares in his company and her in his bed. So beautiful, more so now than when he'd first married her years ago. Just looking at her made him hard. She wouldn't resist him this time. It didn't matter if she did.

"I'll never go back with you again, David. Stop this. Stop this now. Go back to your wife."

He loved it when she begged, but her defiance inflamed him.

"I don't want her! I want you! Now, come here, or I'll get that little brat in the house and you'll be sorry!"

Furious, he spit out each word. Jenna couldn't stall any longer. She had to get him away from Lily. She promised herself this time would be different and she'd stop him.

He grabbed her when she moved forward, spun her around so her back pressed against his chest. He rubbed his groin against her bottom and ran his hand down over her breasts and belly. She shuddered with revulsion. He took it as acquiescence.

"I've missed you, my sweet. It's been so long since I've had you."

"Don't touch me. You will never have me again." She pulled away, but his arm locked around her waist and the knife handle dug into her stomach. She didn't want to get cut. She didn't want any more stitches, or worse, to bleed to death in the woods.

"I will have you if I want you. You'll beg me to take you." He grabbed her arms and pulled them behind her, tying her wrists together with the rope. The bandana around her mouth came next. No matter how she struggled, he held on to her.

"Scream, or call out in any way, and you're dead. I'll come back for the kid." He yanked on her hair and pulled her head back. His lips pressed against her cheek and he spoke into her ear. "Understand? Maybe not today, or even tomorrow, but I will come back for her. Count on it."

She tried to shake her head yes, but his hand gripped her hair too tightly. She tried to say the words, but the bandana gagged in her mouth prevented any sound except a muffled gasp.

Sally leapt, grabbing David's arm and biting him. He tried to shake Sally off, but the dog wouldn't let go. He released her in favor of using the knife to stab Sally in the belly. Jenna screamed behind the gag. Sally gave out a yelp and went limp. David kicked the dog, rolling her into some brush and turned back to her.

"Stupid dog. Get moving." David's arm bled down his sleeve and hand, but not bad enough to slow him down.

He grabbed her arm, digging his fingers into her skin, bruising. With a sharp tug, he led her deeper into the woods and down a long path, away from the house, heading down along the tree line. Tears spilled down her eyes for poor, devoted Sally. She hoped someone found her soon. She hoped some of Jack's men were out scouting the pastures and checking on the cattle and horses and would spot them.

They stayed inside the trees, but sometimes she saw the pastures clearly. Scared and resigned to her fate, she walked in front of David, praying she'd live through this and see Jack again.

"Hey, it's me. Is Jenna around?"

"Hi, Jack. No, Lily came in a little while ago for lunch, but Jenna stayed out back to finish planting flowers. You want me to get her?"

Relieved to hear she was okay, he hated to interrupt while she worked in the yard. She'd been planning the project for more than a week, and he was happy to see her treating the house like her own. "No, tell her I called and we're finished at the auction. We're off to the courthouse, and then heading to my buddy's ranch. I'll call her when I'm on my way back."

"Okay. Anything else?"

"No. Is everything okay there?"

Jack's bad feeling had stayed with him the whole trip. He couldn't shake the uneasiness that something was wrong. It grew worse in the last hour. He didn't want her scared every time he left. He'd just make things worse by harping on her about it.

"Everything is fine. The flowers Jenna and Lily planted

are lovely. Lily is having ice cream before her mama picks her up."

"Hi, Uncle Jack," Lily called to him.

"Tell her I said hi."

"I will. I'll tell Jenna, too. Bye."

"Bye." Jack's gut was working overtime. Maybe he should have had Beth go out back and check on Jenna. Before he called her back to do just that, Caleb called out for him to join him across the street at a diner for lunch. Beth said everything was fine. No need to upset Jenna by nagging her about not being safe without him there.

Chapter Thirty-Five

JENNA'S LEGS ACHED thanks to the fast pace David kept, pushing her along. Each time she slowed, he shoved her or punched her in the back. She'd fallen twice already, and with her hands bound behind her back, she couldn't use them to break her fall. She'd torn her jeans and cut her knee badly. Limping, she tried to keep up. She'd rather have sore muscles than be punched in the back again.

They came to a halt standing just inside the tree line next to an empty pasture. The ranch stretched across the land in a long rectangle with the valley of pastureland down the center and the trees and hills on each side. That's part of what made the landscape so beautiful, the rolling hills with trees that came down to a wide-open green valley. Jenna and David stood at the shortest distance between the two sides of the tree lines on both sides of the valley. They'd have to cross about three hundred yards of pasture to get to the other side. In some areas, several miles separated the hills and trees.

"We're going straight across. You had better run and hope no one sees us, because if they do, you're dead."

Unable to speak with the gag, she nodded. Shoved from behind again, she ran across the field. She stole a glance both ways, but didn't see any of the ranch hands. No cattle or horses grazing on this piece of land, so none of the men were out checking on them. They made it to the other tree line and into the woods without being seen. Jenna's spirits dropped. She'd hoped someone would have seen her and David and try to help her. She didn't want anyone to get hurt, but she didn't want David to take her off the property and someplace else. He could hide her forever, and no one would find her.

The guards didn't patrol this part of the property. That's how David had gotten past them. They'd concentrated on Summer's and Jack's houses, not the outlying forested areas. Her nightmare had come back to haunt her again. He'd taken her and no one knew.

Jenna screamed in her head for Jack to come and save her. Deep in the woods, David used a compass to keep them on some course she couldn't determine. Each time she slowed, he'd hit her in the back, in the head, in the shoulder, like she was some kind of punching bag. Biding her time, she waited for the right opportunity to make her move.

They finally cleared some of the trees and rough terrain and came to a narrow dirt road. They headed down the road for about a mile when they came upon

David's jeep. Open with roll bars and no doors, covered in dirt. Additional rope along with a black canvas bag sat ominously in the back. She didn't want to know what it contained.

No way was she getting in that car. If he took her somewhere else, he'd kill her. How many times had the cops told her, never let him take you to a secondary location? Time to take a chance and try to get away, because if she didn't . . . She didn't want to think about what would happen if she didn't.

David spun her around and slammed her up against the side of the jeep. He hooked a finger in the bandana and dragged it out of her mouth and pulled it down around her throat.

"Scream all you'd like. No one will hear you."

The truth of that threat hit her hard, like a fist to the gut.

"Where are we going?" she asked to distract him.

"A special spot I've picked out. I went back to the cottage after the last time we were together, but you'd already gone. You're fast. I'll give you that. I've been searching for you ever since.

"I didn't want to marry that bitch, but my family insisted. All I want is you. You're everything I ever wanted.

"You and I are meant to be together. Fate carried me right to you at the college campus. From the moment I looked into your eyes, I knew you were my destiny."

The hairs on the back of her neck stood on end. He called it fate, but now she wondered if he'd targeted her.

"You're usually much better at hiding, but this time

you made an easy mistake. Did you think I wouldn't find out about the trust you set up for this land?"

"I did it for Jack." She didn't see the blow coming. He struck her with the knife handle on the side of the head above her temple and across her brow, cutting her above the corner of her eye. Blood ran down her cheek. He hadn't hit her hard enough to knock her out, but white flashes of light obscured her vision and she stumbled back a few steps.

"I don't want to ever hear another man's name come out of your mouth."

She didn't want to instigate a fight, knew his jealousy would feed his rage. Better strategy, shut up and keep her wits about her.

WORRIED, FRUSTRATED AS hell. Irrational, Jack knew, but as the day dragged on his gut got worse. Jack tried Jenna on the phone again. No answer, just the incessant ringing. He figured Beth went home early and Jenna was still out in the garden unable to hear the phone. He tried her cell, but got voicemail again. He and Caleb had another hour left of their drive to his buddy Rick's place. Reluctantly, he stuffed his phone back in his pocket and tried to remember she was okay by herself. He didn't have to be with her every minute of every day. She was fine. That became his mantra over the next hours.

Chapter Thirty-Six

JENNA HADN'T EATEN lunch. Her stomach pitched and rolled, a sour taste left her mouth bitter. All the walking—well, jogging really—had made her tired and thirsty. Scared, she just wanted to run away, get away from David before he really hurt her. She needed to make a plan, find the best possible escape, so David couldn't catch her and hurt her even worse. David held the advantage and she needed to find a way to turn things in her favor.

She didn't know if this would be one of the incidents where he just tried to convince her to come back, or if he'd hurt her like the last time. He'd never brought a weapon with him. He'd always used his fists or something handy. The knife was a new, very bad twist. His eerily calm monotone voice chilled her.

"Time to go." With a shove to her shoulder, she tripped on a rock and fell at his feet. His heavy booted foot stomped down on her thigh. She screamed in pain and tried to move away. Her legs shook, making it near impossible to get them under her and stand. Unable to lift her weight, she settled on her hip and waited for the throbbing to ease.

"Did I say take a break? Get up."

No one around for miles, no one close enough to hear her screams. Which meant he didn't need to worry about nosy neighbors calling the police. He could take his time with her.

"You need to understand, you belong to me. Only me."

Those ominous words rang in her head.

Stunned into silence by his last words, still on the ground, he kicked her again. "You bitch! Get up! I'm not carrying your ass."

"David, don't do this. Let me go," she begged.

"Let me go. Let me go," he mocked in a menacing voice and grabbed the front of her shirt and pulled her up to her toes, his face in hers. "I'll never let you go. You belong to me. We belong together. Accept it. You understand me?" he shouted.

David was going to kill her. She'd accepted that fact a long time ago. She'd fought to stop it from happening, and now that it was near, she wished with everything in her heart that she was somewhere else with Jack. She wished she could close her eyes, sleep, and wake up from this nightmare.

Jack, please, come get me.

"I'll leave that other bitch, and we can be together."

"Do you really think it's that easy? To go against your family and your wife's, divorce her after a few days of marriage, and live happily ever after with me? You're insane."

He'd completely deluded himself into believing he could make this happen without any consequences.

"Shut up. Just shut up," he shouted, shoving her back a step and releasing her. He pressed his bloody arm to his middle. A weakness. Maybe one she could capitalize on.

David pulled out a bottle of water from his bag, doused his bleeding arm, and took another gulp of water, trying to calm himself. It didn't work, and that was bad news for her.

"You're all I want. Why can't you understand that? I can have any woman I want. Women flock to me, but you won't return my love, my adoration for you."

His kind of love and adoration hurt. She felt it even now, swelling her face and wrists, throbbing in her bruised and battered back and thigh. Obsessed, she had become a virus to him, infecting his system, destroying his rationality.

"Why do we keep doing this?" she asked, futilely trying to get him to see reason where he clearly had none.

"You can be a good wife. I know we'll be happy together, like in the beginning."

"Things were fine until you accused me of cheating on you with every man within five feet of me. You did this. You destroyed our marriage and any chance of us being together. You killed our baby. You're a monster. I won't go back. Do you hear me? Never," she screamed at him now. She couldn't take this anymore. Years of fear and abuse drove her anger.

His face contorted with pure fury. "My fault! You're the lying, cheating bitch. The baby probably wasn't even mine. Stop playing games. I've had enough of you running away, making me chase after you to prove my love. I've had enough," he shouted, spittle spraying her cheek.

"You've had enough. You've had enough. I'm the one you tied up and kidnapped, you delusional, twisted—"

He rushed forward, grabbed her by the hair, yanking her face to his. His breath came out in harsh bursts.

"David . . ." She began, but his words stopped her cold. His tone flat and menacing, every word he deliberately spaced out to emphasize the finality of their meaning.

"Either you come back, or . . . I. Will. Kill. You."

"You won't get away with this." Her gaze locked on his, letting him know she meant every word. "Jack will find me. He'll save me."

She'd done it this time. Gone too far. If she hadn't said the last, he might have left her and walked away to hunt her again someday. But she'd retaliated the only way she could, used her words to hurt him and piss him off.

Right in her face, their gazes still locked, he shoved her. She stumbled back several steps, momentum sending her down onto her bottom and back with a thump on the hard-packed dirt. Straddling her, his nose pressed into her cheek, he grabbed the bandana around her throat, twisted it tight and choked her. She gagged and tried to buck him off. Too heavy, too strong, she lost this fight. Again. Her eyes rolled back in her head and the blackness closed in. Unexpectedly, he released the bandana and fisted his hand in her hair. She gasped for breath, but he ignored her difficulty.

"I told you, I don't ever want to hear you say another man's name." He pounded her head backward into the ground and the rocks beneath her. Pain shot through her skull, bright lights exploded in her eyes, and blessed darkness took over and blanked out all the fear and pain.

JACK TRIED JENNA again that evening when they arrived at Rick's ranch and delivered the colt. Past dinnertime, he thought she should be in from the garden by now. No answer. No answer on her cell phone either. Beyond worried, even Caleb grew concerned now that Jack had told him he couldn't get her on the phone.

Jack had enough. He dialed the head guard's cell number.

"Where's Jenna?"

"She was gardening until this afternoon. That's the last we saw her outside. There's a light on in the kitchen and upstairs. She's in the house."

"Why isn't she answering the phone?"

"She's probably in the shower. She and Lily were full of dirt last time I saw them outside."

"Is everything quiet there?"

"Yeah. No problems. Nothing to report."

Maybe she was in the shower, or working in the office and ignoring the phone. Sometimes she did that, thinking it was just another rancher calling him about business. Still, he'd left her several messages and she hadn't called him back. She hated when he was too overprotective, but her circumstances called for it and she understood.

"Go in, check on her," he ordered.

"She told us to remain in the background."

"I don't care what she said. I'm telling you to go in and see if she's okay."

Something nagged at him. They hadn't been apart in the last three months. She'd answer the phone wanting to talk to him. Wouldn't she? Couldn't she? That question haunted him through the next ten minutes while he waited for a call back to let him know Jenna was safe. Or not.

Chapter Thirty-Seven

JOSTLED, DRAGGED UP to her feet, Jenna woke, David's hands fisted in her shirt to support her weight. *Oh, God.* She shivered from the cold. While the temperature was a nice high seventy-something during the day, it dropped to the low forties at night. She didn't know how long she blacked out. Minutes? Longer? Instinct kicked in and she yanked herself free of David's hold and took several steps back. Unsteady on her feet, she shook her pounding head, making even more stars flash on her closed eyelids. Her stomach pitched, bile rose up her throat. About to throw up, this time it wasn't because of the pregnancy.

"Time to go. Quit stalling."

Stalling? He'd knocked her out cold and he excused his behavior, put the blame on her by saying she'd been stalling.

Something sticky ran down the back of her neck and in her hair. Blood. He'd cracked open her skull. Her brain pulsed to the beat of her heart and her vision blurred in and out of focus.

No wonder my head hurts. Jack, please, come help me. Oh, God, please.

"That's a nice ring you've got on. You think I'd let you marry someone else. I'll see you dead first, you bitch."

"Seems to me," she rasped out, "you almost got your wish."

He'd worked himself into a rage. "You made me hit you. It's your own damn fault you can't follow the rules and insist on provoking me by whoring around with other men."

I am going to marry Jack. He loves me, and I love him.

Her silence pissed him off. He slapped her across the mouth and split her lip.

Something in her face must have given away her thoughts.

He grabbed her around the throat. "You'll never marry anyone but me. Do you hear me?"

His voice softened, but the anger behind his threats didn't lessen. "You've punished me enough for your clumsiness when you fell down the stairs. It wasn't my fault. All of this is your fault, but I can make it better."

"It will never be better, David. The only way you know how to love is to hurt."

"Don't you think you've hurt me by staying away? You're all I want," he raged.

"I won't go back!" she screamed at him, hoping, for once, he'd hear her and understand.

"Yes you will." He slapped her again and her head

snapped to the left, but she stood her ground with the help of his hand clamped to her throat.

"No. I won't go back."

"Say it. Say you'll come back," he shouted.

"No!"

Barely able to speak now, shivering, the back of her head throbbed, and now her lip bled down her chin.

Oh, God, Jack. Please come get me. Help me.

He slapped her again. Again, her head twisted to the left, spit flying out of her mouth, landing in the dry leaves. He grabbed her hair into his fist. "Say it. You love me. Only me. We'll be happy together. Don't make me hurt you. Come back."

"Never."

She rose to her toes and slammed her forehead into his. He fell backward. Her momentum carried her forward and she landed with a thump on top of him. Her face pressed to his chest. She straddled his waist, gained her feet, and pulled back, her head knocking into his chin as he rose with her. His teeth came together with a loud crack. He grunted in pain. With her hands tied behind her back, she used the only weapons she had, her throbbing head and her feet.

"Bitch."

Her shoulder hit him square in the chest and she knocked him off his feet again. Nearly falling herself, she stumbled forward, caught her balance and tried to run. His hand snaked out and he grabbed her ankle, toppling her to her knees and down onto her belly. Her hip hit a sharp rock.

"Ow!" She kicked and screamed, "Let me go."

She rolled out of his grasp, scrambled to her feet, and ran for the trees.

"I'll never let you go!" he bellowed.

Almost to the trees, she felt him behind her and took a chance and glanced over her shoulder. Gaining fast, he raced toward her, the knife in his hand. She zigged to the right, but he grabbed her shirt and spun her around. Her shoulder knocked his left arm aside. Momentum and his rage propelled him forward, the knife plunging toward her chest. Adrenaline surging, she shifted to the side, but not far enough. The blade sliced her ribs, the handle catching on her elbow. When he pulled his hand free, the knife sliced her side again. White-hot pain exploded and blood flowed, sticking her shirt to her skin.

She kicked out with her left leg connecting with his knee, sending him down. Knocked off balance again, she fell with him. Unrelenting, he came after her, but she pulled her knees to her chest and he landed on her feet. She pushed as hard as she could, sending him stumbling backward. She rolled, shimmied her knees under her and sat back on her heels. The fight nearly out of her, she lunged to her feet and ran.

His footsteps pounded behind her, but she hit the trees, dodging branches and bushes. Out of control, the rage blinded him, stole his every rational thought. "I will kill you. When your mother inherits all the shares you took from me, I'll convince her—in my own way—to give them back. I'll take back what you stole."

Gasping for air, she ran, but something inside her still

wanted to stand and fight. She called over her shoulder, "I changed the will. Jack . . . gets . . . everything."

Unsure she could really outrun him in her condition, she issued one last threat. "He'll tear your company apart piece by piece, and there's nothing you can do to stop him," she huffed out.

"*No!*"

Everything inside her reverberated with the rage he expelled with that single word. She desperately needed to find someplace safe to hide. Out of his mind, if he caught her, he'd kill her.

Nothing but the sound of their footsteps pounding over the dried leaves. A branch hit her face. Without her hands, she couldn't dodge all the low hanging limbs. No matter how fast she ran, he kept coming. Her side bled freely, her head throbbed, her legs were numb and the rope around her wrists rubbed them raw.

She dodged several large bushes, turned left and spotted a hill, large boulders rising out of the ground. This could be her chance to find a place to hide and rest her battered body. She rounded one of the larger boulders, scrunched herself between the cold stone and an evergreen growing against it. She gulped in deep breaths to her burning lungs and pressed her arm to her bloody side, just managing to stifle a pain-laced groan. The pounding of his feet on the ground grew ever closer. She did her best to slow her gasping breaths and be quiet. She prayed she'd put enough distance between then and he didn't find her.

Unable to catch sight of him, his quick steps faded

into the distance to her right. Desperate to put space between them, she backed further into her hiding spot. The moist earth gave way on the far side of the boulder and she rolled, sliding down a steep hill on her bottom, rocks and brush jabbing into her back. Her feet hit the bottom, momentum tumbled her forward as earth and debris rained down on her prone body. The lights winked out.

David lost her in the thickening trees. Who knew she could run so fast—and in her condition? The drops of blood he spotted and followed earlier were harder to see in the fading light. At some point she'd turned and he'd lost sight of her. Halted beside a huge fir tree, he leaned against it and sucked in deep breaths.

"Shit. Where the hell are you?" he yelled.

Nothing. Not a sound, but the wind rustling the leaves. Not even a damn bird taking flight to indicate which direction she fled.

"I hope you die out here, you stupid bitch."

He leaned forward and braced his forearms on his thighs. His lungs ached and his arm throbbed from the scratches and puncture wounds from the damn dog.

"Fuck!"

Everything went wrong. He had a plan. This time she'd do as she was told. He never expected her to fight him. He should have known better. Her strength and defiance both set him off and excited him. One of the many things that drew him to her.

He never meant to actually use the knife. He could still feel the blade slicing her open, the red blood staining her clothes. Funny, the fact that she could take it and still fight him off made him feel proud. An exceptional woman. His.

He took a deep cleansing breath. It hit him hard, he hadn't gotten everything he wanted. If she died out here—and he believed her threats—the company shares would be in the hands of that rancher. He needed a plan to get them back. With a dozen lawyers on retainer, he'd make sure they tore her will apart and the shares went back to him. He'd get back what she stole, even if he had to kill the rancher to get them.

Resigned that he'd lost her, and fearing someone from the ranch had noticed her absence and began looking for her, he took out his compass and headed back to the jeep. He searched for any sign of her, but found none.

The stillness settled into him, washing away the last of his anger and clearing his mind. This game hadn't ended the way he wanted, but she'd left him alone and wanting her for years. Now she'd be the one left alone—in the darkening woods. He wasn't worried about her. The damn woman had nine lives. No doubt she'd run again. He looked forward to the next time he found her. The thought put a smile on his face.

Chapter Thirty-Eight

THE BAD FEELING haunting Jack since this morning was getting worse with every minute that ticked by and the guard didn't call him back. He tried not to panic and thought about Jenna and all the wonderful times they had shared over the past several weeks. They had so many more memories to make.

God, I love you. Where are you, Jenna? Please be safe.

He'd put the ring on her finger and gotten her promise to marry him just this morning. She was going to be his wife. He already thought of her as his. His to love. His to protect.

Caleb and Rick met him on the driveway and he announced, "We need to head back. Right now."

"I promised to pick up some new baby furniture for Summer. We'll haul it back in the horse trailer," Caleb said, knowing Jack hated to delay any longer.

"We'll have to make another trip. We're leaving. Now."

"Relax, man. I'm sure everything is fine. Summer said the ranch is quiet. Jenna's probably working, or down at the barn visiting Blue. You know how she loves that horse."

"If everything is fine, then why won't she answer the damn phone? Why hasn't she called me? Damn it, my gut is telling me something's wrong."

His cell phone beeped, indicating he had a text message. He hit the button and read the display.

Jenna missing. We're beginning the search.

Jack held the phone up for Caleb to see. "Tell me I'm overreacting."

"Shit. Let's go."

"Rick, can I leave the horse trailer? I need to get home fast."

"Sure thing, man. No problem. I hope you find your lady."

"I will. And God help the bastard who took her."

JENNA WOKE GASPING for breath and inhaled deeply, lying flat on her stomach in the dirt. Her head rested on a pile of crisp dead leaves, her bound hands lay on her lower back. Her legs felt sore and numb. She shivered from the cold and sleeping on the ground most of the evening. She caught her breath, rolled, and struggled to sit up, checking all around to make sure she was alone. The breeze whispered and the birds chirped in the trees. She let her frantic nerves and racing heart settle.

I'm alive. Oh God, the baby. No cramps. Despite her many injuries, she felt fine. *Thank you. Thank you. Maybe*

*the baby is okay. I need to get out of here and back to Jack.
Is Lily okay? Please, God. Don't let him have gone after
them. I need to get out of here.*

Hands flattened on the ground behind her, she
squeezed her hips through her arms and brought her hands
down her legs and over her feet. Finally, her hands in front
of her, she bit at the ropes, trying to untie the knot. She
worked at it for several minutes, her split lip opening and
bleeding down her chin and onto the bindings. Her efforts
paid off and her hands were free. She wiggled her swollen
fingers and rotated her chafed and bleeding wrists. They
hurt so bad, tears stung her eyes, but the diamond on her
hand sparkled and she brought it to her lips. Such a small
thing, but it boosted her spirits, reminded her of Jack and
the promise of a future she desperately wanted.

The sun sank behind the hills, darkening the sky
quickly. Stars winked on, beautiful, but not a lot of help
for someone lost in the woods. She assessed her situation. No flashlight. No idea where she was in this vast
forest. The thick trees had been a blessing hiding her, but
they also disoriented her. Never good with direction in
the first place, no matter which way she turned, nothing but trees and more trees. Frustrated, she looked up at
the hill she'd slid down and knew going back up was impossible. Assessing her many aches and pains, she pulled
the blood-soaked shirt away from her side and gasped at
the two deep gashes. Without something to staunch the
bleeding, her situation was becoming more dire by the
minute. She needed to find her way home, or at least to a
road in hopes of flagging someone down.

She rose on unsteady legs, clamped her hand over her bleeding side, and made her way around the hill in hopes of finding something familiar and a way back to the dirt road. Running for her life, she hadn't paid attention to where she was going or how to get back. Constantly on alert for any sound David was following her, or hiding in the bushes, or behind a tree, she plodded along on unsteady legs. Despite walking for some time, she was more disoriented now than when she began.

Deflated, hopes dashed, she settled back against a tree dejected. Tired and thirsty, she hadn't eaten anything since breakfast. Her head pounded. Dried blood matted her hair and soaked the collar of her shirt. The unbearable pain in her ribs, where the knife had sliced her open, throbbed with every breath she took. She rested her head back against the tree and closed her eyes to rest. Once her energy came back, she'd start walking again in hopes of finding her way home.

She ignored the fear and thinking David was coming back to finish her off. She let her thoughts drift to Jack. She held a picture of him in her mind. Thoughts of him lessened the fear and kept her sane.

Maybe Jack already knew she was missing and he'd sent men out searching for her. She hadn't heard anyone, but knew she was far from the ranch.

No, he's probably not home yet. No one knows I'm gone.

Jack, where are you? Come and save me. Oh, please. Come and save our baby and me.

Chapter Thirty-Nine

JACK AND CALEB arrived home after dark, the ranch eerily quiet. The Camaro and Mustang were both in Jack's driveway where they'd left them. Several of the ranch hands' trucks were still parked outside the barn, indicating the men were out searching the grounds for Jenna with the security guards. Jack hadn't received an update in over an hour.

The front of the house looked great with all the flowers Lily and Jenna had planted. Jenna had put a woman's touch on the place. Too bad he couldn't enjoy it. Nothing seemed right. His insides turned cold. A familiar feeling he'd lived with before meeting Jenna. He'd hoped to never feel this way again. It hit him hard just how much light, warmth, and love she'd brought into his life. He didn't want to go back to the dark days where war and death intruded on his thoughts. He didn't want to add anything bad happening to Jenna to his daily nightmare.

If something happened to her ... He couldn't bear to think about what his life would be without her.

They made their way up the front porch steps. Jack dreaded entering the empty house.

"The flowers look great." Caleb broke the silence with his mundane statement.

Jack ignored him and went in first. The kitchen light was on, along with a light upstairs, but the house was too quiet. A shiver danced up his spine. His skin went cold.

He ran up the stairs two at a time and checked the bedroom. Nothing appeared out of place, or even changed since he left. All of Jenna's clothes were in the closet, and the bathroom was clean and orderly.

Where is she?

Jack was losing his mind. No one had seen her since this morning. She could be anywhere by now. He didn't know what to think, but his mind conjured one nightmare after another.

He met Caleb in the Great Room. "She promised she'd stay here with me. We're supposed to get married. She wouldn't leave."

He paced back and forth trying to think. He replayed their last few conversations in his mind. Nothing stood out. She hadn't indicated anything about being unhappy with him, or that she wanted to leave. They were happy. She was happy.

"He took her. I know that bastard came here and took her. She wouldn't leave me."

"Jack, calm down. We don't know anything yet. The

house looks intact. There's no sign of a struggle. Maybe she went somewhere and just didn't say."

"No. The truck and the Camaro are both here. He took her. I know it. This bad feeling has been eating at me all day. Something's not right." The quiet in the house disturbed him. Something tickled the back of his mind, and then it hit him. "Where's Sally?"

Caleb looked around and shrugged. Jack pulled out his phone and dialed his sister.

"Summer, we're back. Do you have Sally?"

"No. Sally was with Jenna, like always. I spoke with the men searching this side of the property. No one has seen anything. I'm on my way." Summer hung up.

Jenna's gone.

Panic gripped Jack's heart like a vice, threatening to squeeze the life out of him. He didn't want to think about all the things that could have happened to her, but his mind conjured one gruesome image after another. She could be dead. He flashed back to her lying unconscious in front of the fire in the cabin and seeing all the wounds down her back and thigh. About to lose it, he dug the heel of his hand into his eye to erase the horrible images.

The guards and ranch hands were searching. Running out of other options, Jack flipped open his cell and dialed.

"Ben, it's Jack. Where is she?"

"What are you talking about?"

"Where's Jenna? Did she call you? Is she on the run again?"

"She hasn't called. Isn't she with you?"

"I just got back. No one has seen her since this morning. I'm losing my mind."

"She hasn't contacted me, and she would. That's the first thing she does when he's caught up to her. Did she take her purse?"

"No, it's on the kitchen counter where she always leaves it."

"Check it. There should be a set of keys to lockers at a local health club. That's where she keeps her emergency suitcase and money. If she runs, she wouldn't leave without them."

Jack rifled through her purse, found the keys tucked into a slit in the lining. "They're here. I didn't even know she'd set this up over the last few months. She shouldn't have had to do this. She should have been safe on the ranch with me!" he shouted, letting his rage slip the reins.

"She probably hoped she'd never need to use it again. What do you think happened?"

"There's no sign of her. It's like she vanished. Where is he?"

"My last report confirmed he got married a couple days ago in San Francisco and left to an undisclosed location for his honeymoon. I'll call my contact and see if I can get a definite location, or even a rumored one."

"Do it. I'm calling the sheriff. We'll need their help searching for her."

Jack hung up with Ben. Caleb watched him shake with frustration and worry. Overcome with pent-up rage, Jack hauled his arm back and punched the wall. A huge hole gaped where his fist broke through the drywall. He didn't feel the pain or the abrasions on his knuckles. Without Jenna, he couldn't feel anything.

"Better?" Caleb asked, worried.

"No. Where the hell is she?"

Summer and Lily walked in the door. Summer's gaze went from his bleeding knuckles to the hole in the wall. Frowning, she asked, "Feel better?"

Jack glared and tossed the phone to Caleb. "Call the sheriff."

Jack headed down to the barn to find his men, the guards, anyone to ask if they'd seen anything. He knew the answer, but at least it was something to do. He didn't even know where to start looking for her.

He'd failed her. That's all he kept telling himself. He'd said he'd protect her, and he'd left her alone.

JENNA WOKE TO the stars above her. She stared at them for a long while, shivering, she curled up as best she could to keep warm. The pounding in her head wouldn't stop, she lost focus often. She closed her eyes and opened them again. The stars blurred and fell from the sky. At least, that's how it appeared in her hazy condition.

Noises came from the brush. She lay very still, unsure if it was someone looking for her, or an animal zeroing in on the smell of her blood. Watching and waiting, out of nowhere came a huge buck. He walked into the clearing about ten feet from her. He stood still, studying her before he turned to look behind him. A doe and faun followed. The deer took off with a leap, sprinting back into the trees. Tears blurred her vision and dripped down her cheeks. A family. Would she survive to have a family with Jack? She wasn't so sure anymore.

Exhausted after only a short while, she laid her head back and slept.

Help me, Jack. Please, help me.

Chapter Forty

JACK ARRIVED BACK at the house in time to meet the sheriff and some of his men in the Great Room. The sheriff, a tall man with a huge potbelly and a sandy grey mustache in need of trimming, commanded the room. His shrewd brown eyes narrowed on Jack.

"How long has she been missing?"

"Since early this afternoon, maybe a little before one o'clock. Nearest we can tell. She was out back planting flowers, and now she's gone."

"So, less than twenty-four hours. Are you sure she's not off visiting a friend?"

"She doesn't have any friends." Jack frowned at the thought. "She promised not to leave the ranch."

"I've known you and your family a long time. I'm not saying you had anything to do with the woman's disappearance, but still, I need to check every possible angle. Where were you this afternoon?"

Statistically the person closest to the victim was usually responsible. He wasn't upset the sheriff zeroed in on him, but wasting time annoyed him. Time Jenna didn't have if she was at David's mercy.

"Caleb and I attended an auction, went to the courthouse to sign some papers, and headed over to a friend's ranch. He was with me the whole time. I've been calling most of the day. She hasn't answered. Her purse is in the kitchen along with her cell phone. None of her clothes are missing. None of the cars are gone. None of my men or the guards has seen her."

"Mommy, why are the police here?" Lily asked.

"We can't find Jenna, so he's going to help us." Summer hugged Lily close.

Everyone knew, but no one would say it. David could have taken Lily too. The thought of that evil man touching a hair on Lily's head was reprehensible.

"Maybe she's still with that man," Lily said, working on a Popsicle, her lips cherry red. Every head in the room turned toward her. Her big blue eyes went wide as everyone stared in disbelief.

"What?" Jack came over to Lily and kneeled beside her, Summer's arms locked around her protectively. "What man, Lily?"

"The man in the woods. He looked like a bush, but his face was mad."

"You saw a man in the woods?" Jack asked softly, though he wanted to demand she tell him everything. He reminded himself she was little more than three.

"Yes, he watched us plant the blue flowers. Jenna didn't see him at first, but I did. He tried to hide."

Jack's heart sank. His worst fears had come true. "What did he do then?"

"Jenna told me to go inside for lunch. I did, but I watched out the window."

"What did you see?" Jack was torn up inside. His niece saw what happened to Jenna. He hoped it wasn't anything that would haunt her.

"The man came out of the trees. He had a really big knife."

"Did he hurt Jenna?" Jack asked carefully.

"No. Jenna went into the woods with him. Sally followed and I had lunch."

"Why didn't you tell anyone about the man?" Jack didn't know what to do. She was only a little girl. She didn't know something bad happened to Jenna.

"Because I thought she knew him."

The sheriff spoke up then, having written everything down. "What did he look like?"

"I don't know." She shrugged her small shoulders.

The sheriff tried again. "Was he tall? What color hair did he have?"

"Dark. He was bigger than Jenna. His clothes looked like a bush."

"What do you mean he looked like a bush?" the sheriff asked, as confused as the rest of them.

"Lots of green, like Daddy and Uncle Jack when they were in the Army. I saw pictures."

Jack spoke first. "Camouflage. That's why she didn't

see him sneak up on her. If she heard anything in the woods, she probably thought it was one of the guards."

"What guards?" The sheriff's interest increased.

"We have guards watching the property. Jenna's ex-husband has a habit of finding her and," he considered Lily, "let's just say, hurting her."

The sheriff got the picture and nodded with a frown tilting his mustache. "Who's the ex?"

"David Merrick. Last I knew he was in San Francisco. His wedding was a couple of days ago. I have someone checking to see where he is now. I don't know, maybe he came and took her. Maybe he had someone else take her. From what Lily said about the man, my guess is it's David. Her description fits. Where Jenna is concerned, he likes to do his own dirty work."

"Okay, we'll check him out. Let's send some men into the woods behind the house, see if we can't find tracks. She could still be out there." The sheriff's blunt statement made the situation that much more real. It was a real possibility she was lying dead out in the trees behind the house. Every instinct Jack possessed told him to rush out there, search every square inch of land until he found her, but reason and training prevailed. They needed a strategic approach if they had any hope of finding her and thwarting whatever diabolical plan David had in store for her.

"She's been gone all afternoon. She could be anywhere," Jack said, distracted by his wandering thoughts.

"Let's begin the search where she was last seen, and see if we can't determine which direction they went."

"Fine. The men have checked most of the immediate area around the barns and family cabins. We'll meet you outside and work our way north along the pastures."

The sheriff and his men headed out to the back patio, taking out their flashlights to look around for clues. It would be slow going in the dark.

"We'll find her, Jack. I know we will," Summer tried to reassure him again. It didn't help.

"I pray she's alive when we do. Take Lily home. You need your rest. We'll call when we find her."

"Jack, call Sam. We talked about this, remember? It's time." She'd spoken to Jack shortly after Jenna decided to stay. They agreed Sam could help in some way if Jenna got into trouble. This was big trouble and Sam's FBI training and experience would be invaluable. Jack knew his twin brother would keep him sane if something bad happened to Jenna.

"I hate to take him away from his work, but you're right. We need him." Jack pulled out his cell phone and dialed Sam's number. As usual, he got his voicemail. "Sam, it's Jack. I need you to come home. It's an emergency." That's the only message he left and all he needed to say.

Lily squirmed excitedly, squealing, "Uncle Sam is coming? Yeah!"

"Come on, Sunshine. You and me are going home. Uncle Jack and Daddy will look for Jenna.

"Call me no matter what time and tell me when you find her. She's okay. I know it. She's a survivor. We just need to find her."

Jack hugged his sister. Her body trembled and tears rolled down her face. She didn't need to be here enduring this stress when she was pregnant. "Go home, little sister. Take care of yourself. Caleb and I will call when we know something. Have one of the guards stay with you. I don't want to take any chances."

"I'll have one of them stay on the couch."

Caleb hugged his wife and daughter. "I'll be home when I can. Get some rest." He held them close for a few moments.

Jack's arms were empty, making him ache as he watched Caleb and Summer. He turned his back on them and walked away, needing to do something besides wallowing in his misery and thinking about what might be happening to the woman he loved. She was out there, and he needed to find her.

Chapter Forty-One

JENNA WOKE AT dawn, cold to the bone but alive. For now. The sun peaked over the hills, brightening the horizon. She welcomed it because it meant the temperature would warm up soon. Groggy and thirsty, she turned to her side and awkwardly pushed herself up and leaned back against the tree. She didn't hear anyone looking for her, only the sound of the wind in the trees, birds chirping around her. Didn't anyone know she was gone? Jack would know. He'd come for her.

Help me, Jack.

With single-minded determination, she stood, gained her balance as her head spun. She braced herself against the tree. Her hands hurt, everything hurt. The pain sometimes overcame her. She had to stay awake. Move. Find Jack.

Face raised to the sun, she tried to picture the ranch, figure out the route David brought her. Hesitant about her decision, but needing to do something, she made the decision to head east toward the rising sun, and hopefully Jack.

I love you, Jack. I'm coming home.

EXHAUSTED, FRUSTRATED, AND going out of his mind, Jack almost believed he heard Jenna calling him. Crazy, just the exhaustion and his conscience calling to him. They spent all night looking for her, only to discover Sally, badly injured and near death in the brush out behind the house. Caleb rushed her to the animal hospital, hoping they'd found her in time. Sick over the dog's injuries and the possibility he might lose her, even more devastating, Jack knew the bastard had a knife and was willing to use it.

No telling what he'd do with the knife on Jenna. How far would he go this time? That thought set Jack's muscles solid as stone and had him desperate to comb every house, barn, farm, acre, mile to find her. Whatever it took, he'd never stop searching.

They hadn't found a single trace of her. She'd vanished into the woods. Jack was thankful they hadn't found her dead, but with the temperature dropping at night and the fact she'd been gone for so long, his thoughts turned morbid. If she were alive out there, she wouldn't last another night. Jack knew it, and it was eating him alive.

What if she wasn't on the property anymore, but somewhere else? The enormity of that thought swamped him in misery.

Caleb crashed on the couch. Jack drank coffee, trying to stay awake and alert. Midmorning now, the sheriff organized the men to start searching the other side of the property. Jack hoped they'd find Jenna soon. They had to find her. If he lost her, he didn't think he could live.

He'd talked to Ben again. Jenna hadn't called him, or his office, to say she was on the run. Ben's source reported no news about Merrick's whereabouts. The honeymoon remained a closely guarded secret, kept under wraps from the press.

The sheriff tried contacting Merrick International, only to be told David was on his honeymoon. He hadn't really thought the sheriff would have any better luck getting information from the Merrick family or the corporate office. David had gotten away with this many times before, but he wouldn't get away with it this time. Jack would make sure of it.

The phone rang and Jack jumped to grab it.

"I'm on a plane. I'll be home in an hour." Sam received Jack's message and knew he wouldn't have called unless the situation was dire.

"Thanks, Sam. You don't know what this means to me."

"What's going on? Is it Mom and Dad? Summer? The baby?"

"No, they're all fine. It's Jenna. She's been kidnapped. Just get here," Jack said wearily.

"Who's Jenna? And who kidnapped her?" Sam didn't hide the surprise in his voice.

"Jenna is my fiancé and her ex-husband kidnapped her yesterday."

"Fiancé! Well, I'll be damned, brother. Okay. You got the local guys looking for her?"

"We've been out all night. We think he took her into the woods on the property, but he could have had a car stashed and taken her anywhere. He stabbed Sally. She's still at the hospital. We don't know if she'll make it. We really have nothing."

"I'm sorry about the dog, man."

Jack appreciated the sentiment, but with Sally in good hands, his thoughts were on Jenna and finding her.

"So he's armed and dangerous. All right. Who's the ex? Maybe I can start with him?"

"David Merrick. You heard of him?"

"As in Merrick International?"

"That's the one."

Sam whistled. "That's big money. If he's got her, he could take her out of the country and hide her forever."

"I don't think he did. He just got married. I think he came to tie up loose ends. Namely, Jenna. She owns a big junk of Merrick International. He wants it back, in addition to being obsessed with her. It's a long story. Get here, and I'll tell you everything."

"On my way. We'll figure this out, and we'll find her."

"We need to find her. She's everything, Sam. I can't lose her."

"So it's like that, huh. Your Jenna must be something special to bring you out of your stupor and back into the real world. I'll do everything in my power to make sure we get her back," he assured Jack. "I thought maybe you'd end up like me, spending too much time working and not enough time living."

"I'm only alive when I'm with her," Jack responded, choked up.

"We'll get her back." Sam hung up.

JENNA SPENT THE morning walking and resting in intervals. Weak from blood loss and lack of food and water, she had to rest more often than she liked. Her head cleared in the warm sun, making it easier to concentrate on her surroundings. At one point, she realized she'd walked in a circle. Her vision doubled and she pressed the heels of her hands to her eyes. Frustrated, she found a relatively soft patch of grass, lay down, and closed her tired eyes. She didn't think she'd run this far from the dirt road, but maybe in her panic she'd covered more ground than she realized.

Rested and refocused, she rolled to her hands and knees, hissed in a ragged breath when she pressed on the scrapes and cuts on her right knee, and cocked her head to the side to look down at the damage. Something off in the distance caught her eye.

"No way. I was this close and didn't see it." The dirt road lay no more than fifty feet ahead of her. Difficult to make out for all the trees and shifting limbs in the wind, but there it was right in front of her.

Back on her feet, she moved slowly on rubbery legs and made it to the deserted road. Still alone. Deep tire tracks rutted the road where David must have taken off in the Jeep, reassuring her he was gone. The coil of rope lay as an ominous reminder of what David had planned for her. She didn't think he'd really stayed in the woods, but with all the spooky noises at night, she had scared herself good, imagining him out there stalking her.

Chapter Forty-Two

SAM PULLED INTO the driveway, noting all the men standing around, eating lunch and drinking coffee. He parked behind the classic Mustang and wondered who it belonged to. Nice ride. He got out, grinned, and caught Lily when she launched herself into his arms.

"Uncle Sam! You came."

"Yes, darlin'. Where's Mommy and Uncle Jack?"

"They're in the house. Uncle Jack is very sad. We can't find Jenna. The bad man with the knife took her."

"You saw the bad man?" Sam didn't like the idea of his niece being exposed to this kind of danger.

"Yes. He was big and he took Jenna into the woods. He hurt Sally." Her little lip quivered.

Sam kissed her sweet cheek and carried Lily up the porch stairs and into the house with him. "Did the bad man say anything to you?"

"No. I watched out the window. Jenna made me go

inside. I didn't think she saw the bad man, but now, maybe she did see him, and that's why she made me go in."

"I think you might be right." Sam and Lily walked into the kitchen. His sister smiled and Jack looked beat.

"How did you get here so fast?" Summer grabbed Lily and gave him a huge hug, holding on to him for a long time.

"Jack called. I came." Sam put a hand on his sister's rounded belly and gave her a wink. Happy for her, but his concern for Jack overshadowed everything at the moment. "Any word, brother?"

"No. The teams just came in from searching the woods behind the barn and out along the pastures. We'll grab something to eat and head out again in an hour. It's already late afternoon and we haven't found any clues. Nothing. Not one damn sign of her."

"Tell me about her, the ex, everything. How did you get involved with her? Another thing, how come I didn't know you were getting married? I might be busy, but I'm never too busy to answer the phone and talk to my brother about his upcoming wedding."

"Summer, take Lily outside, or home, something," Jack pleaded. "She doesn't need to hear about how we found Jenna and got involved."

Summer headed out with Lily, kissing Sam's cheek as she passed.

"Okay. Here it is . . ." Jack told Sam the whole story, everything he knew about Jenna. Sam listened, asking questions only for clarification. When Jack finished, he let out a long sigh and put his forehead down on his crossed arms on the kitchen island.

"This is quite a mess she's in. You think she's still alive?" Sam had his doubts at this point. He'd seen too many similar cases that ended in tragedy.

Jack raised his head, meeting Sam's eyes. "My gut says she's alive. I feel it. We need to find her, Sam. She's been out there a long time."

"We'll go with your gut. Mine's usually right, so we'll trust yours. Who's running the search, and where do we have left to look before we take this off the property?"

"The sheriff is running things with some direction from me. I sent the guards with pictures of her to check all the bus stations, airports, car rental places, anything and any way he could take her out of here. Nothing.

"We've searched the woods behind the house where we found Sally. I don't think he would have continued back through there, because he'd have come to the family cabins. Too many people back that way. Someone would have seen him. I think if they were on foot, he'd have to cross the valley and go into the woods on the other side, back behind the barn. We've searched there, but nothing. Depending on how far he got with her on foot, the next place to look is the hills farther past the fire road. It runs through the forest and back toward the main road and the lake. But, Sam, that's damn far for him to take her on foot."

"But possible. We have to assume he wanted to get as far away from the ranch with her as possible. She probably went willingly to get him away from the house and Lily. He probably stashed a car on the dirt road and took her out that way. Let's check it out."

What Sam didn't want to say was that she might not

be on the property any longer, and they might never find her. Deep down, Jack already knew, but wasn't ready to admit it.

AFTERNOON ALREADY, THE sun descended toward the west. Darkness would fall quickly once it passed the hills. Jenna needed to cover as much ground as possible before she lost daylight.

Walking down the road was much easier than trying to dodge branches and see a clear path through the dense forest. Still, it was slow going. Exhausted, she needed food and water. She hoped she'd come to the creek, or some kind of water she could drink. Maybe then she'd feel a little better, and she could make it to the ranch. She needed to make it back to Jack.

She didn't come to the creek, but managed to walk for several hours, talking to herself in her mind to keep from going crazy.

Just a little farther, take one step at a time. Jack's waiting for you. You can make it. Keep going. Think of the baby. Don't let that bastard win. You've survived every other time. You'll make it this time, too. Find Jack.

Thanks to the mostly downhill grade, she managed to cover a good distance before sunset. Worn out, she was determined to make it around the next bend before stopping to rest. She dragged her feet, putting one foot in front of the other. If she lay down again, she might sleep through the night, and she couldn't afford to spend another night in the cold.

She came around the bend and spotted the edge of the lake past the open meadow. Unable to help herself, she started laughing. With her hoarse voice and mouth so dry, the odd sound came out more like a series of squeaky croaks, but she was elated. Maybe just hysterical.

Water. The lake meant she was close to the main road and only about five miles from the ranch. Not that far. If she could get to the main road, someone would see her.

Excited, her energy surged and she made her way to the lake. Lake water was better than no water. She knelt on the bank and leaned forward to drink. Nothing like tap water, the lake water was gritty from dirt and silt she stirred up, but it would do. Her knees and the bottom half of her legs were soaked through, making her even colder. Violent shivers shook her. Maybe getting wet wasn't such a good idea. Thirst overrode common sense.

More tired than she'd ever felt, she couldn't get her legs to lift her and fell back on her heels. She needed to rest. So close, but she just couldn't go any further. Everything ached, but not as much as her head. She collapsed onto her side, her feet and knees in the water, and passed out curled on the muddy bank.

Chapter Forty-Three

JACK, CALEB, AND Sam rode through the low area on horseback, past the large pastures to the part of the property where the tree lines on both sides of the valley were closest. None of the men found any sign of Jenna, but they all thought this area the most logical place to search. This part of the valley was a long way from the main house, but the best place to cross from one side to the other without being seen.

They made their way through the forest to the dirt road high in the hills. They'd seen several broken branches and disturbed dirt, but it was difficult to tell if it was man-made or from the animals. They'd make their way back down the road past the lake to the main road, searching for any sign Jenna or a vehicle had come this way.

As they rode on, Jack noticed something up ahead. Deep tire impressions in the dirt and gravel and something else he couldn't quite make out in the setting sun. They reached the spot and found the rope. "He had her here. These tire tracks are fresh. He must have tied her up at some point." Jack fisted his hands on the reins, his knuckles going white and his hands aching.

They dismounted and Caleb searched the area. "Where is she now?"

They fanned out, calling out for her, but received no response. Some brush and dirt had been disturbed. Sam searched the road in a zigzag pattern, stopping every couple feet and bending down to take a closer look.

"Check this out," Sam called. They rushed to his location and stared down at the drops of dried blood.

"That doesn't mean anything," Jack said, unwilling to believe she could be dead.

"It's not a lot of blood. Something happened here. Take a step back and look at the disturbed ground. The footprints start here. They're widely spaced and headed for the trees. She ran."

"He ran after her," Caleb said, indicating the larger prints that followed Jenna's smaller ones.

"Yes. She ran. Despite the blood, the evidence in the disturbed dirt and gravel indicates a scuffle. Hopefully she was able to get away."

Sam took a closer look around and walked several yards into the trees, following the trail and other bits of evidence. Broken limbs, trampled weeds, disturbed dirt and dried leaves. He came back to the road and walked along the edge further up the road. Spotting something, he bent and pivoted on his toes and looked down the road where he and Caleb waited.

Sam made his way back and spoke first, because Jack couldn't form a single coherent thought, let alone speak his worst fears.

"All indications show they fought, ran, but . . ."

"But what?" Jack demanded.

"I found her footprints coming back out of the trees about a quarter mile up. Headed this way. Makes sense. This road has a downward grade. If she escaped him, she'd head downhill in hopes of finding the main road or even the ranch. Maybe she's up ahead."

Jack held on to Sam's optimism. He didn't even want to consider that maybe Merrick had killed her and taken her body somewhere else.

Mounted, about to head out, Jack's radio squawked to life.

"Jack, this is the sheriff. You read me?"

"Did you find her? Where is she?"

"One of my men reported seeing what looks like a body down by the lake. He's up on the hill and making his way down to the lake now."

"We're on our way. We're not that far. Call an ambulance, have them meet us there."

Jack, Caleb, and Sam kicked their horses into motion, racing down the road as fast as the horses could run. They knew it was Jenna. She'd made it all the way down the hills to the lake. Jack prayed she'd be alive when he got to her.

As the three men approached the lake, the sheriff's man came out of the woods on the run, too. Jenna lay sprawled in the mud, partially in the water.

Jack, Caleb, and Sam jumped off their horses and ran over to her. Covered in dirt and mud, dried leaves and twigs tangled in her hair. Her swollen and bloody hands lay limp in front of her. Several of her nails were broken and torn. Blood covered her neck, hair, and shoulder from a cut on the back of her head. She didn't move at their approach.

Jack placed a hand on her ribs, barely able to feel the shallow rise and fall as she breathed. Cold to the touch, Jack's insides froze with fear. He bent his head low to her ear. "Jenna, baby, wake up. Wake up, baby, please."

Her lips formed Jack's name, but he couldn't even hear her voice.

Gently, the men rolled her onto her back, and Jack saw the blood and open wound. "She's been stabbed." Covered in blood and mud, the cuts looked bad. "Oh, honey, it's all my fault. I shouldn't have left you alone."

Jenna's eyes fluttered, but she never got them open. She softly spoke, "Lily?"

"What, honey? What did you say?"

Jenna's cracked, split lips mouthed, "Lily?"

"Lily's fine. Everyone else is fine. He didn't hurt Lily."

"Water."

"Yes, honey. We'll get you some water, and we'll take you to the hospital." Jack tore off his jacket and tucked it around her.

Jenna passed out, unable to stay awake any longer. Caleb brushed the hair away from her face and neck and untied the bandana covered in blood from Jenna's head wound. The men starred at Jenna's bruised neck.

"He tried to strangle her," Sam said, shocked. How did she survive in the woods after being strangled and stabbed? "My God, she's one amazing woman."

The ambulance finally arrived after what Jack considered an eternity. The sheriff's men, Caleb, and Sam stood back while the paramedics carefully put Jenna on a stretcher and into the back of the ambulance. Jack refused to leave her side for even a second. They'd started an IV for her dehydration, covered her in several blankets to get her warm, and Jack climbed in to ride to the hospital, despite objections from the paramedics.

Sam and Caleb watched as they drove away. "Caleb, let's take the horses back to the barn and meet Jack at the hospital."

"Can you believe what that bastard did to her?" Caleb asked.

Furious, Sam saw a lot of horrible things in the FBI, but seeing a woman or child hurt always made him sick. And this was his future sister-in-law. He'd seen the devastated look on Jack's face, felt his deep pain all the way to his own soul. He hated the bastard who'd done this and made his brother and Jenna hurt.

"You should have seen her the last time," Caleb said on a weary sigh. "I don't know how she survives that asshole. He better hope Jack doesn't find him before the cops do."

Chapter Forty-Four

JENNA WOKE IN the emergency room, people all around her. Someone was cutting off her clothes and a man next to her issued orders with machine-gun rapid-fire precision. He said something about an X-ray and she panicked. She grabbed his coat and yanked, despite the pain in her hands. He leaned down and she whispered, "Baby."

"What did you say? Can you say it again?"

She took a deep breath, and although it hurt her throat and ribs, she said, "Baby."

The doctor locked eyes with Jenna and she nodded yes.

"No X-ray. Let's get an ultrasound machine in here," he ordered a nurse, who rushed to get the machine. "Don't worry. I'll make sure everything is fine. I'll give you something for the pain, but it won't hurt the baby. Do you know if you have any broken bones?"

Jenna couldn't even attempt to speak again. She shook her head no and her heavy eyelids drooped. The doctor barked more orders, but she drifted off into blissful numbness.

Sam joined Caleb, Summer, Lily, and Jack in the waiting room after he spoke to the sheriff about finding David Merrick.

"What did the doctor say?" Sam whispered to Caleb.

"Jack's waiting for an update. The emergency room people have been very closed-mouthed so far."

"The sheriff contacted Merrick's lawyers," Sam explained. "They're already spinning things, saying Merrick is on his honeymoon and Jenna is trying to cause trouble for her ex, jealous of his new wife, shit like that. If David has a solid alibi, it'll be the same story, her word against his."

"Lily saw him," Summer volunteered.

"Who's going to take the word of a three-year-old?" Jack frowned and shrugged at his little niece. He believed her, but he wouldn't put her through that kind of scrutiny. Furious, Jack wanted Merrick found, so he could kill him.

"When will they give us word on Jenna?" Summer asked, worried.

Jack wouldn't be okay until he saw Jenna, and the doctors told him she would make it. "They won't say, and they won't let me see her. Something about a complication they weren't expecting when she came in. Covered in mud, dirt, and blood, I couldn't tell how bad she was hurt. God only knows what he did to her out in the woods."

"They'll clean and patch her up, and then they'll let you see her," Sam assured him. Jack wasn't so sure he believed Jenna's wounds wouldn't be severe, if not life-threatening.

The doctor came into the waiting room a few minutes later. Jack closed the distance in two long strides. He introduced himself, but before he could get any further the doctor spoke to Summer.

"I'm Doctor Weber. I know you're all anxious to hear what I have to say about Jenna. She's very upset at the moment, and I need some answers so I can calm her down. Are you Lily?" he asked Summer.

"I'm Lily."

"Jenna's asking for you. She's very concerned. Would you like to go see her? Maybe she'll respond to treatment better if she sees you." Addressing the group, he added, "I've never seen anyone in Jenna's condition so determined to find out about another person. She wakes up agitated and demanding answers."

"I'll go see her. Is she really sick? Did you give her a pokey shot?" Lily asked with a deep frown.

"I'm afraid I gave her several pokey shots to help make her better."

"Did you give her a lollipop for the shots?"

"No, but I'll try to find one for her," he said, unable to ignore Lily's earnest question.

"Okay," Lily said, satisfied.

Doctor Weber bent down in front of Lily and spoke directly to her. "I don't want you to be scared, but when you see Jenna, she might look different than you remember. She was hurt very badly, and she has some cuts and bruises. Do you understand?"

"Yeah. Does she look like she did when she came to stay with Uncle Jack?"

The doctor gave Jack a questioning, worried glance at hearing Jenna had suffered similar injuries in the past. "She looks bad, and I don't want you to be afraid. Jenna is very upset and wants to know that you're safe. Okay?"

"Okay." Lily needed some reassurance and glanced up at her Mom and Dad. They nodded their encouragement. Jack felt much the same as the doctor. It might not be a good idea for Lily to see Jenna, but Jenna needed to see Lily to put her mind at ease.

"I'm not sure about this one," Doctor Weber said. "Does anyone know about a ring?"

"I have the ring," Jack said, relieved he could give that back to her. "The paramedics were concerned about her swollen hands, so we pried it off her in the ambulance."

"She wants it back. In fact, she's quite adamant about getting it back."

"I'll be sure to give it to her as soon as you let me see her. How is she? What kind of damage did he do to her?"

Summer grabbed Lily and walked down to the nurse's station away from the doctor and his evaluation of Jenna's injuries.

"She's severely dehydrated. We're giving her IV fluids, and she should recover from that quickly. She's got two severe lacerations along her ribs on her left side that took quite a few stitches to close up. She has a gash on the back of her head, which also required several stitches. The head injury resulted in a severe concussion and a cracked skull. I don't know how she's survived that injury out in the woods overnight in the cold. Those are her worst injuries. Other than that, she has bruises and cuts all over. The bruises and abrasions around her throat are particularly severe. She's in a lot of pain."

"You've given her something for the pain though, right?" Jack didn't want Jenna to suffer anymore. He couldn't stand to think of her enduring any more pain.

"Acetaminophen. She simply refused anything more. She's very strong and seems to be enduring the pain. I have to go by her wishes."

"Why won't she take anything? Can't you put it in her IV? Take the pain away. That's your job!"

Undeterred by Jack's outburst, the doctor simply answered, "I have to go with what she wants. Maybe once you talk to her, you'll understand. You can go in and see her now. She's extremely tired and might not wake up, but I think it would do her a world of good to see Lily and the rest of you.

"Also, she needs rest, so only two visitors at a time and for a few minutes only. We've cleaned her up and bandaged all the wounds. You may want to warn Lily again before bringing her in."

"Thanks, Doc. Is there anything else we should know? I feel like you're holding something back." He just wasn't sure what it was, or why.

"She'll have to tell you the rest, doctor-patient confidentiality. She'll need to stay here for a few days, at least until we're sure her concussion is healed."

The doctor left the waiting room, onto his next patient, leaving Jack confused about the things he hadn't said. Patient confidentiality. Bullshit. Jack needed to know what wasn't said.

Chapter Forty-Five

JACK HELD LILY'S hand and walked to Jenna's room.
They entered quietly and found Jenna asleep in the bed.
A bandage covered the back of her head and more were
wrapped around her wrists. The sheet covered her body
and all the other injuries. Nothing he could see should
scare Lily.

If not for Lily, Jack would have cried at the sight of
her. Pale, her eyes sunken with black circles marring her
translucent skin. The cut above her eye had small bandages keeping it closed, and the cut on her swollen lip
would heal on its own. Jack's heart sank at the sight of
her. He'd failed her. His mind wouldn't let him forget, he
didn't protect her after he'd promised no one would hurt
her again. Now, look at her, in the hospital, having come
too close to dying. Again.

Lily scooted around the bed and touched Jenna's hand
with her tiny fingertips.

Jenna's eyes fluttered open at the touch. At the sight of Lily, tears filled her eyes and skated down her cheeks. "Come here, Sunshine." Barely able to hear Jenna, her voice came out like a hoarse croak.

Jack lifted Lily onto the bed and Lily laid her head on the pillow next to Jenna's. Jenna winced when Lily bumped her. She tried not to show the pain etched on her face.

"You're okay, right?" Lily asked.

"Yes," Jenna answered, her voice no more than a rasp. Tears rolled down her cheeks. She couldn't seem to stop them, so relieved to see Lily safe and sound. Unable to concentrate very well, her head pounded and ached, but Lily was okay and that's all that mattered.

"I'm having a baby," Lily announced. "Mommy told me I'm going to be a big sister. Maybe Uncle Jack can get another puppy when Mommy has the baby like he did when mommy had me."

Jenna bent her head and whispered into the little girl's ear, so Jack couldn't hear her.

"Uncle Jack is having a baby, too?" Lily positively beamed.

Jenna's gaze fell on Jack and she nodded her head yes.

Stunned, tears rolled down Jack's face as he bent over her and laid his head gently on her belly looking up at her. She ran her bandaged hand through his hair and smiled.

"You're going to be a Dad." Her voice almost didn't get the words out, but Jack heard them loud and clear.

He lifted his head and kissed her softly. "Thank you. I love you so much. I'm so sorry I let you down."

"No. You didn't let me down. You were with me the whole time."

"I should have been with you. Honey, I'm so sorry." Jack gazed down at her lying beaten near death, holding on to his niece, and carrying his baby. He didn't think this much love could fill his heart. It ached for her.

"In my heart, you were with me. You found me. It's not your fault. I love you."

Jenna's eyes drooped closed, simply too tired for any more.

Jack scooped up Lily and took her out to her mother. Summer, Caleb, and Sam all turned to him expectantly. "She's okay."

"Jack's having a baby, too, mama." Lily beamed.

Everyone's eyes went wide with shock. He'd never seen all of them speechless. "She's pregnant. He took her and hurt her and she's carrying my baby. I didn't do anything to stop him. In fact, I made it easy for him to take her because I wasn't there. She said he always managed to get her, but I thought she'd be safe."

Summer took Jack into her arms and whispered into his ear. "This is not your fault. We'll get him. He won't get away with this again. We'll all keep her safe."

"I need to talk to her. Is she awake?" Sam asked.

"She's in no shape for it tonight." Jack tried to keep the anger and anguish out of his voice, but his words came out too harshly. "I'll try to convince her to let the doctor give her something for the pain. Then I hope she'll sleep through the night. I'm staying with her. You guys go home, and I'll see you tomorrow."

Sam gripped his shoulder. "I'll light a fire under the sheriff and see if I can get anywhere with him. Be back first thing in the morning. The three of us will come up with a plan to put a stop to this once and for all. Go back to her, Jack. Don't let her wake up without you there. I've seen plenty of victims, and she'll probably have a rough night if she won't let them knock her out."

"Thanks, Sam. Thanks for coming, and thanks for helping. You too, Caleb. I don't want to think about what would have happened to her if she'd been outside another night."

They made their goodbyes. Before Summer left with her family, Jack pulled her aside and asked her to take care of a few small surprises for Jenna.

Chapter Forty-Six

JACK WAS ONLY gone a few minutes, but even in that short time Jenna was desperate to see him again. When he returned, the doctor and a nurse were checking on her. Only half awake, she struggled to concentrate on what the doctor said. Just seeing Jack made her cry again.

"Honey, you're okay. I'm here, and I'm not going anywhere. Okay?"

She couldn't help it. She clung to his hand and cried.

"Doc, what's going on? Is everything all right with the baby?"

"Jenna's in a lot of pain and she's overwhelmed. I know your head must be pounding like bass drums. I want to give her some medication, but she won't let me."

"Jenna, please, baby. Take the medicine. You need to rest. I'll be right here with you all night."

"Jenna, what I'll give you won't hurt the baby. I promise. I'll do an ultrasound right now, so you can see the baby is okay. Then, if you take the medication, I'll come in and check on the baby during the night. The pain and stress you're under is overburdening your system. It's not good for you or your child. I'll make you more comfortable, so you can sleep. Both of you will be better for it."

Jenna noted Jack's and the doctor's concerned faces. Jack kissed her palm and held it to his cheek. "Please, Jenna. Take the medicine. Rest, so the baby can rest."

"I want to see the baby first. I need to know he's okay."

Doctor Weber pulled the covers back from her abdomen and put some clear jelly on her lower stomach. Cold, she flinched. He took the wand from the machine set up next to the bed and moved it over her stomach. His brow creased as he studied the monitor. Then, he smiled and pushed a few buttons. The sound filled the room.

Jack wasn't sure what exactly he was hearing, but it sounded like a train chugging down the tracks, the steady rhythm strong. Jack looked to the doctor for an explanation.

"That is their heartbeats, and these," he pointed to the screen, "are your babies."

Transfixed by the figure on the screen, Jack stared at his baby inside Jenna. His focus on the tiny heart beating. Overwhelmed with love, he turned to Jenna. Tears streamed down her face, and she never looked away from the baby on the screen.

"Is the baby okay? Did David harm him when he hurt me? I'm not losing another baby because of him. I'm not." Her voice shook and she clutched Jack's hand.

"I think you missed what I said. Not baby, babies.

See here, two heartbeats, two babies. They're perfect. There doesn't seem to be any problems. It's early in the pregnancy."

Jack finally registered what the doctor was saying. "You mean we're having twins?"

Jenna chimed in, too, her voice a little stronger. "We're having twins?"

"Yes. Identical twins. I suspected as much when I first examined Jenna in the emergency room, but she wasn't very cooperative at the time, so it was difficult to get a good look. We were too concerned about her other injuries."

"But they're okay. Nothing's wrong. Twins?" Jenna asked again.

"There's nothing wrong. And yes, twins. They appear to be perfect. They're in a great position. So long as you take care of yourself and rest, you shouldn't have any complications. I'll recommend a few obstetricians for you. I suggest you start seeing one soon, so they can monitor the pregnancy. Right now, I'd say you're about ten, eleven weeks along. The babies' hearts are strong. Now, let's let them rest. I'll give you something to put you to sleep and relieve your pain. Your blood pressure is too high due to all this stress, and that's not good for them."

"Um, Doc. You're sure everything is okay? The babies won't cause any complications for Jenna to recover?"

"No. Her body will heal and the babies seem to be doing just fine after the ordeal she's been through. We'll monitor them while she's here to be sure, but I don't expect any problems. All of them will be fine. Congratulations. I hope you have a big house."

The doctor shot a syringe full of drugs into Jenna's IV before she protested further, her eyes closed and she fell into a deep sleep.

"We do have a big house. Even if we didn't, we'd build one. Nothing will be too good for Jenna and these babies." Jack made sure Jenna was asleep before continuing. "Be straight with me, Doc. Did he rape her?"

"No, he didn't." His serious voice convinced Jack he wasn't holding back on him at Jenna's request.

Relieved, he put his head down on Jenna's arm and breathed deeply, letting that fear slip away.

"She'll rest now," the doctor continued. "Like I said, the drugs I gave her won't harm the babies. If nothing else, they'll help because she won't be fighting the pain and her blood pressure should come down. I'll be back in a few hours. I'll do another ultrasound. It isn't necessary, but you can reassure her I did check and all is well."

"Thanks, Doc. I'm staying with her tonight. I don't want her to be alone."

"I'd recommend you go home and get some rest, but I can tell you'd probably just punch me if I tried to get you out of here."

"You got that right, Doc. I'm sitting right here and making sure that if she wakes up, she knows I'm here, keeping her safe. I shouldn't have left her in the first place."

Doctor Weber shook his head and left Jack to watch over Jenna.

Jack brought the chair over to the bed, sat, and stared at her. Resting soundly, he placed his hand over her lower belly and contemplated being a father. His babies were resting, safe and sound. With everything she'd been through, she'd kept their babies safe. She'd kept herself alive—again.

She slept most of the night without stirring. Doctor Weber came in and did another ultrasound. Jack watched in awe, his babies resting inside Jenna. The doctor assured him the babies were fine. Jenna wasn't having any contractions or spotting blood. They were safe, all of them.

Jenna woke up screaming before dawn. Actually, she'd sat bolt upright in bed with her mouth open in a scream, but nothing came out but a raspy whoosh of air. Breathing heavily, she collapsed into Jack's arms and cried herself back to sleep.

She woke up again late in the morning, disoriented, but Jack still held her hand, comforting her. It hurt her head too much to open her eyes, so she simply lay still. Her body ached, her head hurt, her ribs burned with each breath, and the images in her head wouldn't go away. She'd never forget the crazed way David looked when he'd come after her with that knife.

Crying again, Jack gently wiped her cheeks. He whispered in her ear, such soft loving words. Just like when she'd first met him, that soft honey of a voice soothed her. He always knew just how to make her feel safe.

"You're okay, honey. I'm here with you. You're safe."

"Make it stop. I can't do this anymore. Make it stop."

"Oh, God, honey. I love you. You're going to be fine, and we'll go home and have a wonderful life. I promise."

"He won't stop. Even in my head, he won't stop. You should walk away. Get as far away from me as you can. I'll only ruin your life."

Crushed by her outburst, Jack's heart ached. She sounded so defeated, barely able to speak at all. Nothing but a rasped-out whisper, making what she said even sadder.

"You're not ruining my life. You're the best thing in my life. We're going to get married, raise our babies, and be happy on the ranch. We'll stop him one way or another, even if I have to kill him myself."

"He's too evil to die. I can't get his eyes out of my head. They were so crazed and empty at the same time. It's like he wasn't even there and some monster was inside him."

"Look at my eyes, honey. What do you see?"

Jenna opened her eyes, tears spilling out and rolling down her cheeks. "I see home. I see love. Jack, I'm sorry. I don't want you to go. I love you so much. I don't want you or your family to get hurt. I was so afraid he'd done something to Lily. I couldn't stand it if something happened to one of you."

"I can't stand it that something did happen to you. We'll put a stop to this. I promise. Whatever it takes."

"I want to believe we'll get married and raise these babies, and I'll get to see them grow. I'm so afraid to hope for that."

He rested his brow on hers.

"Believe it, honey. It will come true. Rest, baby. I'm right here. You're safe."

She didn't need much coaxing. Her eyes already drooping, she fell back into a deep sleep with Jack watching over her and holding her hand. Safe.

Chapter Forty-Seven

JENNA SLEPT ON and off for the rest of the day and night. Jack sat by her bed, never leaving her side. Sam, Summer, and Caleb came by to check on them. Jack refused each offer to leave and get some rest. They would stay with her, but if she woke up, he wanted her to see him and know she could count on him. He'd let her down once. He wouldn't do it again when she needed him the most.

He held her when she woke from a nightmare and whispered words of love. She didn't stir for much of the night. He hoped she was finally overcoming some of the shock and trauma.

Jack fell asleep shortly after dawn, only to wake up with Jenna's hand gripped in his hair. His eyes flew open, only to see hers wide with shock and utter fear. His heart slammed against his chest. He had no idea what had her so scared, but his whole body jolted with adrenaline, making him ready to defend her.

"Jack, you better tell her who I am before she rips your hair out," Sam said from the door.

"Jenna, honey, did I forget to tell you I have a brother, a twin brother. That's Sam."

His head rested on the bed next to her side, and she still had a death grip on his hair. Her head turned from him to Sam and back and forth again.

"That's right, honey, my twin. Sam lives in Virginia, and he doesn't get back to the ranch often enough. I can't believe I forgot to mention him. Now, will you let go? Please."

She immediately released Jack and ran her hand over his face to say sorry.

"Don't worry about it. Sam, this is Jenna, my fiancé, and the mother of my babies."

Jenna smiled warmly and nodded her head in a kind of hello.

"Did you say babies?"

"That's right. Babies. Identical twins. Imagine that."

"Yeah, imagine that." Sam smiled at them both. "There's nothing better than having an identical twin. Jack and I were very close growing up, like having a built-in friend from birth."

"Jenna can't talk. Her voice is completely gone, and the doctor wants her to rest it for a few days."

"I can't believe you didn't mention me, show her pictures of the two of us, anything. Have I been gone that long?"

"All the pictures in the house look like me," Jack pointed out.

"No matter. How are you feeling, Jenna?"

She simply shrugged her shoulders. The action set off a wave of pain and she rolled her eyes.

"Honey, you can't move around like that, remember your ribs," Jack scolded.

She gave him a dirty look. "Right, how could you forget," Jack said, and tried to smile for her.

"Well, I guess that answers the question. Since Jack obviously didn't get a chance to tell you I'm here, or that I exist for that matter, I guess I'll explain why I came, besides the fact you were kidnapped. I'm an FBI agent, and I think I can help you."

Jenna shook her head no. Then her concussion kicked in, blurring her vision, making her dizzy. She closed her eyes while she regained her equilibrium.

"Jenna, I didn't call in the FBI," Jack said, squeezing her hand. "I know how you feel about the cops, and the hospital for that matter. I called Sam because he's my brother, and I needed help finding you. He's the best, and once I told him what's been happening to you, he said he could help. You were right, the sheriff was no help in getting to David."

Jenna shook her head no. "He'll kill you if he knows you're helping me," she rasped out. "He killed my bodyguard a year and a half ago. I won't let that happen again."

"Jenna, you aren't supposed to talk."

She waved his protest away with her hand. The bandage on her wrist a grim reminder of what she'd been through. Her throat hurt each time she talked, but she needed to get her point across. She didn't want anyone else in danger. "I don't want you to help me. I'll take care of this my way."

"If you run again, I swear to God, I will find you and bring you back. Please, honey, you can't run again. Think of the babies. Think of me. I can't live without you." Jack was so afraid she'd run. She could lose herself somewhere and it would be difficult to find her. She had the money and the means to do it. Hell, she'd done it countless times and he didn't have David's resources to find her.

She'd been so down yesterday. He hoped some of her strength had come back and she'd be back to her fighting self. She was a survivor. Hearing her talk about him leaving her, and that she didn't want to ruin his life, worried him. It wasn't her nature to give up.

"I'm not running. It's time I put an end to this. Although I planned to do it in another few months, it's past time I get it done."

"What's your plan?" Sam asked. "Maybe if we work together, we can put a stop to him forever. I have a lot of resources at my disposal. Like Jack said, I'm the best," Sam reassured her.

"He has your confidence," she teased Jack. "What did the doctor say about the babies last night? Did you see them again?"

"They're fine. I got to watch them for a few minutes while the doctor checked you out. They're snuggled in tight like they should be. Now stop changing the subject and tell us what you have planned. Ben is working on something for you, so what is it?"

"Jack, I can't do this right now. I'm in a lot of pain, my

throat hurts, and I'm tired. I promise when we go home, we'll sit down and I'll give you all the details."

"Okay, honey. We'll wait till you get home. You rest, and I'll get the doctor to give you some more medication for the pain.

"Sam, stay with her while I rustle up the Doc. I'll be right back, honey. I want you to stop talking and rest. I'll find you some tea, too."

Jack left the room to find the doctor and Jenna seized the opportunity to enlist Sam's help. She didn't want Jack taking unnecessary risks, but Sam was a trained federal agent. She needed to trust someone. Her future brother-in-law, for better or worse, had her trust. She prayed she didn't get him hurt or killed.

"Sam, do you really want to help me?"

He moved closer, so he could hear her weak voice. "Absolutely. I can do things to help you because I'm a federal agent, but more importantly, I'll do things for you because you're family."

"I'm not family, yet."

"Yes, you are. Those babies you're carrying are Turners, too. There's nothing I won't do for family. To tell you the truth, I can't wait to see those little ones. I'm happy for you and Jack. You and those babies are the family he always wanted. I envy him. You're an amazing woman."

Taken aback by his praise and easy acceptance of her into the family, she swallowed the lump in her throat. "You do realize my ex may try to kill you. Look what he's done to me. He's killed before. I wasn't kidding when I said he killed my bodyguard. I can't prove it, of course. It was a well-planned 'accident,' but I know he did it just the same. I don't want you getting hurt."

"When I'm finished, he'll be even more dangerous and unpredictable."

"What do you want me to do?"

"I want you to start a fake FBI file on my death. Do you have someone at the FBI who will do you a favor? Someone who can go see David and make a little noise."

"Yeah, I have a few favors I can call in. I've already put in a request to have someone on him round the clock. We'll know where he is at all times, until we can spring whatever trap you have planned. Why don't you want me to do this?"

"Because once he finds out I'm really dead, he'll come after Jack." She pointed to him.

His face told her he understood. They could set a trap for David if he didn't know Jack had a twin brother who was an FBI agent.

"And why would he come after Jack?"

"Because I told him Jack is the beneficiary of my will. The money, my piece of the company, it all goes to Jack in the event of my death. He wants his company shares back. He'll contact Jack to attend the big board meeting being held in a week. Jack owns enough of the company that he has a seat on the board and voting rights. I usually vote by conference call, so I don't have to be in the same room as David, but Jack will tell David he'll be there. Then I'll spring the rest of my plan at the board meeting. I'm going to take everything from David. And that will make him very dangerous. I have no doubt he'll come after me.

With you by my side, I'll have hard evidence from a federal official. I'll get him for everything he's done."

"What do you have planned for the board meeting? Will you vote against David on something major for the company?"

"No. I'm taking over the company."

Sam's mouth fell open in shock. Merrick International was a huge corporation. Taking it over was a monumental undertaking, but she'd had her plans in progress for several years, and it was past time she saw them through.

"How can you take over the company? Doesn't his family own majority shares?"

"Right now they hold controlling interest, because collectively they own the majority of the stock. The board has eight members, four of which are Merrick family members: David, his father, his mother, and the patriarch of the family, David's grandfather.

"David and his grandfather are the ones who run the company, but his grandfather is looking to transfer power to David over the next year. David's parents vote on the board and serve as figureheads at events for the company. They don't actually oversee any of the business operations.

"I received a large portion of the company as part of the divorce and hold a seat on the board. The three other board members are shareholders from other companies that have a stake in Merrick International. One of those board members is Cameron Shaw. You might know the company he heads, Ortel, Inc."

"Yeah, I've heard of it. They're very influential in

building contracts here and overseas. It's basically a huge construction and finance company. Very high end buildings and factories."

"That's right. Cameron Shaw is president and CEO. He's brilliant. He also has a large voting share in Merrick International. I plan to make him an offer he can't refuse. With the shares I hold and Cameron behind me, I'll have more than I need."

"I think I see where you're going with this. Consider yourself dead. I'll contact the field office in Denver and put an announcement out over the wire that the former Mrs. David Merrick was found beaten and stabbed on a ranch outside Denver, and she later died at the hospital of hypothermia and her injuries."

"Perfect. Get the hospital's cooperation. Have Jack take me home today before the press arrives. We'll stage some sort of medical emergency to convince the hospital staff. You need to get a camera and take pictures of my injuries. Send a set to Ben for my murder book and use the other set for your agent to take to David."

"Hold it. Your murder book? What the hell are you talking about?" Sam asked angrily.

"How much did Jack tell you about my past?"

"Everything, I think. He mentioned your relationship with Ben, how you use him to help you hide, your password with him, and how David has 'hunted' you unmercifully."

"Then you know the precautions I take. I send pictures to Ben each time David hurts me from the very minor to"—she swept her hand down the length of her—"the very serious."

"What does that have to do with a murder book?"

"A cop show on TV showed that every murder is documented in what's called a 'murder book' detailing the crime. Since I always believed David would kill me, I asked Ben to create my murder book."

Sam winced at the description. He must think her crazy. What sane person keeps a scrapbook of stalking and beatings hoping it can be used in the event of her death?

"In addition to the photos, I write him a detailed account of what happened to me in my own words. I sign it and send it with the photos. He has an accounting of every incident, whether it was some note, or call, or worse."

"How have you survived and still stayed the generous, kind-hearted person Jack describes and I see before me? You're the strongest person I've ever met."

"I don't feel very strong at the moment. I just want this to be over. I want a life with Jack. Will you help me, knowing this could be very dangerous for you and Jack?"

"What's dangerous for Sam and me?" Jack came in carrying a cup of tea for her, the doctor right behind him.

"I'll let Jenna explain. I have a few things to work on, including finding a camera. My condolences, brother, on the death of your fiancé."

"Death of my fiancé? What the hell are you talking about?" He was talking to a closed door, Sam was already off and running.

"Jenna, what is he talking about?" Jack asked again.

"Doctor, I need a favor. I need you to stage some sort

of medical emergency and declare me dead and let me go home today."

Both Jack and Doctor Weber looked at her like she was crazy. She simply smiled weakly and explained the first part of her plan. She left off the part about taking over the company. She'd outlined her plan for Jack weeks ago, leaving off many of the details, despite Jack's badgering her about how it was possible for her to do it.

So much for being quiet and resting.

Doctor Weber agreed to assist by declaring her dead to the press. He didn't want to release her today, but knew if he kept her in the hospital he couldn't keep her secret. They'd stage her death and wheel her out of the room as if she were dead and being transferred to the morgue. Jack could sneak her out the back of the hospital without the press knowing any different.

The doctor checked her out and did another ultrasound to show her the babies were doing fine. He gave her some samples of prescription medication for her pain and some prenatal vitamins. She couldn't very well fill a prescription if she were dead.

Sam returned as soon as the doctor left, carrying a camera. Her spirits sank deeper. She hated being exposed, hated even more that the pictures were necessary. Without the photos, she couldn't prove what David had done to her. She'd tried to file charges the first several times he'd hurt her, but the police were always bought off; the district attorney, pressured by David's lawyers, would say they didn't have enough evidence; or David would simply supply an airtight alibi. It was easy for him to get people to do his bidding. She may have a lot of money, but she lacked power, especially after he smeared her name in the press. Not for long though.

"Okay, Jenna. Let's get the pictures done. You can write your report for Ben. I'll email the photos to my buddy and have him confront David as soon as he's located. Are you sure you want to do this now? You look completely wiped out."

"Let's just get it over with before I fall asleep again. Jack, honey, you don't need to stay for this."

"The hell I don't. I know he hurt you. I saw what he did the last time. I'm not leaving you to deal with this alone."

"You're sure? You haven't seen what he's done, and maybe you shouldn't. I don't want you to think of me looking like this. It's bad enough you had to stitch me up the last time."

"Honey, to me you're beautiful no matter what. It'll be okay. We'll get through this together." His hand cupped her cheek and their eyes met. She leaned into his palm and fell into his eyes and the warmth of his love.

"Will you help me up so Sam can take the pictures?"

He put his hands under her arms and lifted her to a sitting position on the side of the bed. "Come on, honey. Take it slow. You don't want to hurt your ribs."

"It's not only that, my leg and back are killing me."

"What do you mean?"

"Sam, are you ready?"

"Yeah, all set."

Jenna stood with Jack's help. The nurses had put a

gown on her that simply hung over her shoulders, open in the back. She held on to Jack as she stood and, facing Jack, turned her back toward Sam.

Sam hissed in a breath when he saw the damage. Black and blue from her neck down to her panties. She'd been punched multiple times in the back, and it appeared each one left its own hideous bruise. She looked like she'd been the loser in a heavyweight title fight.

His gaze fell down her spine to the back of her thighs and the long scar where Jack had stitched her up the last time. The injury healed well and would fade even more over time. Several small bruises covered her legs, but one was large and nasty looking, the perfect impression of a man's hiking boot. He could almost make out the tread in the impression of the bruise, making him sick. Maybe he could get his forensic guys to match the impression to one of David's shoes.

None of them had realized just how badly David had hurt her. She'd lain in the bed not complaining or wanting to take anything to make the pain go away. How she managed to even get up, he didn't know.

Jack held her arms as she stood facing him. He hadn't seen any of her, except her face and stomach for the last day. He wasn't sure what the rest of her looked like. Sam's face fell, agony and sadness filled his eyes at the sight of Jenna's back. Jack took a step to the side of Jenna, still holding on to her, and saw her back. He couldn't believe the black and blue marks spreading across her entire backside. Severely beaten, the bastard had kicked her in the thigh. His insides quaked and he wanted to rage.

"Jack, honey, don't hold my arms so tight. You're hurting me."

"Oh, honey, I'm sorry. I'm just so angry at what he did to you."

"Sam, take the pictures, then I'll turn around and you can do the front."

"I don't know if I want to see the front if it's as bad as the back of you," Sam said sadly.

"Please, just take the damn pictures. I can't take this much longer."

Sam snapped pictures of her back and thighs in quick succession. About ready to pass out on them, she hoped this humiliation would be over soon.

"Jenna, turn your head so I can see your face. That way, no one will dispute these pictures are of you."

She did what he wanted. He snapped two more pictures of her backside. "Okay, turn around."

She kept her eyes on Jack as she slipped off the gown, her back to Sam. She cupped her breasts in her hands to cover them. Her panties would cover her a little, too. A large bandage below her left breast covered the knife wound.

"Jack, take the bandage off my ribs."

Sam watched her try to cover herself so he couldn't see all of her. No way to make her more comfortable, he kept his face blank. She must feel humiliated to stand there almost naked in front of him, her future brother-in-law. She did it though. She had guts.

"This is going to hurt." Jack peeled the bandages away and swore under his breath at the long double lines of stitches. Too many to count before she turned toward him.

"Hurry up. Take the pictures."

Sam didn't say a word. He took pictures of the nasty knife wounds that went from almost the middle of her chest around her ribs to her back. Next came the bruises on her other side, the scrapes and cuts on her knee, the cut above her eye, and her split lip.

"Jack, take the bandage off her head, so I can take a picture of the cut and stitches back there."

Sam snapped more pictures, his stomach in knots. The cut was about three inches long, swollen into a large ball the size of a lemon. Multiple stitches kept it closed. She must have one hell of a headache.

"Okay, Jenna. You did a great job. I'll email the photos to Ben and my buddy at the FBI to use on David."

She hadn't moved, just stood with her face buried in Jack's chest, his arms loose around her. Jack nodded to Sam to leave.

Sam didn't need a reason to escape. He'd seen enough.

Jack gently sat Jenna on the edge of the bed. Without a word, he put the bandages back on her ribcage and the back of her head. He slid the gown up her arms and draped it over her shoulders. Helping her lie down again, he leaned over and kissed her softly for a long minute. He put his brow to hers as her eyes drooped closed again.

"I am so proud of you. I know that can't have been easy to do in front of Sam. I had no idea how bad . . . Sleep now," he finished, unable to voice his concerns about her condition. "I'll help Sam get things ready for you to leave. I want you home in our bed."

He didn't think she heard him. So peaceful looking

with her eyes closed, but he knew she didn't have any peaceful thoughts in her head. He stood to leave, but she called to him.

"Jack."

"Yeah, honey. I'm here."

"I didn't break my promise."

"What promise, honey?"

"I promised I wouldn't leave the ranch. I never did. At least, I think I was on the ranch the whole time." She gave him what appeared to be a crooked smile and opened her eyes. He couldn't help himself, he smiled back.

"Smart ass. Even in your condition, you're being a smart ass."

"I got you to smile. Don't worry about me. I'm okay. I promise. Please don't be mad at me."

"I'm not mad at you. I love you. You and our babies are everything to me. The thought of losing you breaks my heart. I was so scared when I couldn't find you. I finally found the woman of my dreams, and I let you down and almost lost you and the babies. Now stop talking, or your voice will never come back."

"You never let me down. You can't be with me every second. We thought I'd be safe. I'm safe now. Kiss me goodnight."

He did kiss her again and, reluctant to leave her, held her hand until she slept. He left her room quietly. The guard he'd posted at her door nodded as he left. No one would get into her room except the doctor or one of the family members.

This time, Jack wasn't taking any chances.

Chapter Forty-Eight

SAM ISSUED ORDERS over the phone, detailing the story to appear in the news regarding the death of Jenna Caldwell Merrick. Jack stood near, listening. His face said it all: If they couldn't pull this off, David may decide to come back and finish the job. After everything they'd been through the last few days, thinking about losing Jenna even in theory about shattered Jack's control.

Sam finished his call and studied his brother. This was really taking a toll on him and it wasn't over. He hoped Jack and Jenna would get beyond this and have the happy life they deserved. He wished he had a woman half as special as Jenna. He'd only known her for a few hours really, but from what he'd seen and been told, she was remarkable. He didn't think there was anyone else like her.

"Jack, you need a shower and a shave and about two days of sleep."

"Yeah, well, it's been a shitty couple of days, and it isn't over. You just killed my future wife, and I have to say, I'm a little pissed about it."

"You're being irrational about this. I had to kill her for her own good."

Jack couldn't help it. He busted up laughing. "I know, it's bizarre. Tell me what your friend at the FBI is doing about her death."

"He'll take the photos I sent to him and confront David. He'll make it appear the FBI is investigating the death of the late Jenna Caldwell Merrick. He might also drop the hint that her funeral is being held two days from now."

"Is that so? And just where is the funeral taking place?

"At the cemetery. Where else would we hold a fake funeral? This has to look real, Jack. You're going to have to cry like a baby." Sam smiled and punched his brother in the arm.

"I'll make it look real, but I will not be crying like a baby. I know Jenna's life is on the line, and now ours as well. What are we doing with her while this is all going down?"

"She'll be at the ranch with three very big guards. I've already assigned guards at the gates. I've doubled the detail around the ranch. Two guards are assigned to Lily and two more to Summer. They'll appear to be family members at the funeral.

"No one gets on the property from the main road, or through the woods like that bastard did. There'll be black ribbons on the gates, indicating we're in mourning. I'm sure the press will set up camp trying to get information about where Jenna's death occurred. They'll definitely want to know about your relationship, which will set off David."

"How did you manage all of that this morning?"

"Jenna gave me Ben's number. After that, everything was easy. We have unlimited funds to pull this off. You're a very rich man."

"I know. She's worth everything to me."

"That's not what I meant," Sam corrected when he saw Jack's confusion. "Didn't she tell you?"

"Tell me what?"

"You inherit everything. You're the sole beneficiary of her estate. All her money, her shares in the company, everything. She left it all to you."

"She didn't."

"Oh yes she did. She changed her will back in July after you took care of her when she first came to the ranch. Do you know what she's worth?"

"Everything."

Sam smiled. It wasn't about the money for Jack. He loved her, and she loved him. Rare, that was enough.

Jack ran a hand through his hair and over his face, unable to believe Jenna's generosity and faith in him.

"I know, Jack, it's big. She loves you. If you ever had a doubt about how much, I think her leaving everything to you, trusting you to take care of her assets and finish things with David says it all."

Jack couldn't answer. What was there to say?

Summer walked toward them, carrying a small duffel bag. He'd asked her to bring some clothes for Jenna, in addition to doing a few other things for him. "Did you take care of everything I asked you to?"

"Well, hello to you too, brother. You look like crap, by the way. You need a shower and a shave. Didn't you get any rest? How's Jenna this morning?"

"I'm sorry. Hello. Thanks for the compliment. No, I didn't get any rest. Jenna was up and down most of the night. She's having a hard time. She could use a friendly face. Did you take care of everything?"

"Yes. Here is the gift. The house is ready. Can I go in to see her? There's a big man outside her door, looks like a wrestler."

"That's her guard. Don't wake her. She had a hard morning. Sam took pictures of her, and she's dying in an hour or so."

"What?" Summer said stunned.

"I got to see her naked." Sam winked, setting off Jack's already combustible temper.

Sam fell back against the wall from the blow to his jaw. He knew that comment would get him decked, but Jack needed to let out some of his pent-up aggression. He'd take one from his brother to make him feel better. Now Jack could think more clearly.

"You really want to provoke me today when Jenna is going to die."

"You need to blow off steam, and I don't have time to take you home and wrestle with you in the front yard like we used to."

"What the hell are you two talking about? Jenna's dying?" Summer asked, clearly stunned.

"Yes. No. I mean we're killing her in the press," Jack explained.

"Would you talk sense? Sam, explain what this idiot is talking about. Is Jenna dying?"

Sam rubbed at his jaw. "No, she isn't dying. But she will be dead in a little while."

He put up his hand to make her give him a minute to explain. She fisted her hand, ready to deck him again. Willing to help Jack relieve his stress, he didn't want to take a pounding from both his siblings in one day.

"We're faking her death. I've got the FBI putting out a press release that Jenna has died. The funeral is in a couple of days. Do you have a dress?"

"Do I have a dress for Jenna's funeral where she won't be dead? Yes, of course I do. Why would you think I wouldn't have a dress for such an occasion? Now, if you'll excuse me, I'm going to see my not dead future sister-in-law."

"Don't wake her yet. She and the babies need to rest," Jack reminded her.

Summer stopped in her tracks and turned slowly around on her toes to face them. "Did you just say babies?"

"That's right. Babies. We're having twins. Identical twins," Jack said with a broad smile.

"God help her if they're anything like the two of you."

Jack and Sam looked at each other and back to their sister.

"That wounds us. We're perfect angels, little sister." Jack and Sam gave their sister a wicked smile.

"More like the devil times two. I think I'll just warn

Jenna what she's in for. Maybe a few stories about your childhood should do it."

"Be nice, Summer. We want her to recover, so she can die later."

Summer shook her head at the two of them. She loved them deeply, knew better than anyone they were two peas in a pod.

Jack hoped they knew what they were doing. This scheme was one for the books. Sam and he had cooked up some good gags over the years together, but this one topped the creativity list. Not only that, this one could get them killed. Jenna too.

Chapter Forty-Nine

JENNA WOKE AND found Summer reading a magazine in the chair next to her bed. Her head pounded to some unknown tempo. She closed her eyes again hoping it would stop. Her tongue stuck to her desert-dry mouth and swallowing hurt her scratchy throat. She wanted to curl up and pass out again. She rolled onto her side and curled up as much as she could manage. She pulled her arms over her head and covered her eyes, unable to hold back the moan of pain and frustration.

Summer rose from the chair and clicked the button for the nurse. She ran her hand over Jenna's hair, careful not to touch where she'd been hurt.

"It's okay. You must be in terrible pain. I buzzed for the nurse. She'll be here soon to give you something."

"I need water." The words came out on an exhale of air barely above a whisper.

Summer poured her a glass from the pitcher on the

bedside table and held the straw to her cracked, dry lips. Summer put the cup down and closed the blinds on the window, turned down the lights in the room, and sat back beside the bed. Jenna concentrated on the feel of Summer's fingers combing through her hair and tried to relax.

The nurse came in a few minutes later carrying a syringe of medication. She shot it into the IV and left as quietly as she arrived.

"Congratulations on the babies. Jack told me you're having twins. You must be so excited."

"I am happy, but afraid I won't live long enough to have them and hold them."

"Oh, Jenna. Yes, you will. Sam and Jack are working right now to make sure you're safe from now on."

"It's just so hard to believe this could actually be over. I want to stay on the ranch for the rest of my life without having to worry that maybe today I'll have to leave everything and run. You have no idea what it feels like to never feel part of someplace, of something. It's so hard to live your life looking over your shoulder and wondering if today will be the day that everything ends."

"Don't talk like this. You're the strongest person I know. You're going to get through this, and we'll raise our babies together. We'll be real sisters. I've been stuck with those two devilish twins my whole life. It'll be nice to have a sister."

"I would really like that."

Tired, she closed her eyes again while Summer sat stroking her hair. The bodyguard's deep voice warned someone they were not allowed to enter. Several voices spoke at once and the door opened.

"Miss Caldwell . . ."

"She's Mrs. Merrick," David interrupted.

Summer's hand stopped and protectively covered her head. Jenna turned to see David standing in the doorway, a doe-eyed nurse looking up at his handsome face with worship. No doubt he'd paid her many a compliment, pouring on his sickeningly sweet charm to get her to bring him in here. One of his many lawyers entered behind him, Gucci briefcase in hand.

"I'd be happy to escort them out," the guard said, blocking them from getting close to her and shooting David a glare over his massive shoulder.

"That won't be necessary," David turned on the charm. "Jenna will see me. Won't you, darling."

"Summer—"

"Summer, is it?" the bastard interrupted again, controlling the conversation. "I'm David Merrick. I heard my ex-wife had a tragic accident. I was in Denver and wanted to stop by and check on her, since I was . . . in the neighborhood, let's say."

David stood stunned, unable to believe she survived out in the cold woods. He shouldn't be surprised. Damn woman was invincible, and he admired her for it. Made the challenge that much more fun. As a child, he'd always tested the limits of everything and everyone around him. He so enjoyed taunting others, making them bend to his will. Jenna's spirit and strength added an extra thrill. She wasn't an easy mark, and he so enjoyed playing with her.

Jenna froze. Her whole body went on alert and adrenaline pumped through her veins. She bolted upright, pulling some of the stitches free, opening one of the gashes on her side. Blood ran down her side. She grabbed Summer and pulled her close to whisper in her ear.

"Go tell Sam to cancel the press release. Hurry. It can't go out now."

"I'm not leaving you alone with him," Summer protested, unconcerned that David overheard.

David's eyes narrowed, letting her know he didn't like people thinking he was responsible for Jenna's injuries. It put a crimp in his public image. She was going to throw a wrench in it if it was the last thing she did.

"Jenna and I have a lot of catching up to do. I haven't seen her in quite some time," he said, trying to add credence to the false alibi he'd already supplied to the police. "I'm sure she'll tell you, we'll be just fine together."

An order, if ever she'd heard one. If she didn't get Summer out of there, David might decide to punish her later for not obeying his request. Teaching her a lesson was David's favorite pastime.

"Summer, David is right. We'll be just fine together. Perhaps you could check with the doctor about my release."

"Jenna?"

"It's okay. You can go. Make sure you see Sam on your way to find the doctor."

Summer didn't want to leave her alone. Jenna tried to make her voice strong, so Summer knew she was all right, even though she was anything but. David had a way of making things happen. If he somehow managed to get her out of the hospital, she'd be dead.

Summer left quickly. The starry-eyed nurse followed her out. More hesitant to leave her alone with David, the guard locked gazes with her, silently asking for her decision for him to stay or go. She nodded her approval for him to resume his post outside the door. Too many witnesses in the hospital for David to do anything drastic. Right?

Jack and Sam were not going to be happy with her for sending the guard out. David gave his lawyer the same type of nod she'd given the guard and he moved outside the door too. Silence settled and they both took a moment to absorb where they were and how they got here.

David moved further into the room, so his back wasn't to the door, yet he could block her attempt at escape easily.

"I see you're doing well."

"Sorry to disappoint you again." Jenna got out of the bed to stand. No way would she look the victim or appear passive.

"You always disappointed me."

"Yes, well, the same is true of you. What happened to you, David? You were such a lovely man when we met. I really thought you were wonderful. You turned into such a monster. Maybe you always were, and I just never saw it."

"You wanted to get your hands on my money and my company. My family tried to warn me. I couldn't see past that lovely face and body, or my own need for you."

"No. I never wanted the money. I wanted you. As stupid as that turned out to be. You have no heart, David.

You're incapable of love, or seeing it when it's given freely to you."

"You don't know what you're talking about. I love you. I love you with such passion that you're all I think about. I can't even work for thinking about you. No one will ever love you like I love you."

"That's not love. That's obsession. Go back to your new wife. End this here and now before I destroy you."

"You? Destroy me?" His laugh turned sinister. "After all these years, you think you can do anything to me. I can find you anywhere you go. That new man of yours just might have an accident, maybe that pretty little girl will turn up missing, or perhaps that nice ranch will burn to the ground. Take your pick. They might all happen if you don't do what I want you to do."

His voice grew louder as his anger built. If she wasn't careful, he just might go into a rage again, unable to control himself, even knowing they were in a hospital with lots of witnesses.

"Threats, with people right outside the door," she warned. "Listen to me. Stop this now, or I will destroy you and everything you hold dear."

He took three long strides toward her so fast, she didn't have time to react before he was standing over her. Squared off, toe-to-toe, the strength she thought spent surged and allowed her to stand her ground.

"You want to end this. Come back to me. That's all I ever wanted. I can't live without you. If you don't, you know what will happen, only this time you have a lot more to lose."

Hard to sound strong when your voice rasped out no louder than a whisper, but she managed. "I'll never come back to you. Not now. Not ever. If you even think about harming one of the people I love, I'll do more than destroy you. I'll kill you. Now get out." She hadn't realized that as she spoke, she'd actually backed him into the wall by the door.

"You'll regret this, Jenna. My lawyer is here so you can sign over the shares. If you do, I'll leave you alone."

"No. You wouldn't leave me alone just for the shares. I know that. I've known that from the beginning. You enjoy hunting and hurting me. You'll keep coming back for more. I won't allow it. I will destroy you, David. You'll see."

She didn't see the slap coming, should have anticipated his instinctive reaction to lash out and hurt. Her head snapped to the side from the blow. She held her ground again.

"You can't threaten me," he said outraged. "There's nothing you can do to hurt me. I'll be seeing you soon."

"You're wrong. I can hurt you, and I will. You'll see. This time, I'm coming for you."

She'd never been able to shake him. The worried look on his face gave her some satisfaction.

David moved toward the door, but stopped in his tracks at her final statement.

"That's the last time you'll ever lay a hand on me, David."

He walked out without looking back.

Jenna's heart pounded against her aching ribs. Despite

the fact she was shaking, it was a powerful feeling to have stood up to him. The guard looked in, she gave him a half-hearted smile to let him know she was okay and he closed the door.

She shuffled back toward the bed, grabbed the phone, and dialed.

"It's Rabbit. I need Ben," she told the receptionist.

Ben came on the line within seconds.

"Rabbit. Please tell me you aren't on the run. I talked to Sam earlier, he said you were putting your plan in action and you were due to die today."

"Not anymore. Make sure the story about my death doesn't go out. David just stopped by for a visit. We can't go with that plan now. He'll know it's a hoax. I need to know if Mike finished my project."

"David was there. He actually came to see you. Did Jack kill him?"

"Jack wasn't here. I spoke to David alone. He threatened me."

"Are you okay? Did he hurt you?"

"Just a parting slap to make me understand he can get to me whenever he wants and it doesn't matter where we are."

"Oh, Rabbit. Are you okay?"

"I'm okay. Did Mike finish my project?"

"Yesterday. After this last incident, we finished the last push to get it done. I have all the papers ready for your signature. We'll turn all the corporations that hide the assets into your name."

"Great. Get on a plane and meet me at the ranch. Bring everything, including my murder book."

"You want me to come to you? I'll actually see you in person?"

"Yes. It's time to end this. Since my death plan didn't work, we need to go back to the original plan. I hate to expose myself like this, but I have no choice. I hope Jack won't mind seeing my pictures splashed across the front pages."

"I get to see you in person." He'd wanted to meet her for a long time. He'd offered so many times to come and get her and protect her from David.

"Ben, keep up here. Get everything ready. Oh, what is the name of that paper I own?"

"It's called—get this—*The Daily Dirt.* I have no idea why you wanted me to buy a rag like that."

"You'll see. Bring the murder book and all the papers. Hire a private jet if you like and get here ASAP. You'll be away from your office a few days. I'll see you at the ranch."

"A jet. Really? Cool."

"Yeah, Lily thought so, too. Hurry up. Get moving. The board of directors meeting is in a few days and we need to get ready. I'm going to San Francisco."

She hung up with Ben completely drained. In too much pain, she didn't have the energy to climb back into the high bed. She put her back to the wall and slid to the floor. With her head against the wall, her legs outstretched, she waited for Jack, Summer, and Sam to come for her. She barely registered the stream of blood running down her side and pooling on the floor.

Chapter Fifty

SAM'S HEAD SNAPPED up as Summer burst into Doctor Weber's office panting. "Where the hell have you two been?" she demanded of him and Jack. "He's here. He's in there with her."

"Who's here?" Sam asked.

"David Merrick. He's with her right now."

Jack and Sam bolted to their feet and ran for the door. Summer stopped Sam. "You need to call off the press release. He won't believe she's dead now, he'll know it's a trick."

"Shit! No wonder the agents helping me haven't been able to find him. He's been here the whole time."

He grabbed the phone and canceled the press release. As Sam issued orders, Summer left the office, running after Jack back to Jenna's room.

JACK BURST PAST the guard and into Jenna's room. The empty bed set off a wildfire of panic through his system, squeezing his heart, nearly stopping it cold. He rushed further into the room and found her sitting against the wall next to the bed. Head back, eyes closed, her whole body trembled.

Relieved beyond measure, he exhaled and the fear washed away. He kneeled in front of her and put his hand to the red outline of David's hand imprinted on her cheek. He bent and kissed it gently.

"Jenna?"

She didn't respond.

"Are you okay?"

"I stood up to him. I told him I'm going to destroy him. He thinks I'm bluffing. I'm not. I will end this. Ben is on his way. Take me home, Jack. I want to go home."

"Come here, I'll help you into bed until we can get you checked out of here."

He helped her stand, noticing for the first time her blood-soaked gown and the blood running down her leg. He didn't panic. He'd seen a lot worse, but he hated seeing her hurt. It did something to his heart that he felt echo through his whole being.

"Jenna, you tore your stitches. You're bleeding."

"Will you fix it?"

"I'll get the doctor to stitch it for you. I'm not poking you with needles anymore. It hurts me too much to do that to you." He cupped her cheek and brushed his thumb across her soft skin.

"I love you. You're so sweet."

"That bastard comes in here, slaps you, threatens you,

and you still try to make me feel better. I'll kill him. And the guard for letting him in."

"I told the guard to leave. As for David, you don't need to kill him. I'm going to take away the one thing he can't live without."

"You already left him."

"Not me. I'm taking the company away from him."

"Can you do that?"

"I couldn't before, but I can now."

"Whatever you need, I'll help you. I know I haven't done a very good job protecting you . . ."

"Jack, stop. Just stop it. You haven't let me down, and none of this is your fault. You're the best thing in my life. If you keep blaming yourself for what's happened, I don't think I can take it. I need you to take care of me. Do that, and I'll be happy."

"I love you so much. When Summer said he was alone with you, I thought I'd lose you forever. I was so afraid he'd take you, and I'd never find you again."

"Don't. Don't think about it anymore. I want to go home, now. We have a lot of things to prepare for, and I want to be with you in our bed tonight."

"I'll get the doctor to stitch you back up."

Summer came barreling through the door. "Jenna, he hurt you," Summer said, disbelieving what her eyes saw. "You're bleeding. I'm so sorry. I shouldn't have left you."

"It's okay. I tore my stitches. Don't feel bad. I made you leave. I couldn't have the press release go out. Did Sam stop it?"

"Yes, I think so. You're okay, really?"

"I will be once Jack gets me home."

"Sis, get the doctor. I'm not leaving Jenna."

Summer left the room just as Sam came rushing in, a pained look on his face. Jenna pointed a finger at him and said, "You did not let me down, so stop thinking that. Did you stop the press release?"

"How did you know what I was thinking?" Sam asked surprised. Jack laughed.

"Because you and Jack are exactly alike. He's feeling guilty, and now so are you. Stop it, both of you. The press release?"

"Canceled. Now what are we going to do?"

"He never makes anything easy," she complained. "Looks like we do things the hard way. It'll be more dangerous, but it's the only way. I'm taking over the company."

"Whatever you want, I'll take care of it," Sam said, and squeezed her foot to reassure himself she was okay.

"We'll make all the arrangements when we're back home. Go away, Sam. Jack's going to kiss me, and I want to be alone with him."

"Kiss me. You'll never know the difference."

"Get out, Sam. She's all mine." Jack wrapped Jenna in his arms and kissed her softly. He held her close and they lost themselves in each other. Jack was the best medicine, and she drowned in a huge dose of his love.

Chapter Fifty-One

JACK STAYED WITH Jenna while the doctor repaired her stitches. She held his hand, eyes locked on him while the doctor worked. Long looks, a touch here, there, a soft kiss. Connected.

Jack helped her get cleaned up and dressed. Summer brought a loose sheath dress and button-up sweater for her to wear. The dress accommodated Jenna's wounds without pressing on her back or ribs. Jack brushed her hair, and while she was enjoying the closeness, he draped something around her neck.

Jenna looked down at the gold chain, her diamond engagement ring hanging from it.

"Your hands are still swollen, but I wanted you to be able to wear your ring. The doctor told me how upset you were when they had to remove it."

"I thought I'd lost it," she said and held the ring up, letting it catch the light and sparkle.

"I'd buy you a dozen more if it meant you were always safe."

"I don't deserve you."

"It's me who doesn't deserve you. But I'm selfish and I'm keeping you."

"I'm keeping you, too. We need to get married soon. I want to wear a nice dress, and since you gave me two wonderful gifts, I don't know how much longer I'll actually fit into a dress. I'll need a tent in another few months."

"You're beautiful now, and you'll still be when you're round carrying my babies. I don't care what you wear as long as you say 'I do'."

"I do." She liked how that sounded. "Take me home. I hate hospitals and Ben will arrive soon."

"Let's go."

JENNA LEANED INTO Jack, his arm wrapped tight around her while she rested against his shoulder with her eyes closed in the back seat of the car. Sam drove and spoke with his friends at the FBI, setting things up for their trip to San Francisco. He'd already increased security at the ranch. He wasn't taking any chances. They'd underestimated David's ability and determination to get to her for the last time.

They arrived at the ranch house. Jack traced lines up and down her forearm with his fingers to get her attention. "Jenna, wake up. We're home."

"That's the best thing you've ever said to me."

"Just wait. I have a surprise for you."

"A surprise? Really?"

She turned from the car and glanced at the front yard for the first time since she and Lily had planted the flowers. Beautiful, the house truly looked like a home. Then the memories of everything that happened came flooding back again. She remembered how close David had come to Lily, how he'd stabbed Sally, and how he'd looked when he came after her. She couldn't take it. She needed time to adjust.

She turned away from Jack and Sam and limped to the barn. She wrapped her hands around her middle and kept her head down as she made her way along the gravel drive, her every step a painful reminder of what David did to her.

"Jenna?" Jack called.

She didn't say anything, just kept walking, trying not to be upset that Sam had three men following behind her. That they were necessary.

"Where's she going?" Sam asked.

"To see Blue. I don't know if bringing her back here was such a good idea. Did you see her face? She couldn't even go inside the house."

"Give her time. Let her get her bearings back. Who is Blue?"

"You'll see. She'll be out in a minute."

Jenna walked out leading Blue by a rope, the three guards following. Blue sidestepped and nearly knocked down one of the men.

"You let her ride that stallion. Are you crazy? He'll kill her."

"Watch. That horse is the meanest sonofabitch I've ever put into that barn. He's bitten just about every ranch hand on the spread. Given a chance, he'll kick the shit out of you."

"And you trust him with your pregnant fiancé?"

"Patience," Jack said and smiled with pride.

Jenna stopped just outside the doors and stood in front of Blue and rubbed a hand down his long nose. He bent his head and rested it between her breasts and down her chest and belly like he did every time she came to see him. She rubbed his ears and his face.

"Oh my God. She just turned that big, giant stallion into a puppy."

Jack's pride swelled. She was amazing. "Just watch, Sam."

Jenna kept rubbing and talking to Blue. Blue raised his head and rested it over Jenna's shoulder and down her back as if giving her a hug. She wrapped her arms around his head and neck. He raised her right off her feet. He put her down gently again. She whispered into his ear and walked to his side. She pulled on the lead rope indicating she wanted him to go down to the ground, and he happily obliged.

Sam watched in astonishment as the stallion literally kneeled on the ground with his front legs and allowed Jenna to mount him. Still very high off the ground, even when kneeling, but Jenna managed as if she'd done it a hundred times. Then she gave him a tap in the side with her heels and the horse stood up.

"Amazing," Sam said. "That horse is in love with her."

"Yes, I know. I hate to admit it, but sometimes I'm jealous."

Jenna turned to Jack and pointed to the pasture, then made a circle motion with her arm. She gave Blue a gentle nudge and they walked to the pasture.

"Where's she going?"

"To take a walk around the field. She needs time to think. Normally, when she's trying to work something out in her head, she'll take off at full speed and let Blue have a good run. She likes the speed and the freedom. Today it will be a nice walk. Her ribs can't take the run. And I imagine she knows it wouldn't be good for the babies. Blue will take care of her, and she'll feel better when she gets back."

Sam raised his hand, indicating the three guards watching Jenna to follow. He indicated, much the same way Jenna had, for them to spread out and circle around the pasture to keep her in site. The pasture beside the barn wasn't that large and the guards took positions like a triangle around her. She and Blue walked in wide circles.

The sun warmed her face. Thanks to the full skirt of her sundress, her legs stayed covered as she rode. Blue read her mood and kept the pace slow and steady. She took in the trees, the grass, and finally the house with the garden out front. She was home.

She returned Blue to the barn and Pete, who would take care of him for her. She walked out of the barn and couldn't help but smile at the two men in the driveway. Identical down to the way they stood, both men leaning over the engine of the Camaro Jenna had given to Jack a few short months ago. She made her way up to them.

"I'm going inside to take a nap before Ben arrives. Will you come with me?"

"Yeah, honey. I still have a surprise for you."

"Oh, God. I forgot. I'm sorry. I needed to—"

"I know," he interrupted and pulled her to him and hugged her. "It's okay. Let's go inside."

Sam slammed the hood of the car and they all walked up the front walkway into the house. As soon as Jenna stepped inside the front door, the quiet and something else hit her. The house didn't feel right.

"Jack, there's something missing." And then she figured out what was bothering her. "She's gone and now the house is empty. I'm sorry. He killed Sally, and it's all my fault," she cried, taking in the empty house.

Jack stood in front of her and cupped her face in his warm hands. "Nothing is your fault. This house could never be empty. It's ours, yours and mine, and soon it'll reverberate with the sounds of babies. This house has a family, our family."

"But Sally. She was more than just a dog to you, to me."

"Come upstairs with me. I have a surprise I think you'll like."

Jack led Jenna to their bedroom door. He pushed the door open and let her go in first. Beautiful. He'd redecorated to reflect them both. Before, the bed had a blue comforter, but now a beautiful amethyst silk quilt accompanied it along with matching pillows. He'd added an antique dresser for her. On top sat a beautiful set of glass perfume bottles and a huge crystal vase full of Stargazer lilies. Their sweet scent filled the room. Between the bed and the large window sat an antique cradle lined in pale green fabric with a small white ruffle.

"Jack, it's beautiful. You didn't have to change the room for me. I liked the way it was, even if it was a little single-guy blue."

"Single-guy blue? That some new weird color name?"

"No," she laughed. "Why did you add purple?"

"Because it's our room, and I wanted you to feel at home. You like to wear purple and it looks good on you. I figured it must be one of your favorite colors, and, well, it went well with my blue."

"It does make a nice compliment."

"You've been scrunched into my closet and small dresser. I thought you might like the antique dresser. The perfume bottles where my great-grandmother's."

"They're beautiful," she said and traced a finger over the delicate crystal. She smelled her favorite jasmine perfume. "It's been a long time since I had something pretty in a room. Most of the time the places I stayed were sparsely decorated, and everything belonged to someone else. Isn't it funny? I have tons of money and hardly any possessions. What little I managed to keep, I sent to my mother."

"Honey, this is your house, too. I thought that, since we are engaged, I'd try to show you this room is ours. It's not just the bed we share, but everything."

"That bed looks really inviting. I'm so tired. You must be too."

"You haven't seen all of your surprise yet. Look inside the cradle."

"It's beautiful. Was it yours when you were a baby?"

"Mine and my brother's, Summer's, and my father's and his siblings and his father's. It's been in the family for several generations. I think it was carved by my great-great-grandfather. There might be one more great in there. Now we'll bring our babies home and they'll sleep in it. I'm beginning to really like all these traditions, now that I have you."

"I can see that. So, what's in the cradle?" She walked past the bed and nearly fell to her knees when she saw Sally sleeping on a dog bed on the floor at the foot of the cradle, her midsection wrapped in bandages.

"Jack, Sally." She covered her mouth to hold back the happy sob of tears. A puppy jumped up in the cradle, large paws dangling over the side. She let out a happy bark.

"There's a puppy in the babies' cradle."

"Sally made a friend at the hospital," Jack joked.

"She's okay."

Sally wagged her tail and raised her head to look at them.

"She will be in a week or so. She needs lots of rest, but she'll be just fine. Like you."

Jenna knelt beside Sally and pat her softly on the head. Jack kneeled behind her and rested his hands on her shoulders.

The puppy let out a bark and pounced back and forth, trying to get their attention. Sally whined, but lay back down.

"So, what do you think? She's four months old and she's already housebroken."

"How did you do all this? You were at the hospital with me."

"Busted," he said and grinned. "Summer helped. I told her what I wanted, and she and Beth took care of the house. Summer picked up Sally this morning and called to tell me about the pup, who needed a home. I wanted something special for you to come home to."

"It's a wonderful surprise. She's so cute."

Jenna scooped up the puppy, who turned into a ball of energy. She licked Jenna's hand and pawed at her as Jenna tried to keep a good hold and not hurt herself in the process.

"I think she needs a name."

"You didn't name her?" she asked.

"I thought you'd like to name her," Jack said, and gave the fur-ball a pet.

"Really?"

"Yes, so what do you think? What are you going to call her?"

"Anything I want?"

"That's kind of a long name for a puppy, but if you want to call her that," he smiled and shrugged.

"Funny. Anything-I-Want sounds like a racehorse, actually."

"She's a golden retriever, not a racehorse. So what's her name?"

The puppy rolled around on the floor, trying to bite Jack's boots. She barked at his feet and pounced again. Bored with the boots' lack of response, she bounded onto the dog bed with Sally, gave her a lick on the nose, plopped down and cuddled up to Sally for a nap.

"I'm thinking. How about Trixie?"

"I like that. Trixie will suit her fine. It's a spunky kind of name, just like her."

Jenna went into Jack's arms. "Thank you, for all of this. It's wonderful."

Jack kissed her softly and tilted her head back, so he could take the kiss deeper. "I'm so glad to have you home." He kissed her cheeks and her forehead and trailed kisses down her neck. "With you wrapped around me, I finally feel whole again."

"I feel the same way. I know it's the middle of the afternoon, but I really need to lie down." Jenna rested her head against his chest. "Will you crawl in bed with me? You must be exhausted. You've hardly slept for days."

"That's the best offer I've had today, but more than I need to sleep, I need a shower and a shave. Why don't you get in and I'll join you in a few, once I'm cleaned up."

"How about I join you for that shower, and then we both get in bed together. You can shave later. I kind of like you all scruffy looking."

"You do, huh?"

"Oh, yeah."

She kissed him again and followed him into the bathroom and a hot shower. Jack helped wash her hair. After drying her with soft strokes, he carried her to the bed, laid her down in the soft sheets and showed her how much he'd missed her. All the emotions he'd held inside, he poured into making slow, sweet love to her. He stroked her softly and kissed her gently. When he entered her it was with slow aching strokes that had him melting into her. He kept his hands gentle on her hips and kissed her with all the passion and love he had in his heart.

The sweetness of the leisurely rhythm relaxed her and made her feel even closer to him. She clung to his shoulders and pressed her hips to his, taking him deeper. She held him inside her and clung to him with her face buried in his neck. She couldn't get any closer to him, yet she tried.

She needed the closeness more than anything. He kept his pace unhurried and rocked his hips harder and deeper into her. Her passion built, her inner muscles squeezed tight, and he increased his speed. He drove home again and again, and they both reached the peak together. He held her close and kissed her long and slow until the flame inside both of them simmered to a smolder. He remained awake, stroking her hair softly until she fell into a dreamless sleep nestled against his chest.

Chapter Fifty-Two

WITH JACK'S ARM draped over her, his palm covering her breast, she woke a few hours later feeling absolutely wonderful. Her future husband's soft breath whispered through her hair, her babies lay nestled in her belly, and her new puppy snuggled in at the foot of the bed. Sally rested comfortably on the floor, alive and well on her way to a full recovery. What more could she ask for?

She didn't want to wake him. He'd had a rough few days searching for her and keeping watch over her in the hospital. She moved his arm to his side and gently pulled her hair out from under his face. He grumbled something under his breath and rolled over and away from her, drifting back into a deep sleep.

Once she stirred, the puppy immediately jumped up and followed her into the closet. Trixie had already chewed through a pair of Jack's sneakers and dragged out one heavy work boot. In addition to his cowboy boots, that made three pairs she'd ruined. Jenna noted all her shoes were intact and patted the puppy on the head, letting her know she was a good girl. Trixie immediately rolled onto her back for a belly rub. Jenna obliged her, and then found an amethyst slip dress to wear. She drew on a cream sweater to cover her shoulders and keep her warm, but it wouldn't hide the bruises around her neck. It didn't matter; between that, the cut above her eye, and her still swollen lip, it was quite obvious she'd been through the ringer. The only good thing, she'd survived and the wounds would heal in time.

The doorbell rang downstairs and, barefoot, she went down to answer. Sam had said he'd be working in the office most of the afternoon, and she wasn't sure if he was still on the phone.

Jenna opened the door to a very handsome man. About the same age as Jack and just as tall, he had brown hair cut short and the warmest brown eyes. He wore gray slacks that fit him well and showed off his trim waist and legs along with a very elegant dark blue cashmere sweater. His appearance signified he might be a businessman or a lawyer. Remembered photographs transformed into the image of the man in front of her.

"Ben?"

"Rabbit." Her name came out on a whoosh of air when she launched herself into his chest and grabbed him around the neck. He dropped his heavy briefcase and held on to her, though not as tight as she held him. "It's okay, Rabbit," he soothed.

"I'm so happy to see you," she said into his neck.

"Let go of my future wife," Jack hollered with a note of teasing and pounded down the stairs behind her. "It's all right, she's fine," he said to the guards standing ominously behind Ben.

Jenna hugged Ben with everything she had. They'd never met in person, but Ben had been the single most important person in her life while she was on the run.

Ben tried to step back, but she held fast. "No, don't let go. I'm not done hugging you. Thank you," she said and held him tighter. "Thank you for everything you ever did for me. Thank you for always talking to me and helping me to survive and stay sane all these years. Thank you for always being there at every possible inconvenient time I called on you. Thank you for being my friend. Thank you, most of all, for sending me to Jack. I love you more than words can say for all you've done."

With each expression of thanks, she'd held him tighter, crying all over him.

"I don't think I've ever been hugged so well, or felt so much love from one person," Ben said and squeezed her, though not enough to hurt her.

He turned his head and whispered in her ear, "You're welcome, Rabbit. I love you, too.

"I wish we could have met years ago. I'm sorry I sent you to Jack. The lucky sonofabitch had to go and steal your heart before I got a shot at capturing it myself."

"And here I thought lawyers were smart," Jack said.

"We're also conniving," Ben added. "I might steal her back."

"Not a chance."

Jenna laughed at their antics. Ben was about to let her go, but she held tight.

"Jenna, honey, at least let him in the door," Jack said with a smile.

Jenna stepped back from him, but kept her hands on his shoulders. "I'm so happy to see you."

"I'm happy to see you, too, Rabbit. Finally. Are you okay?"

"I am now."

"Then stop crying. It kills me when you cry." He wiped the tears from her cheeks with a soft brush of his thumb.

"Jenna, let him come in," Jack said again and put his hands on her shoulders.

"Oh, sorry. Come in. Let's get you settled."

Ben and Jack shook hands.

"You lucky SOB. I knew you'd take care of her if I sent her to you. I never thought you'd keep her."

"Yeah, well, tough shit. You got to hug her, now keep your hands to yourself. She's all mine."

"Yeah, he's already marked his territory," Sam said and walked out of the office. "He put a ring on her finger and knocked her up with twins." Sam grinned, the same cocky grin Jack had on his face.

"Sam!" Jenna scolded, outraged by his audacious comment.

"Well, it's true. Hi, Ben, I'm Jack's brother, Sam. Don't let the resemblance fool you, we're exactly alike."

"We'll get along just fine then. Did I hear you say something about twins?"

The two men shook hands while Jack put his arm

around Jenna and pulled her to his side. "Yeah, she's having identical twins. Imagine that."

"See, he's territorial, too." Sam pointed to Jack and Jenna. "So does she really own controlling interest in Merrick International?" Sam asked bluntly. "I want to make sure everything is in place in order to carry out Jenna's plan. I don't want to walk into a hornet's nest only to find out we don't have what we need to take down David."

"She does. Jenna, Mike finished the transactions. Between your personal assets and all the corporations both false and real, you now hold the majority share of Merrick."

"Excellent. Did you contact Cameron Shaw and request a meeting?"

"The meeting is set. He's very interested in what you have to say."

"I'll bet he is. I'm about to make his dreams come true."

"You'll fill us in on the whole plan? You have controlling interest, what are you going to do with it?" Sam asked.

"That's a very good question. I'll answer it after Ben and I do some business and we all have a nice family dinner together. I've asked Beth to prepare a lovely family meal of fried chicken and mashed potatoes with all the fixings."

"That sounds much better than airline food," Ben said, unable to take his eyes off her. Her injuries were more devastating to see in person, and Jenna hated to finally meet Ben, only to have him see her looking like this.

"Okay, where do you want to do this? You have about sixty companies to take back and put into your name. You'll have carpel tunnel syndrome by the time you finish signing all these papers."

"Fifty-eight companies. Let's go into Jack's office and get started. Jack and Sam, we'll see you guys in a little while for dinner."

"Come here, honey." Jack pulled her into his arms and gently wrapped them around her. Looking down into her eyes, he asked, "Are you sure you want to do this? You're poking at a sleeping lion. Poke too hard and he'll bite."

"I thought you wanted me to end this."

"I do. I don't want you to get hurt anymore. If you do this, he'll come after you. I don't want to lose you."

"Trust me. We'll work out a plan for what will happen after I go to the board meeting. *We* will end this. Together."

She put her hands on either side of his face and brought him down to her for a kiss, gentle and loving, promising everything.

"Do they put you through this often, Sam?" Ben asked.

Sam smiled and grumbled, "Yeah. They're in love. It's really starting to get on my nerves."

Chapter Fifty-Three

THEY ENTERED THE office, cozy with an overabundance of books lining the walls, a leather sofa with soft suede pillows in blue, of course, and wood tables with crystal lamps. It invited you to sit and read, or simply enjoy the peaceful setting. She wanted to put all this business behind her, curl up on the sofa, read a good book by the light of a fire in the corner river-rock fireplace.

"Are you sure you want to do this now? We can keep the bodyguards and protect you around the clock until you're feeling better. I don't need to change the companies into your name just yet. We can wait."

"It has to be now, Ben. The board is due to meet. David won't expect me to attend. Not after what happened. We need the element of surprise on our side."

To prove how ready she was to end this, she took the seat behind the desk and held out her hand for Ben to pass her the papers. She scrawled her name next to every tab, indicating "Sign Here". She reviewed each one, noting the name of the company and the transfer of the name back into her own, then signed—one step closer to destroying her nightmare for good.

"So what's the plan for the board meeting?"

"It's going to be explosive, I can tell you that. The Merricks are very arrogant. They set up the board and the rules that govern them, so whoever holds majority share, namely them, controls the company and the board.

"I was never able to fight David. Physically, he's stronger than I am. As you can see by my appearance, he always wins that fight. He won't give up trying to get me back, even though he's married. He says the family forced the marriage because the woman comes from a good family and has a lot of money."

"She does," Ben confirmed. "The Merricks have gone through a lot of their liquid funds. Most of their money is tied up in the company. They got wind a few weeks ago someone's buying up shares. They've tried to maintain their majority share by buying more stock themselves. I don't think they suspect what's going on, as the shares we bought have been spread out over time and all these companies, but they're suspicious."

"I'm sure they won't be relieved when they find out there's a takeover about to happen, and it's coming from within the company."

"So how does Cameron Shaw play into your plan? He holds a seat on the board and is president of Ortel, Inc., but why do you want to meet with him?"

"Because I'm making him president of Merrick International. I'll maintain my seat as CEO, but he'll run the company. I'll give him power to do what he's done for Ortel, but on a much larger scale. It's the deal of a lifetime for him. He's good, and I have no doubt he'll make Merrick even better than it is now. He's been trying to get the Merricks to make some strategic changes that could have made the company millions upon millions over the past several years, but they constantly vetoed him. Now I'm giving him the opportunity he wants and deserves. He'll be a very rich man, and I'm going to have babies and reap the rewards."

"You have it all thought out then."

"Not everything. The board is easy. David will be unpredictable. His volatile temper is not something I look forward to facing again. His parents will put up a fuss, but they don't actually work for Merrick. David's grandfather plans to retire and turn the company over to David. I hope he'll see this as the better alternative. He's a shrewd businessman. He'll realize Cameron will make him a lot of money. Still, it won't be a Merrick in charge, and that will piss him off. David, on the other hand, will go off the deep end. I expect he'll come after me."

"What's your plan to handle David?"

"I'll ruin him professionally at Merrick, and then personally in the press. He's gotten away with hurting me for too long. Everyone will know what he's done. I may not have gotten the police to do something to help me over the years, but now the world will know."

"Is that why you wanted the book?"

"Yes. Do you have it?"

"It's right here in my briefcase. Are you sure you want to look at it? It's filled with a lot of bad memories. You've just been through the latest nightmare, and I don't think it's a good idea to compound that by reliving all the others, too."

"Give it to me, Ben."

"Please, don't put yourself through this."

"Did you bring the name of the man who runs my paper?"

"I have it."

"Good, I'll need that, too."

"You aren't publishing the book," Ben stated unequivocally, concerned. "You can't. Think about Jack."

"Jack will understand I have to do this. It's the only way. Taking Merrick away from David will be a big blow. This will be an explosion. Do you think it's wrong for me to want to ruin him?"

Sad and contemplative, he answered truthfully, "It isn't your nature to destroy, but to help. You've helped me with my charity projects and strangers. This is the only way you can help yourself. I know you well enough to say, it kills you to do it by destroying a person, even one as evil as David.

"Having said that, I think it's about time he gets what he deserves. He's used his money and power to do the things he's done to you. Taking that away and going public with the abuse is the only way to really pay him back and put an end to this. You're right, there's no other way. Besides, I'm tired of going up against his dirty lawyers and losing."

Jenna reached across the desk and took Ben's hand, squeezing it to let him know she appreciated his support.

"Will you ask Sam to come in here? I have to set up a few things with him. Catch up with Jack. Have a drink, and we'll all have dinner together."

Ben came around the desk and pulled her up from her seat. The bandages on her wrists peaked out from beneath her sweater. "It makes me sick to see you hurt. Even worse to look into your eyes and know I didn't stop the sadness and heartbreak you've suffered. I'll help you any way I can to stop it now, for good."

He kissed her forehead above the cut over her eye. "I'm sorry I didn't do more to protect you."

"You did everything you could. We both know that. Now we'll end it together."

"Yes, we will. I'll get Sam."

She waited in the office, picking up the book, which was actually a three-inch leather binder filled to capacity, and held it to her chest. The pages contained every photograph she'd ever taken of herself after David attacked her. It had an accounting in her words of each incident and the few medical records she'd managed to keep. Notes he'd written to her. Some flowery and sweet with an undertone of demand. Others threatened and terrorized, promising retribution. The record of the last two plus years of her life. Her murder book.

She didn't need to open it to remember what happened. She simply closed her eyes and saw each one, heard David's ominous voice cruelly cutting her down. David never spent a single day in jail for any of it. She vowed there wouldn't be another incident to put into the book.

Sam walked into the office, dragging Jenna out of her dark thoughts.

"You wanted to see me?" he asked gently.

"Sam. I need you to do me several favors. If you say no, I'll understand."

"Name it. Anything for family."

She rested her hand protectively on the book afraid to let anyone see it, knowing she didn't have a choice. "This is my murder book. I want you to contact this man at the paper I own and tell him to print my story. The story I want you to put together should consist of some of these photos and notes and an overview of what happened to me since I married David. Every detail is in this book."

She handed him the business card for the paper and waited for his response.

"I can do that, but are you sure? The press will hound you for more details and interviews."

He reached out to take the book from her, but she wasn't ready to let it go and he pulled his hand away.

"I know I'm putting myself into the public eye by doing this. It's a sensational story. That's why I trust you to put together something that will tell the story accurately. I want people to know who David Merrick really is, not just the most eligible bachelor who goes out with starlets and lives the rich life. I want them to see the monster hiding behind the elegant facade."

"I'll make sure everyone knows. What else? You're holding something back."

"I want you to promise me Jack will never see this book."

"I promise you, Jenna, I won't let him see it. Even if he did, he wouldn't feel any different about you. He loves you."

"I know he does, but if he sees this, it'll kill him. He's seen, twice now, what David has done to me. I don't want him to see all the ways David's tortured me over the years. This book should never have existed. I should have put a stop to this when I divorced David. I wish I had been able to. Promise me you'll use only what is absolutely necessary, and you'll return this to Ben, so he can lock it away again."

"I promise. I'll do exactly what you ask, but Jack will see the papers."

"I know. I also know you'll do your best not to hurt me, or him, with what you choose to have published."

"You have my word. What else?"

They sat in the office a long while talking about their plans for San Francisco and the board meeting. Then they planned for what they knew would happen afterwards. She was trusting Sam with her life.

She'd been married to David and had years to plan her revenge. She'd planned well.

Chapter Fifty-Four

DAVID STOOD IN the moonlit room, staring down at the wrong woman sleeping in his bed. Despite her protests, he'd exhausted her with his ferocious lovemaking, punishing her in his own way for taking a place in his life that he'd given Jenna even before they'd said their vows. Vows he considered sacred and unbreakable. A promise he might have spoken twice, but only held credence the first time. After all, you only had one soul mate.

Patricia was nothing more than a placeholder. She served a purpose. At times, she was even a pleasant distraction. Like tonight.

His family thought he'd moved on, forgotten about Jenna and his love for her. Never.

David entered his study and sat behind his desk. He pulled the left side drawer open and took out the framed photo of him and Jenna on their wedding day. She smiled brightly up at him and he traced a finger over her lovely face.

"You're so beautiful. We were so happy."

He thought of the last time he'd seen her. Not so pretty after she'd shot off her mouth and made him put her in her place. Still, her strength and determination shined when she threatened to destroy him. He had to admit, her conviction gave him pause. He dismissed the threat then and now. He was David Merrick. No one could touch him. No one said no to him. She knew that. Perhaps she needed reminding. Again.

He knew just where to find her this time. No way would she leave her new protector, that stupid rancher. A smile spread across his face as he planned his next move.

JENNA BRUSHED DOWN Blue, trying not to think about
the board meeting tomorrow. Jack, Sam, and she would
fly to San Francisco in the morning. The more her mind
tried to predict the events and outcome, the more her
nerves built.

She'd asked Ben to return to Chicago. She hated to
do it, but he had other business. She wanted to keep his
involvement a secret from David. She couldn't afford for
David to take away her protector if things went terribly
wrong tomorrow.

Sam had David under constant FBI surveillance since
his return to San Francisco with his new wife. As far
as Jenna knew, David remained unaware someone was
watching his every move.

Sam spent most of the last two days coordinating security needed for the trip and on the ranch. He'd hired
a couple of bodyguards, and with Jenna's help, he'd sent

Caleb, Summer, and Lily on vacation to Hawaii, just what their family needed before the new baby arrived. It would also keep them out of harm's way if David decided to come after Jenna after the board meeting.

A private jet would fly her, Jack, Sam and their security team to San Francisco and back to Colorado the same day. Best not to make herself an easy target by staying overnight in San Francisco.

Jack was nervous about the trip, afraid for Jenna and the babies. He didn't like having Jenna anywhere near David. He'd been so sweet to her over the last two nights. They would lie in bed and talk about what it was going to be like when the babies arrived. They came up with names and changed them several times. They speculated about whether the babies would be girls or boys, would they look like Jenna or Jack, and what would they be when they grew up.

Dreaming about the future with Jack was far simpler to think about than what might happen in San Francisco. She knew all the possibilities. She, Jack, and Sam went over all the what-ifs and maybes and planned for any and all contingencies.

Tomorrow everything would change. Once the plan was set in motion, there would be no turning back.

She brushed and stroked Blue with the curry comb. Her body healing slowly, the stitches still itched and pulled, but she would get them out in a week. The bruises on her back were beginning to fade and brushing Blue helped work out the knots. The injuries and abrasions around her neck were still too difficult to look at, a sick reminder of how close she'd come to being killed. Her voice grew stronger. Each day she talked a little bit better. She'd been quiet as much as possible, so her voice would be strong when she addressed the board.

She grabbed a brush and stroked Blue's neck. He nudged her with his big head wanting more. Caught up rubbing down Blue, she didn't hear Jack come in behind her. He put his hands on her shoulders and gave her a squeeze. Jenna jumped and almost lost her footing. Ever protective, Jack steadied her by wrapping his arms around her and drawing her back to his chest.

His voice came out low and husky at her ear. "It's me. Leave my horse alone and come to bed with me."

She leaned into him, savored his warmth and strength wrapped around her. "You scared me. I'm all wound up about tomorrow. I thought a little exercise would help me sleep."

Blue shifted and nudged Jack's shoulder.

"I think your horse is jealous." Jenna gave Jack a sweet smile over her shoulder.

"Yeah, well he can join the club. So far, Sam and Ben fit into that category, too. They both think I don't deserve you. I'm sure they're plotting to steal you away from me."

"No way," she said, astonished and embarrassed. She turned in his arms and placed her hands on his chest.

"Sam's convinced he can get you to leave with him. He doesn't even mind the babies are mine, because, well, technically we have the same DNA, so no one can prove they aren't his."

"Good lord. Is this what you guys talk about while you're watching ball games and drinking beer?"

"Nah, mostly he and Ben talk about how they'll get rid of me and hide my body."

"Stop it. That's not funny. Besides, that'd be hard to do these days with all the guards. Three are watching us right now."

"Not us, you. They're plotting how they can get rid of me and still keep an eye on you at the same time."

"All right, that's enough. Take me to bed and claim me as yours."

"I've already done that, it doesn't seem to convince anyone. They still want you for their own."

"Enough, Jack." She couldn't help smiling and laughing with him. Blue gave her a nudge as she passed him. She came to his head and stood in front. He bowed to her chest and she kissed him on the forehead.

"Goodnight, Blue."

"Sam's right, you've turned this mean beast into a puppy. Speaking of puppies, have you seen what Trixie did to my shoes? I don't think I have a pair left that she hasn't sank her teeth into."

"That's not true. I put several pairs on the shelf in the closet. She's going through a phase. She'll grow out of it. Where is she?"

"Locked in the kitchen, gnawing a bone, indulging her chewing fixation. Sally made it down the stairs on her own. She's working on a bone of her own."

"She's getting better every day," Jenna said, thankful for small blessings.

They walked back to the house, three guards following behind them. She tried not to resent them.

Jack held her hand and she took pleasure in that small kindness. Jack showed her she was loved. He did it in the smallest of ways, but they never failed to pass without her noticing or touching her heart.

Jenna headed upstairs to their room and Jack let Trixie and Sally out of the kitchen. She changed into a soft pink silk nightgown and sat on the bed. Jack, Sally, and Trixie came into the room.

"I'm nervous about tomorrow," she confessed. "I don't know if I can confront him. I don't know if I can stand there and not be afraid. At the same time I need to be strong and powerful and take over a company. Oh, God. I'm taking over an entire company. Why did I think I could do that?"

"Because you can. You are strong. You'll go in there and show him he can't hurt you anymore. You'll make him pay for everything he's done."

"It's just that, now that it's time to do it, I'm nervous."

Jack stood in front of her while she put her arms around his thighs and rested her head on his stomach. He brushed his hands through her hair. Careful not to touch the stitched wound, he found the latch to the necklace he'd given her to hold the engagement ring and unclasped it.

"Your hands aren't swollen anymore. Let's see if this ring will fit again."

He kneeled in front of her and slid the ring back onto her hand. It sparkled in the light from the bedside table. He kissed her fingers, sealing it in place. "Will you marry me?"

"Oh, Jack. Yes, I will marry you. I don't know what I did to deserve you. I hope this ring never leaves my hand again."

"Me too."

Jack pulled a small velvet box out of his jean's pocket. "I bought you a good luck gift for tomorrow."

He opened the box. Inside lay a gorgeous green heart-shaped stone. Jack slipped it onto the necklace, held it up, and it sparkled as it caught the light.

"I saw this and thought of your eyes. It's a green amethyst."

"It's beautiful. I've never seen a green amethyst. You shouldn't have done this."

"When I saw you in the diner the first day we met, your eyes amazed me. I think I fell in love with you then. Now when I look in your eyes, I see the promise of the future we'll have together. Some of the sadness is gone. I hope once all of this is over, I'll see happiness in them every day."

"You make me very happy, Jack. You've given me my life back and so much more. You've given me a family. I haven't had that in a long time."

He bent and kissed her gently and clasped the necklace around her neck. He leaned back, looking into her eyes, the same shade of green as the stone. How had he gotten so lucky as to have this woman in his life? How'd he manage to get her to love him so much?

He kissed her again softly. When she buried her

hands in his hair and pulled him close, he deepened the kiss. His arms found their way around her. As he stood, he picked her up and slid her further onto the bed. Still locked in the kiss, he slid his hands down her body awakening every nerve. He trailed kisses over her face as his hand found her breast and gently kneaded. His fingertips found her already aroused nipple and traced its shape. Her intake of breath spurred him forward as he ran kisses down her neck to the valley between her breasts.

Completely overwhelmed by Jack's attention to every part of her body, she arched into his every touch. His warm hands smoothed over her silk nightgown from her breast to her thigh. He gripped the hem and slid the nightgown up and over her head. Naked under him, his hands and mouth continued to heat her skin.

She grabbed his shirt at his back and pulled it up over his head. His chest rested against her breasts and the feel of his strong muscles and warm skin sent her into oblivion. She stroked her hands over the muscles of his back and up into his hair where she brought his mouth back to hers for another deep kiss. Their tongues smoothed over each other as their passion built, and she lost herself in the feel of Jack, the taste, the warmth, his love.

His mouth and tongue made a trail of kisses down her neck to her breast, made even more sensitive due to the pregnancy. With each kiss and stroke of his tongue she came more and more unglued. She arched into him and dug her fingers into his thick hair, holding him to her.

Her nails dug into his shoulders. Every moan he brought out in her made him feel powerful, masterful. He rubbed and caressed her body and trailed kisses down her stomach. His hands had a mind of their own, seeking every sweet spot on her body. He kissed a path down her stomach across her hips and thighs and once his mouth found her center and his fingers moved over her heat she exploded from the fire he'd built inside of her. His fingers continued stroking along with his tongue, and when he found the sensitive little nub, he licked softly and sent her higher. Just when she was ready to fall over the crest again, he thrust his finger deep, leaning over her, he swallowed her groan with a deep kiss.

While they were lost in the kiss, Jack managed to get his jeans off and settle between her thighs. His throbbing erection pushed against her opening and she wrapped her legs around his waist. When he didn't come to her fast enough, she used her legs to pull him into her. Buried to the hilt, he groaned, pulled back and thrust deep again. They moved in a slow and steady rhythm. He sensed she needed the closeness, so he wrapped his arms around her and held her tight.

She moved her hips up to meet him, taking him deep. He moved his hand down her back and grabbed her bottom and pulled her up to him, increasing the pace. When she crashed over the edge, her body tightening around him like a fist, he followed her over with one last flex of his body and a deep, satisfied groan.

Spent, he lay on top of her breathing heavily into her hair. He held her close, cocooned in his warmth, mindful of the amount of his weight he put on her and where. She felt so good pressed underneath him.

"You're squishing me and the babies."

He rolled onto his side and gently took her with him. They lay facing each other still linked together in a tangle of arms and legs.

"I'm sorry, honey. Are you okay? I didn't hurt you, or them?" He couldn't believe his babies were inside of her. He was going to be a father. The enormity of that hit him at odd times.

"We're all fine. That was wonderful, Jack. I've never felt better." She nuzzled his neck and gave him a love bite. "My nervousness is gone, it's hard to feel anything but warmth and love when I'm close to you."

"You feel good to me. Your belly is already starting to swell from the babies."

"Did you just call me fat?"

"You're beautiful. I can't believe two babies are growing in there."

"I don't know how beautiful you'll think I am when I'm as big as a house, and you can't even get your arms around me in a few months."

"I can't wait to see you all round. You'll be beautiful even then. I think it's a wonder you're having my twins."

"You won't be saying that when I'm swearing at you in the delivery room."

"Swear at me all you want, so long as you and the babies are healthy after the delivery. I'll pass out cigars."

"You're ecstatic about these babies, aren't you?"

"I couldn't be happier. *Soon*, we'll be married. Nothing but happiness from now on."

"I can't wait to marry you. Once we're back from San

Francisco, I hope we can concentrate on planning the wedding and put all of the bad behind us."

"We will. You'll see. It'll all work out in the end, because you're taking back your life tomorrow. I'll be right there to back you up."

"This nightmare will end tomorrow. Nothing and no one will get in the way of our future happiness again."

Chapter Fifty-Six

THE JET SAT in front of a large airplane hangar at the
San Francisco airport. Jenna paced the length, waiting
for Cameron Shaw to arrive for their meeting before they
went to the Merrick International offices. In addition to
the flight crew, Jack, Sam, and five bodyguards accompanied them to San Francisco. Tension filled the air on
board the long flight.

The pendant Jack gave her rested in the V of her dark
green Armani suit jacket. She thought it the perfect
touch. The diamond earrings she'd bought on her shopping trip with Summer and Lily sparkled at her ears, and
her engagement ring was the perfect complement to any
outfit. She also knew it would drive David insane to see
her wearing another man's ring.

She wore her hair up in a chignon and had worn a
light touch of make-up. The cut above her eye was healing and with the make-up it wasn't that noticeable. The

collar of the jacket covered most of the bruising around her neck, but you could still see it at her throat. She hoped the large green amethyst would attract people's attention and not the bruises. Wishful thinking.

Rehearsing her speech in her head, Jack's soothing voice broke into her thoughts. "Honey, he's here. The limo just pulled up. I thought maybe you'd need a minute to get ready."

"I'm ready, Jack. If you'll let him in, and then give us some time, I'd appreciate it."

"Whatever you need, I'm here. This is the easy part. I hope Cameron comes through for you."

"He will. He has to. Otherwise, I'll end up running a company I don't even want."

Jack gave her a smile and a quick hug for support. A minute later, he showed Cameron onto the jet. Jenna waited in front of a small table near the rear of the plane.

"Thanks, Jack." She winked before he turned and left her with Cameron.

"Thank you for meeting me, Cameron." She shook his offered hand. "I know it's a little cloak and dagger bringing you here in secret, but it was necessary. Can I get you anything?"

"I'm fine, thanks. I am curious why you asked to meet. Ben said something about an offer I couldn't refuse. I found that intriguing, since we've never met, even though we serve on the same board. I've often wondered why you never attend any of the meetings in person. Your insights into business and making deals are quite astounding. I enjoy watching the Merricks' faces when your points or ideas go against them."

She was a beautiful woman, distracting. To say her request to meet intrigued him wasn't giving justice to his curiosity. She'd been married to David Merrick and the marriage ended in scandal. He wondered if there was any grain of truth to the gossip, or if the press put a spin on things.

She kept well-informed about the company. When she voted it was always in favor of whatever was good for business, and not necessarily what the Merrick clan wanted. She wasn't afraid to use her vote to go against them, as he'd done countless times.

Her keen business sense interested him. A very successful businessman, he could read most people easily. She was anything but easy to read. He noted the bruises on her neck, the cut above her eye, and the way her voice wasn't quite the sultry sound he usually heard on conference calls. He wondered what happened to her.

"Let's sit. What I have to tell you is difficult to reveal, but it'll all come out today in the papers and at the board meeting. I want to prepare you for what's to come."

"Will you meet with the other board members, or is this courtesy reserved for me?"

"Just you. See, once I tell you my story, I'm going to make you an offer I hope you won't refuse."

"All right. Let's hear the story so we can get to the offer. You've made the anticipation more than I can take. I don't get many offers from beautiful women, and I find myself quite enjoying the anticipation."

She couldn't help but laugh. Cameron was one of the most handsome men she'd ever seen. Women probably threw themselves at him on a regular basis. It was a wonder there weren't women beating down the jet door to get to him. His smile hinted at mischief, but under the surface he too seemed sad. She wondered about that, but let it pass.

Dark hair, cut short, of course, for the business world he moved in set off his shrewd silver-blue eyes. His tanned and lean frame told her he spent time outdoors. Not one to spend his life stuck in his office. Tall, maybe six-two, his broad shoulders and strong thighs couldn't be hidden behind the cut of his well-tailored suit. He had great hands, strong with long fingers.

"I'm sure plenty of women try to snag you—often. However, I like your get-to-the-point attitude. I've found over the years that you have a great head for business and an even better sense of future trends. You've made quite a name for yourself running Ortel. I hope you'll find my offer will further your career ambitions and ultimately benefit both of us."

"Go on. So far you have my attention."

"Let's start with why I haven't been to any of those board meetings. You know, of course, that I was married to David and the marriage ended very badly. That part came out in the press. What no one knows is the divorce came about after a particularly bad incident where David threw me down the stairs, and I lost my baby."

"My God. I'm so sorry. I remember the stories in the papers. Sounds like you made David pay for being a bastard. You got half of his share of the company and a large cash settlement as I recall."

"That's right. What you don't know, what nobody knows, is that for the last few years David has been hunting me all over the country, despite all my efforts to remain hidden. When he finds me, he terrorizes me and sometimes inflicts as much pain as possible before returning to his plush life here in San Francisco." She pulled the collar of her jacket back to reveal even more of the bruises around her neck.

"I'm guessing that's not all he's done to you, not to mention the psychological damage he's inflicted." Cameron fisted his hands until his knuckles shone white. Jenna relaxed, confident he didn't believe in hurting women.

"You're right on both counts. This last attack included a concussion, stab wounds, and other bruises." She pointed to her throat. "He won't stop, so I'm here to make him stop, once and for all. He is going to pay for what he's done. I'm going to take away his life, like he took away mine."

"That explains the muscle you brought with you. Several large men blocked the entrance to this plane. One gave me a very thorough pat down."

"It's extremely dangerous for me to be here. If David manages to get to me again, I have no doubt he'll kill me this time. He is mentally unbalanced, completely out of his mind when it comes to me."

"So what are you going to do? Why are you here now?"

"This afternoon, this paper is coming out."

Cameron scanned the photos of her over the years

and all the attacks. His stomach soured just looking at them, knowing she sat before him in the same shape as some of the pictures. Overwhelmed with sympathy, he read the article. How could she have survived all these years and still be sitting in front of him the confident woman he saw? He admired her for her business sense over the years, but now he respected her for the strength and perseverance she'd used to survive. He couldn't help but think of his small daughter, Emma.

"You're going to ruin David in the press? What does that have to do with me?"

"This is just the icing on the cake. The main course I'm serving at the board meeting."

"And just what will you be serving?"

"Pink slips."

Leaning forward, her arms on the table, she went on. "In a nutshell, I took the money I got in the divorce and invested it in what a lot of people would have considered risky companies. Seems I have a knack for picking companies that explode with growth, and I've made millions in returns. I took those millions and bought shares in Merrick International. Under the various names of those companies, of course."

He sat still and continued to listen. He believed he was getting the picture of what she'd done.

"I now hold controlling interest in Merrick International."

He knew it. "I see."

Smiling, she said, "That's it? You must be a very good poker player. You don't give anything away."

"It's wise to listen and know all the facts before speaking and inserting your foot in your mouth. So you're taking over the entire company and squeezing David out. Charles has, essentially, increasingly let him run things and plans to retire at the end of the year. We both know David's parents don't really make any business decisions, so they'll only object to your taking over because you aren't a Merrick anymore."

"Exactly. At today's meeting, I'll reveal I've gained controlling interest and assume control."

"That's great as far as I'm concerned. You seem to have made quite a lot of money over the last several years. I won't mind making more with you running things. You and I usually vote the same way on most deals and acquisitions, so I imagine we'll have no problem working together. Is that why you wanted to have this meeting? So we could solidify a working relationship?"

"No. Now, what kind of offer would that be? I told you, I had an offer you couldn't refuse."

"You're enjoying this, aren't you? I like that about you. You get the same kind of thrill I get when a deal goes particularly well. So let's see your cards. Lay it on me. What's the deal?"

"I want to make you president of Merrick International. I'll maintain the CEO position that comes with controlling interest, but you'll run Merrick."

He closed his open mouth and took a second to absorb the surprise. "Are you kidding? You've done all this and you don't even want to run the company. You obviously have the ability to do it. Why wouldn't you?"

"I only did this to make David pay. Revenge isn't very pretty, but it is sweet."

She smiled. It was hard not to. With Cameron sitting in front of her impressed with her accomplishment, it was hard not to feel her success. "David took away everything from me. I've finally found someone to spend my life with, who loves me and treats me like I deserve to be treated. I want to have a life with him. I'm pregnant with twins. I'm going to be a mother and a wife, and that suits me just fine."

"David did that to you," he pointed to her throat, "and you're pregnant?"

"He doesn't know about the pregnancy, not that it would have stopped him. So, will you accept my offer and take over Merrick for me? I'll keep my hand in the business and vote on the board, but essentially, you'll have the power to run the company as you see fit. I promise to try to keep my nose out of things as much as possible."

"It's quite an offer, but I run Ortel."

"Ortel is small beans compared to Merrick. I don't say that to insult you. But heading Merrick would give you the opportunity to work your magic at a bigger international level.

"You took a fledgling company and grew it into a very competitive organization. I imagine letting someone else take over is difficult, but not impossible. Running Merrick would be a coup. You'd be one of the youngest presidents to run a company the size and scope of Merrick International. This is a dream job for someone in your position, and I'm handing it to you. You'd be crazy to pass up this opportunity," she finished.

Ortel was his baby, but she was right. He couldn't pass this up, despite the fact it would be detrimental to his personal life and what little time he had with his daughter. A pang of guilt gripped his heart when he thought about Emma. He wanted so much to give her a good life.

"You have a deal. I'll run Merrick's day-to-day operations, but I want you involved even if it's just a weekly conference call. Anyone who can take over the company the way you have deserves my respect and admiration. I'd be a fool to let you step back completely and not use your uncanny sense of trends and business savvy. No way I'm letting that asset go to waste."

She had to admit, talking to Cameron put a lot of things into perspective. She really thought the two of them could run the company together. In fact, she was excited about it.

"Deal. We'll work together, but it will have to be long distance. I want to live in Colorado on the ranch with Jack and the babies. I won't give that up. But I will meet you halfway. I'll fly into San Francisco when necessary, but never for more than a day or two."

"Great. We'll work out all the details later. If I understand what you have planned for the board meeting, we'll also need to restructure the top levels of the company. I have a few people in mind for some key positions. We can discuss this at a later date."

"We'll do it by phone and webcam. Once we're finished today, I'm getting back on this plane and going home. Unfortunately, David may have other ideas. Sam and I have a plan to deal with him. I only hope it works."

"With your security, David can't get close to you, unless you want him to."

"Exactly."

Cameron frowned, not understanding her cryptic answer. She was about to explain, but Jack and Sam headed toward them, looking grim.

"It's time to go. The board meets in an hour and we don't want to be late." Jack gave Cameron the once-over. "Did you two come to an agreement?"

"We're all set. Stop glaring at Cameron. He was a perfect gentleman. Don't worry, Cameron, he's jealous of his horse, too."

"I am not." Jack's smile said otherwise.

"Are too. It's cute though. Let's go."

Time to face her past and take back her future.

Chapter Fifty-Seven

JENNA'S MEETING WITH Cameron went so well, her confidence soared. The limo took them down the crowded
city streets, followed by another car full of her security
people. She stared out the window at the people and
buildings while Jack, Sam, and Cameron talked about . . .
Well, she didn't know what they were talking about. Her
thoughts were on the upcoming board meeting and the
possibilities of what might happen.

Jack held her hand. Even though the guys carried on
with their conversation, they remained focused on her.
Even Cameron understood the stakes, and that she was,
essentially, walking into the lion's den.

They arrived in front of the Merrick International
building and stepped out. What a sight they made. Three
of the most handsome men around, dressed in their best
suits, and her in her finest business attire flanked by five
other large men, who despite their suits couldn't be mis-

taken for anything but bodyguards. They drew everyone's attention in the lobby of the building as Cameron led the way to the elevators to take them up to the conference room on the thirty-sixth floor.

Nervous, her palms were sweating. Jack still held her hand and leaned in to say, "You'll do fine. He can't hurt you. Go in there and do what you came to do. Sam and I have your back."

The elevator doors opened and Jack released her hand. They exited the elevator and headed to the conference room door. He understood she needed to stand on her own. She entered, Sam and Jack right behind her. Cameron followed along with the five bodyguards, who spread out around the room. Jenna headed to the large table and looked at the other occupants already assembled.

Charles Merrick, Nathan and Marion Merrick, and the other two members of the board appeared surprised to see her. She settled her gaze last on David, seated to Charles's left at the head of the table, his parents on the right. She noted his furious expression. Mr. Jamison and Mr. Richards were seated beside David's parents. Cameron took the seat next to David, watching him with a predatory glare.

Jenna stood at the head of the table at the opposite end from Charles waiting a moment to gather her strength. Jack and Sam sat in the chairs behind her against the wall. As she continued to stare at David steam, Charles broke the silence that ensued once she walked into the room.

"Good afternoon, Jenna. We weren't expecting you.

It's a pleasure to see you. I'm happy you've decided to actually attend the board meeting, instead of simply calling in."

"It's nice to see you, too, though I doubt you'll think it's such a good afternoon when you find out why I've come today, Charles."

She'd always liked him. A shrewd businessman, he believed in hard work and an honest living. He'd never approved of David's personal life, but stayed out of it so as not to draw David's temper. He hadn't liked the fact Jenna won part of the company in the divorce settlement, but he hadn't approved of David's treatment of her either. Married for over forty years to his beloved wife before she died of a heart attack, Jenna knew he still missed her, even after her death more than ten years ago. She didn't want to hurt him, but she couldn't allow David to run the company when he retired.

"What the hell are you doing here? I thought you were in the hospital," David seethed.

"I'm sure you did. How's your new wife. Still alive and in one piece, I hope."

"You bitch!" He stood and slammed his hands on the table. Every one of the guards tensed. Jack and Sam stepped forward ominously. David fell back into his chair.

"Shut up," she snapped. "I'm not putting up with you anymore. I warned you in Colorado to leave me alone, or suffer the consequences. I'm here to deliver the consequences."

"Jenna, we have business to discuss. I'm sure you can deal with your personal issues with David after the meeting, which I'll remind you is not open to anyone but board members. I'd appreciate it if you'd ask these men to leave the room, while we conduct that business."

"Charles, respectfully, I'm sorry, but I can't do that. These men are here to protect me."

"Protect you from whom? Nobody here will harm you. It's simply a business meeting."

"No, Charles, this isn't just any business meeting. I'm sure you remember the circumstances of David's and my divorce. My safety is at issue here. The men stay."

"All right, if it makes you feel better, I'll make an exception. Let's get on with the meeting."

"Charles, I hate to interrupt you, but I have business to discuss before we can go any further. I realize you and everyone else are quite surprised to see me here today, but I have a very good reason for coming. Unfortunately, the consequences David has to face will also affect you and David's parents. It's unfortunate, but unavoidable at this point. David pushed me too far. And now, I'm pushing back."

"She's crazy. I haven't seen her in years, except to visit her in the hospital a few days ago after she had an accident. Meredith and I were on our honeymoon in Denver when we heard she'd been hurt." He tried to sound sincere. He didn't want his grandfather to rethink his upcoming retirement. He wanted Merrick International all to himself. Soon, he'd have it. If it's the last thing he did, he'd have his shares back from Jenna, too.

Jenna shook with fury. She placed her briefcase on the table in front of her and crossed her arms over her chest.

"Is that so, David? You haven't seen me in years? Liar! Bastard!"

"You got what you wanted. You took my shares in the company and millions in the settlement. What more do you want? You were a gold digger then, and you're still one," he spat out.

"Aren't you going to congratulate me on my engagement?" She'd thrown him with that one. She refused to allow him to continue acting like the last few years hadn't happened. He simply stared at her, furious. She held up her hand and admired the diamond ring.

"It's beautiful, don't you think? Jack and I are getting married. This is Jack, everyone." She pointed to Jack behind her and gave him a big smile. "He's a very successful rancher in Colorado. Did I mention, David, we're expecting? Twins."

David fumed. Sweat broke out across his brow and his ears turned red.

"Charles, I apologize. You were interested in the business I have to discuss. First, let me say I'm truly sorry to do this to you, but there's simply no other way. I'm sure if you think about the future, you'll see what I'm about to do is best for the company. You'll profit for many years to come. David," she turned and locked gazes with him, "although you'll profit from the shares you still hold at Merrick, you'll be the most hurt by what I'm doing. You'll be ruined, both personally and professionally. Just know you deserve it and so much more."

"There's nothing you can do to me. You couldn't when we were married, and you can't now."

Jenna smiled at him and then at Cameron. "I wouldn't be so sure about that."

She opened her briefcase and took out the copy of the newspaper she'd shown Cameron. She walked around the table, passing behind David, and handed the paper to his grandfather.

Charles read the headline and snapped his head toward David. He turned back to Jenna and took a good long look at her. Everyone waited in silence while he read the article. Jenna returned to the other end of the table, giving Jack a wink as she took her position. He and Sam sat at her back keeping an eye on David and the rest of the board.

Charles handed the paper to David's mother and father. They took one look at it and gasped. Marion Merrick looked at Jenna with tears in her eyes. "No, Jenna. This isn't possible. He didn't do this."

"It's true. Every picture. Every word. I asked for your help the first time he came after me after the divorce. Back then, he wasn't quite so physical, but still you wouldn't believe me, or help me. This family has sheltered him, giving in to his every whim, and in doing so, you've condoned his behavior with your indifference. He killed your grandchild," she finished, driving her point home.

Marion's gaze fell to her lap in shame. Nathan simply sat like a stone starring at his son.

"What's in that paper? Why are you all so upset?" David demanded.

Nathan Merrick threw the paper on the table in front of his son. "How could you? You aren't the man I thought you were. I taught you better than this." He indicated the paper with a disgusted look on his face. "You don't hurt people, especially women. What kind of person does this to someone?"

David stared at the headline.

DAVID MERRICK – HUNTER
JENNA CALDWELL MERRICK –
THE HUNTED

Several pictures of Jenna were printed beneath the headline, all in color, along with an accompanying article. His whole face turned red with rage. He stood, about to go after her when one of the bodyguards grabbed his shoulders from behind and sat him forcefully back into his seat. Jenna felt Jack's body heat as he stood directly behind her, his arm banding around her protectively, his hand resting over her belly.

"I wouldn't do that if I were you, David," Jenna warned. "These men have orders to protect me. They'll do just that."

"You can't be serious about this. I'll sue you for libel and defamation of character. No one will believe you when I'm finished with you, you bitch."

"Go ahead, but I have the pictures. If a picture speaks a thousand words, I won't need to say anything. I only printed a few, but I have an entire book full of pictures of all the damage you've ever done to me. Push me and I'll print the whole damn thing. Sue me and I'll bring them to court."

"You can't do this."

Jenna patted Jack's hand, and he released her and took his seat again. "I already have. I've asked you ... No, I begged you to leave me alone. You continued to hunt me down. I spent year after year hiding, fearing the day you'd show up to hurt and punish me. No more. You won't ever lay a hand on me again."

"I'll kill you for this, you stupid bitch!"

"Be careful what you say, David. Sam here is an FBI agent. You wouldn't want to go to jail for threatening my life."

"Jenna, what do you want?" Charles asked, trying to defuse the situation and turn the conversation back to civil. "How can we make this right for you? Do you want David arrested?"

"Having David arrested wouldn't make up for what he's done, but it would be a start. If only I could have him arrested and prosecuted for what he's done."

"You'd never win," David said, a sneer on his face.

"I should have stepped in during the divorce proceedings," Charles interjected before David could wind up again. "I turned a blind eye, allowed David to handle the situation. It was a bad decision, and one you've paid for dearly. I'm sorry, I wish I could make this right."

"Charles, I appreciate the sentiment. But you can't make this right. David spent a great deal of time making sure records disappeared. He'd only pay people off to get his way in court. He'd tie us up in court for years. Frankly, at this point, I don't have the time or inclination. David had a chance to do the right thing and leave me alone. He chose not to, and now I'm taking everything he holds dear away from him."

"So what?" David thundered. "The paper will come out today. There'll be press for a few days maybe a week and the next story will come along and everyone will forget. You won't have accomplished very much," he said arrogantly.

"You're wrong. It will be hard for people to forget those pictures, and you know it. You'll find your name isn't on so many dinner invitations. You'll still be rich, of course, but let's face it, the way you live, even that won't last. That pretty new wife of yours might decide being married to you is too great a risk to her health. Or has she already found out what it's like to be David Merrick's wife? Tell me, do you allow her to speak with her friends and family? Do you slap her after a dinner party because she's spoken to another man? Maybe you throw her down the stairs because you think she's having an affair with a man she doesn't even know!" Jenna screamed at him.

Marion wept openly and Nathan sat stone silent glaring at his son. Charles simply shook his head in dismay. David was furious, but wise enough to remain seated this time.

"Is that how you treat her? If she leaves you, will you hunt her like you've hunted me all these years? Will you take a belt and beat her because she refuses to come back to you? Maybe you'll take her from her home and into the woods where you'll stab her and leave her alone to die. Is that how you'll treat your new wife? Will you tell her you love her, and you can't live without her, and then slap her with your next breath?"

"Shut up! Just shut up!"

"No. You'll listen to what I have to say. After today everyone will know what you are, David. They'll all know the kind of monster you are." Her voice cracked, but she'd gotten her point across. Each word she spoke put another nail in David's coffin.

"You can't do this. I'll sue you for everything you have. I'll make you pay."

She had no doubt, given half a chance, he'd kill her the first chance he got. This time he'd make it slow and painful to the bitter end.

"You and I both know you can, but you won't win. It'll just be a huge waste of money. If my research on you is correct, I've got more than you do. So don't waste your time, or mine."

"You checked into my finances. What the hell is wrong with you? You can't do that."

"Yes, I can. One of the first rules of war, and business, is know your enemy. I know everything there is to know about you, David. I know exactly what makes you tick. And now I'm going to use all of what I know against you."

"What more can you do? So the article comes out. I'll get past that."

Jenna took out two stacks of papers from her briefcase and walked around the table again. This time David followed her progress turning to face her as she passed. She held her ground, counting on Cameron and the men guarding her to protect her, should David make a grab for her. She handed the papers to Charles and returned to her position at the other end of the table.

She waited for Charles to review the papers and look up at her. He did so with eyes resigned to the inevitable. He understood he'd just lost his company to her because of David.

"I'm sorry, Charles. This has nothing to do with you. I wanted to wait until after you'd retired to see it through. As you can see by the newspaper and my appearance today, David has made that impossible. It has to end—now."

"Nothing I can do, David's been battling you for years. You've found a way to win the war. As a business strategist, I tip my hat to you. You've outflanked us all, especially David. I'm ready to retire and live a life of leisure. At least, I know the company will be in good hands—yours. Go ahead. Make your announcement."

She placed her hands on the table, leaned toward David, locked eyes with him, and fired her death shot. "I hold controlling interest in Merrick International. You're fired."

David stood and planted his hands on the table, mimicking her. "What? You can't possibly own that much of the company. Between my shares, grandfather's, and my parents', we hold controlling interest collectively. You can't fire me."

"Yes, I do. And I can. You've spent the last few years hunting me. I've spent that time making money and buying shares of Merrick stock. Your goal was to stalk me and terrorize me. My goal was to destroy you. Now I have, both publicly and privately. I own controlling interest in Merrick, and as such, I *can* fire you."

"A Merrick has run this company for more than eighty years. You can't do this. I'm taking over when grandfather retires at the end of the year and that's final. There's nothing you can do about it."

"David, sit down. She's already done it. The papers are in order. She owns majority share, and therefore she's CEO of the company now."

"Charles, you understand why I've done this. The only way to get to David was to take away the only thing he has and held over me—the company."

Charles nodded, a frown deepening the lines on his face.

"She can't do this, Grandfather. You're CEO. No one can vote you out."

"You forget the charter for the board of directors, David." Jenna gained his full attention. "Majority owner is CEO by default. Also, there's something else you've neglected to remember, or maybe it's that you're so arrogant you simply believe you can make the rules up as you go. The charter also states that as majority owner, the CEO appoints the board members. While the Merricks collectively have always held majority share, that rule worked out great for you. Now that I have majority ownership, it works against you. As of this moment, everyone at this table with the last name Merrick is relieved of their duties on the board."

"What the hell are you talking about? This is Merrick International and the Merricks run this company."

"Keep up, David. I run this company now. The Merricks no longer sit on the board. Charles, as of this moment you are retired and will receive your full benefits package. Mr. and Mrs. Merrick, you only serve on the board as figureheads and don't actually contribute to the running of the business. I'm sorry to do this, but I feel it's in the best interest of the company to replace you with board members who will work toward expanding this company. David, like I said, you're fired. You won't run Merrick International, either on this board or in any other capacity."

Finally sinking in for David, he simply stared at the table, his face red with fury, his hands fisted. An animal tensing, ready to pounce.

"Mr. Jamison. Mr. Richards. It would please me very much if you'd remain on the board. I believe that together we can work toward our common goals. Mr. Shaw has told me a lot about the both of you, and I feel we could make a good team."

Both a little shell-shocked, they agreed to stay on.

"You can't really mean to run this company. You have absolutely no business skills."

"David, are you really this stupid? I have a degree in computer graphics and programming. I've taken over your company without you, or this company, being any the wiser. You're right, though. I'm not going to run this company. I'm appointing Cameron Shaw as president. He'll take over running the company immediately. I'm also changing the charter for the board, so this kind of thing won't happen again. In the future, majority holder will need a majority vote from the board of directors to earn the CEO position. They'll have a seat on the board, but they need to be voted in as CEO. So if you think you and your family can pull your resources and gain back the majority and the company, you're wrong. By the looks of your parents and grandfather, I'd say you'd have a hard time convincing them to back you."

"I'll make you regret this."

She recognized the menacing tone. One he knew she'd understand from their many past encounters.

"Watch what you say. We're surrounded by witnesses. You've dug this hole for yourself and taken all of your family down with you. Don't make this any worse. For yourself or them."

Nathan Merrick, with no choice but to accept the inevitable, stood with his wife, came around the table and stopped in front of her. She wasn't sure what to expect, but having them embraced her was not what she'd anticipated.

"I'm sorry we didn't help you. I'm sorry we didn't know what's happened ever since. We ... I'm sorry. I don't know what else to say." Nathan's stoic face transformed into a mask of disappointment and regret.

"There's nothing to say. I don't blame you. David's the only one responsible."

They walked from the room without looking back at their son.

Charles stood and came to her next, holding the documents she'd given to him. "I'll clear my office in a few days. I think I'll take a long overdue vacation, someplace warm. I've been meaning to do some fishing."

"That sounds wonderful. Enjoy your retirement,

Charles. You've served this business gallantly. I only hope Cameron and I can carry on in the same professional and respectful manner with which you've always conducted yourself."

"I have no doubt you'll handle things. You made a wise choice in Cameron. To tell you the truth, in other circumstances, he'd be my first choice as well." Charles nodded his approval to Cameron with a satisfied grin.

"I thought you'd see it that way." She smiled softly for him. She'd always liked Charles.

"You're a very brilliant woman. I'm sorry I didn't see that before and use it to my advantage." He gave her a smile and a hug. "I am sorry. I should have realized . . . Well, what is there to say now, but it shouldn't have happened. Take care of yourself and the babies you're carrying. Perhaps you'll keep in touch and let me know how you're doing. Maybe you'll need my professional opinion and expertise in the future."

"I'll be in touch. You can count on it."

Charles left with Mr. Jamison and Mr. Richards. They were setting up a golf date, if Jenna heard them right. Jenna nodded to Sam and he left the room.

"You're still here, David? Security will show you out. I'll have your desk packed up and your things forwarded to you."

"Do you really think I'll just walk away from this?"

"You don't have a choice. It's done. I'm going home with *Jack*. Cameron and I run the company now. There's nothing you can do about it. Follow your grandfather's example and accept defeat like a gentleman."

"I'll never accept this. You'll pay for this, and you know it. You know what I can do to you. What I will do to you."

"David, go before you make things worse. Jack has sat quietly and patiently, even though he wants to rip you apart. He did that for me. If you don't go, I'm afraid he won't be patient much longer. It also appears Cameron would like to have *his* conference room to himself. I think the site of you offends him. It absolutely offends me. You make me sick. I hope you rot in hell for what you've done. Once that paper hits the stands, you won't be able to go anywhere without the press hounding you. Maybe then you'll know what it feels like to be hunted everywhere you go."

"I hate you, you bitch. Wait until I get my hands on you. I'll make you pay."

She didn't know what possessed her to keep pushing him, but she couldn't stop herself. "Come after me and I'll take away everything you have left. You won't have a dime to your name when I'm done. Don't believe me? Well, I took the company. That should tell you what *I'm* capable of.

"By the way, I spoke with your wife this morning. She wasn't very pleased by the newspaper left on her doorstep. I believe she mentioned something about moving back to her parents' estate. She also mentioned something about marrying a monster. I told her she had my sympathies."

He tried to go after her, but Cameron and Jack blocked him from her just as Sam and two security guards walked into the room. Her bodyguards took up positions around her. Jack shoved David back. "Don't even think about it." The tightly controlled words conveyed his pent-up rage.

Sam grabbed David by the arm. "Let's go." With the security guards, he led David to the door, screaming and threatening retribution all the way down the hall to his office.

Chapter Fifty-Eight

"THANK YOU, GUYS. That was close. I thought for sure he'd take a swing at me." Jenna took a deep breath and tried to settle her nerves. All this stress couldn't be good for her and the babies.

"He won't get anywhere near you." Jack gave her a reassuring smile, cupped her cheek and brushed his thumb across her cheek. "I'm so proud of you. You stood up to David and took over the company. You amaze me."

"Thank you, honey. I couldn't have done this without you. I wouldn't have wanted to." She closed the distance and brushed her lips against his. A simple touch, it calmed and centered her again.

Sam came back and took his position by the conference room door while Jenna and Cameron gathered their papers and got ready to leave.

"Cameron, I want to thank you for your support and all the long nights you're about to put in. Make me a list of potential board members and we'll go over them. Let me know what kind of upper management changes you want to make, and who you want to move over here from Ortel. I've prepared a press release. Take a look at it, then send it out. We'll get started on Monday via telephone and go from there."

"I'll do all that, but first I want to say congratulations. You did it. I can't believe all those things you said about David and what he's done to you."

"I have twenty-seven stitches across my ribcage to prove it. They're not as nice as the ones Jack put in my thigh several months ago, but they'll do." She smiled at Jack. "Let's go home. I'm tired. It's been a busy day and these babies are hungry."

Jack gave her a huge smile. "Oh, yeah. What do they want to eat? I'll call the pilot and have him get dinner ready for us."

"Not airport food. This calls for a celebration. I want cake or pie. Ooh, ice cream. Chocolate."

"Sounds like the babies need a sugar rush," Jack teased. He kissed her softly and patted her belly.

"Cameron, will you join us?" Jenna asked.

"I'd love to. I know this great place. Best bakery in town. Lines out the door. It's called Decadence. I think we deserve a little indulgence after such a boring board meeting," he joked. "You'll love it. We'll grab a bottle of champagne from the limo and celebrate."

Chapter Fifty-Nine

DAVID SEETHED WHEN security escorted him out of the boardroom. This was his company, his building. These people worked for him.

He allowed them to walk him to his office where he promptly entered and shut the door in their faces. He headed straight for his desk and unlocked the side drawer. Taking out the gun, he held it up looking at the cold metal.

She won't get away with this. She's not leaving this building alive. She thinks she can get away with ruining me. I'll see her in hell first.

He put the gun in his suit pocket and headed back to the office doors, where security guards waited on the other side to escort him from the building.

He opened the door and turned toward the board-room. "I just need a word with Mrs. Merrick before I go." He increased his pace. He both hated and secretly loved calling her Mrs. Merrick. She belonged to him. And he'd show her she couldn't betray him again and get away with it.

She stood talking with Cameron just through the open doorway. Other men stood around, including that stupid rancher, but he only had eyes for her.

His vision tunneled in on only her. His heart raced, his mind raged with all the anger and contempt he felt for her, for everything she'd done. He took the gun from his pocket, raised his arm toward her, and fired.

Chapter Sixty

THE EXCITEMENT IN the boardroom was only overshadowed by the anticipation. They didn't have long to wait. Sam yelled for everyone to get down. Jack pushed her from behind and shoved her to the floor, covering her with his body. Shots rang out. Someone cried out in pain. Jack cursed, snapping her out of her haze. She tried to look up, but Jack kept her head down. Two more shots rang out before everything went eerily quiet.

"Jenna, are you okay?" Sam called to her from the doorway.

"Fine," she answered automatically, unsure about anything at the moment.

"Everyone else okay?" Sam asked.

All the men indicated they were fine, but she didn't hear Jack among them. Jack eased his weight off her and slid aside. Cameron helped her to her feet and the two bodyguards flanking her made room for her to pass.

Jack leaned against the wall, blood running down his left arm, a gun in his right. She flung herself against his chest and held on to him, unable to look through the doorway where the first shots originated.

Sam was excellent at his job. In his background check on David, he'd discovered David's gun permit. Using some of his less-than-reputable contacts from the FBI, they'd had someone break into David's house and office to locate the weapon. David actually owned quite a few guns, only one registered, which he kept in his office, locked in his desk drawer. They assumed David would be in a rage before he left the boardroom, and his rage would make him pick up the gun and come after Jenna. Provoking him was risky, but it was also the only way to end David's terrorism.

Knowing David would be volatile, she and Sam had sat in the office at the ranch planning what they'd do to prevent the inevitable. They figured David would probably try to get to her before she got back on the plane. She never thought David would come after her before she'd even left the boardroom.

"What the hell were you thinking? You weren't supposed to have a gun. I'm going to kill Sam," she said and grabbed his lapels and shook him.

"Later, give me a kiss."

She pressed her lips to his. Warm, alive, she thanked God he was alive. She helped him off with his suit jacket, revealing the deep furrow on the outside of his arm.

"Looks like this time you get the stitches. Maybe if you need a pokey shot, Lily will give you a lollipop." She gave him her most sugary sweet smile, even though they both knew she wasn't happy about the situation. A tear slid down her cheek. "I could have lost you."

"Now you know exactly how I felt when he took you."

The relief overcame her fear. She pressed her forehead to his and took a moment to savor the closeness and the fact that they were both alive.

She took a calming breath before addressing Sam. "Is David dead?"

"Yes, just outside the door. Jack got him."

"I told you I'd kill that bastard."

"I never wanted you to have to live with this."

Jack shrugged it away, but she saw the conviction in his eyes.

Sam was a trained FBI agent. She thought he'd handle this better than Jack. It wasn't supposed to be this way.

"I'm only sorry I didn't kill the fucker before he grabbed you at the ranch and hurt you."

"Jack . . ."

"This is the only way. You knew it, even though you tiptoed around it with Sam. He can't hurt you anymore."

Jenna pressed her forehead to Jack's, understanding everything he said and didn't say. Jack promised to keep her safe. The only way to do that was to take David out once and for all. With his military background, Jack knew any other tactic would only result in a longer campaign of terror. "You did this for me."

"I told you before, I'm selfish. I want you all to myself." All joking aside, he said, "I want you to be happy. Above all else, I want you safe. I love you."

"The police are on the way," Sam interrupted. "We've got a lot of explaining to do. Cameron, you okay?"

"Fine. Thanks for giving me a heads up, by the way."

"Sorry. We weren't sure he'd actually try to kill her. Well, we suspected it, but didn't think it would happen while she was still in the building. Looks like his rage got the better of him, and he wasn't thinking clearly."

"Yeah, looks like it." Cameron grabbed the lapels of his jacket and adjusted it over his shoulders nervously.

Unsteady on her legs, Jenna walked out the doorway, everyone watching her. She stood looking down at the man who had hunted and terrorized her. It was over, truly over. Relief washed over her spirit, the weight of the world lifted from her shoulders. She looked upon David's lifeless body. He appeared peaceful. He must have been shot in the chest and fallen forward. She couldn't see any blood and his eyes were closed. She didn't have a mean bone in her body, but for a second she wished he'd suffered a fraction of the pain she'd suffered at his hands.

She turned her back on him for the last time and went back to Jack.

Chapter Sixty-One

THE POLICE ARRIVED and they spent hours in the conference room answering questions about why David tried to kill her. Every detail of the last two years was discussed along with her reasons for coming to the board meeting today with several bodyguards and an FBI agent in tow.

"So he came back to kill you after you showed him today's newspaper?" the lieutenant asked again.

"Actually, Lieutenant, the newspaper is a fake," Sam supplied.

"What do you mean it's fake? It's supposed to come out today." Jenna didn't understand why Sam hadn't set up the paper to be printed and distributed as they'd planned.

"We knew David would try something, so I asked the paper to print this newspaper with the story on Jenna, but they won't distribute it.

"It isn't necessary to expose you like this, Jenna.

You've accomplished what you wanted, and there's no reason to publicize the abuse you've suffered. Since you own the paper, I threatened you'd shut the place down if they didn't keep this a secret."

She went into his arms and held him close. She hadn't considered they could accomplish this without the paper going out. "Thank you, Sam."

"I see, so what Mr. Shaw said about you having a copy sent to David's wife was incorrect?" the lieutenant asked.

"I made David believe a copy was left for his wife this morning. I lied. I've never spoken to her, nor did I have a paper delivered to her." Jenna had just been egging David on, hoping he'd make a mistake they could use against him. She never actually believed he'd end up dead.

"So you provoked David?"

"Yes. He pushed me. I pushed him back, knowing his penchant for violence. I warned him several days ago after he almost killed me to leave me alone, or I'd take everything that mattered from him. Today I made good on that threat by taking over Merrick International and firing him."

"So you're saying this is simply a case of employee rage. You were using the bodyguards and an FBI agent as self-defense."

"That's what I'm saying. That's all I'm saying."

"There's a lot more to the story. You planned for this eventuality when Mr. Merrick would snap and go after you, Mrs. Merrick."

Jenna didn't say anything. Taking a page from Cameron's book and remaining silent, she waited the lieutenant out. The less she said, the better the chance she didn't incriminate herself.

"There simply isn't any evidence Sam or Jack Turner shot the man in cold blood. Mr. Merrick fired his gun several times into the boardroom, where you were standing. The pictures in the fake paper confirm David Merrick was a deadly threat."

Relieved the lieutenant saw things her way, she decided to get out of there before he changed his mind and took her in for more questioning. "If you'll excuse me, we're flying home. If you have further questions, you can contact my lawyer."

"You're free to go, but I'll be in touch until the case is officially closed."

Jenna nodded her agreement, walked past David's grieving family, and left Sam to handle any further details with the police.

JACK HADN'T NEEDED stitches, which annoyed Jenna just a little. She was always the one getting stuck with needles. Actually, she was relieved Sam and Jack were both okay. They boarded the plane, and after taking off they removed their bulletproof vests and settled on the couch for a much-needed rest. Jenna brought each of them a beer. She sat next to Jack and turned toward Sam and punched him as hard as she could in the arm.

"Ow! What's that for?"

"Giving Jack a gun. What the hell were you thinking? He could have been killed. You got your brother shot."

"I didn't shoot him. I gave him the gun so he could protect you and himself. He knew we were plotting behind his back. What'd you expect me to do?"

"Honey, it's not Sam's fault. If he hadn't given me the gun, I'd have brought one from the ranch. I wasn't going to let David hurt you ever again."

"Instead, he shot you. You could have been killed. You're lucky he has terrible aim."

Jack squeezed her to his side, kissed the side of her head and held her close. "Honey, calm down. It's not good for the babies. It's over now, and we don't have to worry about him anymore. Sam will handle the police until they close their investigation. It shouldn't take long. Then this whole mess will be behind us."

He was right, and she was having a delayed reaction to the stressful and traumatic events. Snapping at him allowed her to let off steam and Jack understood. It was finally over.

"We never got to have cake at Decadence. Now, that's a great name for a bakery. I think next time we visit the city, we should definitely go there."

"Whatever you want, honey." Jack kissed her head and held her close. She laid her head on his shoulder and closed her eyes, finally able to sleep, free of the suspense of wondering if David was out there, somewhere, hunting her.

Chapter Sixty-Two

Six months later . . .

UNABLE TO SLEEP, Trixie, full-grown, engulfed the space at her feet, making Jenna uncomfortable. Jack lay at her back with his hand on her thigh and his breath soft in her hair at the back of her neck. Sally, completely healed and vibrant as ever, lay down the length of his legs. The two babies, that had been putting up a fuss for hours now, swelled her belly to capacity. A piercing pain in her lower back wouldn't go away. Nervous and excited, she got out of bed to stretch and walk, hoping to calm the babies and ease the nagging pain.

She managed to get out of bed without waking Jack. He was used to her getting up several times a night to pee. Neither of the dogs stirred more than enough to cozy up to Jack. She knew exactly how they felt. Who wouldn't want to be snuggled up against all that strength and warmth.

She headed to the bathroom to take care of her over-taxed bladder, and then went to the closet to dress. She settled on a loose-fitting turquoise dress and slid her feet into a pair of black flats. She went to the bed, leaned over, and shook Jack's shoulder to wake him.

"Jack, honey, wake up. It's time to go."

Jack didn't budge. She shook him harder, pressed a hand to the small of her back, and breathed shallowly through the pain as her abdomen contracted. "Jack. Wake up. It's time to go."

"What, honey? Time to go where?"

"To the hospital. Your babies want out."

Jack sat straight up, eyes wide. "What? The babies. Now?"

"Yes, now." To demonstrate they wanted out, her water broke in a gush down her leg. She stared at the puddle at her feet. Another painful contraction bent her forward, making her groan in agony. She held on to Jack's arms as another pain overtook her body. "Oh God, Jack, it hurts." The pains intensified and grew more insistent and the ache in her back turned to a real kick-ass sting.

Jack jumped out of bed and threw on his jeans and shirt. He helped her change her clothes again and put her in the car and rushed her to the hospital. The whole way, he held her hand, soothed her with calm, loving words, and hated every second she was in pain.

The babies were delivered several hours later and Jack and Jenna were happily holding them when Caleb, Summer, Lily, and little baby Jacob arrived. Caleb carried Lily, who was lost behind a huge bouquet of Stargazer lilies. Summer pushed Jacob in his stroller. The little dark-haired cherub of a boy slept soundly, sucking his finger. He resembled his father, Caleb, right down to his muddy brown eyes. Summer came over to the bed and hugged Jenna around the bundled in her arms.

"Oh, Jenna, they're beautiful. Are you okay? Everything went all right?" Summer asked, probably remembering delivering Jacob only a few short months ago.

"Everything went well. I'm fine. The babies are fine. I don't know if Jack will ever be the same again, though." She smiled at her husband as he stood holding their other son.

"What do you mean? I held your hand and panted with you through the whole thing."

"He turned a little green for a while. The nurse even put a chair behind him just in case he passed out. He held it together in the end. Once he saw the first one arrive, his fatherly pride kicked in."

"They look just like Jack and Sam did when they were born." Summer touched a finger to the baby's soft hair. "I remember pictures of the two of them bundled with their little caps of almost white hair sticking out."

"It's uncanny how they look like their Dad already."

"So, what are their names?" Caleb asked, holding Lily up so she could stare at the baby in Jack's arms.

"I'd like to introduce Matthew," whom Jenna held, "and Jack has Samuel." Jack moved closer to Lily and Caleb, so Lily could get a good look at Sam.

"Does Sam know you named one of the babies after him? He must be so excited." Summer beamed.

"I called him early this morning and told him. He's

on some assignment. Ever since they moved him to the San Francisco office, he's been working like a demon. He'll try to come for a visit soon. He said he misses us, but I think he just misses Jenna." Jack smiled. "He's still jealous."

Jack winked at his wife. He couldn't believe after everything ended, they'd finally been married. The image of Jenna in a white gown walking toward him was never far from his mind. They'd gotten married at the ranch with flowers, friends, and family surrounding them. Ben walked her down the aisle. Jenna's mother attended and stayed for a month. Jack arranged for the visit as a wedding gift. Jenna cried that day. For the first time in a long time, they were tears of joy.

"They're so cute, Aunt Jenna. Maybe they can play with baby brother, Jacob," Lily said, handing over the flowers to Summer to put on the bedside table.

"I think it will be a little while before they can play together. When they get bigger, I'm sure you'll all be good friends."

"That's right, honey. You'll all grow up on the ranch and play together." Jack couldn't imagine anything better than the ranch with all these children, and hopefully more to come, running around and riding the horses. Thanks to Jenna, the children would someday have children, and they'd play on the ranch, too. He hoped the future generations would be as close as they all were today.

He thought of Sam back at work and wished he could have been there with them to celebrate the day the twins were born.

Jenna pictured the children growing up together on the ranch. It was a nice image, one she'd hoped and dreamed about for a long time. She looked around the room at all the faces of her family. She had everything she'd ever dreamed. Jack caught her gaze and held it. He mouthed I love you, their son in his arms. Her heart was so full. She was healed, home, safe and loved.

*Read on for a sneak peek at the next
in THE HUNTED series,*

LUCKY LIKE US,

*by Jennifer Ryan
on sale April 9, 2013
from Avon Impulse*

An Excerpt from

LUCKY LIKE US

A WISP OF smoke rose from the barrel of his gun. The
smell of gunpowder filled the air. Face raised to the night
sky, eyes closed, he sucked in a deep breath and let it out
slow, enjoying the moment. Adrenaline coursed through
his veins with a thrill that left a tingle in his skin. His
heart pounded and he felt more alive than he ever remembered feeling in his normal life.

Slowly, he lowered his head to the bloody body lying
sprawled on the dirty pavement at his feet. The Silver Fox
strikes again. The smile spread across his face. He loved
the nickname the press had dubbed him after the police
spoke of the elusive killer who'd staged eight deaths.
Who knew how many more? He did. He remembered
every one of them in minute detail.

He kicked the dead guy in the ribs. Sonofabitch
almost ruined everything, but you didn't get to be in his
position by leaving the details in a partnership to chance.
They had a deal, but the idiot had gotten greedy, making
him sloppy. He'd set up a meeting for tonight for a new
hit, but hadn't done the proper background investigation.
His death was a direct result of his stupidity.

"You set me up with a cop!" he yelled at the corpse.

He dragged the body by the foot into the steel container, heedless of the man's face scraping across the rough road. He dropped the guy's leg. The loud thud echoed through the cavernous interior. He locked the door and walked through the deserted shipyard indifferent.

Maybe he'd let his fury get the best of him, but anything, or anyone, who threatened to expose him or end his most enjoyable hobby needed to be eliminated. He had too much to lose, and he never lost.

Only one more loose end to tie up.

JENNIFER RYAN lives lives in the San Francisco Bay Area with her husband, three children, her dog, Bella, and cat, Shadow.

When she isn't writing a book, she's reading one. Her obsession for both is often revealed in the state of her home and how late dinner is to the table. When she finally leaves those fictional worlds, you'll find her in the garden, playing in the dirt and daydreaming about people who live only in her head until she puts them on paper.

Please visit her website at www.jennifer-ryan.com.

Visit www.AuthorTracker.com for exclusive information on your favorite HarperCollins authors.

Give in to your impulses . . .
Read on for a sneak peek at a brand-new
e-book original tale of romance from Avon Books.
Available now wherever e-books are sold.

SEDUCED BY THE GLADIATOR
By Lauren Hawkeye

An Excerpt from

SEDUCED BY THE GLADIATOR

by *Lauren Hawkeye*

In Lauren Hawkeye's second erotic romance
featuring the fierce gladiators of Ancient
Rome, Lilia is the rarest of commodities—a
champion female gladiator. When Christus,
a warrior with the body of a god, is sold to
the *ludus* that owns Lilia, she finds herself
forced to defend her position and guard her
body against the erotic sensations only he can
bring. But beneath the tantalizing flesh of the
gladiator, Lilia finds a man determined to protect
her—and to love her—no matter the cost.

AN AVON RED NOVEL

"What are you doing?" My words were a hiss as I looked frantically around the room. We were alone for the moment, thank the gods, but someone could come in at any moment.

Weak was the least of the things that I would appear to be if someone were to come upon this scene, me flushed from the steam, Christus' sure fingers lightly massaging the purpling skin of my ankle.

Every touch of his fingers sent a lick of fire straight between my legs. Though I tried to swallow it down, a groan escaped my lips.

His touch felt so incredibly *good*.

"I cannot let myself be seen like this." There was no point in denying that I found his touch pleasurable. Against my better judgment, I closed my eyes for a moment—just a moment—and let sensation wash over me.

When I again opened my eyes, Christus' fingers had

trailed upward to my calf. His eyes burned brightly and were fixed on my own.

"I told the men that anyone who bothered you while you bathed would find himself without a cock." My mouth fell open at the words, and inexplicably a giggle bubbled up from my throat.

I clapped a hand over my mouth as it escaped. I never giggled. I rarely even laughed.

Sobering myself, I tried to tug my leg from Christus' reach. "That does not mean they will listen."

"I assure you they will." Christus did not allow me to pull my flesh away, instead trailing his fingers ever higher. My breath caught in my throat as he stroked the tender skin beneath my knee.

"If it eases you, Darius is keeping watch. No one will disturb you. No one will disturb us."

I heard the double meaning in his words, and though I felt as though I should run, I found myself doing nothing of the sort. Instead I reached out, my hand shaking, and ran uncertain fingers over the stripe of his cheekbone.

I shuddered as my fingers made contact with his skin. It had been so long since I had been touched with anything but violence or desire that was twisted at its root. Darius touched me sometimes, but his caresses were friendly and reassuring.

They did not affect me in nearly the same way that these small caresses did.

"Christus. I cannot do this." I wanted to. I could no longer lie to myself. I wanted this man, wanted the moments of pleasure that he could bring to me in this strange life that I called my own. "If the men found out that I took you as a lover, we would both be under attack."

My voice had a breathless quality to it, one that I had never heard before. I was feeling things that I had never felt before, too, as Christus lowered his head and laid his lips on my knee.

When he again looked up, the expression on his face—the longing, the desire—was my undoing.

"Why should anyone find out? It is no one's business but our own." The fingers that still softly stroked the skin beneath my knee moved with excruciating slowness, tracing a stripe up and up, until they found the edge where my leather wrap met my skin.

"Christus." What was happening to me? I was not weak—I made my own decisions. Yet I could no more have stopped this encounter than I could have stopped breathing.

Slowly, giving me time to say no, Christus worked at the knot in my leather. When the fastening was loose, he pulled the garment away from my body, hanging it on the edge of the tub.

Leaving my skin bare from the waist down.

I felt my lower lip tremble, but apart from that small movement I was still, tensed, my breath caught in my throat with anticipation. With his eyes on my own, drinking in every nuance of my expression, he inched his fingers up, then up again, trailing them over my inner thighs as the muscles beneath quivered.

I inhaled sharply when those fingers grazed over the heated skin between my legs. Christus paused at the noise, again giving me time to say no.

I waited a long moment, my innermost thoughts whirling through my head in a great rush. Sex had been tied up with violence for so long, it had made me feel cheap at best. The idea that I could embrace it for pleasure was strange and oddly thrilling, if I could but take that leap.

My eyelids lowered, I looked down from the edge of the bath, where I still perched, looked at the god of a man who was rising out of the water at my feet. He was golden and sleek and beautiful, and he wore an expression of reverence and of need that looked to be nearly painful.

It was this exact combination that pushed me the last step. With an exhalation of the breath that I had been holding, I covered his wrist with my hand, holding his fingers in place even as I arched my hips to meet his touch.

"You are certain that we will not be disturbed?" I could not quite believe that I was prepared to accept his word when he nodded. The Lilia of even a day before would never have taken anything at face value, would have had to see for herself.

But this man inspired trust. Trust, as well as lust.

For the first time since I had come to the ludus, I decided to embrace the sensations.